MW01139722

Regal Hearts: Season 2

The Unlikely Story of a Princess, a Popstar,
an Amish Girl, and an Average Girl

By Livy Jarmusch

Copyright 2019 ©

Dear Reader,

Before you begin *Regal Hearts: Season 2*, I'd like to remind you of the time-frame of this story. *Regal Hearts* takes place two years after my debut novel, *The Coronation*.

If you haven't read *The Coronation* and *The Rebellion* (books 1 and 2 in *The Tales of Tarsurella* series) yet, and you want to maximize the full enjoyment of this season, I recommend checking them out!

Just be forewarned that if you haven't read *The Coronation* and *The Rebellion* yet, there are some spoilers in this season!

If you don't plan on ever reading *The Tales of Tarsurella*, then I guess you have nothing to worry about! Carry on! :)

Lots of Love,

-Livy Lynn

P.S. Find *The Coronation* and *The Rebellion* on Kindle or in Paperback!

Episode 1

Lena's tired shoulder presses against the tiny airplane window. Her legs complain, begging to find a more comfortable position. She wiggles in her seat, but the belt is too snug, and her legs are trapped in tight quarters. She glances at the tall, friendly giant seated beside her. Poor Jack's knees are nearly up to his chest. The private plane allows them to avoid long security lines and flight delays, yet now they are paying for the quick convenience with their vast discomfort.

She cranes her neck backward, attempting to settle into the bucket seat. The headrest is too small, and it hurts her neck to lean in that direction. She wiggles once more, turning her hips slightly toward the window. There's nothing to do but think and stare out the window.

As emotionally drained and physically tired as she is, she knows the flight isn't long enough to take a nap. Her tired eyes observe the glorious outdoor scenery. Lacy white clouds, fluffy enough to bounce upon, float beneath them. Clear blue skies remind Lena of a lovely ocean backdrop. Theodore would've enjoyed being in an airplane. Oh, how he would love to soar above the clouds!

But now, instead of ever being given the chance to fasten his seatbelt beside Lena, he is instead dancing through the heavens at an altitude far, far higher than she. Her heart aches to think of his precious little face and darling dimples. She still can't believe he's gone.

Her bottom lip quivers, as thoughts of Grandmary and Theodore twirl around in her heart.

"Your Highness, do you mind if I share some advice with you?" Jack asks, interrupting her mournful thoughts.

Lena removes her gaze from the window, welcoming the temporary distraction from her grief. As much as she misses Grandmary and Theodore, she knows that she cannot allow it to pull her into a pit of depression. There are far too many important reasons to keep her chin up. She knows sorrow desires to drain the very life out of her. Joy is the only strength that will carry her through this trying time.

"Of course." Lena gives him her full attention. She severely lacks the knowledge needed to run a country. Her heart is wide open to all the advice he has to offer.

"The king you are meeting with today, though he is young, is not inexperienced. Tarsurella has been one of Bella Adar's greatest allies for centuries. Still, I would advise you not to enter the meeting assuming all is well. Just because King Addison's parents backed up our nation doesn't mean he will necessarily follow in their footsteps. You must be confident that you have Tarsurella's financial, political, and military support. Though I am not an expert in international relations, I advise you not to leave before you have a solid contract in writing. Be shrewd, and don't allow anyone to take advantage of your position."

Lena nods, fully appreciating his advice. Her naive state of inexperience in such matters is unnerving. Without the help of Captain Cepheus, his team of board members, and most importantly God Himself, she would be lost in a sea of cluelessness.

She smiles at Jack. "Thank you. I know many voices will be whispering in my ears over the weeks and months to come. Even though I want to learn everything I possibly can, I must also be on my guard. I know I can trust you, though. Your strong, steady, Christ-like character and unwavering desire to protect and defend the Crown is very admirable. I want you to know that you're not just my security guard, Jack. You are now one of my dear friends."

"I appreciate your kind words, Princess," Jack nods, "but I know my role in this story. I am a Military Cadet, and it's my job to serve the URIA. I do not consider myself to be an equal with your Royal title and would never trick myself into thinking that friendship with Your Highness would be something to count on or foresee enduring into the future. You might not be able to fully grasp this yet, but your decision to embrace your role as Queen has changed everything. In time, the world as we know it is going to be flipped upside down. Just because I'm serving you now, in this capacity, does not mean that in a few weeks' time I won't be marching out with the rest of my platoon."

Lena's kind gaze continues as she studies the young man sitting beside her. She's never allowed herself to spend any time appreciating his handsome features, as these past few weeks have been nothing more than a whirlwind.

From the first night he showed up at their farm, sharing the life-altering news of her royal past on the eve of her birthday, only one thing has mattered: protecting Grandmary and Theodore. She followed the mysterious stranger on a leap of blind faith, believing his words were true and that her unknown royal linage meant the wicked man who killed her birth parents was also after her. She followed Jack upon the promise that leaving home guaranteed Grandmary and Theodore's safety.

Tragically, the URIA could not protect her beloved family members from King Raymond's evil hitmen. Even though the people Lena loved with all her heart had been ripped from the soil of her life, new seeds of hope were slowly being planted. Her nation needed her, and once again she stepped out on the invisible bridge of faith, praying and believing that God would be faithful to guide her through this new unknown adventure.

Her decision to become Queen has only been in effect for several hours, but she can already see sprouts of blessing and provision popping up for this new endeavor—one of them being Jack.

Lena finds herself quietly admiring the man. His strong, noble character has already assisted her through many trials. His faithfulness is unwavering, and his convictions are sharp. Unlike Peter, her spirited childhood friend, he does not bounce from one wave to the next, riding the tide of unsteady emotions. Jack's anchor goes very deep.

When Captain Cepheus told Lena about her trip to Tarsurella, a body guard had been issued to travel with her with whom she had no previous history. Lena asked for Jack to come instead. Captain Cepheus was happy to grant her request, and though Jack was honored to serve in this capacity, Peter was not pleased with the arrangement. He wanted so desperately to come with Lena to Tarsurella, and he insisted that he should. But as much as Lena cared for her friend, she did not think this was his place.

"Next time," she promised, "but I must go ahead, as a forerunner of sorts, and lay the foundation for our future relations with Tarsurella. This is a very important trip. Surely you understand why it is best for you to stay here."

Peter eventually, yet very reluctantly agreed. He offered a grumpy goodbye and tossed a vicious stare toward Jack. Lena knew the two were not very fond of one another, but she wondered why Peter always behaved so cross around Jack. Peter has many wonderful qualities, and Lena knows their friendship is a rare, priceless treasure; even so, his negative attitude toward Jack and the URIA is beginning to concern her.

Lena steals one more shy glance at Jack, considering the weight of his words. *Just because I'm serving you now in this capacity does not mean that in a few weeks' time I won't be marching out with the rest of my platoon.*

Marching out. Though he did not state where they would be marching to, Lena knows.

They would be marching out to war.

A sharp shot of pain zig-zags like a crooked bullet through her chest, rattled by the thought that blood might be spilled in effort to take back the Kingdom. Jack is enrolled in the URIA as a foot solider. And even though he's been assigned a variety of different jobs, his first role is to fight on the ground with the rest of his men. Lena tightly clenches the arm rest. She cannot bear the thought of Jack, or any other innocent men, being injured or killed on the battlefield.

"You don't think it will come down to that, do you?" Lena asks quietly. "War?"

"Freedom isn't free." Courage soars in Jack's voice, "Though no man wants to enlist himself to such a fate, everyone in the URIA has been preparing for the possibility. We're willing to pay whatever price is necessary to release our nation from Raymond, the tyrant."

Lena shakes her head, all at once regretting her decision to lead such a cause. "How foolish could I be?" Her voice is full of fear. "Never pausing to think that my fiery desire to stop Raymond would come at the price of another man's sacrifice! I cannot do it. I have made a terrible mistake! I did not fully count the cost before attempting to rebuild this Kingdom! We must call Captain Cepheus and tell him to turn us back around—"

"No." Jack's voice is tranquil, "You have made the right decision. No man was forced to enlist, to place his life on the line. We love our country. We want our families, our friends, our children, and our grandchildren to know what it's like to live in a free Bella Adar! A nation where liberty, wealth, justice, and kindness endure. Your Majesty, you're carrying forward the destiny of this nation. You're bringing fresh hope to the lungs of every fighter! We've been preparing for years, and now, under your leadership, we are finally ready. Don't regret the decision you have made. It was the right one."

"I, I'm just so afraid," Lena admits, fighting back tears. "What if we don't win? What if Raymond destroys us and every effort to escape his grip is made in vain. What if—"

"Majesty," Jack interrupts, "you will not beat him if you're already defeated in your heart. You must take courage and remember whose side you are on! You are fighting for light and freedom, and for goodness! God is on our side and He is behind our righteous cause! If God is for us, who can be against us? Raymond will be defeated, so long as you don't allow fear to rule in your mind."

Lena takes a deep breath, sucking up strength from his words and allowing them to refresh her heart. Jack is right. She must remember the truth. God's faithfulness will see them through. History tends to repeat itself, and history is sprinkled with miraculous stories of God using the underdog to overthrow wicked rulers. If He's done it once, He can do it again. If He used Gideon, Deborah, Esther, and David, surely, He can use Bella Adar.

"You're right," Lena nods, forcing her thoughts to align with God's perspective on the matter. "God wouldn't have brought us this far only to disappoint us. The overthrow will come. Raymond doesn't know who he's messing with."

~*~

Jittery Lena sits in a lofty reception room, hands shaking as she rests her tea cup on a clattering saucer. The last thing she wants to do is break the Royal china! Her big eyes gawk at the lavish décor items that pose arrogantly, covering each square inch of the velvet room. Ancient oil paintings frown at her from the walls, with their disapproving stares reminding Lena that she is not wealthy nor sophisticated enough to be a Royal.

The overwhelming feelings of inadequacy sink deeper into her gut, as they have been ever increasing since she first stepped into the grand Palace entryway. The Tarsurellian Palace is like something out of a fairytale storybook. Expensive treasures are on display in each extravagant room. Lena is breathless by the sheer size of the Palace, let alone all the gaudy decorations and dozens of hired workers bustling about.

King Addison's lofty home is so far out of her league that she can't help but feel like an imposter attempting to masquerade herself as a Princess. Surely King Addison will see right through her. He will know she's nothing more than a poor, pathetic, uneducated, ill-equipped country girl.

She looks at the two URIA members who are present in the room. Captain Cepheus sent them with her, in another small plane, to see that matters are properly taken care of. The men calmly sip their tea, acting as if the posh room doesn't faze them. They look as if they're waiting to catch a taxi, not to meet with the King of Tarsurella!

Lena glances at Jack, who appears just as tranquil. He is always so dauntless. Perhaps he should be the king. It is obvious he knows much more about ruling a country than she does.

A pair of high heels clicks down the hallway, and Lena cranes her neck toward the closed door. Deborah, the kind and confident secretary who had given them a brief tour of the Palace upon their arrival, enters.

"His Majesty will see you now." She smiles kindly. "We apologize for the delay."

Lena's stomach drops. She is not ready for this.

All too soon, before she has time to prepare herself, the door flings open and everyone stands up. Lena quickly follows suit, assuming that Jack and the other men know what they're doing. Lena lowers her head, prepared to curtsy upon the King's entrance.

Footsteps are heard. She knows the King has arrived.

"Princess Lena," she is greeted with a warm voice, "it is a pleasure to make your acquaintance."

She looks upward, and King Addison holds out his hand. "Welcome to Tarsurella."

Lena is fondly taken aback by his pleasant features and kind tone. King Addison's sparkling blue eyes are shining with twenty-four carats of golden compassion. His youthful appearance, light skin, and sun-kissed hair tell Lena that he must be somewhere in his mid-twenties. His casual pair of blue jeans and blue, knitted sweater are shockingly modern.

She isn't sure why, but she was expecting to see someone far older. Someone ugly and harsh, with a fixed frown and a long beard, dressed in a purple robe and glittering crown. He couldn't be further from the predetermined image in her mind.

King Addison shakes hands with the URIA members then sits across from Lena on the velvet sofa. The rest follow the King's lead and settle into their seats.

"Ah, thank you for the tea, Monsieur Michael." King Addison smiles at the skinny staff member standing nearby, donned in suit and tie. King Addison looks at Lena. "These lemon cookies are my wife's favorite. I'm not sure how long you'll be staying here at the Palace, but you must make it a point to stop by the Royal Restaurant and try their dessert sampler. Clark, our head cook, cranks out some delicious Tarsurellian pastries. It will make your entire trip here totally worth it."

"Thank you, Your Majesty." Mr. Copeland, one of the URIA board members speaks up. "But we do hope to leave here with more than just full bellies."

"Of course!" King Addison sets his cookie down and his joyful smile disappears. "I know the nature of your trip here isn't a particularly joyous one." His gaze turns to Lena again, "I'm so very sorry for your loss."

"Thank you." She looks at him, sensing that his comment is sincere.

"Captain Cepheus has disclosed to me the entirety of your situation," King Addison begins, "and I first and foremost want to tell you that Tarsurella will gladly lend itself to your assistance and support. Although I never had the pleasure of meeting your parents, Lena, my father knew them well. He said they were kind, faithful, God-fearing individuals, and despite all the political struggles your nation has suffered, we intend to remain allies. Our parents forged a strong bond with the purpose of protecting and securing both of our nations, and I intend to keep all the promises Tarsurella has made to Bella Adar."

"Wow. Thank you," Lena breathes as tears form in her eyes. "You have no idea how much that means to me."

"Actually, I think I do." Addison smiles as he leans over, sitting on the edge of the sofa, "There are not many people on this planet who can relate with the stress, pressure, and overwhelming weight of responsibility you're feeling, other than someone who has walked a similar path in life. Now, even though my situation was a tad different than yours, I was handed this nation when I turned twenty-one. I felt like the whole world was on my shoulders; well, the whole country anyway." Addison chuckles before his face turns serious. "I was so afraid of disappointing the people I loved the most. It wasn't until I surrendered complete control to God that I was able to breathe easily and sleep at night again."

Lena is amazed by his words. It's as if someone had revealed to him everything her heart has been struggling with. "Do you have any advice for me?" Lena asks, eager to glean from his wisdom. "I don't know the first thing about running a country, and right now Bella Adar is in such a desperate state. There are orphans living in the capital city, whose parents have been murdered by Raymond. They cannot afford to attend school and are struggling to find enough food to eat. I know this is just one of many overwhelming problems we need to fix. I don't even know where to begin."

"Sometimes, tackling the problems we face in today's society feels like emptying the ocean one tiny glass at a time." King Addison sighs, "The burden is real. But you must remember that you're not called to carry it all on your own. When you surrender it to God, He is always faithful to bring others along to support your righteous cause. Captain Cepheus mentioned that you have several sisters? If I've learned anything through my journey, it's that family is everything."

"I do," Lena nods, "although they are each very preoccupied with their lives. I don't foresee any of them wanting to leave their home country to join the fight."

"Have you spoken with them directly about this, expressing the burden that weighs on you?" Addison asks.

"No." Lena shakes her head slowly, beginning to wonder what might happen if she did, "Captain Cepheus suggested it might be best for them to stay where they're at, for safety purposes, as well as just not wanting to add to the complexity of the situation."

"Captain Cepheus could be right," Addison shrugs, "but he could be wrong. I know I wouldn't be able to get through the struggles in our own country without the help and support of my siblings."

"Do you really think they'll come?" Lena's eyes grow wide, electrified by the thought. "Oh, it would be such a blessing to have them here with me!"

"I guess you'll never know until you ask." King Addison leans over to refill his teacup. "There's a lot of power in unity. Especially the unity of a family."

"Speaking of unity," Mr. Copeland speaks up, "the URIA would like to discuss Tarsurella's partnership and involvement in our military operations. We're currently developing a strategy that will…"

~*~

In New York City…

"Aurora! Bradley!" A spunky reporter calls out from where the two pass by on the red carpet. "Is it true? You're dating?"

Aurora stops in her tracks. She's trying to make her way into the pre-party for New York City Fashion Week's spectacular kickoff. Her tour rehearsals have ended and tomorrow morning she's scheduled to return to California for three precious days of rest, before flying back to New York to launch her massive tour at Madison Square Garden. As much as Aurora adores Fashion Week, tonight's pre-party is the only opportunity she'll have to participate in the festivities.

Aurora clenches her jaw, resisting the urge to show her frustration with this reporter. She's only been out of the limo for three minutes and has already heard this question dozens of times. Can't the media ever just chill out and mind their own business?!

"No ma'am, we're just hanging out together in preparation for Aurora's big tour!" Bradley jumps in, offering a kind, classy response to the woman. "It kicks off next weekend, and we are stoked!"

Aurora glances at Bradley, who clearly knows the drill. When reporters ask about your nonexistent love life, redirect their question to talk about your work.

"But Aurora, in an interview with *Totally Teen* last fall, you exclusively revealed that Bradley was your celebrity crush! Does this mean you've taken the posters down from your bedroom walls?"

Aurora is roasting with embarrassment. She cannot hide the color in her cheeks. "I have a boyfriend," Aurora manages to spit out, "and he's amazing." She continues marching her gold, sparkly high-heels down the carpet, determined not to respond to any more questions.

The venue doors open for her, and she rushes into the air-conditioned building. The cool air envelopes her as a sudden chill creeps down her legs. Now she's questioning her outfit of choice. *Maybe I shouldn't have worn such a short skirt. It's freezing in here.*

Nevertheless, it is Fashion Week and she wants to make a statement. Her turquoise mini-skirt is ruffled like a silk tutu, showing off her gold statement shoes. Her glittering tank embossed with gold sequins is hand-crafted by one of her favorite designers. She'll brave the cold to look this cute.

She opens her clutch, seeking a text message from Jeremiah. If he's responded, she'll send him a selfie, letting him know how she wishes he was here.

Her heart falls when she unlocks her screen and discovers her phone is lacking notifications. *What is with this boy?* Aurora frets, having received only a few lines from him the day before. *Can't he make the time to reply to a simple text?*

The past few days he had several excuses as to why he had to cancel their evening Facetime dates. Something about his brother getting ready to ship off to Iraq, and they had lots of family around and wanted to cherish those moments. Aurora can understand that. But is he really *that* busy?

"Whatcha doing? Updating Twitter?" Bradley asks from behind. "Making a mass public service announcement that we are *not* together?" He chuckles.

Aurora sighs and stuffs her phone back in her clutch. "No. But I probably should. The media sharks just don't know when to stop."

"Aw, don't let it get you down." Bradley tries to be positive, "Look on the bright side! We're in The Big Apple, attending an event so exclusive I didn't even know it existed." Bradley smirks, appearing to get great joy and amusement out of his own stale jokes.

"Yeah, I didn't know you were into fashion." Aurora's eyes narrow, wondering all at once what his true purpose for attending is.

"I'm not." Bradley shakes his head, his brown curls bouncing out in every direction. "It wasn't my intention when I woke up this morning, but I felt like God wanted me to come."

God? Aurora is about to ask why the Lord would care about whether or not he attended, but a flock of familiar faces wearing pastel cocktail dresses flood Aurora's personal space. They greet her with flattering hugs and half-hearted air kisses. Aurora greets her industry friends, attempting to act just as excited as they are.

The girls frivolously chat about who's attending and who is missing out, but Aurora's thoughts are not with them. She's distracted by Jeremiah's silence, and resists the urge to gnaw on her French-tipped nail. Is something wrong between them? Did she do something to irritate him? Is everything going to be okay when she lands in Cali tomorrow?

"Oh, I see you brought a friend!" Patricia Dart, last season's Academy Award winner for Best Actress, acknowledges Bradley's presence. "How long has this been a thing?"

"We're not dating," Aurora grumbles, wondering if she should write a post-it note on her face exclaiming the facts. "Goodness, can't a girl go out with a friend, without the world assuming they're a 'thing'?"

"I totally agree!" Another actress buds in, "It is so anti-feminist of the media to think you have to be in a relationship. Like, catch up June Cleavers, this is the twenty-first century! We can walk around with arm candy if we want to."

"Get it girl!" Another cheers her on, expressing her own feminist-driven thoughts on the matter, "I am *over* guys thinking they own us. We should be able to do whatever the heck we want to! Forget the lame relationship boxes. The word 'date' is too inclusive. I think we should create a new term. Just because we make out one day and never talk to each other again, doesn't mean anything! This is a free country; it's about time we act like it!"

Bradley can't hide the confusion on his face. "Well that's odd. Am I hearing you right? It sounds to me like you want guys to be *less* committed and even more flighty than most dudes already are? Or is this one of those double standard things, where you want to be free to cheat, but are going to demand the guy play nice and follow the rules you're constantly changing on him?"

Aurora's eyes grow wide. Yikes, Bradley is asking for it. He just dove head first into a conversation with some of the most fiery, radical feminist leaders in Hollywood. His traditional views on dating, marriage, and doing things 'God's' way, are not going to be tolerated.

"See, that's just the thing!" Patricia shakes her head, "The terms we're using in this conversation are way too constricting. Like, what does 'cheat' really mean anyway? One person's perspective of cheating might be another person's expression of freedom and self-expression. These labels are choking us."

Bradley shakes his head, "That's what I don't understand about this whole movement. You claim that you want to be free to do whatever you want and not have to answer to anyone…but at the end of the day, rules, boundaries and expectations still need to be in place. If one person comes into a relationship thinking, 'This is a genuine, selfless commitment of love and faithfulness', and another person enters it thinking, 'Oh, this is just a temporary, spur-of-the-moment infatuation and I can use you until I get bored and want to leave,' then there are going to be major problems. That's why God's original intention of a lifelong commitment of marriage between a man and a woman is pretty solid. Dare I say genius even."

"Marriage?" Patricia raises an eyebrow, "Woah, we're all teenagers here, right? Nobody is thinking about marriage! This conversation is about dating or not-dating, or self-exploration or whatever we want to call it. Nobody our age is thinking about weddings. Unless…you're not one of those old-fashioned, Bible-thumping, side-hugging, Baptist freaks, are you?"

"I'm not Baptist," Bradley hides a chuckle, although his eyes are clearly amused, "but I am a Christian. And I believe in doing life the way God lays it all out for us in the Bible. So, what's the purpose of dating or hooking up, or whatever elusive 'no labels' thing you girls are talking about if it's not going to end in a dedicated, life-long commitment of a lasting marriage and true love? Doing things God's way can save you some serious heartache."

"Wow, I never pegged you as one of those purity ring guys." Another actress pops into the conversation, "Isn't that like, some kind of a cult?"

Aurora's face is turning colors again. She shuffles her heels, wondering if she should walk away. She's growing more uncomfortable with each passing second.

"Christianity isn't cult." Bradley calmly explains, "We simply believe that Jesus is the Son of God, and He came to this broken world as a man, to die on the cross and take the place of punishment for our sins. Everyone who believes in Him will be saved and have eternal life; and once we experience His love and forgiveness, we're never the same. It's like, this amazing transformation takes place on the inside, and we want to do everything in our lives to please Him. All of a sudden, living the way the Bible teaches makes sense, and there's nothing more amazing than experiencing His love and direction in our lives. Choosing a lifestyle of purity is something Christians do because they *want* to. My decision not to date and wait for the woman God has for me is a personal one, and not everybody who follows Christ makes that decision. To each their own. But, there are some major blessings and perks involved with doing things His way. Like I said, less heartbreak. His boundaries bring truer freedom."

"I get that you have freedom of religion and I respect that," Patricia offers a haughty response, "but how have you *never* been on a date? Are you trying to convince us that you haven't even kissed a girl?! That's insane."

"It's true," Bradley nods. "It might sound a little bit cray, cray; but I'm totally down with living my life by God's design."

"Meanwhile, you're judging the rest of us heathens," Patricia spits bitterly. "The whole essence of your religion is based on labels and rules. It's guys like you who oppress women and try to make us feel like sluts, body shaming us for showing skin; thinking the meaning of our existence is to settle down, get married, and multiply. It's disgusting. Christians are holding all of humanity back, freezing us in the past, and trying to suck the life out of every leap women make toward a better tomorrow! You should be ashamed of yourself, and everything your stupid Bible stands for!"

"Patricia, not all Christians are like that." Aurora feels the need to speak up. As uncomfortable as the conversation is, she hates that Bradley is being persecuted. "You put just as many labels on us as you think we do on you. But the truth is, just because Bradley isn't dating around and treats women with respect and kindness, doesn't mean he's judging people who don't live the way he does, or is trying to push us back to the 1950's. There's nothing wrong with being old-fashioned about some things."

"Oh, my starfish, Aurora!" Another actress bursts out, "You're not a Christian, are you?"

Aurora's cool feet are suddenly extremely warm. Seven intense pairs of eyes are locked on her like lasers of fire, anxiously awaiting her response. Aurora gulps. She knows she can't lie. But siding with Bradley is going to make her look *so* bad right now.

"I, um…" Her eyes flash toward the ceiling. "Yeah, I mean, I am, but that doesn't mean–"

"How did we not know this?!" the girl continues. "You do *not* come across to me as the Christianly type. But wait…you're not like, into all that purity stuff too, are you? I mean, you're always out mingling and making things happen, am I right?"

"Of course!" Patricia gives her two cents worth. "She's Aurora Jasper! The Aurora we know *gets. her. man.*" The young woman adds an animated snapping sequence at the end, hoping to add a dramatic flair to her words.

Aurora's mouth is dry. She knows what the tabloids say about her. She knows that to these girls, Aurora appears to be a woman of the world, following the same social trends and thoughtless ways of living. Aurora doesn't know what to say. "I mean, I um…" Aurora anxiously touches her long, gold, dangling earing, "I date, if that's what you mean."

"See, she's no purity ring girl!" Patricia laughs, "She knows how to get what she wants!"

Aurora anxiously glances at Bradley. She doesn't want him to get the wrong idea about her. Yet, she doesn't want her friends to think she's a total geek burger either. "I'm not like a serial dater!" She quickly explains, "The media seems to think I have a new boyfriend every week…but that's totally not the case. I take my relationships seriously, and I'm not just going to throw my boyfriend away when I get tired of him. Jeremiah is amazing, and we have a deep, mutual respect and love for one another. Just because I'm a Christian doesn't mean I can't have an amazing love life. With boundaries, of course," she quickly adds.

"Boundaries?" Patricia asks, "Like what? *Oh. Girl.* Don't tell me you're not kissing your man. What's the point of having a boyfriend if you're not kissing!?"

Several of the girls laugh.

Once more, Aurora's face is flush red. She cannot hide her true emotions. She bites her lip, not wanting to lie again. She and Jeremiah were so close to having their first kiss. Several of her songs *do* talk about kissing. So maybe it's not a huge deal if she simply shakes her head and stretches the truth slightly. "No, no, I mean, of course we kiss. Like, who doesn't want to kiss their boyfriend?"

Bradley appears disappointed by her answer. Aurora scratches her arm, abruptly wishing this conversation never happened.

"Well, it was a pleasure chatting with you ladies, but I think I hear the food table calling my name." Bradley kindly excuses himself, and Aurora wishes to follow him and explain herself. But that would look ridiculous. Besides, isn't she currently trying to convince the world that she's not still 'in-like' with Bradley? Avoiding him for the rest of the night certainly sounds like a smarter and safer plan.

She can explain things to Bradley later. Maybe.

Because it shouldn't matter to Aurora what Bradley thinks about her, right?

Yet, it does.

~*~

Aurora doesn't want to peel her eyes away from the colorful runway. A line of paper-thin models strut blue and green peacock dresses. Yes, peacocks. Even though Aurora would never wear such a hideous thing, she can't seem to look away. But now, she really has to go to the bathroom. Her VIP seat in the second row doesn't make it simple for her to escape without everyone noticing. Nevertheless, nature is calling, and Aurora finally gets up.

She excuses her way past several long rows of celebrities and fashionistas much more popular than she and escapes the auditorium. The hallways are quiet and well lit, offering clear directions to the nearest restroom.

Her heels tinker down the floor and Aurora is tempted to take them off. Her feet are aching. *Why did I wear these?!* She scolds herself. *Nobody is looking at you. You're not even on the runway! You should've listened to Emma and just worn sneakers.*

She glances over her shoulder and when she's confident no one else is present, she leans against the wall and slips off her shoes. "Ahhhhhh." She sighs happily and collects her heels in her left hand. *Once we get back to the hotel, it's straight to the hot tub for you, Miss Jasper.*

She walks barefoot down the flat carpet, passing a worker who rolls an empty cart which used to display food, into a door marked "Kitchen." Aurora smiles at the worker, but she doesn't make eye contact with her. The worker's frown doesn't disappear.

Hmm, she must not be a fan, she thinks before turning toward the restroom.

After, she reemerges from the ladies' room and eyes the kitchen. A familiar sight catches her attention as she passes. She pauses to do a double-take. She can see Bradley's almost-afro sticking up from where he's chatting with several workers. Aurora slowly steps toward the open door, curious as to why he would be talking to them. Is he asking for more food? Did he come in search of seconds for his favorite dessert? Why isn't he watching the fashion show?

"Can I pray with you, man? I know this life isn't easy, but when you accept Jesus into your heart, He just floods you with so much peace and joy, and there is nothing like it in the world," Bradley tells one of the workers.

Aurora's breath catches as she watches in nervous anticipation.

Aurora cannot hear the worker's response, but next thing she knows, Bradley's head is bowed, and she can hear his prayer.

"Lord, you know everything about Diego. You know his life and what he's going through, and all the hard stuff he's facing. You know that his wife has left him, and times are hard. But You love Diego, and you have a plan and a purpose for him."

Tears form in Aurora's eyes. She's never seen anyone be so open and fearless about their faith. Is this why Bradley believed God wanted him to come to this event? To share the love of Jesus with others? Aurora wants to cry, and smile, and hide from her own shame, all at the same time.

"Lord, my brother here knows he is a sinner. He knows that he's messed up and missed the mark, and he wants to ask for Your forgiveness. So Lord, I'm standing here, in support of my brother, asking that You hear his prayer and accept His cry for forgiveness and for Jesus to come live in his heart. Now Diego, why don't you tell God what you're feeling? Ask Him for a second chance. Repent and ask Jesus to come make His home in your heart."

The conversation goes quiet, as Aurora knows that this man is praying. Others in the kitchen are praying as well. As astonishingly beautiful as it is, Aurora pulls herself away from the scene. It's wrong for her to stand in the shadows and listen. It's even *more* wrong of her to pretend she's a Christian. Her heart pounds with conviction. She walks down the hall.

God, what am I doing?! She screams out a silent prayer from somewhere deep inside. *I claim to know You, but I am so afraid that I don't! It's been so long since I've walked with You. So long since I've prayed. I'm afraid Lord! I'm afraid to speak Your name in front of my friends. I'm afraid to surrender and let go, and live unashamed of You. Why am I so afraid to speak the name of Jesus, when Bradley is bold enough to speak about his beliefs and pray with strangers? Oh God, forgive me! Forgive me for falling short and allowing our relationship to wither away!*

Aurora slows, not ready to return to the fashion show. She stops completely and allows herself to slide down the wall.

She hugs her knees and sniffs back tears. "Oh Jesus, I've chosen so many things over You," Aurora whispers, unable to hold it back any longer. "I've hurt so many people. I've hurt You and my parents and Emma and Miss Maggie and my sisters…and I've hurt myself. I hate the way that I'm living! It's like I'm the stupid center of my selfish, selfish world. I know I don't deserve it, but I want a second chance, God. I want to make You everything. Lord, please. I don't know how to make things better. I don't know how to be better. I don't know how to trust You, and I don't know how to let go…but I want to. So please, please be here to catch me."

~*~

Aurora's eyelashes flutter open. As she attempts to suppress a yawn, her face makes a twisted expression which the paparazzi would find quite unglamorous. She rubs her eyes. Instead of flopping over in her fluffy hotel room comforter and reaching for several more minutes of sleep, she props herself up on her pillows. A sweet peace, a peace which she hasn't felt since she was a little girl, is still present. It's been with her all night, sweetly rocking her to sleep then gently waking her up at the sound of her alarm. She can't help but smile. She knows God's presence is with her.

"Good morning, Lord," she whispers. "Thank You. I know that you're here with me now."

She ponders the ginormity of that truth. The God who breathed out the stars, the same God who created the entire planet and every person on it, is right here with her. In this very room. She takes a deep breath, wondering what to do next. How can she live today in a way that will be pleasing to God? How can she learn more about Him and be faithful in her newly recommitted faith walk?

She stretches across the bed and opens the bedside drawer. There, just as she expected, is a Bible. She opens it, places the KJV in her lap, and closes her eyes once more. "Lord, I know this is Your Word, so speak to me, and help me understand it. Amen."

And with that, Aurora opens her eyes and begins her hungry search in the diamond mine of God's Word.

~*~

Aurora's fingers speedily respond to Emma, typing out a text message close to five pages long. Sure it's teetering on the edge of novel length, and it's way too many words for what the texting app was invented for, but Aurora doesn't care. She can't wait to return home and tell Emma everything that's happened. She needs to share all this bubbly excitement with someone. Besides, she's got lots of time to kill. It'll be another two hours before she boards her flight back to LA.

Miss Maggie enjoys a pack of M&M's while flipping through a magazine. The two pass the time, just past the security checkpoint in a private area of the John F. Kennedy Airport.

Their waiting room is quiet, an exclusive area set apart for Aurora and other high-profile humans who want to fly without all the craziness that can happen on a public airline. Even though Aurora isn't quite wealthy enough to have her own private jet yet, this exclusive airline program for celebrities works just fine for her. The only other first-class flight members she has to tangle with are actors, wealthy businessmen, and reality TV stars; people who understand life in the limelight and respect one another's privacy. It makes the entire flying ordeal much more chill.

"How did Chelsea Bedru get a feature in *People*?" Miss Maggie exclaims, "Goodness, we are really slacking on your publicity! I'll call them as soon as we get to LA. Just because you have a sold-out tour doesn't mean we can lay low on your publicity. If we're not careful, girls like Chelsea are gonna come and steal your fans right out from under your nose!"

"That's ridiculous." Aurora looks up from her phone, "Chelsea doesn't even sing."

"Not according to *People*!" Miss Maggie waves the magazine around excitedly. "She's working on her first solo project right now! And apparently *Cowboy Carson* is a musical. We should get you in a musical."

Aurora doesn't respond. She's busy typing out her message to Emma.

"Yikes, out of M&M's!" Miss Maggie announces for no one but herself to hear. "Better get some more for the flight!"

She stands up and exits the small room in search of the sweet snack.

Aurora finally finishes her message and puts her phone away. She leans back in her chair happily, wondering what the next few days will have in store. It'll be nice to be back in LA, sleeping in her own bed, hanging out with Emma, and of course spending time with Jeremiah. She can't wait to see him. She feels as though their romance is like an epic movie that was put on pause. As soon as she lands, she knows they'll pick up right where they left off.

Before last night, Aurora was getting concerned. This long-distance relationship thing doesn't seem to be working too great for them. Apparently, Jeremiah isn't much on texting and Facetime. But now, Aurora knows everything is going to be okay. She trusts that God will work it all out. Worrying is just a waste of energy.

A familiar figure walks into the small waiting room. Bradley enters, carrying his laptop bag and guitar case. A small entourage of his management team follows. His untamed curls are bouncing about in every direction, and Aurora can't help but wonder if he even bothered to brush his hair today. Well, it is 6 AM, so she can't blame him. And, the messy look works for him.

"Morning." She smiles.

"Is it morning?" Bradly plops into the seat beside her, "It still feels like the middle of the night to me."

"Well, it's 3 AM in California; so, if you're still on Cali time that might be why."

Bradley pulls his grey hoodie over his head and leans back in the chair, closing his eyes. "Goodnight."

"Wait—before you go to sleep!" Aurora quickly blurts out.

Bradley's chocolate eyes open and turn toward her.

"I wanted to ask you a question."

[26]

"Shoot."

"Did um…did you ever find out why God wanted you to go to the fashion show last night?"

"What do you mean?" Bradley cocks his head slightly to the left.

"Like, did He show you why you were supposed to be there? Or did anything significant happen?"

"You mean like, when I was in the kitchen praying with several staff workers and you were standing in the hallway spying on us?"

"I wasn't spying on you!" Aurora gasps, surprised to hear that he knew she was there. "I just happened to be passing by, and I saw your afro sticking out and–"

"Aurora, I'm joking." Bradley laughs. "And to answer your question, yes. Talking to Diego about Jesus was my assignment."

"Assignment?" Aurora asks with a giggle, "What, like God gives you these top-secret, undercover missions or something?"

"Pretty much." Bradley grins, "I want to live my life with intention and make the most of every second I'm given. Hollywood is a crazy place, and I'm not here to make a name for myself, make a bunch of money, and die. I wanna live with more purpose than that! So, whenever I'm out, I ask God for an assignment. Someone to connect with, talk with, minister to. It doesn't always go the way I hoped, I mean sometimes I'm just planting seeds and then praying God does something with it. But last night? Last night was awesome. It's moments like those that keep me going. I mean, who knows? My daily, simple obedience to Christ just might change a life."

"It definitely did." Aurora nods, admiring so much about the faith and boldness of the young man sitting beside her. "And it wasn't just Diego's life who was effected. Last night I–"

"Oh, my Butterfingers, I just found the M&M pretzel flavor!" Miss Maggie announces as she reenters the room. "Arden has been telling me about these, and I didn't think they were a real thing! Ha, I'm going to have to take a picture of them on my phone and show him!" She suddenly notices Bradley, "Well, if it isn't Mr. Bradley Cason! On the same flight as us! How fun! Oh, how would you like to snap a photo of me holding my M&M's? Arden will get a kick out of it!"

Aurora crinkles her nose, wondering why Miss Maggie can be so kooky sometimes. Aurora can't help but laugh and shake her head. Despite Miss Maggie's zany request, Bradley is a gentleman and snaps a photo of Miss Maggie.

Aurora realizes that her conversation with Bradley has been cut short, so she redirects her attention to her own phone. As much as she wants to tell Bradley what happened last night and how his boldness influenced her decision and recommitment to follow Christ, it looks like it will have to wait.

~*~

In Amish Country...

Elizabeth nervously twirls a fork in her fingers. She glances upward at Da as he devours the noon meal. Her eyes flicker to Ma. She takes small, polite bites, waiting to speak until she's been spoken to. Elizabeth knows it isn't right to bring up topics of conversation at the table unless Da initiates them. Women are to be submissive and quiet. But Elizabeth's tongue burns with a question. She must ask it.

"Da," she manages to squeak out anxiously.

Da's thick, bushy eyebrows shoot upward. His fork pauses in the air.

Elizabeth gulps. "Why do we not study the Bible on our own? Why do the Bishops say we should only listen to their interpretation of the Scriptures?"

Da sets down his fork. "'Tis easy for the devil to get a foothold. The Holy Scriptures must be read with a pure mind and without questions or doubts. Private Bible study has led to the development of false doctrine. When you were just a youngin', about two or three perhaps, a man from our Community led a Bible study, a secret group within our own Church. The men who read and attended the study got so puffed up with pride, they started questioning the Ordnug, challenged the Bishops, and eventually left the community."

"Does that mean there are things in the Bible that do not line up with the Old Order?" Elizabeth asks.

"Where are these questions coming from?" Da frowns. "Are you having doubts about the faith? Doubts about joining the Church? I see that your time in the world has planted ungodly leaven in your mind." He shakes his head with disappointment.

"No, Da! That's not it!" Elizabeth argues. She attempts to explain a reason why, but she cannot. Oh dear. Maybe that is it.

"Are you lying to me Elizabeth?" Da asks, his voice hot with an undertone of fear and anger.

Elizabeth looks shamefully toward her plate. "I am sorry, Da. I confess. I do…I do have…questions."

"Oh, Abraham, I knew we never should've let her go!" Ma cries.

Da places his napkin on the table and folds his arms. "Elizabeth, you must confess this sin to the Bishop. If you do not repent of your doubts and ungodly thoughts, the devil will continue to lead your mind astray."

"But Da, I–"

Da puts a hand up, as if to silence her, "No excuses! I will schedule a meeting with the Bishop tomorrow. Perhaps he will help you turn back to the Lord before it is too late."

"I am not turning away from God!" Elizabeth argues, bravely standing up for herself and her stirring convictions. "It is quite the opposite! I do not understand why my questions would be a bad thing! Surely they will help me grow closer to Him instead of–"

"That is enough!" Da barks, his volume shocking Elizabeth into silence. "We will speak no more of it. Tomorrow you will speak with the Bishop, confess your sins, and forget everything that happened while you were in the world. The time has come to put away childish things, Elizabeth. Baptism classes are about to begin. It is time you make your decision. If you stay lukewarm, the Lord Jesus will surely spit you out of His mouth. It is time to commit yourself to the Church."

~*~

Elizabeth's heart is heavy as she sits on the porch, snapping the ends off a large pile of green beans from the garden. Da's heated words had frightened her. The lack of compassion and understanding in his response hurt her heart. Didn't he trust his own daughter? Why did he think her questions were evil? Did he really think she would choose the ways of the devil and abandon her people? It hurt Elizabeth to know her parents don't trust her, yet they're not open to discussing any of these matters either.

Elizabeth tosses another bean into the bowl then glances at her mother who performs the same chore. Elizabeth wants to speak but she doesn't. She knows whatever she says will only end in an argument. That's how all their conversations have been going.

The tearing of her heart in two opposite directions grows more painful with each passing day. She longs to know how her sisters are doing. She deeply misses their companionship and all the joyful times they had together. She misses Emma too, and cupcake baking, and giggling while stuffing their faces with that delicious pizza pie.

Elizabeth would never admit it to her parents, but there are some ways about the Englishers' lives that make sense to her. Flush toilets, for example! Not having to go outside to use the privy in the middle of the night is a convenience Elizabeth can appreciate. As well as motor cars. Though they were terribly frightening to her in the beginning, she can now see the purpose behind them. Traveling so quickly can connect family across many miles.

But the one thing which makes the most sense to Elizabeth in the Englisher's world, is freedom to study the Bible. Surely their Church is missing out on a great joy and comfort from not being able to study the Scriptures on their own. Elizabeth finds it hard to believe that the devil could use the Bible to lead people astray. Lena seems very confident of her faith in Christ, yet she did not grow up with the Ordnug. It is all so puzzling to her.

Elizabeth sighs, wishing for a way to discover answers for herself. How can she explain to the people around her that her questions have nothing to do with a desire to leave the Church? She merely wants to know more about God and His ways, and perhaps have a peace in her heart that her sisters might not be eternally condemned to hell. As much as she loves her sisters, Ma and Da are her first family. Her true family. She would never think of leaving them. She is content with life in their Community and wouldn't want anything to change.

Elizabeth looks upward, surprised to see a buggy pulling up their long drive. It is an odd hour of day for visitors. Perhaps whoever is inside has come to see Da about a milk order? She continues working on her green beans when Ma suddenly lets out a little gasp.

"Elizabeth, it looks like we have a visitor!" she exclaims excitedly.

Elizabeth looks up again and her face turns warm. The features of the handsome buggy driver are clearly seen. It's Jonah!

She quickly brushes off her hands and adjusts her Prayer Cap, feeling a flurry of nervousness stir up in her stomach like a miniature windstorm. She tries to appear busy while waiting for him to walk up the long drive, park his ponies, and ascend their squeaky porch steps.

"Good afternoon, Mrs. Stoltz," Jonah nods respectfully, "Miss. Elizabeth."

Elizabeth cannot suppress her smile. She never tires of hearing her name upon his lips.

"Is Mr. Stoltz in the barn?" Jonah asks, attempting to keep his eyes fixed on Mrs. Stoltz.

"Yah, he is." Mrs. Stoltz smiles, "He will be pleased to see ya, Jonah."

"Thank you, ma'am." Jonah nods once more then turns on his heel. Not before tossing a quick smile in Elizabeth's direction.

Jonah takes long strides toward the barn, and Ma squeezes Elizabeth's hand. "I think he is here to ask about you!"

"Ask about me for what?"

"For a courtship, silly girl!" Ma laughs. "Our prayers have been answered! Despite your time in the world, Jonah has come back and made good on his word!"

Elizabeth's heart skips a beat. Could it be true? Could Jonah be standing in the barn right now, this very second, asking Da for permission to enter an official courtship? Elizabeth cannot focus on snipping beans any longer. She has to know what's going on! Her foot taps nervously on the wooden porch as minutes stretch into what feels like an eternity.

Finally, Jonah rounds the house and appears before them again. Elizabeth holds her breath.

"Miss Elizabeth, would you do me the pleasure of being my company this fine afternoon, as I escort you for a buggy ride?"

Elizabeth anxiously looks at Ma for permission.

Ma nods gladly.

Elizabeth sets down the bowl of beans and slowly rises to her feet, feeling like she's floating on a daydream. Jonah offers a friendly arm to help her down the steps and Elizabeth takes it. Normally, she can get down the steps just fine. But right now, she might actually need his help from falling on her face.

As they walk to the buggy and climb in, Elizabeth can't help but praise God. Jonah's invitation proves that He still has a plan for her life! A plan right here, at home, in Amish country. And, if things are going in the direction Elizabeth believes them to be, this plan is far more beautiful than she could've possibly dreamed!

With a short click of the tongue, Jonah's horses pull out of the drive, marking the first moment of what Elizabeth hopes will be a lifetime of endless memories just like this one.

"Beautiful day, isn't it?" Jonah starts with small-talk, glancing at the lovely girl seated beside him.

"Indeed." Elizabeth grins. But she's not talking about the blue skies above.

"I have to admit, I had trouble keeping my breakfast down this morning."

"Oh no." Elizabeth tosses him a compassionate glance, "Are you well?"

"Not then I wasn't!" Jonah laughs, "But it had nothing to do with my ma's cooking. It was only because I had decided that today would be the day. The day I rode to Elizabeth Stolz's house and asked her Da permission to court his daughter."

Elizabeth can't help but giggle.

"But now? Oh, now I feel wonderful! I feel like I could eat a whole feast!" Jonah smiles, "But there is no need. My soul is feasting on this moment alone. That is enough for me."

"I must apologize for leaving so abruptly, after the last Singin'," Elizabeth breathes. "Did Da explain to you? A strange emergency came up and–"

"No need to explain." Jonah waves a hand through the air, "All is understood. Your da rode over the next day and shared what took place. It was no bother to me though. I knew that as soon as you returned home, I would ask. Elizabeth, I have prayed my entire life for a woman like you. And I believe wholeheartedly that you are the woman God has for me to marry."

Elizabeth's eyes grow wide. Did Jonah just say *marry*?!

"I hope my frank speech isn't bothering you." Jonah suddenly sounds as if he might be concerned about being too forward, "It's just, I want you to know, Elizabeth. My heart has belonged to you since the time we first met. Four years ago, at the Anderson's barn raising. Do you remember?"

Elizabeth can feel her heart melting into a soppy puddle of happiness and bliss. "Yah. I remember." She nods, a small smile pressing onto her lips. "Naomi's cat had a fresh litter of kittens, and all of us children were playing with them. All the hustle and bustle must have frightened her cat, as she bolted up a tree and wouldn't come back down. We tried everything to coax her, but it wasn't until you climbed up the tree and rescued her yourself that she was safe on the ground. I thought you were very brave."

"How funny!" Jonah laughs, "I am glad to hear that my plan worked! Truth was, the only reason I climbed up that tree was to impress you."

Elizabeth joins in Jonah's laughter.

A delightful stillness settles over the two, and after a few moments, Elizabeth speaks again. "I too, have had my heart fixed on you, ever since that day. It almost feels too wonderful to be real. I have prayed, asking for God to send me a man like you, Jonah Yoder. And I am humbled that He has answered my prayer and made provision for a–" she pauses before allowing the strange new word to slip off her tongue, "husband."

"My ma always said that if you leave the match making up to God He will never disappoint you." Jonah grins, having trouble keeping his eyes on the road, "And she was right."

Elizabeth and Jonah talk in a carefree manner for the next ten minutes, laughing and chatting about everything under the sun. Elizabeth is wonderstruck by how natural everything feels. All her nerves melt away, and each new word with Jonah causes her to feel like they've been close friends their entire lives.

Jonah turns his buggy off the main road, down a bumpy path toward the river. Elizabeth recognizes the place. She and her cousins used to play down here often, as young children.

"Where are we going?" she asks.

"To have a picnic by the river."

"A picnic? But we have not packed any food."

"You have not packed any food." Jonah grins mischievously, "But I have."

Several moments later, they're settled on the bank, praying and thanking God for the delicious meal set before them. After the "amens" they dive in, continuing their immensely enjoyed conversation.

"I will begin my Baptism classes this week," Jonah reveals. "I am ready to take the next step of commitment to the Church."

"Oh." Elizabeth pauses from placing a small chunk of cheese in her mouth. "Da signed me up to begin classes as well."

Jonah's eyes narrow suspiciously, "You do not sound very pleased."

Elizabeth freezes, wondering what to say next. Should she tell Jonah of the doubts and questions she's been struggling with? Or will he respond in the same way her parents have? Will Jonah understand? Or will he grow angry and wish to throw away the entire courtship?

She takes a deep breath, knowing that if she is going to build a strong relationship with this young man, she must be truthful. "I confess I have been struggling with doubts and questions." Elizabeth sighs, hating she has to admit this to him. "I am meeting with Bishop tomorrow to confess my sins and pray for forgiveness."

"Forgiveness for what?"

"For having so many questions," she explains.

"What is sinful about having questions?"

"Questions can lead to deception and false doctrine."

"I suppose that is true." Jonah shrugs, "But at the same time, questions can also lead to truth and discovery about God and His Holy ways."

Elizabeth is surprised by his words. "So, you do not think I am wickedly sinful for battling with the questions that plague my heart?"

"Of course not!" Jonah reassures her, "I think it is foolish to blindly believe everything people tell you, even be it your parents or the Church. You must know in your heart of hearts that what you believe is true. Otherwise, it is not your faith, and you are merely riding on the coat-tails of someone else. Asking questions is wise. Jesus said to seek and you will find. To knock, and the door will be opened to you. I know that if you are praying to find truth, you will know what to believe."

"Are not the Holy Scriptures truth?" Elizabeth asks. "I cannot understand why we are discouraged to keep from studying them on our own. Is the Bishop fearful of what we might find inside? Fearful of something that will change our minds, or show them to be in the wrong?"

"Though it is frowned upon in the Church, my parents have always encouraged me to study the Scriptures," Jonah reveals. "My studying has not pulled me away from the Amish way of life, but rather it has drawn me closer, giving me all the more reason as to why I desire to live according to the Old Order! Da explained that there are things in the Bible that do not match the Ordnug. The Old Order is a strong doctrine passed down from generation to generation, and it is a beautiful, holy way of life. But my parents wanted me to know it is not the way to Salvation. Just ask our Mennonite neighbors! We may have differences in dress or tradition, but we always have one thing in common. Jesus is the only Way of salvation and eternal life."

"Do you mean to say, someone who is not Amish can be saved from damnation?" Elizabeth's eyes widen with hope.

Jonah nods, "In the Gospels, The Lord Jesus makes it very clear that there is only one way to be cleansed of sin and have eternal life. And that is through Him. But don't take my word for it. Read the words in red for yourself."

Elizabeth is speechless. All at once, Jonah speaks the words her heart has been aching to hear. His insights give her hope. Perhaps her sisters will be saved after all! Perhaps the Amish way is not the only way! But like Jonah says, she cannot be sure until she reads the words for herself. Then she will know what to believe.

"Thank you," Elizabeth breathes. "Thank you for sharing your wisdom, and for listening to me and not condemning my questions. I feel like now you have given me the courage to find answers."

"Joining the Church isn't something to take lightly." Jonah continues, "Nobody should enter such a commitment blindly. I think it is fear that causes parents and the Church leadership to push young people into making that choice, afraid that they might go astray. But my parents were wise. They allowed me to study on my own, ask questions, and search for answers; to make an educated, informed, and heartfelt decision. I am confident that joining the Church is God's will for me. 'Come out from among them and be separate.' That is God's will for me. I pray of marrying a wife who believes the same, someone who is content and humble and kind. Someone who desires to raise their children in the Lord's Way and be a blessing to serve the Community. I truly hope and pray that you are that woman, Elizabeth. But if not…" Jonah timidly looks away for a second, as if it pains him to speak the words, "If God has another path for you," he looks back at her, "then I pray that you will find it."

~*~

Elizabeth turns over in her small bed, readjusting the quilt on her legs. She stares upward at the dark ceiling, wondering what time it is. She does not know the hour, but it has to be late. She's been struggling to fall asleep for hours.

Everything that happened today with Jonah was pure bliss. He's every bit as wonderful as she hoped he would be. Yet, Elizabeth still doesn't have peace in her mind. A deep unsettling causes her to feel disturbed, and she doesn't know why.

She flops over, wondering why things have to be so complicated. Like a ball of knotted-up yarn, she can't seem to untangle her mind from all the things that are bothering her so deeply. She sits up and crosses her legs, closing her eyes in prayer.

"Lord, I need help," she whispers. "I am so very confused. I need to know the truth for myself. I need to know what I believe and why I believe it. Guide me into the truth."

Her eyes pop open as she thinks about the family Bible downstairs. Should she dare go down and read it? Sneaking downstairs to study without her parents' permission can't possibly be sinful. Can it? Surely there is nothing sinful about exploring the Bible! If her parents discover what she is doing…well…they're just going to have to be okay with it.

Elizabeth slips out of bed, careful to avoid all the sensitive floor boards in her room. Ma and Da are snoring in the room just beside her. She must be quiet as a mouse to guarantee they do not awake.

She unlatches her bedroom door and steps into the small hallway. She tiptoes down the stairs, careful to skip the second to bottom step, which always makes a loud creak when landed upon.

Once downstairs, she feels her way along the wall through the dark. Only a small sliver of light is coming in the kitchen window from where a half moon hangs above. She reaches the empty fireplace where the thick Bible rests on the mantel.

Elizabeth's heartbeat picks up as she nervously reaches for the Book. She glances over her shoulder, fearful that Da might come down the stairs at any moment and find her. Elizabeth takes a deep breath, scolding herself for being so timid. She should be confident in her decision and believe that God will stand by her righteous cause. She places the heavy book beneath her arm and sneaks out the squeaky front door. She will go to the barn to read.

She dashes barefoot across the yard, feeling a wet dew on the long blades of grass. She doesn't have much time. Dusk will come soon. She enters the dairy barn and quickly climbs the loft, hoping to find a secret place where no one will find her. She plops onto a hay bale near the loft window and narrows her eyes, opening the dusty book. Where should she begin? Her fingers lead her to the book of John. She quickly reads the first two chapters. Then Chapter 3 arrests her attention.

The text is about a religious leader named Nicodemus, who wanted to listen to Jesus' teachings but was fearful as to what might happen if he got caught. Elizabeth instantly connects by the similarity of her situation. Her heart sops up every word like a thirsty sponge, wondering what all of these wonderful words truly mean.

"For God so loved the world that he gave his only begotten Son, that whosoever believeth in him should not perish, but have everlasting life. For God sent not his Son into the world to condemn the world; but that the world through him might be saved. He that believeth on him is not condemned: but he that believeth not is condemned already, because he hath not believed in the name of the only begotten Son of God."

Elizabeth's eyes scan the first line again, "whosoever believeth in Him should not perish." Does this mean Jonah is right? The only requirement to be saved is to believe in Jesus? What about their manner of dress? And their work habits? What about whether or not they use machinery or drive vehicles? What about cooking Englishers' food or singing songs that are not in the old Hymn Book?

A cranky old rooster suddenly interrupts her thoughts. She anxiously looks up, fearing that the sun will rise soon. She must get back inside before Da sees her. She closes the Bible and descends the loft, pondering those mysterious words in red.

Whosoever believes...

~*~

Elizabeth gathers eggs, searching for any peculiar places their old hen may have hidden them. Sometimes she leaves them in the oddest of spots.

A gentle rumbling is heard in the distance. Elizabeth looks up, curious as to what the sound might be.

A silver car, sparkling in the early morning sunshine, pulls up their driveway. Elizabeth watches with tired eyes. All at once it dawns on her. She excitedly drops her egg basket and races toward the parked car. The passenger door flings open and Lena races out.

"Elizabeth!" she cries, flinging herself into her sister's arms.

"Oh, Lena! Lena!" Elizabeth squeals excitedly, relishing the embrace. "I cannot believe it is you! Oh, praise God, I am so happy you have come to visit! I have missed you dearly!"

Jack climbs out of the driver's seat and reaches his arms into the air. It was a long drive from the airport to Elizabeth's home in the middle-of-nowhere. His eyes are pleased to see the girls' happy reunion.

"I have missed you too!" Lena exclaims. "So very much!"

The screen door opens and Ma anxiously steps onto the porch. "Elizabeth? Elizabeth, who are these strangers?"

"Oh Ma, this is my sister!" Elizabeth explains excitedly. "Lena, meet my mother!"

"I am pleased to meet you, Mrs. Stoltz." Lena quickly climbs the porch steps and offers a hand of greeting.

Ma frowns. "Why are you here?"

"Ma'am, you don't need to be concerned," Jack speaks up. "We're only here for a visit. The URIA isn't going to take her away."

"And who are you?" Ma crosses her arms.

"Jack Conway, Lena's escort for this visit, a URIA cadet."

"Well," Ma places a questioning hand on her hip as she examines the young man, "I suppose you've had a long journey. Why don't you two come in for breakfast?"

"Oh, thank you, Mrs. Stolz, you're too kind!" Lena curtsies politely, sensing that the woman still doesn't trust them.

Ma opens the door and Elizabeth grabs Lena's hand. "Come, we were just getting breakfast on! You'll have to tell me all about your journey!" She leads her inside as they breeze past Ma.

Jack's heavy boots clomp up the stairs, and he offers Mrs. Stoltz a polite nod before entering her home. "Thank you, we really do appreciate it. I know this hasn't been easy for you."

"Do you?" Mrs. Stoltz huffs, "If you and the URIA knew it was so challenging for us then why did you not stay out of Elizabeth's life and mind your own business?"

Ma saunters off toward the barn, leaving Jack alone in the doorway. He wants to say something to comfort the woman, but she's already halfway toward the barn. Realizing that there's nothing else he can do, he steps inside and finds the girls excitedly chatting in the kitchen.

"Oh, things have been so very dull around here!" Elizabeth tells Lena. "As much as I adore my family and our little Community, it is lonely not having sisters to cook and eat and laugh with! I am overjoyed by the fact that you've come! How long will you be staying?!"

"Elizabeth," Lena starts slowly, cautiously trying to find the right words, "I did not just come for a leisurely visit. Much has happened since we left New York. When I returned to Bella Adar, I found..." A lump surfaces in her throat, and she struggles to speak what she knows to be true. "Grandmary and Theodore are dead."

"Oh, Lena." Elizabeth's heart aches with compassion for her sister. She grabs her hands and squeezes them tightly, "How horrible! I am so very sorry!"

"It...it hasn't been easy." She sniffs then offers a brave smile. "But God is walking with me through the midst of the pain. I don't know why He allowed this to happen, but I believe that

He has a plan in all of it. Elizabeth, that is why I am here. Raymond, the same evil man who killed our birth parents and has been oppressing the people of Bella Adar, murdered my Grandmother and brother. He is a wicked, heartless man, and many in our nation are suffering because of him. I need you, Elizabeth. Our country needs you. I've come to ask you to return to Bella Adar with me."

~*~

Episode 2

"There must be more to this provincial life!" A loud brunette with a full soprano voice belts out onstage. Emma watches from the front row as Jeremiah struts onto the stage, owning each step as haughty Gaston. The role is quite perfect for him. As much as Emma detests the guy, she cannot deny the fact that he's a fantastic actor. Either that or he's just being himself.

"Oh, how beautiful are your eyes my dear, Belle!" Jeremiah tells the strawberry-blonde girl named Savannah. She attempts to act as if she's completely uninterested in the self-absorbed villain. "When I gaze into your eyes, I see the reflection of my own dashingly flawless face!" Jeremiah proudly grabs his invisible shirt collar and gets a bit of laughter from the younger audience.

Emma glances at the young girl sitting beside her and smiles. The perky eight-year-old, who she spoke to on the first day of practice, dangles her feet, happily kicking them back and forth from her elevated position in the red theater seat. Several days into rehearsals, the spunky little girl had shared that her name was Emma; and once the munchkin knew that big Emma was her name twin, she took a strong liking to her.

"Your name is so lovely, as sweet as a rose, but it will be even greater once it's seated next to *my* last name!" Gaston continues to pursue his distracted love interest. Belle peers into her book, blocking out the world around her.

You go, Belle! Emma mentally cheers her on, *that guy is a creep! Books are way better than boys.*

Gaston is persistent. "Once you become my wife, life will be bliss, you'll cook and clean for me and we'll have ten kids—

each of them strapping young boys, taking after their incredibly good-looking father."

Belle snaps her book shut, "Gaston, I already told you! I have no interest in becoming your wife! Now if you'll excuse me, I have–" All at once, Savannah giggles uncontrollably.

Emma frowns. The immature actress is having a struggle staying in character.

"I'm sorry!" Savannah covers up another giggle with her hands, "Jeremiah is making me laugh! Stop making that face!" She pushes him playfully in the arm and Emma resists the urge to roll her eyes.

They've been trying to get through this scene for a full fifteen minutes, but Savannah can't seem to control her giddy emotions. Doesn't she have the personal willpower to stop flirting with Jeremiah and stay in character? Emma makes a disgusted clicking sound with her tongue.

"It's okay, let's take it from Gaston's line." Julie's voice is patient, "Once you become my wife…go."

Emma is beyond impressed with Julie's personal aptitude for patience and long-suffering. She clearly has the heart of a saint. If Emma were in charge, she would've already booted giddy Savannah and cast someone who can look at Jeremiah without melting into a helpless pile of teenage crush.

"Gaston, I already told you!" Savannah slams her book shut, "I have no interesting in becoming your wife! Now if you'll excuse me, I have, I have to…uh, what do I have to do?" She turns sheepishly toward Julie.

"Get to the bookstore and find this sequel," Emma grumbles, having already memorized the script. "I'm in the middle of a most exciting tale, and I cannot be interrupted."

"This is boring," Little Emma announces, declaring that she too is done with the ordeal.

"I know it can be tiring waiting around like this," Emma whispers, "but rehearsing each scene takes a lot of hard work."

"I didn't even get a big part!" Little Emma crosses her arms grumpily. "I'm just a stupid fork in the cupboard."

"Hey now, in theater there's no such thing as a small role!" Emma tries to cheer her up, "Being a fork is a *way* bigger deal than you might think. Without the fork, the *Be Our Guest* number would be totally dull!"

"But I really wanted to be Belle!" she insists. "And every time I try out for something I get a super small role. Maybe I should just give up acting."

"Do you know who Aurora Jasper is?" Emma asks.

"Duh!" She looks at Emma like she has just suggested an alien from Mars is running for president. "Everybody does!"

"When Aurora was a little girl, she used to get small parts too. One time, in the *Jungle Book*, she was part of a snake. Not a snake. *Part* of a snake. Meaning, she had to walk under this big costume with other kids, and she didn't even have any lines! She hated it and wished she had a lead role like one of the older cast members. She thought about giving up her dreams of performing too. But she didn't. Know why?"

"Why?" Emma asks with wide eyes, clearly drawn into the story.

"Because her director said that having a small roll in any production is a huge honor. There's so much you can learn from each show, and as long as you have the right attitude and focus on having fun, it will prepare you for bigger opportunities in the future! Her director also said to never give up on her dreams. I for one am glad that she didn't. I mean, can you imagine a world without Aurora Jasper's music? Aurora didn't give up, and neither should you."

"Wow, I didn't know that about her." Little Emma smiles, "That kind of makes feel better! Are you a fan of hers?"

"I guess you could say that." Emma shrugs.

"Cool." Little Emma leans back in her velvet auditorium seat, "Maybe being a fork isn't so bad after all…"

After rehearsal, Emma collects forgotten scripts left behind from the younger kids. She checks beneath the seats, wrangling up a myriad of lost items. She, Julie, and the rest of the team must make sure the auditorium is perfectly clean after each practice session.

Loud laughter floats from the stage. Emma glances upward, watching with suspicious eyes as Savannah and Jeremiah chat with one another.

"Obviously, I'm having my struggles," Savannah admits. "But with school and cheer practice and everything else, I haven't had any time to go over my lines. It would be great if we could get together and practice."

"I agree." Jeremiah nods, "I have a pretty crazy schedule too, but we should definitely make it happen. Here, let me give you my number."

"Ohhh, getting the digits of the cutest guy in town. I'm flattered." Savannah giggles.

Emma curls her lip upward, grossed out by Savannah's desperate clawing for him. She listens intently, wondering how Jeremiah will respond. Will he tell her to back off and boldly state that he's got a girlfriend? Or will he continue to welcome the illegal attention?

"The cutest guy in town?" Jeremiah laughs, "Yikes, I don't know about that. I mean, come on, let's be realistic. That's a pretty insane claim, how about…best looking guy in this production?"

"You're so humble!" Savannah giggles then continues in a teasing tone, "Now I see why they cast you as Gaston!"

Emma angrily closes her ears, fuming about the fact that *this* is her best friend's boyfriend. Could she have chosen much more of a jerk?!

She continues her search for forgotten items. Savannah bids Jeremiah goodbye and slips out the back door. Jeremiah leaps off the stage, landing just several feet from Emma.

"Finding some good stuff in these seats?" Jeremiah asks in a friendly tone, acting as though they've been buddies for years.

Emma shakes her head, wondering how the guy can be so clueless. Doesn't he get the message? She doesn't want to talk to him! Are her non-verbal signals of rudeness not clear enough?!

"Oh, you know, just the usual." Emma keeps her voice steady, "Scripts, candy wrappers, pencils, forgotten girlfriends."

"What?" Jeremiah makes a twisted face, missing the meaning of Emma's passive-aggressive message.

"Oh, don't pretend like you don't know what I'm talking about," Emma snaps. "You're a good actor, but you're not *that* good. My best friend is crazy about you, which I have no idea why, but she is. And if you think I'm just going to sit here and watch you flirt with every girl who walks by while your girlfriend is out of town for a few days, then you have severely underestimated mine and Aurora's friendship."

"Oh, come on, Emma!" Jeremiah attempts to explain himself, "I wasn't flirting with Savannah! What, you think just because Aurora's gone I'm trying to move in on some other girl? That's insane! Aurora is amazing! In fact, I've got an epic date planned for tomorrow night. We're going out for lobster and then we're gonna hit some waves, two of Rory's favorite things. Now, I don't know what your definition of 'flirting' is, but me talking to Savannah? That is most definitely not it. Hey, maybe you should third wheel on our date tomorrow night. Then you can see some real flirting in action." He winks.

Emma's eyes widen. "I'd rather be forced to go to a party and talk to a bunch of strangers, which for me is a very unpleasant experience." Emma shakes her head before turning away, "I don't know what Aurora sees in you. But if you hurt her, I–" Emma pauses, suddenly realizing that none of her threats will hold any weight with him.

"You'll what?" Jeremiah chuckles, "Hit me with a book?"

"Let's just make sure you never have to find out," Emma grumbles.

~*~

"Lord, I lift Your name on high! Lord I love to sing Your praises! I'm so glad you're in my life! I'm so glad you came to save us!"

Emma struggles to sing along with the praise band at youth group, feeling slightly guilty for the way she tore into

Jeremiah earlier. As much as he deserves it, maybe Emma needs to calm down. Maybe she's overreacting. Maybe Jeremiah really isn't a bad guy.

But Emma just can't seem to force herself to trust him. Emma knows she shouldn't be so emotionally invested in the outcome of Aurora's relationship, but she is. The last thing she wants is Aurora's heart to be shattered into a million pieces. This is the first time she's opened up and given her heart away. Jeremiah holds so much power in his hands. And Emma can't bear to think of him breaking the heart of her best friend.

After worship, Emma sits among a small group of teens. She doesn't know any of them very well, as her church attendance has been sporadic over the past several years. Emma had invited Arden to come, but he had a meeting with *Bubblegum* and the band. He sounded really interested though. So maybe next time.

"Alright guys, we've got a special treat for you tonight!" Pastor Brian clasps his hands together, "My lovely, amazing, and incredibly beautiful wife is going to be sharing with you guys! Now, brace yourself folks because things might get a little bit mushy-gushy up in here, as we're going to be talking about our love story."

Several of the students laugh, and one girl lets out a little cheer. Emma smiles. Pastor Brian and Julie are so adorable together.

"Let's not get ahead of ourselves!" Julie laughs, "There were certainly no warm fuzzy feelings when we first met. In fact, I couldn't even stand you." She laughs again at the memory, "You seemed so full of yourself! I thought you were the know-it-all pastor's kid who wanted to appear more spiritual than everyone else."

"You guys met in youth group?" one of the girls asks.

"Uh-huh," Julie smiles, "but again, I'm getting ahead of myself. Let's back up and return to the beginning. Several years before we met. I wasn't in California yet. I was on the East Coast in North Carolina with my family, and we attended a tiny little Baptist church. One night, at a youth rally, a speaker came and talked about purity, relationships, and trusting God with our love stories. Now, this was back before the whole purity ring thing was a trend, so this was the first I heard about any of this. I had dated several guys throughout middle school and, uh confession time, elementary school also; and because of our culture, I just thought that was the 'thing to do.' It was like, if you saw a cute guy, you're supposed to take a chance and see if you might end up together, right? Like Ken and Barbie? That's how I thought things were supposed to be, and I had no idea that God had a different design for my life."

Emma smiles, loving that Julie and Brian are talking about this. *If only Aurora was here*, Emma thinks sadly, wishing her best friend could have a wiser approach about relationships. *She really needs to hear this.*

"You see, my love story with Brian started long before we ever met. It started when I made the decision to surrender my whole heart to God, including the area of purity and relationships. Don't get me wrong, I wanted a boyfriend just as much as the next girl!
There was a need in my heart for attention and affection that I so desperately desired to have filled, and I thought the only place I could find it was through dating. But dating only brought me more and more brokenness. You see, God is the

[53]

only One who can fulfill that deep desire that we have, to be loved! And as young people, we each have a choice to make. Are we going to trust God with every area of our lives, believing He is the only One who truly satisfies and brings joy?

Or are we going to follow along with the world and search for something that no person will ever be able to give us? Our emotional needs and desires can only be fulfilled in Jesus Christ! Dreaming of someday becoming a wife and mother, or a husband and father, and having a romantic, wonderful relationship isn't a bad thing! God gave you those amazing dreams. But what *isn't* amazing is trying to make that happen outside of His perfect timing. Take it from someone who knows. You can trust God with your love story! He is fully aware of your desire to find true love and live out an incredible happily ever after…but why go looking for that before you're at the age to be married and enter a lifelong commitment? I believe God has a special someone out there for you. But trying to find them on your own is going to bring a whole lot of extra mess. If we can trust Him with the salvation of our souls, can't we trust Him to someday introduce us to the person He wants us to spend the rest of our lives with?"

As Julie continues to share her story, Emma feels a twinge of conviction in her heart. As much as she wants Aurora to hear this message, maybe Emma needs to hear it too.

Afterward, Pastor Brian invites everyone to come up to the altar and make a commitment to purity. "A commitment to trust God with every part of your life. Including your love story," Pastor Brian explains.

Emma's heartbeat increases as she feels drawn to stand up. Thoughts flash through her mind as she thinks of Logan and how mindless she had acted around him. Even though she would never label herself as "boy crazy," it was clear that she wasn't immune to the magnetic pull of wild emotions.

God, is this something you have for me? Emma silently prays. *Choosing to refrain from recreational dating sounds a little bit old fashioned, but if that's the path You have for my life, I'm willing to trust You and give it a try.*

Emma slowly stands, feeling as though it's an important moment in her life. She's going to do it. She's going to make the decision and surrender to God with a whole new level of trust.

At the altar, Pastor Brain prays for her, asking the Lord to grant her the wisdom and strength to endure temptation and trust Him no matter what comes her way.

After whispering, "Amen," Emma has a question for Brian. "Um, can I ask you something?" she asks shyly.

"Sure, of course!" Brian smiles.

"I um…I want to keep my commitment and my promise to God, but you were talking about having parents help hold you accountable. I guess, the thing is…my dad isn't around, and my mom isn't really that involved." Emma fumbles over her words, "I mean, I don't know if she's really going to get this, or honestly even care. So, like whenever the time does come, and God brings that person into my life…do you think maybe you could, oh I don't know…check him out for me? Make sure I'm actually hearing from God and stuff?"

"Emma, I would be honored." Brian gives her hug, "You're an amazing girl, and I am more than willing to keep any guys away with my shotgun."

Emma bursts out laughing, "Oh goodness, I don't know if that's necessary! It's not like a parade of guys are storming down my front door or anything. But I don't know, maybe someday someone will show up." She shrugs, "And I might need help navigating through all of that craziness."

"Absolutely." Brian's smile continues to shine from his eyes, "Both Julie and I are here for you. Whatever you need, you can count on us. We're family and we're in it for the long ride, kid."

~*~

Emma floats into the living room, feeling a light-heartedness that she hasn't experienced in a long, long while. Somehow, the daily burden of living life feels lighter. She can breathe easier knowing that God is in full control. Emma flops onto the couch, smiling toward the ceiling, wondering how she'll describe what's happened tonight. She can't quite put her finger on it, but something about her has changed. Even so, her lack of words and understanding don't bother her. She just knows it's a God thing.

The sound of jiggling keys is heard as the backdoor unlocks. Emma lifts herself from the couch, ready to greet Aurora and her mother.

"Emma!" Aurora bursts across the threshold, leaving her heavy luggage behind. Emma welcomes Aurora with open arms and the two giggle as they hug.

"Woah! What's with the intense hug?" Emma laughs, "You're acting like you've been gone for months!"

"It sure feels like it! I've missed you! We have so much to catch up on! There are like a million things I want to tell you."

"Me too." Emma smiles, truly happy to see her again.

"I'm next, I'm next!" Miss Maggie squeezes her daughter, "Things just weren't the same without you in New York!"

"Thanks, Mom." Emma hugs her in return, "I missed you guys too. Sometimes." She cracks a smile, "I mean, I'm not gonna lie, it was kind of nice having the house so quiet. But actually, there's something I want to tell you. Like, something kind of huge, I'm not really even sure where to start."

Miss Maggie's phone rings and she glances at her palm, "Oh I'm sorry, honey, I have to take this! But I look forward to what you have to say, promise!" She quickly answers it, "Hello, Maggie Bates. Yes, I just landed! Mmm hmm, I'm already working on the paperwork for next week…"

Emma sighs as her mother quickly escapes the room.

"Don't worry, Em." Aurora squeezes her hand, "I wanna hear all about it. So, tell me! What's your news?" Aurora suddenly gasps, thrilled by the thought which pops into her mind, "Wait! Is it about a guy?"

"Kind of." Emma cocks her head slightly to the left, wondering how this is going to go. Will Aurora understand her choice to refrain from dating and wait on God? Or will she think she's completely bonkers?

"Is it Arden?!" Aurora blurts out, far too excited than she should be.

"What?!" Emma is shocked by Aurora suggesting such a thing, "Of course not!" Emma viciously shakes her head, "No, when I say it's about a guy, I don't mean an actual living, breathing guy. It's about my future husband. Which I mean, I guess he's alive out there somewhere, which would technically mean he's living and breathing, yes, but what I mean is—"

"Husband?!" Aurora stops her, "Em, are you in love with someone? Did you meet someone at this community theater thing?!"

"No! Aurora, stop!" Emma wishes she would just calm down and close her mouth, "Would you just listen to me for a second?"

Suddenly, one of Bradley's hit songs, *Celestial Starfish*, floats out of Aurora's purse. She excitedly dashes toward her luggage, recognizing the ring tone. "It's Jer! Just give me two seconds, okay?"

Emma places impatient hands on her hips and lets out a frustrated huff. Of *course*, Jeremiah would call right in the middle of their conversation.

"Hello?" Aurora answers casually, trying her best not to sound completely obsessed with her beau. "Oh hey, babe!" Aurora greets him happily, "Yes, I just got back to the house! Aw, I know, I can't wait to see you! Are you kidding? I missed you more! No, I missed you way more! No, I missed you more! No, I missed you so much—"

Emma rolls her eyes and slowly backs out of the room. There's nothing more nauseating than couples arguing about who missed who more. She heads for the stairs when Aurora's tone changes.

"Wait, what do you mean you talked to Emma today?" Aurora's voice is full of question.

Emma pauses, not allowing her Converse-clad toes to touch the stairs.

"Play practice?"

Uh-oh. Aurora is about to find out that neither she nor Jeremiah mentioned the fact that he's in *Beauty and the Beast*.

"Oh. Wow. Okay, no Emma didn't mention anything. Yeah. Okay. Can't wait to see you tomorrow too. Mmm-hmm, four is good. Okay, bye love."

Aurora shuts her phone and Emma twirls around.

"Why didn't you tell me?" Aurora asks in a simple, calm, and somewhat confused voice, "I mean, we're best friends. We're supposed to tell each other everything. I've been driving myself mentally crazy these past three days, wondering why Jer won't text me back when apparently he's at play practice…talking to you?"

"I wanted to tell you." Emma returns to the living room, "And I guess it was stupid of me not to, but I wanted to protect you. I mean, if Jeremiah never mentioned it to you, then I don't know, maybe you guys aren't as close as you thought you were."

"Protect me? Protect me from what?" Aurora snaps, crossing her arms. "It's obvious there's something you're not telling me. Otherwise, you never would've hidden this from me in the first place!"

Emma hesitates. This conversation is *not* going well. She was planning on telling Aurora about her suspicions with Jeremiah and his faithfulness to her, but not like this. Not when Aurora already has her defenses up and her cannons loaded! The girl can easily explode at any moment. But Emma isn't enemy. She shouldn't be the one under fire!

"I just…" Emma stumbles, struggling to find the right words, "I just think…" she sighs, "I've seen the way Jeremiah talks to other girls. And it's not just one girl. It's a lot of them.

He's got his own little fan club of groupies following him around at play practice. And from what I've seen, he doesn't seem to be discouraging them. At all."

"So, what, you think he's cheating on me?" Aurora hisses.

"No! I mean, maybe? I mean…I don't know!" Emma throws frustrated hands in the air, "See, this is why I didn't want to tell you! I don't have any kind of real evidence to back up my suspicion. It's just a gut feeling."

"You've been trying to sabotage this relationship since day one." Aurora shakes her head, "Why should I even believe you? It's like you're so set on us breaking up that you're making up all these fake stories to get me thinking Jeremiah is something he's not."

"Aurora, I would never lie to you!" Emma raises her voice, attempting to defend her dignity.

"Oh yeah? Then why didn't you tell me Jeremiah was doing this play with you?"

"Since when am I the bad guy here? Jeremiah didn't tell you he was doing the play either!"

"I'll deal with Jeremiah later. Right now I just…. I don't know if I can even trust you anymore."

"Aurora!" Emma crosses her arms, "That's not fair."

"Whatever." Aurora presses anxious hands to her tired head, "I'm exhausted. Just…forget it. I'm going to bed."

"Rory, wait!" Emma attempts to stop her, but Aurora is already halfway up the stairs.

~*~

Emma doesn't bother to look up from her book as Aurora leaves for her date with Jeremiah. Miss Maggie agreed to drive the two to The Lobster House; and even though she won't be dining with them, she wants to remain nearby and keep an eye out for unwelcome press hounds. Miss Maggie invited Emma to come, but she turned down the invitation. Neither she nor Aurora have spoken to one another all day.

The living room door closes and Emma breathes a sigh of relief, thankful the house is quiet again. She has no other plans for the day than to sit and read. She attempts to focus on her page, but her thoughts just aren't with it. After several tries of reading the same sentence but to no avail, she stands up, tosses her book on the couch, and heads to the kitchen. She's not hungry but she's bored, so she's going to eat anyway.

She opens the fridge and stares intently into it for a solid five minutes, hoping something will pop out at her. When nothing does, she closes it then opens it again, wondering if something delicious magically appeared inside. Of course not. That's ridiculous. She closes the fridge once more, and a knock is heard on the front door.

She cautiously makes her way back into the living room and stands on her tippy-toes to peak out the peep hole. She smiles, recognizing the face. She unbolts the door and opens the screen.

"Hey Arden. You just missed my mom. She and Aurora are going on a date with Jeremiah," Emma tells him.

"I'm not here to see your mom," Arden smiles. "I'm here for you. You busy?"

"Not unless you count staring into the refrigerator as an important item on the To-Do list."

"Come on," he nods his head outside, "I'm going to the mall. And you need to get out of the house."

"Why?" Emma asks with a sly smile. "There's nothing wrong with my hermit life."

"Eh, yeah. Keep telling yourself that. Come on, the bus leaves in ten minutes. Get some fresh air, and maybe some cheese fries. Trust me, you need them."

Emma can't help but laugh. She wants to ask more questions but getting out of the house for a few hours doesn't sound half bad. "Let me just grab my cell phone. I'll shoot Mom a text and make sure it's okay."

~*~

"Like HEY I've finally found the one, and HEY I'm coming so undone, and HEY I'm not the only one, the one in love with youuuuuu!"

Emma hopelessly shakes her head, attempting to hold back laughter as Arden sings into a thin-necked ketchup bottle. She doesn't want to encourage his goofy antics. But the guy is truly gut-splittingly hilarious.

He carries on in a mellow-dramatic, horribly off-key voice, "So IF you dare to look my way, and IF I dare to smile and say, that HEY I'm tota-lly nutty, a maniac in loooovvvveeeee!" Arden pauses from his bazaar reenactment of *Kennetic Energy's* music video and allows the guitar solo to carry on.

He sits down in their booth in the food court, pleased to have completed his performance, and stuffs some curly fries into his mouth.

"You know you sing *really* bad for a popstar," Emma tells him from across the table.

"Thank you, thank you very much." He winks cheekily.

"Come to think of it, I've never actually heard you sing." Emma reaches for a fry, "I mean, when you're actually trying *not* to sound like a dying cow. Maybe I should Google you?"

"Noooo! Please no. Those YouTube covers are so bad. My voice was still squeaking like a thrown-around-doggy-toy in the mouth of a pit bull."

"Oh, come on, you can't be *that* horrible. My mom seemed to think pretty highly of those videos."

"Thankfully, *Bubblegum* required that I take them down. They wanted me to start with a clean slate. Fresh identity with the band, you know?"

"Makes sense." Emma nods before popping a fry into her mouth. "So, tell me more about this new identity of yours. Has the label chosen a band name yet?"

"Yep." Arden nods, "But I'm not going to tell you what it is."

"What?! Why?"

"I want you to find out when everyone else does. Tomorrow morning at 6 AM on KDP-LA."

"I'm homeschooled. I don't get up at 6 AM."

"But our first single drops tomorrow!" Arden's eyebrows dance around, adding choreography to the song of his excited voice, "KDP will be the first station we get airtime on. Ever. It's going to be amazing. We're going to perform live, do an interview, and then they'll play the studio version. Man, those words sound so crazy on my lips. I just can't believe this is all happening."

"So, you're happy with the way things have turned out?" Emma asks cautiously, "I mean, with you being in a band rather than a solo artist?"

"I was obviously really disappointed at first, but then I realized I can't have that kind of an attitude," Arden tells her, his passionate eyes penetrating into hers. "I need to be grateful for where I'm at. The opportunities *Bubblegum* is giving me and the guys only come along once in a lifetime! If I have to conform a little bit and stick my own ideas and opinions on the backburner, I can handle it. Why would I complain about being on KDP radio?!"

"I guess you're right." Emma nods, "I mean, as cool as it would be for you to write and release your own songs, this is a great starting block for you. Maybe in the future more opportunities will open up, and you can crank out a solo album."

"Exactly," Arden nods, "and in the meantime, I'm just going to enjoy the ride."

"Well, just don't enjoy it too much," Emma cautions him. "Hollywood is crazy. It can really put people through the ringer."

"Oh, come on, Emma, it's not like I'm going to end up like all those messed up kid stars who derail their lives with drugs and alcohol and crash into a brick wall. There's no way Hollywood could change me."

"I hope you're right." Emma sighs, suddenly worried about what might happen if his band truly takes off.

"Trust me, I'm not like those other run-of-the-mill, self-conscious, egotistical, posh popstars. I mean, would Logan Sparks or David Carter ever do this?" He reaches for several fries and begins stuffing them up his nose.

Emma gasps and quickly covers her eyes, completely grossed out by the gesture. "Ew, ew, stop, that's barbaric!"

"Look Emma, I have curly fry nose hairs!"

Emma doesn't open her eyes. "That's disgusting!" she rants. "Ugh, you are such a boy!"

Arden removes the fries and hides them in a napkin, grinning proudly. "Take that, Hollywood!"

Emma finally opens her eyes and shakes her head, unable to stop the laughter. "Okay, I admit it. You're nothing like those cookie-cutter popstars."

"To be completely honest, I'm actually really nervous about tomorrow." Arden's' tone changes, focusing the conversation on more serious matters. "*Bubblegum* said KDP's response to our single could make or break our career. We desperately need good audience feedback or else we might be toast."

"Wow, yeah I bet you guys feel like you're under a lot of pressure. Just remember that no matter what happens, God is in control of the outcome. As much as you love the idea of becoming an overnight sensation, that might not be the best thing. Building your audience at a slower, more sustainable rate might be the better way to go."

"Not according to *Bubblegum*." Arden shakes his head, "For them, it's all about the money. And apparently, they need it. I heard a few of the executives talking and it sounds like finances might be getting a little tight. They took a huge gamble on us, and they're hoping we're going to pay off."

"It's not right of them to be putting that much pressure on you guys." Emma shares her personal thoughts on the matter, "Your music should be about your message, and the fun you have sharing it, not about selling songs."

"You know, you're actually kind of encouraging and fun to be around when you try." Arden grins. "Maybe we could have you run our fan club."

"Yeah right!" Emma laughs. "I am *not* a groupie. I don't even know what your silly band is called yet or if you guys even sound half decent!"

"Why don't you come find out tomorrow morning? Just think, you can witness history in the making! Us three guys, first time ever on radio airwaves, blasting through So Cal."

"At 6 AM?" Emma asks with pleading eyes, "Can't I just sleep in and hear the recording later?"

"Oh, come on Em, you'll love it! Or you could at least pretend to love it. Show up for moral support?"

Emma purses her lips, contemplating if she should say yes. Six is early. But it would be *kind* of fun to hear what this manufactured, synchronized, auto-tuned boyband sounds like. And strangely enough, it sounds like Arden really wants her there.

"I guess I'll come," she tells him slowly. "But I'm not buying any fan club t-shirts."

~*~

At *Napp Resort...*

"I thought you would be my cowboy, I thought you were my dream come true, but reality hit like a thousand-pound brick, and now I don't know what to do!"

Eleanor scrunches her face in deep, analytical thought as Chelsea Bedru lip-syncs to her sob-inducing breakup number. It's supposed to be the climax of the story, the tear-jerking moment where Cowboy Carson and Andrea realize they will never be together, but Eleanor finds it far more laughable than tear-worthy.

Chelsea, her face caked in far too much makeup for any normal girl on a working farm, is strutting through the barn in her designer boots, pausing to lean dramatically against the old wood, crooning about how all she has left in life is her horse.

Eleanor grips Prince's bridal, waiting for her que. Soon, Prince is to come thundering in with Logan running behind. Eleanor glances at Logan, who stands several feet away. She wonders how a guy as thoughtful and down to earth as he is, can partake in such a cheesy musical.

"I thought you would be my cowboy, I thought we had it all, as you smiled and said my name, my heart began to fall."

Eleanor shakes her head, knowing perfectly well that the young teens in Logan's target demographic are going to eat this stuff up like pumpkin pie on Thanksgiving. Even though Eleanor can't appreciate it, she knows Logan and Chelsea's fans will be beyond thrilled with this movie.

"I thought—" Chelsea's song is interrupted by a small screech. Chelsea jumps up, swatting away a fly, "Bug, bug!"

"Cut!" the director yells, impatience heavy on his voice.

"Someone kill it, someone kill it!" Chelsea cries out in horror.

"Looks like Cowboy Carson rode away on his horse just in time," Logan leans over and whispers to Eleanor.

She can't help but smirk.

"Okay, take five everyone! Take five!" the exasperated director tells his crew.

Prince impatiently brushes his hoof on the ground. Eleanor sighs. This scene has been taking far longer than anyone expected. They're already three hours past quitting time, and it's starting to get dark outside. With only a few days left to finish their film, it's crunch time. Nobody is crazy about working extra-long hours, yet Jack Heart won't let anyone stop until he's satisfied with their production.

"Looks like Prince is tired of waiting," Logan tells her.

"Yeah, I'm gonna let him stretch his legs."

"Mind if I join you?" Logan asks.

Eleanor shrugs, truly not minding the company. The more she learns about Logan, the *real* Logan, the more respect she has for him.

The two lead Prince out of the barn, and Eleanor takes a deep breath of fresh air. Darkness has nearly settled in, but rustic lamp posts light the path for them. Loud crickets chirp in the background. Eleanor finds that sound far sweeter than the annoying song that's been on repeat in her brain. They reach the paddock and Eleanor unhooks his lead rope. Prince happily lowers his head and begins mowing on the delicious, leafy grass.

"So, I'm thinking about getting a horse after this film wraps," Logan tells her, patting Prince's side affectionately. "These animals are starting to grow on me. Any suggestions on where to look?"

"You are?" Eleanor smiles. "That's awesome! And sure, I have some tips. The first being, don't buy from a breeder. There are enough orphaned horses out there who need a home, without spending tens of thousands of dollars on some purebred. We actually have a few rescued mares here who could use owners. They're all really gentle and great for novice riders." She pauses, suddenly remembering who she's talking to. "But wait. Don't you live in the city? Where would you keep your horse?"

"Actually, I'm thinking about buying some land in Colorado."

Eleanor's eyes widen. It sounds so strange to hear someone her age talking about purchasing acreage. She still struggles to save up enough money to buy new clothes and shoes. "Wow. Colorado? It's a beautiful state. My Aunt and Uncle have a ranch out there. But why Colorado? Don't you spend most of your time in Cali?"

"Eleanor!" Jack Heart calls from the Barn opening. "Where's your dad? He's not in the office. Apparently, we've got too many lights hooked into the outlet, and we just tripped a breaker. We're gonna need some more power to finish up this shoot. Do you have a generator?"

"Oh yeah, let me go find him." Eleanor quickly climbs the fence and leaps over the other side. She jogs toward the house, knowing that on this set, time is money. She pounds up the back steps, opens the screen door and lands in the kitchen. Just as she's ready to open her mouth, a loud, unhappy noise is heard.

"Get out of here! I do not want to see your blasted face ever again!"

Eleanor slowly closes the door and cringes. The voice is coming from upstairs. It's Jasmine.

"You cannot kick me out of my own house!" Jonathan shouts back at her, "You have no authority to speak to me like that!"

"Fine! I will go! But this is not over!" the woman screams. "If you think I am leaving without taking what belongs to me, you are wrong! Dead wrong!"

Eleanor is shocked by their hateful words. She knew things have been strained between them, but she didn't know it had escalated to such an intense degree. Her mom and dad never used to fight like this.

After more shouting, Jasmine pounds down the stairs, almost plowing into Eleanor before slamming the front door behind her.

Eleanor stands in fearful silence, wondering what she should do. Should she go upstairs and check on her dad? As much as she and Jasmine have their occasional tizzy, Eleanor's heart still aches for her father. She bites her lip and prays for courage, slowly taking the stairs and entering her father's open bedroom door.

"Um, Dad? Are you...okay?"

Jonathan is sitting on the edge of his bed with defeated hands held up to his head. His gaze is fixed on the floor, and Eleanor's heart drops. He sniffs and straightens up his back, setting his gaze on his daughter. "Hey, honey," he speaks, his voice just above a whisper.

"Dad, what's going on?" Eleanor asks quietly, her voice trembling slightly. She sits beside him, and he pulls her close in a hug. She hates seeing him like this!

"Jasmine wants a divorce," he tells her in one short breath.

"Dad, I'm so sorry." She hugs him tighter, wishing there was some way to take the pain away. "I can't even imagine how awful you must feel right now. But maybe she just overreacted?" Eleanor suggests. "You know how arguments can be…surely she didn't mean it."

"No Ellie, it's true." Dad shakes his head sadly, "She's already signed the divorce papers. They were waiting for me as soon as I got back from Pennsylvania."

Silence blankets the room, and Eleanor searches for the right words.

"I wish there was something I could say to make you feel better." Eleanor resists the urge to cry, "I know you loved her. A lot."

"I still do love her, Ellie." Jonathan sighs, "I know Jasmine can be a bit intense at times, but when we said, "I do," we made a lifelong commitment before God to love and care for one another, no matter what happens. And I don't take that commitment lightly. When she first started talking about divorce, I resisted the idea. We're supposed to be a family, Ellie. And families don't just give up on each other. But now that I see how unhappy Jasmine is, and she's determined to find a way out…maybe I will have to let her go."

"Oh, Dad." Eleanor sighs, feeling deflated by the heaviness of the moment, yet suddenly remembering the power outage in the barn. "I know this is really bad timing…but Jack Heart sent me to get you."

~*~

Back in Amish Country…

"Lena, did not your Grandmary ever tell you that you must not eat more berries than you pick? Your bucket is nearly empty!" Elizabeth playfully teases her sister.

Lena peers into her thin bucket. Only a small line of raspberries fills the bottom. "But they're just so good!" She licks her fingers excitedly, "At least my bucket isn't as empty as Jack's! Goodness, you've hardly collected any!"

Jack looks up from where he's seated beneath a tree, casually whittling a stick with his pocket knife. "Raspberry picking is not in my job description."

"But if you want pie, you're going to have to help," Lena tells him.

"No, thank you, I'll pass on the pie. Too many seeds. They get stuck in your teeth."

Lena shrugs, at peace with the fact that Jack doesn't wish to be involved with their berry escapade.

"Doing these chores are so much more enjoyable with you here." Elizabeth smiles, "How long will you be staying?"

Lena sighs, trying to be gentle yet as honest and up front as possible. "Not long." She glances at Jack, "We need to get back to Bella Adar very soon. In fact, Jack and I are planning to leave in the morning."

"The morning?" Elizabeth's face displays obvious displeasure, "Oh. I was dearly hoping you would stay a bit longer."

"I know." Lena sighs, "But as I mentioned before, I didn't come for a social visit. Elizabeth, I want you to consider coming back to Bella Adar with me."

"You know that is impossible." Elizabeth turns away and focuses on the berry bush, her busy fingers reaching for more pie filling. "I cannot leave my family."

"I know this is hard for you to think about." Lena reasons with her, "Everything is changing so fast, and this has all happened rapidly, but would you at least pray about it? God has shown me that He has great purpose for me being in Bella Adar, and I believe He does for you too. I know you love your family and everyone here, but aren't I your true family? I have to believe that God reunited us for a purpose. Elizabeth, the people of Bella Adar need you. They need us. As sisters. Together."

"As much as it hurts my heart to tell you no, I know where my place is." Elizabeth turns to her, "I cannot leave my family. Or Jonah."

"Has Jonah asked you to enter some kind of relationship or commitment with him?" Lena asks gently.

"Yah." Elizabeth nods, "He has," her cheeks flushing red at the sweet memory. "We started courting just yesterday. He believes it is God's will for us to be married."

"Married?" Lena echoes. She pauses before finally asking, "Do *you* believe that, Elizabeth?"

"I have had a special place in my heart for Jonah Yates ever since we first met. Though I didn't dare ask for it in my prayers, there was always a secret hope that he might someday come courting. Never in my wildest dreams would I have hoped that he would ask me such a question." Elizabeth grins, "But this is a very exciting time for me. I deeply care for Jonah, and yes I do believe it is God's will for us to marry one day."

Lena forces a smile onto her face, wishing she could be genuinely happy for her. But she cannot.

Lena isn't ready to give up on Elizabeth just yet. Her smile disappears. "When I was home, Jack took me to a place downtown, where dozens of orphans live on the streets, having nothing more than shabby old tents and a measly amount of food to fill their hungry stomachs. They are all orphaned, their parents having been killed by the same evil man who killed ours. The only ones who can stop this wicked man from doing more damage, from killing more people and orphaning more children, is us! Elizabeth, we have an opportunity sent from Heaven, to make a difference in these people's lives! Their suffering can end, if only we will set aside our personal wants and dreams to sacrifice for them."

"I do not know any of these people whom you speak of." Elizabeth's voice grows sharp, "I am sorry that they do not have food, and struggle to meet their daily needs, but it is not my responsibility. My lot is not in Bella Adar. God's boundary lines have fallen for me in pleasant places, and I know where I am meant to be. Right here. Home. With my family. With Jonah."

"I understand." Lena sighs, accepting the devastating blow of defeat. Her chin drops as she peers into her bucket, "Perhaps it was too much of me to ask. I just thought that perhaps..." Lena looks back up at her with one last wisp of hope, "would you at least promise you'll pray about it? Tonight, before making a final decision?"

"Yah." Elizabeth nods, "I will pray."

But, Elizabeth thinks afterward, *I already know what my answer will be. This is my home. And I am not leaving.*

~*~

The following morning, Lena stands next to their rental car, fighting back tears. This is her final goodbye with Elizabeth.

"Are you sure you don't want to change your mind?" Lena asks once more, desperately wishing she will.

"I know where my place is," Elizabeth tells her confidently. "I am content to stay."

Lena nods, knowing nothing can be said to change her mind. "Very well. I pray that all goes well with you, Elizabeth." She hugs her sister, and Elizabeth clings to her neck.

Tears sting Elizabeth's eyes. Why does it hurt so terribly to see her sister go? Why can't things be different?

This is just the way things are, she tells herself, *and you have to accept it. Lena is an Englisher. I am Amish. Though our paths have crossed, we will always belong in two separate worlds. Our worlds simply have no way of staying together.*

"Thank you for your kind hospitality, Mrs. Stoltz, Mr. Stoltz." Jack shakes Mr. Stoltz's hand.

"And thank you, for not taking away our daughter," Mr. Stoltz tells him.

"It's quite clear that this is where Elizabeth wants to remain, and we can't argue with that." Jack nods, "Blessings on you and your home."

Lena's eyes are pooling as she pulls away from the hug. "I love you, dear sister. Just remember to always trust God, no matter what. Goodbye, Elizabeth."

"Goodbye, Lena." Elizabeth sniffs, knowing full well that she may never see her sister again. She has made her decision. Even though her heart is breaking, she knows this is right. Her feet are right where they belong.

Lena waves goodbye once more, then ducks into the car. Jack turns on the engine and backs out of the driveway. Lena digs in the glove box for a napkin, dabbing her eyes.

"I know the goodbye was hard," Jack says. "But you did your best. It is clear that Elizabeth's heart is not in it."

"I know firsthand how hard it is to leave your family," Lena sniffs, attempting to compose herself, despite the tidal wave of emotions washing through the car. "I never would've left Grandmary and Theodore if I hadn't been told they were in danger. I suppose it is best that Elizabeth stays with her family. But still. I was hoping that maybe, just maybe, I wouldn't have to fight this battle on my own."

"You don't," Jack reminds her, glancing quickly at her before returning his eyes to the road. "Just because your sisters are not willing to armor up for battle doesn't mean that there are not others who are ready to pay the price. The entire URIA is behind you, Your Majesty. You're certainly not alone."

"I know." She sighs. "But it's just so hard to let go of what could've been. Elizabeth has such a beautiful heart, and she would've made a most magnificent Queen."

"So, what do you say, Your Majesty?" Jack asks as he brakes at the stop sign. "Should we change our plans and promptly return to Bella Adar? Or are you still wanting to head out on this wild goose chase in California?"

"Oh no, we're still going to talk to Aurora!" Lena declares. "It may seem like a shot in the dark, but we must take the chance. She is our last hope."

~*~

In California...

Emma's tired hands nervously clench her styrofoam coffee cup. Her stomach tumbles around like socks in a washing machine. An extravagant display of doughnuts is spread before her, but she can't think about eating. Not at a time like this.

She steals a glance at Arden, who appears to be taking it all in stride. His glowing, pearly white grin is flashing as he easily chats with the bubbly DJs. Sam and Pam, the morning voices of KDP radio, are clearly enjoying themselves. Emma looks at her mother who wears a huge smile. Arden's two fellow group mates taste-test the doughnuts. Emma takes a deep breath. There's no reason for her to be nervous. She's not the one who has to sing live for the entire California coastline!

While Sam and Pam reminisce about the first time they met *One Infection*, Arden catches Emma's gaze and smiles.

Emma's stomach does a strange kind of flip-flop, and she wonders what in the world is wrong with her. Why is she so dramatically concerned about Arden's wellbeing? Why does she want, more than anything, for this interview and performance to go well for him?

She feels like the stressed-out parents of an Olympian, watching from the sidelines with bouncing nerves while their champion competes for the gold.

Emma smiles back, warmed by the fact that Arden actually wanted her to come. She breathes again, relaxing a little, reminding herself that everything is going to be just fine. Sam and Pam are completely engrossed, and it's clear that Arden is quite a natural when it comes to these kinds of situations.

"Alright, we're going on air in five minutes!" Sam, who is sporting a huge bald spot, clasps his hands together. "Let's head to the booth, boys!"

Arden raises his eyebrows excitedly toward Emma, "Wish us luck!"

She gives him a supportive 'thumbs up,' hoping the gesture doesn't appear too cheesy. The two other guys ditch their donuts and follow Sam into the sound booth. A glass window separates them, and Emma can no longer hear their conversation.

"Eeep, this is so exciting!" Miss Maggie squeals, clenching her coffee as well. "Arden's first radio interview! Smash it out of the park, boys!"

"Please, have a seat." One of the radio staff wearing a black KDP t-shirt tells the ladies. They scoot into several black chairs beside the band's manager and the other boys' parents. Emma lifts her coffee to take a sip. *Lord, help them. I know this is such a huge moment for Arden. Help him and the guys not to be nervous.* Emma tosses up a silent prayer.

From behind the glass, Emma can see Arden laughing. She can't help but smile. It's as if he has an electric glow radiating out of him, a magnetic field of joy and celestial bliss, as he is clearly smack-dab in the middle of his wildest dream.

Emma almost wishes she could snap a photograph of the moment, feeling as if something special is about to happen. She decides to capture the moment with her Polaroid-mind instead. For some reason, she doesn't want to ever forget this moment. She wants to remember the rain and how it's an oddly-cold morning. She wants to remember how they all dashed through the wet, drizzly drops and wiped their Converse on the rug in the lobby. She wants to remember how her mom anxiously started fussing with Arden's hair, and how the other band members thought it was hilarious. She wants to remember riding the elevator to the thirteenth floor of this skyscraper, and how her stomach fell from her fear of heights when she looked out the window.

But most of all, she wants to remember Arden. Right here, right now, on the other side of the glass, with his million-dollar smile shining from his eyes.

A staff member fumbles with the sound board in front of them, and Emma can hear the legendary KDP radio jingle float through the room. She places her coffee cup between her knees and bites her lip. It's about to start!

"Welcome back to the Morning-Morning Show with Sam–"

"And Pam!" Pam chimes in.

The boys put on headphones, readjusting their sound levels.

"We've got a special treat for you on this drizzly, dreary morning, something that's gonna turn your frown upside and pour a little bit of pep and cheer into your morning brew!"

"That's right!" Pam adds. "You know that we're all about digging up new music and bringing you guys the hottest hits before they're even a thing!"

"Because we're just that hipster," Sam adds.

Miss Maggie chuckles. Emma almost smiles, knowing how much her mom gets a kick out of Sam's dry sense of humor.

"So, we found these three, devastatingly handsome young guys standing on our doorstep this morning, and we had to let them come inside and sing for us." Pam tells her dramatic tale, "And I'm telling you listeners, get ready to freak out. I'm already predicting that they're going to be major stars. Major."

"So, you might be scratching your chin and asking yourself, who are these people? Who did Sam and Pam dig out of the gutter for us this time?" Sam chuckles, "Well, you are about to find out. Please welcome to the studio Matthew Jones, Arden Laverne and Jay Hughes!"

Everyone in the studio cheers. Mrs. Laverne and Miss Maggie squeal and grab one another's hands. Emma smiles and reluctantly claps, unable to keep herself from joining in on the fun.

"So, boys, tell us a little bit about yourselves!" Pam gives them each a chance to talk for a few seconds, briefly explaining how they met and got formed as a band with *Bubblegum*. Finally, they announce the name of their band.

"We are..." the guys exchange glances then join together in unison, "Acid Rain!"

Emma wants to laugh, but she can't. Clearly, Arden is so proud of himself right now. She doesn't want to mess up the moment for him.

Sam tells the guys to take it away, they position themselves at their mics, and Emma holds her breath.

"I've been trying to get your attention," the guy with slick black, spikey hair by the name of Jay begins singing, "been been trying to get your attention, but you just keep looking the other way."

"I wanted to be your superman, but you're treating me like I'm Peter Pan, thinkin' I'm a lost boy, a lost boy, thinkin' I'm a lost boy, ohhhhhhhh," sings Matthew, the buff beach-blonde who sounds like a "Backstreet Boy."

"There's only so many ways you can break my heart, but it's like you've got a check list, and you're killing me right from the start." Arden's voice floats into the mix, and Emma almost falls out of her chair. She does a double take, floored by the quality of what her ears have just heard.

"I write you a letter then I throw it away, 'cause I know my words don't mean a-a-anything,
I'm try'n to be nice but you keep throwing the dice, gambling with all the wrong price,
I hate that I fell, but I'm under your spell, climbing walls just to get your attention, but you're blowing off love like it's a toxic invention, so long love I'm dumb to even mention,
But I'm stuck on you, yeah you're my obsession! Woah, woah! You're my obsession!"

Their voices flawlessly mesh together in a beautifully explosive mind-bomb of harmony and rhythm. Emma is doing everything she can to keep her jaw from dropping onto the floor. To keep herself from squealing. To keep herself from smacking her mother's knee and acting like a mindless fangirl. These guys are *crazy* good.

Emma knows this is only the acoustic version, and the fully produced version of the song will sound far more mechanic and mainstream pop. But still. Nobody can deny that these boys are blessed with a strong dose of raw natural talent. Emma watches Arden in wonderment. There's *no* way that voice can be coming out of him. He's just Arden. Her goofy, offbeat, annoying, and completely unpredictable friend. There's no way this can be happening.

Yet it is.

All at once, Emma is overwhelmed with a devastating sinking feeling. Arden is going to be ridiculously famous. She just knows it.

The thought greatly unnerves her. She's not ready for this. She's not ready to lose him to the big star machine. She's not ready for screaming fans and headlining tours and hour-long interview specials. The posters, the autographs, the pictures, the noise…there must be a way to stop it. Arden can't sell his soul to Hollywood. He just can't!

But she can feel change in the air. She would be foolish to deny it. Even now, this very second, the clouds are brewing, winds are changing, and a storm is swirling. Ears are listening, and busy little fingers are Googling. The inevitable is about to happen.

As much as she wishes to stop it, she knows she cannot. The heavens will open, lightening will strike, and nothing will ever be the same. Ready or not, *Acid Rain* is coming.

~*~

As Emma pushes through the auditorium doors, she attempts to push thoughts of Arden out of her mind. After the early morning stop at KDP, *Acid Rain* is scheduled to return to *Bubblegum* headquarters and host a small press conference. Now that their single, *Obsession,* is out, it's time to promote, promote, promote. They only have a short window of time to pounce on this opportunity and generate some buzz. *Bubblegum* is determined to make the most out of it.

Emma left the KDP tower feeling discouraged, despite everyone's level of off-the-chart excitement. She knows her concern for Arden and his future is legitimate, but she's reminded that she cannot take on such a huge burden. Besides, hadn't she just come to a new place in her life to surrender and trust God with everything? So, she tosses up another prayer for help and tries to set her mind on the task at hand. Making *Beauty and the Beast* one of the best local theater productions possible.

Practice goes much better than the previous day, and it appears as though Savannah and Jeremiah have rehearsed a bit. Emma watches Jeremiah, all-the-while feeling bad for not having patched things up with Aurora yet.

During the snack break, Emma decides to approach him. He leaps down the steps and heads to the back of the auditorium to fill up his water bottle in the fountain by the bathrooms. She stands up to follow him, hoping to apologize for the previous day.

She comes up behind him, awkwardly watching him fill his water bottle. Should she say something? Or wait until he's done?

All at once he turns around and nearly bumps into her. "Oh! Hey!"

"Hi. Um, can I talk to you for a second?"

"Sure. I mean, as long as you're not planning on chewing me out for something I didn't do, then go for it."

"Yeah, about that…" Emma looks down at her shoe, hating that she has to apologize to him. "I feel kind of bad. I think I, um, overreacted a little bit. I haven't been giving you the benefit of the doubt, and I don't know…if Aurora trusts you that much, maybe I should at least try to get along with you."

"Did she tell you to talk to me?" Jeremiah asks suspiciously.

"No." Emma shakes her head, "Actually, we got in a huge argument as soon as she got home. It was about you, go figure. Anyway, I've just been praying and, well I'm a Christian, and obviously Jesus wouldn't have acted the way I did. So, I'm sorry."

"So, this means we can call a truce? For Aurora's sake? Friends?" Jeremiah holds out a hand.

"Maybe." Emma isn't too quick to give in, "But first I need to know something. Why didn't you tell her you're in this musical?"

"I explained it all to her last night, on our date. I didn't want her to feel like I was using her."

"What do you mean?" Emma asks, confused by his answer.

"I love acting," Jeremiah begins. "See, I've been a theater geek my whole life, and I didn't want Aurora to feel like I'm just dating her because of her star status. If she knew that I have aspirations of someday making it in the entertainment industry, I thought maybe she would feel like I was just trying to use her to get somewhere in my career. I shouldn't have hidden it from her, but acting has always been my 'other' identity, you know?"

"Oh." Emma is stumped by how thoughtful his answer sounds. "I guess that makes sense." She slowly admits, "So does this mean the whole 'champion-surfer-boy' thing is just a facade?"

"Not at all!" Jeremiah chuckles, "I love surfing. Salt water funnels through my veins. But I dunno, I love theater too. The stage lights just give me this euphoric high. Like surfing does. Same passion, just two different mediums."

Emma nods, satisfied with his answer. "So, I guess this means we're good. Now I just need to make sure Aurora's going to accept my apology and give me a second chance, or else this whole us being friends thing is going to be a total waste."

Jeremiah throws his head back with a laugh before heading back up front, "Don't worry, I'll put in a good word for you."

After rehearsal, Julie holds a meeting for all the staff and volunteers. The stage has been emptied of children and stray actors, as everyone has been picked up or is at least waiting outside in the parking lot. Emma fully appreciates how quiet things are again.

"Okay, I have several matters to discuss!" Julie tells the small group of adults and teens. "Let's start with the happy items first. I finally found the perfect Belle dress online! I ordered it last night and ahh, I cannot wait for you all to see it! I've been searching forever and was asking the Lord to bring me to the right thing, and I stumbled upon an adorable little Etsy shop where they custom design princess dresses. I got all excited, but then I saw the price tag! Even though it seemed impossible to afford, I messaged the shop owner and told her about our outreach for inner-city kids here, and she decided to donate it!"

"Oh wow, praise God!" one of the volunteers cheers. "That's amazing!"

"Yes, He has been so faithful with every part of this show, it's just, ahhh, beyond perfect! I ordered the dress to Savannah's measurements and it should be here in just a few days. But, that brings me to my more difficult news." She lowers her voice, careful to make sure that if any of the children are left, no one will hear her. "I talked to Savannah's social worker, and things aren't going well in her current foster home. She's struggling in school, arguing with the parents, and displaying a lot of negative behavior that her foster parents are losing patience with. This is the sixth home she's been in, in the past three years." Julie sighs heavily, pressed down by the burden of Savannah's current life situation. "Her case worker said they're looking to send her to a different home in New Mexico. She said the decision isn't final yet, but everything is pointing in that direction. I asked when this change would be occurring, and she said it would happen before opening night. Meaning, if they decide to transfer her, we're not going to have a Belle."

"Oh no!" One of the volunteers shakes her head, "Wow, we definitely need to pray!"

They agree that now is the best time to do so. They all hold hands and begin praying for Savannah and the rest of the kids who are facing troubling situations at home. Emma's heart hurts, realizing she had nearly forgotten the entire reason she signed up to help with this production in the first place: to minister to those who are broken and hurting.

Emma can't help but think about Jeremiah. How did he get involved with this program? Does he have some kind of personal struggles or challenging home life too? Now she's curious to know what Jeremiah is really like. Does Aurora even know the *real* Jeremiah?

After "Amen" and several more matters of discussion, Emma begins collecting stray props still scattered on the stage and puts them in a box. She fills two boxes, then lifts them into her arms.

"Oh Emma, you can just take those out to my truck!" Julie tosses a pair of keys toward her, and Emma wiggles her hand free enough to grab them.

"Nice catch!" Julie is impressed, "And thanks, girl! I wish I could help but, uh," she glances down at her belly, "not sure baby would like it."

Emma laughs. "No worries! It's my pleasure to help. That's why I'm here!"

Emma heads backstage, taking careful steps through the dark. She knows Julie's truck is parked in the back lot, and this will be much easier than hauling heavy boxes all the way around the building.

She finds the red illuminated "Exit" sign and pushes her back against the blue door, swinging into the open air.

A burst of sunlight rushes to her eyes, causing her to go nearly blind as her eyes readjust to the dramatic difference.

She pauses, her back still against the door, trying to process what her eyes are seeing. Emma gasps as the boxes of props nearly slip out of her hands. Just several feet away, Jeremiah is kissing Savannah!

Emma's eyes widen in horror, as she is fuming with rage, disgust, and abhorrent shock.

The passionate kissers suddenly stop. Jeremiah pulls away as he sees Emma standing there. A sense of urgency and desperation sweep across his not-so-innocent face.

Emma readjusts the weight of the boxes and makes a beeline for the truck. She is *not* about to have this conversation. Not with him. Not with the low-life, despicable, wormiest excuse of a boyfriend on the planet!

She angrily plows forward, ignoring his pleas for her to stop.

"Emma, wait! Stop! Let me explain!" he calls after her.

Emma unlocks the truck, tumbles the boxes in the back, then locks it again. Jeremiah catches up with her and fumbles around for an excuse. "Listen, it's not what it looks like! Let me explain!"

"Explain what?" Emma whips around to face him, forgetting everything she said earlier in the way of apology. "The fact that you lied and said there was nothing going on between you and Savannah? Or the fact that you cheated on my best friend, causing her to believe you're someone you're not?! Or the fact that just when I decided to give you a second chance, a little bit of breathing room, you go and do something like...like, that!? As far as I can see, the only explaining that needs to be done is to Aurora where you admit what a selfish, conceited, heartless, two-faced jerk you are!"

"Savannah and I are not together!" Jeremiah's voice is strained with desperation, "Emma, listen to me. Please, it was a mistake! A huge mistake. You can't tell Aurora!"

"You know, Pastor Brian was right." Emma shakes her head, "Teens these days don't have a clue how to steward their hearts. We toss them around from person to person, like they're yesterday's cruddy old football, not even thinking about the priceless masterpieces that they are. And everyone's hurting everyone because we're too blind to see that our worth and value can only be found in One place." Emma shakes her head, "Jeremiah, I feel just as devastated for you as I do for Aurora. And I really hope that someday God does a work in your life, and you learn how to treat women the way they deserve to be treated. Like gold. Irreplaceable, priceless, gold."

[88]

And with that, Emma storms toward the theater, leaving Jeremiah standing alone in the parking lot.

~*~

Episode 3

"I've got so many questions, there's still so much that I don't know." Aurora releases a wobbly song, doubting her lyrics the moment they slip from her lips.

She tries again, this time with a slightly different slant.

"So many questions about you, why am I wondering if your heart is true."

Aurora's fingers slide off the guitar. The steady strum ends, and she quickly slams the brakes on those lame lyrics, eraser dust flying everywhere.

"I can't seem to get my mind off you, you're stuck in there, and I'm stuck on you, something in my heart sayin' this ain't right, but the other part of me wants to see you tonight."

Aurora stops and lets out a frustrated huff. This isn't working. She places her guitar on the bed beside her and flops backward, pressing frustrated fingers to her temples.

She's trying to write a song about Jeremiah, but the stupid lyrics just won't come. Her head is clogged up with heavy thoughts that settled in like a thick fog. Try as she may, she cannot manage to see through the cloudiness. What's wrong with her? Why is she doubting this relationship? Jeremiah is absolutely perfect. And more important than that, *they're* perfect together.

Their date last night was flawless. The whimsical, romantic, euphoric ambiance was off-the-charts glorious. Jeremiah showed up looking adorable as ever, flashing the familiar smile that melts her heart into a pile of happy mush. Their conversation felt heavenly, picking up right where they left off, as no time or space had caused any kind of distance between them.

But as Jeremiah leaned across the table, ready to kiss her and cause the explosion of inner fireworks she's been so desperately aching for, her heart responded with a warning siren. The deep, unsettled feeling which overtook her, quickly pulled her out of their almost-cinema-moment and plucked her back into a strange and cold reality. As she pulled away, Jeremiah opened his eyes, surprised as to why she had refused him the pleasure.

"I, um…not here." She awkwardly looked around the restaurant, rummaging through her brain for an excuse, "There might be paparazzi."

"Are you okay?" he had asked, suspicious of her denial. "Just last week you couldn't wait to kiss me," he added with an impish grin.

"I know." Aurora flashed a smile, hoping to find an excuse that didn't sound utterly lame. "It's just…I don't know…maybe we should, take things a little bit slower, you know?"

Aurora wanted to kick herself for suggesting such a thing. Thinking back on it now, she may have blown her only opportunity to experience her first real kiss, on the beach, before going to New York. Yet somehow, the strangest part of all was that she was oddly okay with that. In some bizarre, unexplainable way, she felt as if God was urging her not to open up that part of herself to Jeremiah. At least not yet anyway. She couldn't quite seem to make sense of any of it, but she had to trust her gut.

Even though Jeremiah continued to act like a complete gentleman all through the night, she couldn't help but wonder if his opinion of her had changed. In their phone conversation this morning, things felt strained. He said they wouldn't be able to meet for a date because of play practice, and then afterword he had to train for an upcoming surf competition. Aurora tried to sound casual, but beneath her cheery tone, it deeply bothered her. Hence the reason she's doggie paddling through such an overwhelming ocean of emotions, trying to write a stupid song about her wacky life.

Aurora closes her eyes, feeling like she has nowhere to go but to the Lord. Emma isn't exactly acting like a huggable koala bear. And Aurora still hasn't talked to her parents. Besides, none of her other "outer circle" friends would even have a clue as to how she's feeling right now.

"Lord, what do I do?" she whispers. A warm, salty breeze flutters through the window. "You know how much I love Jeremiah. But something about us just feels off. I know You want me to walk with You and honor You in all my choices...but I can't help but have this deep, nagging feeling, telling me that Jeremiah isn't the right choice. I mean, he's got me acting like a total coward. I wasn't even able to talk to him about You and my newfound commitment, and everything You've done in my heart. Just like with the rest of the world, I'm scared as to how he might react. I mean, what if he's not even a Christian? What if he's an atheist or Buddhist or something and thinks I'm absolutely off my rocker? Lord, help! I want to live in a way that honors You...but I don't want to give up Jeremiah."

She sighs, disappointed by the fact that the heaviness hasn't lifted yet. If only answers to prayers came as instantly as Instagram notifications. She sits up, wondering who she can talk to that may have even the slightest grid to understand what she's going through. Her eyes dart toward her cell phone as she thinks of Bradley. Surely he's had to make decisions like this before. Maybe he could share something that might help her feel better?

No, she scolds herself, *there's no way you're calling Bradley. You do not call another guy to discuss your relationship with your boyfriend. I've seen enough movies to know how that ends. Bad move, Aurora.*

She stands up and anxiously walks toward her window, wondering if perhaps a stroll on the beach is what she needs right now.

Just then, there's a small tap on her door.

"Come in!" Aurora calls.

Miss Maggie pops her head inside, "Aurora, honey, may I talk to you for a moment?"

"Sure." Aurora plops back down onto her bed, assuming that Miss Maggie wants to go over some last-minute tour stuff.

"I just talked to your parents." Her voice is firm, "They want to come and see you in New York."

Aurora's fingers fumble anxiously with the edge of her white bedspread.

"I told them I thought you'd enjoy seeing them." Miss Maggie adds in a softer tone, "I know this has all been a huge adjustment for you, but they're obviously concerned about the fact that you haven't returned any of their phone calls. They miss you! And they're very worried."

"Can't you see how weird this is?" Aurora struggles to express her perspective, "They're not even my real parents!"

"They may not be your flesh and blood birth parents," Miss Maggie replies tenderly, "but they love you, Aurora. They raised you! They adopted you into their family and gave you every chance and opportunity a girl could dream of. They've always wanted the very best for you, and they still do. I know that if I were in their shoes, I would never want my Emma to shut me out the way you have done to them. It hurts a mom's heart to see her daughter in pain and have no way of reaching her. So please, Rory, talk to your parents. Give them a call and let them know you love them."

Aurora sighs, unsure of what to say next. Thankfully, she doesn't have to say anything as another knock comes to her bedroom door.

This time it's Emma.

"Hey, um…you have a visitor," Emma tells her.

"Visitor?" Aurora quickly crosses the room, wondering if it's Jeremiah. She threads quick fingers through her silky hair and attempts to make herself presentable. She dashes out of her room and turns the curve down the stairs.

She gasps when she reaches the second step. From her lofty view, she can see Lena and Jack standing in the living room.

"Lena!" she screeches, astounded and delighted by the unexpected sight. She races down the stairs and flings herself into Lena. The two hug and giggle, fiercely expressing how much they've missed one another.

"Oh, my cupcakes, you're here! Like in real life!" Aurora squeals, "Lena, there is *so* much I have to talk to you about! Thank God, this couldn't be any better timing! Whatever in the world made you come back so soon? I asked Miss Maggie for some way to reach you, as I've been dying to hear your voice again, but she said the URIA doesn't give out that kind of information and—oh my word, I am so sorry about your Grandmary and little brother! Oh Lena, how are you doing? Are you okay?"

"I am alright." Lena tells her honestly, "My strength is found in the Lord. Without Him I would not have anywhere near the peace and strength I do today. But you're right, Aurora, we have a lot to talk about."

Miss Maggie and Emma land in the living room.

"Welcome back to California!" Miss Maggie hugs Lena and then Jack. Aurora grins, finding it quite comical to see stiff and serious Jack bombarded in a hug by bubbly Miss Maggie. "What are you guys doing here? I had no idea you were coming! Did the URIA send you? Why didn't Jonathan give me any kind of heads up? Is everything okay?"

"We're not here in a state of emergency," Jack explains, "but this is no leisurely visit either." He glances at Lena, "Perhaps the Queen of Bella Adar will better explain the purpose of this trip."

"Queen?" Aurora echoes, her eyes expanding with excitement. "You decided to become Queen? Lena, that's ah-may-zing! Does this mean Raymond is out of the picture? Are you gonna get your own castle? Did you come here to invite me to a fancy ball?!"

"Oh no, Raymond is still on the prowl," Lena quickly corrects her. "The palace is fully occupied by Raymond and his administration. But so much has changed, Aurora. I've changed. God has done a miracle in my heart and helped me see that just like Queen Esther, I have been chosen for this role. I have seen the poverty and turmoil that Bella Adar is in. Hungry children roam the streets and are orphaned because of Raymond's wicked ways; there is so much that needs to change. I know full well that I cannot accomplish any of this on my own, and because of that, Captain Cepheus sent me to Tarsurella to meet with their King. He was very wise, and he counseled that I do not try to move forward without first entreating my sisters. By myself, I do not know how much of an impact I can make. But I know that if we join together, place our differences aside, and march forward in unity, God can use us to make a much-needed difference in our nation."

"Are you hungry?" Aurora asks before crossing to the kitchen and anxiously opening up cupboards. "You guys must be starving after such a long flight. Want some snacks? We've got Goldfish crackers, Cheese-Its, Vanilla Wafers, tons of Nutella—"

Emma bites her lip, all too familiar with Aurora's avoidance tactics. "She's trying to distract you, guys," Emma tells Lena. "Apparently she's not ready to wake up and face reality."

"Shut up, Emma!" Aurora suddenly slams the cupboard door shut, dramatically capturing everyone's attention. "You have *no* idea what it's like to be in my shoes! So quit making your uppity little judgements about everything I do and get a life of your own to focus on, so you can stop psychoanalyzing mine!"

"You think I *want* to be in this position?" Emma snaps, fully fed up with Aurora's selfish ways. "Forced to live under the same roof as you, the Drama Queen who throws temper tantrums every time something doesn't go her way? I'm forever walking one step behind your oversized luggage bags, uprooting my life, traveling, going wherever you want to go and keeping up with your crazy schedule! I'm *always* here for you, cleaning up your messes, protecting you from things that could shatter your heart in two, and keeping my lips zipped when I feel like slapping you in the face and saying, 'Wake up, Aurora!' The entire world is at your fingertips! A whole stinking nation is in need of your help, and all you care about is obsessing over your lowdown, good-for-nothing, wormy boyfriend! Can't you see what's happening here?" She motions towards Lena, "People wait their whole lives for moments like these. I would kill to have a story like yours! A story calling you to slip off the sidelines of an average existence, and play a starring role in an exhilarating adventure, a chance to change the world! People your age never get that kind of power! Yet, you have it! And you're throwing it all away over some stupid infatuation with a boy who doesn't even love you?" Emma's voice calms as she shakes her head slowly, "If you stay trapped in this self-absorbed world of yours and turn down Lena's invitation to find out who you're supposed to be, then I don't know…maybe you were never really the girl I thought you were."

~*~

Emma stares at the dazzling ocean, bewildered by brilliant shades of blue and green, tumbling in a majestic fury of power and beauty. She could stare at the waves forever, and never grow tired of their mesmerizing motions. The rise and fall of each rhythmic beat helps to calm her mind.

"Aurora is driving me literally bananas," Emma vents. "Living with her is severely causing me to worry about my own mental health! Like, I get that she's a self-entitled, boy-crazy popstar, but we never had these kinds of issues in the past! It's like Jeremiah is completely destroying her. He's this toxic waste product filling her lungs, messing with her mind and stealing her breath, but she's far too hypnotized to care."

"I dunno; they say love can do crazy things to people." Arden responds, his tongue hurrying to catch a drip on his chocolate-vanilla-swirl ice cream cone.

"But she's not in love!" Emma argues. "She's just infatuated with this fairytale image of who she *thinks* Jeremiah is. But he's not even that person. She has so many stars in her eyes, when she looks at him, she's not able to see who he really is."

"Makes sense." Arden shrugs, "I mean, I don't know who these 'they' people are, but they do say love is blind."

"But it's not love!" Emma argues. "She's sixteen years old! There's no way she can be in love."

"What, you don't think teenagers can fall in love?" Arden asks, his eyes catching her off guard with the question.

"I—I don't know." She quickly looks away from him, "I mean, maybe, in like some extremely rare cases—"

"You're dripping," Arden tells her, not wanting her to lose any of her sugary goodness in the hot California sunshine.

Emma quickly licks her cone before the drip reaches her hand. "But most teenagers don't even know what love is. Pastor Brian said people our age don't know how to steward their hearts. Most relationships are forged out of selfish desires, and unless both people are placing Jesus first and living the kind of love 1 Corinthians 13 talks about, it's going to be a total fail. We're way more prone to falling into severe *Obsession*, like your silly song says."

"Hey now, I know you're upset with Aurora, but don't go bashing the song!" Arden laughs, "Dozens of stations started playing it. The DJ's are digging it."

"Actually, I think your song perfectly explains what Aurora's problem is. She's too obsessed with Jeremiah to see that her unhealthy desire for him is actually killing her." Emma sighs, "I just don't know if I should tell her what happened at play practice. If I tell her I saw Jeremiah and Savannah swapping spit, she's going to freak out, accuse me of being jealous, and probably bite my head off. But if I *don't* tell her, and she finds out later that I knew, she's going to accuse me of hiding it from her and being a terrible friend. Either way, I lose."

"Not necessarily." Arden grins, "You do have an ice cream cone in your hand. So, I'd say, in the grand scheme of things, you're pretty much winning at life."

Emma laughs, as she's reminded of yet another quality she admires about Arden. When she's got her head in the sand, down in the dumps, and her glass is only half-full of complaints and woe, he comes along and gives her a reason to smile. She tries to hide her grin, but her eyes won't lie.

"Maybe you should just give it some time," Arden suggests. "It sounds like things are really rocky between the two of you, so maybe you should just keep your distance. If Jeremiah really is as much of a jerk as you're making him out to be, then the truth will come out eventually. Trust me, guys like that can only get away with their snaky ways for so long before being caught red-handed. Try to think about it from Aurora's perspective. She's got a ton on her plate. Her job is crazy demanding, and didn't she just find out about her Amish sister? In my opinion, that's a lot to try and handle. I can imagine the struggle to stay sane. You can't blame her for acting a little messed up now and then."

"Okay, enough about my world." Emma shakes her head, ready to change the subject, "How did your day with the press go?"

"Uh, hello! I just bought you ice cream!" He proudly holds up his cone, "Obviously a good sign! I'm usually straight-up-broke so my treat means *Bubblegum* thinks we have a bright future."

"Ohhhh, so that's why you suggested the ice cream." Emma hits herself in the head playfully, "I thought you were just trying to get me to dance on top of a table again."

"Not exactly," he grins, "but I wouldn't hate it if you ran over to that crowd of people and screamed at the top of your lungs about what a massive *Acid Rain* fan you are."

Emma laughs, "Never in a million years! All I said about your performance was that you guys were impressive. That's all. Hardly anything to scream about."

"Yeah, yeah, whatever." He shrugs, "We all know you're secretly fangirling inside."

Emma rolls her eyes, slightly concerned about the unsettling thought that he might be able to see right through her. Can he somehow read her mind? She knows it's impossible. But still. It's freakishly unnerving to think about.

"Let's head to the Pier." Arden quickly gobbles up the last bite of his cone and wipes his hands on his shorts.

"Let me finish my cone first." Emma tries to buy more time before they make contact with the crowds. "I'm really terrible at walking and eating at the same time."

"You're also terrible at eating the same pace of a normal human being," Arden tells her. "I've never seen anyone lick ice cream so slowly. A snail could beat you!"

"Don't judge, I like to enjoy it!" She strongly defends herself and her delicious treat. "Just like my books, I savor them. Dessert is way better when you can make it last for a while."

"That is, if you have anything left by the time you finish. It's going to be all melted!"

"No, it's not!" Emma argues.

"Just stuff it all in your mouth!" He chants, "Eat it! Eat it! Eat it!"

"No way! I'm trying *not* to make a massive mess, thank you very much."

"Yeah, but Emma, it doesn't matter how careful you are, or how slow you go, sometimes life just happens, your plans get tossed to the wind, and you've got a huge mess on your face."

"Are you trying to turn my ice cream into some kind of important life lesson again?" She giggles.

"Nah, not so much." Arden shrugs, "Really, I was just trying to prepare you for–THIS!" All at once, Arden smashes Emma's ice cream cone onto her nose, smearing it down her left cheek.

She releases a horrified gasp as the frozen contents drip down her face. It's like a freaky flashback to their time in New York.

"Arden Laverne!" She spits out his name like it's some kind of wretched disease.

He can't help but laugh and hands her several napkins. "Ready to go to the Pier now?"

"You completely ruined my ice cream cone! I wasn't finished yet!" She wipes off her nose and face.

"Well you are now!" He grins, "Come on, let's go get some cotton candy to wash it down!"

"Oh, and are you planning to smash that into my face too?" she asks sarcastically, wiping off her hands before throwing the wad of sticky napkins into the trash.

"I could," Arden considers, "but somehow I don't think it would be as fun. Race you to the Pier!"

Arden takes off, and Emma shakes her head, wondering why she enjoys hanging out so much with this one-of-a-kind mess. She slips off her flip flops and takes off across the hot sand, determined to beat him. She quickly catches up, but he increases his speed. The two are running at the same stride, but Arden's long arm stretches out and touches the wooden Pier beam just a second before hers does.

"Ugh!" Emma pants, leaning over, attempting to catch her breath after the unexpected dash.

"I should've warned you. I run track in school," Arden tells her.

"Speaking of school, are you planning to keep attending in the fall?" Emma asks as they slowly ascend the steps of the crowded pier. "Or are you going to get a private tutor or something?"

"I'm not sure yet, I guess we'll just have to see what happens. I mean, as much as I love school and hanging out with all my friends, I might be too busy with touring and stuff. Especially if things go well this week, and *Bubblegum* decides for sure that we'll join Aurora's second leg."

They land on the top of the wooden Pier, ready to walk the long boardwalk leading to various stores, junk food venues, balloon stalls, and souvenir shops. The area is swarming with vacationers from around the world, as well as local California natives looking for something fun to do.

"This might sound like kind of a strange question," Emma starts slowly, "but where are your friends? I mean, I know they exist, and I'm sure they all love hanging around Mr. Fun, but why aren't they here? This is one of the most exciting moments of your life, getting your first live radio airplay. And they weren't at the station yesterday or eating celebratory ice cream with us today. I'm a little stumped as to why *I'm* the person you're hanging out with right now…like, are they all out of town or something?"

"Don't get me wrong, my friends are really cool, it's just…they don't really get all of this." Arden attempts to explain himself, "You've been on this whole Hollywood scene a long time, and even though it's crazy exciting, you keep your head cool about everything. Most of my friends would've been begging Sam and Pam for autographs and trying to take selfies with my bandmates, bragging about the fact that they knew us before anything big happened. And I don't know, I just don't see that in you. You're really chill, and you understand this whole process. Even if I do become a big star someday, I just can't imagine you treating me any differently."

"Isn't that the truth!" Emma laughs, "There's nothing fangirl worthy about a guy who dumps ice cream in your face."

"I know you probably get tired of hearing about all this and have seen this kinda stuff happen to your mom's clients, but I just can't believe this is real life!" Arden can't stop grinning, "I mean, we've got a full week of radio interviews, magazine photoshoots, and acoustic performances! It just doesn't seem real. I'll try to shut up about it."

"Oh, no, you don't have to," Emma tells him understandingly. "Sure, I've been in Hollywood a while and I've seen a lot of artists hit it big, but that doesn't make your process any less exciting. To be completely honest, I'm kind of enjoying seeing things through your boyish, rose-colored glasses of bliss–" She bites her lip, stopping herself from finishing her sentence. She almost slipped out with, *and it's kind of adorable.* Her cheeks are touched with a hint of pink, simply from the thought. She quickly looks away, setting her gaze on where they're walking. She clenches her jaw shut, reminding herself to be more careful. She feels so comfortable around Arden, it's easy to forget who she's actually talking to.

"Oh, my goodness, it's that guy from the radio!" A tall, gangly girl, wearing frayed jean shorts and a rose crop-top, elbows her friend, "Isn't he from that new band?"

"I think you're right! I totally freaked out and Googled them after I heard the song! I think his name is...um, Arden?" A young woman with a chocolate-flavored complexion stepped out into their path. "Are you the guy from that new band?"

"*Acid Rain*?" Arden echoes, just as surprised with this encounter as they are.

Emma watches the scene nervously, feeling racked with insecurity, thanks to how freakishly gorgeous the two teens are. She anxiously pushes a stray hair behind her ear, wondering how they get their hair to lay so flat in this kind of heat. Today, she must look like an absolute frizz ball.

Arden is glowing with his ever-constant charm and charisma. Emma glances at him, feeling an unwelcome jealousy stirring in the pit of her stomach. Why does she care that these girls are talking to him? And why is she so devastated by the fact that he appears to be immensely enjoying it?

"Yes! Your song was amazing!" the fair-skinned beauty excitedly tells him, "I immediately texted all my friends and told them to look you guys up!"

"When is *Obsession* gonna be on iTunes? I totally want to buy it!" the other girl squealed.

"I'm not sure yet; we're just doing a radio run right now to see how it goes. But we're going to have a few live shows around Cali this week, so if you check out our site you can find all the details."

"Seriously?! We will totally be there! Can we get a picture with you?"

"Of course!" Arden grins, happy to please the ladies.

"Here, can you take it?" The girl hands her phone to Emma.

Emma bites her lip, unsure of what else to say than, "Sure."

Arden throws his arms around the girls, and they all give Emma their biggest grins. Emma focuses on the elated group then snaps several shots.

"Thank you so much!" the girls squeal in unison.

"Of course!" Arden offers them a cheesy thumbs-up, "Anytime! Hope to see you at the shows!"

~*~

"Obsession is doing fantastic!" Miss Maggie announces triumphantly as she hangs up the phone. "If things continue to go in the direction they're headed, *Bubblegum* is going to finalize them for the second leg of your tour!"

"Awesome!" Aurora nods, carrying a bowl of salad to the table where Lena and Jack are sitting. She sits down beside Lena, "I'm so stoked for tour to begin! Maybe you can come on the road with me too! I could teach you how to play guitar, and we can hang out in between shows. Lena, we would have an absolute blast!"

"As enjoyable as that sounds, you know that I cannot," Lena tells her firmly. "My place is in Bella Adar, with my people."

"I know," Aurora sighs, scooping a small serving of salad onto each plate, "but it's a fun dream anyway." She smiles weakly, "Maybe after things settle down and Raymond is booted out of there, you can come back to the States for a while."

"Aurora, this is not going to be an easy feat." Lena's voice is solemn, "Removing Raymond from the palace is not as simple as it sounds. It's going to involve a highly thought-through and strategic plan, followed by an intense military operation. Even then, once Raymond is gone and we occupy the throne, there will be so much rebuilding to do. And I don't want to do this alone."

"Lena, I understand how hard things are right now," Aurora tells her kindly. "I know your country is hurting, and things are tough. But it's not even possible for me to physically come and help. I'm booked solid for the next four months. I've got thousands of fans depending on me showing up for my tour dates. I can't just cancel on them. And even if I did, it's just not feasible to go to Europe and be part of all that craziness without the press catching onto us and making a huge deal about it. The URIA said everyone is safer if our identities remain a secret, and trust me, pretty much anything I do does *not* stay secret for long."

"Aurora is right." Miss Maggie adds, "And this tour isn't just about the fans. We've signed contracts. With *Bubblegum*, stage management, tour workers, lighting guys, costume design, the set crew...her tour is no small operation! We've got deadlines to meet and bills to pay. If Aurora doesn't follow through with her commitment, hundreds of good, hardworking people would be without a job. This tour is about so much more than just her."

"Oh." Lena sighs, looking down at her plate, not feeling much appetite. She can see that she's not going to get very far with Aurora. She is nearing the end of the road. First

Elizabeth refused to come, and now Aurora. She should've known better. She knew in her heart of hearts that her sisters would not come home with her.

"I'm so sorry," Aurora smiles weakly, "but the timing just isn't right. You know I'll always love and support you. And you're going to be the most spectacular Queen this country has ever seen! But just because I can't go with you right now doesn't mean I'm not with you in spirit. And I promise I'll come visit! You still have to host that big, fancy, ball, remember?" She laughs, hoping to make Lena feel better. "Bottom line is, God has a plan, and He is going to work everything out the way it's supposed to be."

~*~

Back in Bella Adar...

"We will dispatch the troops for ambush in the forest of Siron. There, as they travel on foot beneath the cover of night fall, they'll still maintain the element of surprise," Captain Cepheus tells everyone at the boardroom table. "To the best of our knowledge, it still appears as though Raymond does not know we exist. Hopefully, Raymond's guards will be completely unprepared to face our men when they storm the palace. By force, we will demand that Raymond abdicate the throne, and make way for their rightful Queen. Any questions?"

Lena listens with a sober heart, as Captain Cepheus instructs the military leaders.

When no one speaks, Captain Cepheus continues. "Very well. We will carry forth with this plan and dispatch our men tomorrow at noon. We must pray this operation is successful. Gaining access to Raymond's stronghold is paramount. If we struggle to attain victory and Raymond discovers our existence, it will only make things that much more complicated. We must pray that God is with us and our men, and that the Angel Armies of Heaven will be fighting with us tomorrow. Meeting dismissed."

Lena slowly gets up from her chair, feeling as though she's trapped in the middle of a terribly bitter dream. Tomorrow, the fate of her entire nation will be in jeopardy, and she can do nothing but sit, pray, and wait. She already knows that enduring the dreaded hours' silence will be like torture, as they wait for word on each new development. With nothing to do but turn worries into prayers, Lena already has dozens of fears shooting through her mind.

Her anxious fingers nervously clench the end of her sleeves. Jack will be marching out with a platoon of foot soldiers. Her heart reels with violent concern.

Tomorrow, they will place everything on the line. They will move their chess pieces forward in faith, hoping and praying that victory will come. It is time to conquer the enemy once and for all.

Last night, on Lena's long flight home from the United States, she was greatly discouraged by both Aurora's and Elizabeth's refusal to come. She felt as though she had failed miserably, but Jack had encouraged her otherwise.

"Perhaps it is best that your sisters didn't return with you. It is quite clear that neither of them is mature enough to handle this weight of responsibility. With their petty arguments and immature behavior, let them stay behind and cling to their worthless idols. You've been called to something greater, Your Majesty. God is going to use you to deliver these people. You have made one selfless decision after another, after another, and God will reward you for that. Don't doubt yourself. You've done the right thing. Now there is nothing left to do but rest, and trust God for the victory. The battle is in His hands now."

As Lena walks down the long, earthen corridors, she remembers Jack's words. *The battle is in His hands now.* She thinks of Gideon, and Jehoshaphat, and many others in the Bible who faced impossible odds and came out on top. Surely, God will fight for them in this hour. Surely, He will unveil His mighty arm, and deliver her nation from such unthinkable oppression. Even though her sisters chose not to come and partner with her, God is on her side. And that is all she needs.

Lord, protect Jack. She prays, her quick footsteps making their way toward her shared room with Rachel, her kind assistant. *Protect all the men! I pray that not one life will be lost! I pray they overwhelm Raymond and cause him to surrender quickly, without bloodshed.*

She reaches her door and pushes it open, not at all surprised to see Peter and Rachel chatting over tea. Peter's eyes anxiously dance toward her. "How did the meeting go?"

Lena plops down beside him at their small coffee table, and Rachel bounces up to get a cup of tea for Lena.

"As good as it could I suppose." Lena sighs, "I don't know how else to describe a meeting that discusses putting the lives of so many good people in jeopardy. It makes my heart sick just thinking about it. Oh, I shall never forgive myself if something happens to them."

"Lena," Peter reaches across the table and places a compassionate hand on Lena's forearm, "they're soldiers. Fighting for what they believe in is their job. Nobody is forcing them to go do this. You can't feel responsible for what the URIA has mobilized."

"Oh dear, I think we're out of peppermint tea bags!" Rachel announces. "I know they're your favorite, Your Majesty. I'll go down to the cafeteria and see what I can find."

"Thank you, Rachel, you're too kind." Lena smiles as the woman scurries out the door. She turns back to Peter, "Jack said the same thing. That this is not my responsibility. Yet somehow, I feel like it is. It was *my* parents who were killed. My kingdom that was stolen. The URIA is marching forward with my stamp of approval. If even just one dies...oh Peter, I don't think my heart will be able to bear it!"

"Lena, you must give this heavy burden back to the Lord. It was never yours to carry in the first place." Peter shakes his head, hating to see her in so much pain and distress, "If I would, I would take it all from you in an instant."

"Thank you, Peter." She sighs, "You've always been here for me. A most constant companion even in the depths of my despair. I don't know if I've ever gotten the chance to properly thank you. So, thank you. Truly."

"Lena, you know that thanks isn't needed." Peter continues to stare at her, his Mediterranean-ocean eyes overflowing with endless waves of love and compassion. "You must know that..." he pauses, "I know I haven't exactly said it in so many words, but I've tried, every day of my life for so many years, to express through my actions how I feel about you." His hand reaches for hers, and Lena loses her breath. His warm hand over hers is unexpected. She watches with wide eyes, her mouth dry and heart pounding, somehow knowing what he's about to say next. "Lena, I lo–"

Just then the door flies open, and Rachel is back again. "Well what do you know, there were some extra tea bags in the Captain's Room!"

Peter's eyes flash with disappointment, irritated with the unwelcome interruption. His hand slowly slips away from hers as he clears his throat and stands up. "I guess I'd better go bunk up for the night. Sergeant Crawdad keeps a tight ship. He might have me peeling more potatoes if I'm not back in time. Goodnight, Rachel."

"Oh, goodnight Peter!" Rachel smiles and offers a little wave before returning to her tea kettle.

"Goodnight, Lena," he speaks tenderly, his voice ringing with care and thoughtfulness.

Lena attempts to find words, scrambling to make sense of everything that has just happened. "Oh, yes, goodnight. Um, rest well. Don't forget to pray for the men."

~*~

In New York City…

Invisible electric currents of pure verve pump through Aurora's veins. Gone are the baffling concerns about Jeremiah, her parents, Emma, and her sisters. Every tangling worry that has been suffocating her is miraculously vanishing beneath the promising glow of the soon-to-be stage lights.

The moment has arrived. Aurora is about to go onstage for her kick-off tour show at *Madison Square Garden*. She can hear the deafening roar of elated fans chanting her name, even through the thick cement walls she is standing behind. Her stomach does a lively somersault as she clings to the hand of her drummer. They've all circled together for their pre-show ritual.

"This is it you guys!" she tells her bandmates, backup singers, and dancers. Bradley is in the circle as well. "We finally made it! Opening night! I know you're probably expecting a big, pumped-up speech, but honestly, I don't even know what to say!" She looks at Bradley, "But I do know that we couldn't have made it to this moment without God's grace. So, I think we should pray. Bradley, do you want to lead us?"

Bradley's bright grin causes Aurora's heart to smile. "Of course. Let's bow our heads," he tells the group, well aware that many of them have perhaps never prayed before. "Dear Heavenly Father...wow. Thank you. We come before you with humble, grateful hearts exploding with excitement and overwhelmed emotions! God, we know You brought us to this place, and You have a plan and purpose for us being here tonight. We pray that You would—"

Aurora feels a sudden tap on her shoulder. Her eyes open and she cranes her neck. Miss Maggie is behind her. Her eyes are pooling with threatening tears. Aurora's heart thunders with panic, shocked to see Miss Maggie appear so grief-stricken. Something is wrong. Something is seriously wrong.

"Uh, excuse me, just a second," Aurora quickly speaks up, interrupting Bradley's prayer. "Bradley, I'm so sorry. I um, just a second, I'll be back, hold on." She quickly turns to follow Miss Maggie, who has hidden her face from the rest of the crowd. Aurora attempts to keep up with her brisk pace as they head down the long hallway.

"Miss Maggie, what's wrong?!" Aurora asks, desperate to know what's going on. Whatever it is must be absolutely awful. Or else there's no way Miss Maggie would've interrupted them like that.

"Honey, I'm so sorry." The tears are now falling freely as she closes Aurora's dressing room door and clenches a remote to her chest. "But I had to tell you." She exhales, then flicks on the TV. "Oh, God, help us."

Aurora's bewildered eyes anxiously soak in an unfamiliar scene. The news channel is flashing their obnoxious, "Breaking News!" symbol, as the anchor stands in the streets of an unknown town. "Heartless School Bombing in Bella Adar!" the scrolling letters scream.

Aurora's heart stops as she listens on high alert to the news anchor reporting from the streets,

"As you can see, several hundred feet behind me, there is still smoke rising from their dilapidated school building. Twenty-three women and children are confirmed dead, as well as countless injured, and the death toll is still on the rise. Citizens in the capital city are devastated, as I've already spoken to several mothers who have lost their children. These attacks are believed to be a direct aim at rebel teachers, who have been supposedly indoctrinating the children to believe that their King should be dethroned. Though it seems barbaric and unthinkable to believe any leader would bomb its own children in response to political differences, we're told that this is most likely the reason behind this heartless terror move, in Bella Adar."

The scene flashes back to the news studio in New York City, as the familiar face at his desk tells the world what is newly developing. "It has indeed been confirmed that this attack was a direct terror response from King Raymond, the sovereign leader of Bella Adar, and his military. Sources on the ground tell us that this bombing is believed to be a fear-warning, sent out to dishearten the people of this small nation. This bombing took place no less than twenty minutes after an underground, rebel army attempted to seize the palace and remove King Raymond by force."

The scene flashes to show a gorgeous, strikingly-tall medieval castle, standing beautifully beside a sparkling ocean. But the lovely scene quickly evaporates, and Lena's face is on the TV screen! The still image of her is alongside the photograph of an older-looking man, whose description says, 'Captain Cepheus.'

The anchor continues, "This move was completely unexpected, and was led by the supposed rebellion leader, pictured here, Captain Cepheus, and get this—a teenage girl! Sources are saying that this young woman is the true heir and Princess of Bella Adar! The ambush led by these two was unsuccessful, as dozens of their men are injured and the Captain and rumored-to-be-Princess are reported as Missing in Action. Though it is highly unlikely they survived the backlash from King Raymond after the ambush, we're still waiting for more information."

Aurora tumbles backwards into the chair behind her. "What?! No! Th-that's impossible!"

The scene switches back to a panel of news personalities who are ready to weigh in with their opinion on the crisis.

"We obviously don't have many details yet, as we are still piecing together whatever we can, but I know that everyone who is watching this right now feels the same way we do, with their jaws on the floor. I mean, what kind of leader performs a terror attack on his own citizens?!"

"I don't know, Anthony," a woman shakes her head, appearing disgusted with the false display of power. "Whoever this leader is, surely doesn't deserve to be in that kind of a position. As you mentioned, this story is still developing, and we'll share more details as they come, but from what we know already, this man, their current king, is displaying so many frightening, Hitler-like behaviors. Obviously, the Captain and supposed-Princess didn't know the fullness of what they were getting themselves into, as their army was greatly outnumbered by the Royal Regime. If Raymond succeeded in killing the Princess, this nation is going to be in a startlingly-desperate situation."

Aurora's heart is crumbling. "No! Lena's not dead! She can't be. She can't be!" Violent sobs arrest Aurora's entire being, and she can do nothing to stop them. Her shoulders are shaking, the tears are flowing, and Miss Maggie throws her arms around the dear girl.

"Oh honey! Shhh, shhh, you're okay, you're okay." She speaks in a soothing tone, and tenderly pats Aurora on the back of her head, but Aurora cannot even feel it. She's being carried away in a lava-running-avalanche of turmoil and mourning.

"I can't lose her!" Aurora finally chokes out.

"Sweetie, you don't know that she's gone!" Miss Maggie chokes, "Nothing has been confirmed. Missing in action simply means…Rory, there's still hope."

Aurora pulls away from the hug and wipes her eyes. "That's it. The tour's off. I'm going to Bella Adar."

The news anchors are still speaking in the background. "Now the big question is, will the United States step in and take action? We're still waiting for a response from the President and—"

Miss Maggie shuts the TV off. "Aurora, you know how the press makes everything sound far more dramatic than it actually is. Surely Lena is okay. Right now, we just need to focus on one thing: Your show! Think about all your excited fans out there, they can't wait to see you!"

"Miss Maggie, I'm not doing it. I said the tour is off." She reaches for her phone, "I'm taking the first plane to Bella Adar I can find."

"Woah, Aurora! Honey, I know you're experiencing a lot of emotional turmoil, but let's just stop and think through this before you make any rash decisions! There are thousands of people depending on you!"

"And my sister is more important than all of them!" Aurora shakes her head, "Miss Maggie, I can't think about anything else! There's no way I'm doing the show. I've made up my mind. I am not singing tonight."

Just then, a knock is heard at the door. Aurora wipes her tears once more and opens her Flight Finder App.

"Is everything okay?" Bradly slowly enters, "What's going on?"

"It's a family emergency." Aurora stands up, "I'm not doing the show tonight. I need to catch a flight somewhere. Like, now."

"Oh wow, I'm so sorry!" Bradley is shocked to hear such news, "I'll be praying for you guys."

Miss Maggie sighs, hating that Aurora has already made up her mind. She knows there's no way to steer her in any other direction. She's probably already bought their flight tickets. "I guess I have to be the bearer of bad news…" she sighs, "I'll go tell the rest of the crew."

~*~

In Amish Country...

Elizabeth pushes through the squeaky screen door, entering the familiar general store. She takes a deep breath, pleased with the scent of lavender soaps and fresh cheddar cheeses.

"Good afternoon, Miss Stoltz." Rose greets her from behind the counter.

"Good afternoon, it is a beautiful day God has blessed us with."

"It is indeed! All of this rain has been bringing much delight to my garden. And what about you, Miss Stoltz, you have an extra warm glow about you. Could it be because of your frequent buggy rides with young Mr. Yoder?"

Elizabeth's face flashes pink. She isn't sure what to say.

"Ahh, I knew the two of you were courtin'!" Rose grins, making a satisfied clicking noise with her tongue, "The good Lord did a fine job putting the two of you together! When is the wedding?"

Elizabeth's face is *really* pink now. "It is getting late, I would best find the items Ma has sent me for, Miss Rose." Elizabeth quickly turns away and heads to the other end of the store. Weesh! Some people can just be so very nosey!

The past few days have been filled with many folks asking if she and Jonah are courting. Even though their questions can be tiresome, Elizabeth never grows weary of telling them the answer. *Yes!*

She sighs happily, knowing that each moment she spends with Jonah just gets sweeter and sweeter. Her parents were right. These days spent courting Jonah will be some of the most delightful times of her life. Even when she is old and gray, she will always look back on these moments with a great fondness.

She meanders around the shop, searching for a special gift to present to Jonah on their next get-together. She is searching for something practical, yet meaningful. Even though it is not uncommon in her family to bless one another with gifts, they must be practical, and never vain or wasteful. She thinks of the small necklace her sister got her: an ideal example of something the Amish would never give to one another.

Her eyes gingerly search the premises until something catches her eye. An alarming photograph screams at her. She does a double-take, unable to believe what is laying before her on the counter. Lena's face is on the cover of a newspaper!

Elizabeth's fingers tremble, as she longs to pick up the paper and read it. She knows it is not right for them to read the newspaper, yet it is here because some of the Mennonite families do. She glances over her shoulder, looking around cautiously to make sure no one is watching. Rose is busy with another customer now. Surely she can sneak a glance without getting caught.

She slowly opens the loud paper, and her eyes gulp in the words as quick as she can. It doesn't take long for her to understand the gist of the story: there's been a grave emergency, and her sister might be dead! Elizabeth's heart drops to the floor. She quickly places the paper where it belongs and scurries out the door.

"Miss Stoltz! Are you not going to buy what your ma sent you here to—"

But Elizabeth can't hear her. She's already pounding down the steps and racing up the road. Frantic thoughts invade her mind like flies, but she doesn't pause to dwell on any of them. She just continues to run.

She arrives at the house completely breathless. Even so, she doesn't stop until after thundering up the stairs and into her bedroom. She must find her emergency pager to contact Mr. Jonathan! She must know that Lena is okay!

She frantically opens her dresser drawers, digging beneath her spare bed sheets and nightgown. Elizabeth unfolds her handkerchief, and the delicate, sparkly crown necklace falls into her hand. She cocks her head, puzzled as to why the small electronic device is not there beside it. She digs deeper into the drawer, emptying out each item. She then searches the floor to see if it's fallen. She pushes her dresser away from the wall and peers behind it. Still nothing.

Elizabeth gets on her hands and knees to search beneath her bed. When she doesn't find it, she removes her quilt and sheets, and looks beneath the mattress. Her face is bright red, and she aches to quench her dry throat with a drop of water, but she doesn't stop. Where did it go?

She checks the dresser once more, as her heart begins to ache with fear and confusion. "Dear God, please help me find this!" she prays out loud.

A sudden thought pops into her mind. The laundry.

She catapults herself down the steps and finds Ma in the kitchen. "Is the laundry still drying out on the line?"

"Yah," Ma tells her, not looking away from her bubbling soup. "Where are my fresh cloves of garlic? And the other spices I asked you to fetch?"

Elizabeth gulps, not wanting to explain the reason why she rushed out of the store so abruptly. "I will tell you, but first I must know, have you seen something from the Englishers, in my belongings? It is about yay big, just a small, black, electronic device?"

"I did." Ma's voice is calm, clearly not as concerned about it as Elizabeth is.

"Oh, thank heavens!" Elizabeth breathes a sigh of relief, "Where did you place it?"

"In the garbage. Out with the vile pig-slop, where it belongs."

"Oh Ma, you didn't!" Elizabeth gasps, feeling herself growing angry with the woman, "You should have asked me first! That was very important!"

"Important?" Ma twirls around, wooden stirring spoon still in her hand, "It was one of the devil's toys! And you were hiding it! You should be thanking me for finding it and giving you an opportunity to repent!"

"But Ma, you do not understand!" Elizabeth argues frantically, now wondering what she is going to do to contact Jonathan. "An emergency has come up, and I must use that device! It will allow me to contact Jonathan and talk to my sister. A tragedy has happened in her land, and I must find out if she is still alive!"

"It should make no difference to you. Once you join the Church, she shall be dead to you."

"That is not true, Ma!" Elizabeth's voice cracks with emotion, "She is my sister and I love her!"

"See, the devil has taken over much of your mind! You have set your mind on earthly things, and now he is determined to corrupt you. Elizabeth, you must sever your communication with your sister, Jonathan, and all of the Englishers, once and for all. You know where your place is. You are to join the Church whole-heartedly, marry Jonah, and commit to serving God all the days of your life. You must repent of your sin and put your sister out of your mind. Forever."

"Ma, you cannot ask me to do that!" Elizabeth firmly stands her ground, "I love her! But I also love you and Da, and Jonah, and the Church! Can you not see that there is enough room in my heart to love all of you?"

"You cannot sit on the fence any longer. Your lukewarm state is displeasing to the Lord! You have been teetering dangerously close to the fires of hell, and if you take another step in that direction, I fear you will be lost forever! Elizabeth, listen to me. You must choose. Once and for all, without any backsliding. Your sisters, the Englishers, and their wicked world, or God, your faith, and your family."

"Ma, please do not speak to me so!" Elizabeth fights back tears, "I am not choosing the ways of the world. A most tragic thing has happened, and I need to know if Lena is alright!"

"Fine. If that is what you want, then choose," Ma snaps, losing her patience with her daughter's prodigal ways. "But if you reach out to her, know that you have lost your faith, and your true family forever."

Elizabeth is shocked by her words. Is Ma threatening to…to…shun her?

"Truly, you do not mean it." Elizabeth speaks, just barely above a whisper. "Ma, I told you, I am not choosing this world! I am merely—"

"Either Lena is dead to you, or we are!" she snaps, slamming her wooden spoon upon the counter.

Elizabeth winces, taken aback by the loud noise and even louder words. She gulps, knowing what she must do. She wants so desperately to explain things to Ma. But she won't hear her out. *Lord, help me!* she cries inside. *I know that I must do the right thing! I must check on my sister!*

"If it is a sin to do what is right, then let God be my judge," Elizabeth boldly states, her voice trembling slightly, "not you."

And with that, she dashes out the door.

~*~

Elizabeth's anxious knuckles tap on Jonah's front door. She prays he will answer.

The door slowly opens, and his angelic eyes are revealed. "Elizabeth!" A smile quickly eats up his entire face, and Elizabeth has to be strong in order to not be distracted by his handsome features.

"Something most tragic has happened," she says quickly. "I have a very important question. Do you know anyone who has a telephone?"

"I believe Joseph Dawns, a Mennonite man several miles up the road, might have one. Has something happened? Is it your parents?"

"No, no it is not Ma and Da," she shakes her head, "but my sister needs me."

"Sister?" Jonah cocks his head to the left, his eyes widening.

"I will explain on the way."

~*~

Back in California...

Jonathan Napp struggles to make sense of the wordy documents set before him. "I don't know man, I stayed up half the night looking at this stuff, and can't seem to figure out A from B. What is the bottom line issue here?" Jonathan asks his friend, who doubles as his attorney and is seated across the desk from him.

"The bottom line, is that Jasmine is going to try to nickel and dime you for everything you're worth. And we both know you're worth more than your average Joe! I mean, I've gotta give props to whoever put these documents together, it appears as though Jasmine worked long and hard on this sneaky, underhanded plan." He looks up from the papers, "She wants your ranch, Jon."

Jonathan groans and leans back into his chair. Things are far worse than he thought. After Jasmine's abrupt file for divorce, he received another pile of papers which told him that his marital property needed to be divided, and that Jasmine wanted all of hers in cash. Jon had made the deeply-regretted, harrowing mistake of adding Jasmine's name to their home and property deed, as well as adding her name to several of his bank accounts. He only felt like it was right, as a married couple, to share access to their money, but now Jonathan can see what a massive mistake that was. The day she left, she maxed out three of their credit cards, and withdrew thousands of dollars from several of his accounts.

Even though Jonathan wasn't anywhere near bankrupt, if Jasmine got things her way, he might be. "But that's ludicrous. I mean, there's no way she's going to be able to pull that off, is she?"

"The attorneys she worked with were clearly very skillful and found some clever little loop holes. But I assure you, Jon, I will do everything within my power to keep this from happening. I know how much this ranch means to you and your family."

"Thank you." Jon shakes hands with his old-time friend and business partner, "And please don't mention any of this to Ellie, okay? I can't even imagine how devastated she'd be if she knew the ranch was in jeopardy. Let's not worry her until we absolutely have to, okay?"

"No problem, Jon, my lips are sealed. Enjoy your day!"

Jon waves as his friend leaves, then he sighs at his pile of paperwork. What a ridiculously massive mess. And he's not talking about his desk.

"Hey Dad, is your meeting over?" Eleanor pops in.

"Yep." Jonathan quickly stacks papers which are sprawled out in every direction and stuffs them in a file folder. "Something you wanted to talk to me about?"

"Actually, yes. Logan is interested in buying one of our horses."

"Logan Sparks?" Jonathan's surprise is evident, "What would a big star like him want to do with a horse? Where would he keep it? Surely not in his Los Angeles penthouse."

"We've been talking about boarding options, and he's thinking about purchasing some property in Colorado. Nothing is set in stone though, so until then, he's asked if maybe he can continue to board here? Personally, I think that's a great idea, that way none of the horses have to go through that somewhat traumatic re-homing phase."

"Hmm…well you're a much better judge of potential horse owners than I am, so I'd say if you feel good about him in your gut, then it's fine by me."

"Thanks, Dad." Eleanor smiles, "You know, when Logan first arrived I thought he was this haughty, stuck up, self-absorbed, egotistical popstar without a heart. But it turns out, he has so much compassion for animals, as well as for people."

"Wow, Ellie, I didn't know you had a soft-spot for popstars." Jonathan grins.

"I don't!" Eleanor quickly sets the record straight.

"Not even a guy as good looking as *Cowboy Carson*?" he teases.

"*Especially* not *Cowboy Carson*. Those peppy, smiley, strait-up-caffeinated musical numbers are too much for me." She shakes her head ashamedly.

Jonathan laughs, "That's my Ellie; always far more in love with horses than she is with the cowboys. But that's totally okay, I'm not at all complaining. You make my Dad job much, much easier." He winks.

Eleanor laughs and leaves the office, "Later, Dad!"

She walks down the long isle, pausing for just long enough to check on their two pregnant mares. "Any day now and you, sweet girl, are going to foal." She smiles, giving them each a small sugar cube from her pocket. She kisses them on the nose, then continues making her way toward Auburn's stall.

"Hey lovely, how would you like to meet your possible new owner?" She tells the chestnut mare, "I think you'll really like him. He's good natured, has a patient heart and a soft hand, and I think the two of you will kick it off really well."

"Wow, I never thought I'd hear you speak so highly of me," a voice comes from behind. "I'm flattered."

Eleanor's face turns an awkward shade of pale pink, as she realizes Logan was standing behind her the entire time. She slowly pivots in her cowgirl boots, embarrassed to meet his face. "Auburn is a harsh judge of character. I really had to build you up in her mind, to soften her for the initial introduction."

"Good thinking." Logan smiles, reaching his hand out to meet Auburn. "Hey there girl, pleased to meet you. Wow, she's beautiful."

"My mom found her on a feed lot. She and about six other horses were stranded there without food or water, and they were going to get shipped to the slaughter house. We called Animal Control and even though Mom did the best she could, we could only save two out of the six." She sighs. "Her sister is here too. The fact that Auburn and Ember are alive truly is a miracle."

"Wow," Logan sighs, shaking his head, "it's so infuriating to think that people can be so heartless and cruel. A feed lot? Seriously? I didn't even know that was still a thing. People these days just don't understand the value of life. That's so, so sad."

"Yeah, and even though my mom tried her hardest, she couldn't save all of them. No matter what she did to make a difference, she still had to lay her head on her pillow every night, knowing that there were abused and mistreated horses that she would never be able to reach."

"But at least she was able to save one. I mean, it doesn't seem like a big deal in the grand scheme of things, but it does make an impact. So, what do you say, should we tack up and take Auburn and Ember out for a trail ride?"

"Aren't you busy tonight?" Eleanor tosses him a surprised look, "You only have a few more days on set, I thought Jack would be demanding another all-nighter."

"Not today." Logan smiles, "Thankfully, he decided to lay off and give us the night to chill. We've only got a few scenes left, and things are wrapping up pretty nicely. I think it's our reward for working so many extra hours."

"A trail ride does sound nice." Eleanor wistfully daydreams about the possibility, "But now that Jasmine's gone, I've got a huge mess to untangle in our main computer data-base. All the jobs she was in charge of have fallen off their axis, and someone needs to go in there and organize everything. We've got a lot of important guests this weekend and—"

"Oh, let the uppity guests get their own Macadamia nuts." Logan grins, grabbing his helmet from a nearby bench, "I say we ride."

Eleanor's eyes brighten. His eager, boyish enthusiasm to test out his possible new horse is quite endearing. So, she can't exactly argue with that.

"Logan, bae!" A winey, high-pitched voice floats down the aisle. Chelsea is wearing a pastel-pink cocktail dress, and four-inch-high heels. "Why are you not dressed yet?"

Eleanor looks away from Chelsea's sparkly purse, as the light reflecting off it almost blinds her. Eleanor shyly rubs her eye. Chelsea's outfit should come with some kind of warning label!

"Oh! No, I completely forgot!" Logan lifts a hand to his head, "Can we reschedule? I was just about to take a trail ride here with Auburn."

"Are you kidding? It took me like *three weeks* to book a reservation in this place! I had to bribe the manager to kick out Brad and Angelina. We got their table." She grins, "Come on, find your tux and let's ditch this cruddy little barn. I feel like we've been trapped in the middle of nowhere for weeks! Don't you want to get out and have some fun?"

"Actually, I've been enjoying the change of pace."

Chelsea wrinkles her nose, "This is the horse you're thinking about buying? He stinks!"

"He is a she," Logan corrects her, "and all horses smell like, you know, horses? It's kind of part of the deal."

"Well, I for one do not understand your fascination with these creatures." She stares at Auburn like she's a disgusting, smelly old boot, "Just so long as you don't have to clean up after what comes out the other end." She looks at Eleanor, "But then again, I guess that's what the help is for."

"Hey Logan, aren't you coming to the party?" Jack Heart enters the scene, wearing a fancy tuxedo himself.

"Actually, I was thinking about just hanging out here and taking a ride."

"Oh, come on kid, your riding skills are fine, you look like a pro now! Give yourself a break and come join us at the club. Owl Town, Maroon Seven, and Tustin Jimberlake are going to be playing! Chelsea spent hours trying to get you guys seats! Come on, it's gonna be a good time!"

Logan offers a sympathetic half-smile toward Eleanor. "Can I get a raincheck for next time? I'm a big Owl Town guy."

"Sure." Eleanor nods, attempting not to sound as disappointed as she feels, "Auburn will still be here tomorrow."

"Alright Logan, let's go have some fun!" Jack Heart gives Logan a high five, and excitedly chats as the three walk away.

Eleanor sighs, massaging Auburn between her ears, "Don't worry girl. He'll be back for you. But you know how Hollywood is. Sometimes other things come before horses, I guess."

She gives Auburn a kiss on the face and decides to make her way back to the office. Now that their plans are canceled, it looks like her evening will be spent attempting to reorganize the massive mess Jasmine has made.

Just as she enters her dad's office, the phone rings. Her dad is nowhere to be seen, so she gingerly picks it up.

"Hello, you've reached *Napp Resort*, Jonathan Napp's office, how may I help you?"

"Hello?" a quiet voice asks on the other end. "Is this Eleanor?"

"Yes?" She sits down on the desk, "Who is this?"

"This is Elizabeth Stoltz. Eleanor, I must speak with Mr. Jonathan. It is an emergency."

~*~

Episode 4

Thick, metal elevator doors part, opening exclusive access to the URIA Underground Base. Aurora stands beside Miss Maggie in bewilderment, feeling as if she's trapped in the middle of a freaky sci-fi movie. *What is my life?* she asks herself, unable to wrap her brain around the bizarre action of climbing to the top of a tree fort then barreling down the thick trunk in an elevator, hundreds of feet underground.

Aurora gasps, abandoning her luggage and shooting across the elevator threshold. "Lena!" she cries, crushing her sister in a ginormous hug. Aurora doesn't even bother to stop the waterworks. Her emotions are raw.

Her flight to Bella Adar was a most cruel and unusual form of torture, as her mind was afflicted with unescapable anguish. "I...I thought you were dead," Aurora stutters, clinging to her all the more tightly. She inhales deeply, not wanting to release the grip. She takes a deep whiff, purposing to remember the subtle smell of Lena's soft, coconut milk shampoo. She feels immensely guilty for not truly cherishing everything about her sister until she was assaulted with the threat of her being gone forever.

Miss Maggie quickly dabs her own tears with a Kleenex. "Why didn't you tell us before this?" She looks at Captain Cepheus, "The news report caused it to sound as though the two of you had gone missing! And when the URIA contacted me, they sure didn't say anything that would convince me otherwise!" Miss Maggie's anger is evident, "You could've saved Aurora's heart from a lot of pain if you had only been upfront and honest! And what now, we've left New York, flying here on a wild goose chase only to discover that Lena is alive and well?" Her eyebrows narrow toward Captain

Cepheus, "What is this, some kind of twisted plan to get Aurora to your country?"

"Forgive us, Ms. Bates, that was never our intention." Captain Cepheus attempts to set the record straight, "We are well aware of the false reports circulating about Her Majesty, rumors that say she was with the men when they ambushed the palace. But she has been here, hidden and safe, all along. It is better that Raymond, as well as the rest of the world, believe her to be missing. If anyone outside of the URIA knows her whereabouts, we could be placing her, as well as this entire operation, in grave danger. I hope you understand why we didn't tell you. Even the smallest leak of information to the wrong source could be detrimental."

"It's okay," Aurora speaks up, pulling away from Lena and offering a warm smile. "I'm just so relieved that you're okay. Like, I can't even put it into words. Lena, I don't know what I would've done if…if…"

"Shhh, there is no need to say it." Lena squeezes her hand, "I am perfectly safe here."

"Your Highness," Captain Cepheus addresses Aurora, "welcome to Bella Adar."

Aurora's eyes widen. The Captain's title for her is enchantingly outlandish. *Again*, she tells herself, *there's no way this can be real life.*

"Come," he motions toward the girls, "we shall take your things to your temporary sleeping quarters and discuss matters on the way."

Rachel quickly loads their luggage into the back of their cart, and Lena hops into the back seat. She warmly pats the seat beside her, inviting Aurora to climb on. She slowly steps onto the ATV, unsure of what comes next. She glances cautiously around her, observing the unfamiliar scene. Miss Maggie scoots in beside her and anxiously bites a nail. It's clear that she doesn't want to be here right now.

Aurora clenches her teeth together when Captain Cepheus hits the gas pedal and they lurch forward.

She knows Miss Maggie is not happy with her. Aurora has canceled her shows for the next three days, and according to Miss Maggie, *Bubblegum* is having a hissy fit. Canceled shows mean losing money, disappointed fans, and angry workers who don't get a paycheck. But Aurora puts all of that nonsense out of her mind, knowing there are far more important things to be concerned about. Right now, the only thing that matters is being here with her sister.

All during her plane ride to Europe, Aurora begged for a second chance. She pleaded with God to protect Lena and keep her alive. And now, here she is. Aurora looks at her beautiful sister and smiles. Lena offers her a weak smile in return, and the two grab hands.

"So, what happened to the rest of the army?" Aurora asks, "Was it really as bad as what they were saying on the news or were those just fabricated stories too?"

"Oh no, it was bad." Captain Cepheus sighs, "Our army has suffered a great blow. We lost twenty-eight men in our attempt to overthrow the palace. Raymond was far more equipped than we predicted, and their army greatly outnumbered ours. After just a few short minutes, we had to retreat due to the bloody massacre taking place." Captain Cepheus shakes his head, "And now, after the bombings of innocent civilians, we're forced to take a step back, to reevaluate our plan and consider alternate strategies."

"Oh, my word, what about Jack?!" Aurora suddenly blurts out, as a terrible thought creeps into her mind. "You said he was marching out with the rest of the men, is he…" A lump catches in her throat. Did he make it?"

"Jack is alright, thank the Lord." Lena sighs, "He wasn't on the front line. His platoon was the third to enter and they were ordered to retreat only moments after they arrived on the palace grounds. But that doesn't change the fact that others died." Defeated eyes fall to look down at her hands, "Husbands, fathers, and brothers who will never return home."

"Your Highness, Aurora, would you like me to drop you and Ms. Bates off at your room to retire for the evening? Or would you prefer to stay with your sister?" Captain Cepheus asks.

"Why, where is she going?" She looks at Lena, suddenly concerned that she might be leaving the base.

"I have a meeting with one of our allies. The leaders of Tarsurella have come to discuss possible war strategies," Lena tells her.

Aurora shakes her head, struggling to grasp that this is her current reality. She's in Europe. Underground. Riding around on a cart, discussing massive world political issues with her sister, who is the Queen of this country! Emma is right. This kind of stuff just doesn't happen to people their age. Yet here she is, smack dab in the middle of it, paralyzed with so much shock and bewilderment that she hardly knows what to say.

"I…um," she eventually manages to spit out, "sure. I mean, of course, I want to stay with Lena." She looks back at Captain Cepheus, "I want to know what's going on."

"We'll have to drop Ms. Bates off at your room, as this is a classified meeting." He glances over his shoulder at the irritated woman, "Rachel will help you unpack and see to it that you're comfortable."

"Comfortable? Several hundred feet below the ground?" she murmurs. "Yeah right. Did I mention I'm claustrophobic?"

After dropping Miss Maggie and Rachel off and taking several more twists and turns around the narrow halls of the base, they arrive at the Board Room.

Aurora gulps, attempting to straighten her messy hair. She presses out the wrinkles in her jeans, glancing nervously at Lena. She feels as though they're about to do something very important, and she doesn't want to look like a homeless bum who just rolled in off the street.

Captain Cepheus opens a red door then takes a step backward, motioning for the girls to enter before he does. "After you, Your Majesties."

Aurora allows Lena to go first, as she clearly doesn't have a clue about any of this.

Awaiting them in the small, stuffy little room is a long, ominous looking table, which appears as though it could seat a dozen or so people. The dingy lighting creeping out of dull, mounted light fixtures on the ceiling make Aurora want to shudder. The room could use a serious makeover. The table is empty, but there's a small group of people waiting to meet them.

Standing just several feet away is a young man who appears remarkably paramount. His navy-blue military garb is adorned with a conspicuous-looking row of gold pins and embroidered patches. Although Aurora can't make out every tiny detail, the crest of a roaring lion catches her attention. Below that is a tiny flag.

As striking as this young man's apparel is, the guy tucked inside is far more impressive. The attractive lad is clean shaven, with dark hair that seems a bit too long for the army. Several strands are brushing just slightly over his ears. His warm face is set with magnetic brown eyes that somehow hold an aura of mystery and secrets. Without so much as a smile, the serious expression he currently possesses is compellingly handsome. And of course, Aurora can't help but notice his perfect jawline.

"Captain Cepheus," the young man reaches out a hand., then nods his head politely toward Lena, "Your Majesty. It is a pleasure to meet you, though I wish our meeting was set because of better circumstances."

"Prince Asher, welcome to the underground," Captain Cepheus speaks, having met the young man before. "Thank you for coming."

"I'm humbled to be of service." He nods, "My brother sends his greetings and deepest sympathies to you and all the men, and to their families who lost loved ones. He wanted to come himself, but as you well know, things have been rocky in Tarsurella as well. I hope you don't mind that you got stuck with his kid brother." Asher cracks a smile.

"Thank you for coming," Lena speaks with genuine fervor. "And please, give our greetings to King Addison." She glances at Aurora, "Allow me to introduce you to my sister, Aurora."

Asher's eyes glance at her suspiciously, then he releases a laugh. "This is a joke, right? You're Aurora. Aurora Jasper, the American popstar my sisters are all crazy about?"

"That's right, Aurora Jasper in the flesh." Aurora grins, "Who apparently doubles as an underground, top-secret Princess."

Asher shakes his head, his hair bouncing slightly, struggling to process the strange happening.

"Allow me to place extra emphasis on the *secret* part." Captain Cepheus clears his throat, "Come, let us be seated."

Asher sneaks one last glance at Aurora, and she can't help but wonder what he's thinking.

Aurora sits down beside her sister then watches with wide eyes and tingling ears as the conversation begins.

"I believe our first priority is to increase the size of our army," Captain Cepheus begins. "This will take some time, as finding new recruits and training them as cadets equipped for war isn't going to happen overnight. We believe that Raymond's bombing was an attempt to paralyze the citizens with fear and silence them into thinking there is no hope of change. Though I think his act of terror will have quite the opposite effect: when Her Majesty is revealed and addresses the people as her own, they will be eager and willing to embrace her as their rightful ruler. Although things didn't go quite the way we planned, it appears as though God is using this setback to our advantage. It is giving us more time to place things in proper order, strengthen our numbers, and execute a far more foolproof plan."

"I agree," Asher nods. "Addison and I have spoken with several of our allies, and it's obvious they are disgusted with Raymond. Your tiny little nation is front and center on every news station, and other countries are eager to assist. The United States, France, Germany, the UK, and Ireland have all spoken to Addison about dispatching troops here. They want to help in whatever ways they can, and so do we. So, I guess the first question would be, how many can be stationed here? And should we be holding and training them at another location as well, just in case Raymond somehow finds out about this place?"

The conversation carries on for a good twenty minutes, and Aurora's head bobs back and forth, bouncing from Prince Asher to Captain Cepheus, to Lena then back to Asher. Occasionally, one of Asher's Tarsurella guys speak up and adds a whole new thought to the fascinating dialogue.

As time whisks by, Aurora realizes this is no small matter. This isn't like shopping for new nail polish, deciding what to wear to the *Teen Choice Awards*, or struggling through writing a new hit song. People's lives are on the line! She's never heard a conversation like this in her life.

If what Prince Asher is saying about this is true, and that presidents, armies, and world powers all have their eyes set on Lena's small nation…if they want to see evil shattered and justice triumph for all…then there's no way she's turning down her invitation to be a part of this. It's so much more than an intense game of Monopoly or laser tag. The captains and leaders in this room are planning for war.

Aurora takes a deep breath. Everything about this is real. There's no pause button, no chance to yell 'cut', no makeup artists, and certainly no scripted lines. This is real life. With real guns, real fighter jets, real risks, and real people.

~*~

"Wow. Lena. I have so many conflicting emotions right now, I don't even know where to begin," Aurora tells her as soon as they arrive in their shared room with Rachel and Miss Maggie.

"It's a lot of heavy stuff to process." Lena sighs, taking off her light pink sweater and placing it on her bed. It's much warmer in their room than it is in the rest of the base.

"I feel so stupid." Aurora shakes her head, sitting down on the single bunk-bed where her luggage is piled. "All this time, you were trying to tell me how serious things were, that people's lives were in jeopardy and innocent people were suffering, and I just wouldn't listen to you. I *couldn't* listen to you. My petty little issues seemed way more important than everyone else's. Emma's right. I can't believe how blind I've been! I was so apathetic, only concerned about the things happening in my own little world. Meanwhile, there's a whole bunch of people out there suffering, and I don't have a clue how to help them. Lena, I want to help. But I have no idea how."

"You can help." Lena sits down beside her, eyes burning with passion and desperation as she speaks, "Stay. Fight with us! Once Raymond is removed, we can learn what is required of us to rule these people. Aurora, you are co-heir with me!"

"I can't be a ruler!" Aurora laughs nervously, shaking her head at how utterly insane that sounds, "Lena, you don't know who you're talking to. My life is a disastrous mess. I can't even manage to keep a boyfriend, my friendship with Emma intact, or to focus on growing in my relationship with God, let alone rule a nation!"

"I used to feel the same way. But God spoke to me. He had a different perspective than I! Since the moment I said yes and accepted the job, He has been continually revealing truth to me. And the truth is, that if He has called me to this job, He will surely equip me for it. The fact that I am weak and confused and quite clueless about everything I must be to lead these people, means that I am indeed the right person to lead. Moses surely didn't know what he was doing. Neither did David, or Esther, or Josiah; the boy who became king when he was eight years old! In the midst of my weakness, God is free to work through me. And Aurora, I know it is the same for you as well. While it is true that we are young and inexperienced and at times selfish and immature, there is royal blood coursing through our veins! We cannot change our lineage or erase the fact that God has passed this baton to us. Though we do not feel like royalty, I know we have regal hearts."

Aurora purses her lips together, wishing she could tell Lena yes. But she cannot. There's no way she can uproot her life and move here to Bella Adar!

"Lena, I can't give up my life back home. My career is everything. I'm in the middle of a tour, and so many people are depending on me! As much as I wish I could stay here and help, I know I can't. I have to go and fulfill my commitment. But after! Lena, I promise, as soon as the tour is over, I'll fly back and stay here with you for as long as I possibly can!"

"She's right, honey," Miss Maggie adds, joining the conversation from where she's stirring her lemon tea at the small coffee table. "It's not at all realistic for her to uproot everything. She'd be placing her entire career on the line."

"I suppose you are at a great crossroads," Lena tells her thoughtfully. "You wish to help, yet you wish to do so without making any kind of sacrifice. I do not imagine that royalty can make much of an impact on the world around them without making sacrifices. Jesus said, 'If anyone would come after Me, he must deny himself and take up his cross and follow Me. For whoever wants to save his life will lose it, but whoever loses his life for My sake will find it.' Have you asked the Lord what He wants you to do?"

Aurora looks down at her hands, quiet for a few moments, then meets Lena's gaze once more. Her voice is weak.

"But what would I even do, anyway? I mean, say I were to be absolutely bonkers and throw it all away, move here to Bella Adar to live here with you and these people...like, what would that even mean? What does that look like?" She glances around the room, "How would my fans react? What would the press say? Where would we live? Where would we get out and go for fun? Goodness Lena, this is insane! We're hundreds of feet underground, this room is smaller than my closet, and I don't even know where the shower is!"

"I do not have answers to your questions. Well, I do know where the shower is." Lena smiles, "But besides that, there are many unknowns. I suppose that's all part of trusting God with an adventure such as this. Believing that He will make our paths straight and continuing to trust Him and say yes, even when we don't know the fullness of what exactly we're saying 'Yes' to."

Aurora sighs, her brain on information overload. She doesn't even know how to think right now.

"I remember something Jack told me the first night he showed up on our property and invited me to go on this wild, fearfully unknown adventure. He said, 'You're choosing to do the right thing now, so that you, your family, and your nation can reap the benefits of it later.'
Not everyone would expect you to pay such a high price of sacrifice, Aurora. Some might say, 'It is your life, do whatever you please, whatever makes you feel good'. But it doesn't matter what anyone else thinks. All that matters is knowing

whether or not God has called you to this. And if He has, the rewards of your obedience in the future will far outweigh any temporary pain you may have to endure for the moment."

~*~

Back in California...

"And now, we invite you to relax, pull up a chair, and get ready, as the dining room proudly presents, your dinner!"

The fourteen-year-old posing as a candlestick ducks out of the way. A parade of miniature forks and spoons dance onto the stage.

Emma smiles, spotting her favorite little buddy, Emma junior. She's grinning through her missing front tooth, lifting high knees and kicking her feet in time with the rest of the group.

Savannah, who is trying her best to stay in her character as Belle, wears an astonished face as the silverware entertains her. Emma is so focused on what's happening onstage, she doesn't even notice that someone has slipped into the seat beside her.

"Hey," a voice whispers.

Emma jerks her head away from the stage, slightly frightened and shocked by the unexpected voice. She is even more alarmed to see Jeremiah. He's not needed onstage right now, but still. You don't just sneak up on girls like that!

"Aurora hasn't returned any of my calls," he tells her.

"And whose fault is that?" Emma whispers back.

"Yours, apparently!" he accuses. "Obviously you told her about me and Savannah—"

"Oh, stop jumping to conclusions!" Emma hisses angrily. "I didn't tell her anything! In case you missed the headlines last night, Aurora cancelled the first three days of her tour. She's having some personal, family issues right now."

"Of course I saw that, that's why I tried to call her. But I thought it had to do with me."

Emma resists the urge to laugh, "Do you really think you're so special that she would cancel *Madison Square Garden* for you? Wow, you're even more egotistical than I give you credit for."

"Listen, I don't know why she won't answer her phone, but tell her to call me, okay?"

Emma rolls her eyes, detesting how compassionate and sappy he sounds right now. She bites her lip. She wants to snap, 'Leave her alone, she's out of the country, in the middle of an international emergency!' but she doesn't. She knows better than to spill the beans.

Jeremiah leaves just as quickly as he appeared, going back over to the other side of the theater to quietly chat with his friends.

Emma shakes her head, attempting to refocus on the stage and keep herself awake. She was up until 3 AM last night, video chatting with Aurora and her mom. As soon as Emma heard about the bombing, she and Aurora tossed all their temporary differences and petty misgivings about one another aside, and Aurora told her everything. She colorfully described the underground base, the crazy board meeting with the handsome Prince from Tarsurella, the URIA's plans to take back the palace, and how Aurora desperately wishes she could stay and help.

"Pray for me, Emma. Because right now, I don't know what to do," Aurora had told her. "I feel like God wants me to stay here. But I just can't imagine cancelling the entire tour. It would be like committing suicide to my career! More than that, it might even cause a massive safety issue for Lena and the rest of the underground army, because if the Press finds out that I'm here, Raymond will know we're here too. And that can't happen."

After hanging up with Aurora, Emma struggled to process everything Aurora had shared. She could scarcely believe her ears. How could all of this be happening to her mom and her best friend? Meanwhile, Emma's stuck in nowhere's-ville, California, assisting with a silly little play, with a bunch of high-strung, untalented kids?

Emma sighs. She knows that she needs to change her attitude and perspective. The opportunity to help with this production was obviously an opportunity from God. But it hadn't been going quite as she imagined. And now, being here in this theater feels ridiculously purposeless and unimportant, compared to all the center-staged drama happening in Bella Adar.

Lord, help me, she prays silently, *I don't want to be jealous of Aurora and the other girls. But why is it that they're off on an epic, unbelievable adventure and I'm here collecting gum off the back of people's seats? I know that on opening night we're going to share the Gospel, and maybe some kids will give their hearts to you then, and all this hard work might be worth it...but still. It seems so small compared to what Lena and Aurora get to do—save an entire nation.*

After practice, Julie holds another meeting with the volunteers.

"Before I make this announcement, I just have to say that God is good." Julie takes a moment to close her eyes and lift her hands toward heaven, "He's good in the bad times, and good in the easy times. He's good when everything is going perfectly, and when everything appears to be falling apart. God, we trust you." She opens her eyes and lowers her hands, "I just found out that tomorrow will be Savannah's last practice." She sighs heavily, "They've decided to move her to New Mexico."

"Oh no!" someone calls out, crushingly disappointed by the news.

"Aw man, we did not want that to happen!" another laments. "What are we going to do? We can't do this show without a Belle!"

"Believe me guys, I begged Savannah's social worker to buy us more time. I even asked if we could somehow fly her back up here for opening night, but her foster parents were not in support of that. I tried as hard as I could, and we all prayed, so we can't give up hope yet! Surely God has a plan in all of this. There is an answer. There is always an answer."

"What are we going to do, cast another girl to play the role? We should've foreseen a scenario like this beforehand and cast an understudy."

"That would be crazy, nobody can learn that many lines in such a small amount of time."

"And even if she did, wasn't the dress designed perfectly for Savannah? This is awful!"

Emma bites her lip, her mind racing with the scope of this problem. What *are* they going to do?

"I know this is stressful, but I don't want us to freak out, okay?" Julie attempts to encourage the small group, "We have to keep our joy on! Especially for these kids. They're going to be crushingly disappointed when I tell them tomorrow, and I know it'll be so hard for Savannah to leave all her friends here, so we have to stay positive. Let's just keep praying, and we'll sleep on it tonight and see if any brilliant ideas come to us. If all else fails, I can play Belle. I believe I've subconsciously learned her lines, thanks to running through this show so many times, and the songs are simple enough. I know it wouldn't be the same, but I could do it as a last resort."

~*~

Eleanor opens the refrigerator, searching for a snack. Her eyes scan the contents, and even though it's loaded with food, she can't seem to find what she's looking for. An eerie silence fills the house. She quickly grabs an apple and shuts the fridge door behind her, heading out the sliding screen door. She hates being alone in their home. It feels hauntingly empty.

She bites into the apple, not minding the loud crunching noise it makes as she walks down the porch steps. Even though she's on break, she doesn't like the idea of being by herself. She sighs, wondering why her father left again.

After Elizabeth called, her dad immediately packed up and whisked out the door, promising he would call as soon as he knew the situation was settled. Eleanor couldn't seem to make sense of any it. Why was this company always calling Dad on the spur of the moment, giving him strange assignments with Amish people? Eleanor asked her dad if

Elizabeth was in some kind of danger, and he said he couldn't tell her due to the deal he had with the UR something, something. What is the name of that stupid company anyway? Maybe Eleanor should Google it. If her dad won't tell her anything about this top secret job of his, perhaps she should just do some digging on her own.

She continues walking toward the pastures, pausing to visit the pregnant mares. "Goodness gracious, surely you girls are going to pop any day now!" Eleanor feeds the remainder of her apple to the mare who quickly gobbles it up. "Just hopefully not at the same time." She giggles, knowing the chances of them foaling at the same moment would be quite slim. She runs a careful hand over her belly, hoping everything is okay in there. At the last check, their family vet said everything seemed to be going well, just as expected. But if their sweet mare didn't decide to have this foal soon, she would need to contact the vet.

Eleanor's eyes drift toward a nearby pasture littered with Hair, Makeup, and Costume Trailers. She sighs heavily, knowing that today is the last day Jack Heart's crew will be filming on their land. Tomorrow morning, all the shabby-looking eye-sores will be gone, and the south pasture will be free to use for the horses again. Things will be so very quiet. The thought is bittersweet. The field will look quite bare without those ugly old things propped up in the lawn.

As much as Eleanor had strongly resisted everything about this film, both the cast and crew are starting to grow on her. The more she works with Logan and the others, the more she learns about all the persistent, hard work required to produce movie-making magic. Eleanor had no idea creating a film was such an intensely involved process, and though she never thought it possible, she's starting to respect Jack, Logan, and everyone else involved with the whole ordeal. Well, maybe not Chelsea. She's still a spoiled, bottle-blonde brat. But aside from her, Eleanor might actually admit to being concerned about missing them.

Eleanor looks over her shoulder, surprised to see several workers leading seven horses out of the East Barn. It doesn't appear as if they're prepping them for trail rides, and Eleanor knows their schedule by heart. It's not time for them to pasture.

"Hey," Eleanor calls out, walking toward the young man at the front of the mini horse parade, "Where are you headed?"

"Out to the front, miss," the somewhat newly-hired hand, tells her. Even though the worker hasn't learned all the ropes yet, he's been around long enough to know that Eleanor is Jonathan's daughter, and has a lot of say in what happens around here. "To the front pasture. Miss Jasmine's orders."

"Jasmine?" Eleanor echoes. "Jasmine doesn't work here anymore."

Eleanor quickly heads off toward the barn, wondering if perhaps Jasmine caught wind of the fact that her dad is gone again. If she thinks she can just storm in here and boss everyone around like nothing's changed, that woman has got another thing coming to her!

Sure enough, at the end of the narrow alley, Jasmine is directing several hands to lead three more horses out of the barn.

"Jasmine!" Eleanor snaps, "What are you doing?"

"What do you think I'm doing?" she asks smartly. "I'm back to collect my stuff."

"Your stuff?!" Eleanor echoes. "All your junk is in our house, not this barn! You don't own any of these horses!"

"Relax, I have already called for the moving truck, they are collecting my things inside, then I am leaving." Jasmine brushes her out of the way. "Right this way, boys! Bring those horses out to the front!"

Eleanor jumps in front of her path, blocking her from moving forward. "What do you think you're doing?!" Eleanor's voice is raw with emotion, "Stealing horses?!"

"I am not stealing anything." She explains with angry hands on her hips, "Twelve of these horses are mine. They were a stupid wedding gift from your father. Some men like to buy their brides jewelry or a new car or a vacation to an exotic island—but no, your cheap dad only gave me these measly beasts."

"Liar!" Eleanor accuses her. "Those horses were my mom's!"

"Yes, and now they are mine." Jasmine pulls out legal documents from her purple alligator-skin purse. "Read it and weep." She hands the papers over and sidesteps her, "Hurry up boys, the truck will be here soon!"

Eleanor's eyes frantically search the strange documents in hand. She can't believe this! There's no way her dad would have transferred this many horses into Jasmine's name. Surely these papers are forged! They have to be the working of a con-artist!

She looks up from the documents, realizing that Jasmine is nearly out of the barn, and all of her mom's beloved horses are in the front yard. Her heart pounds, panicking in desperation as she picks up her speed. "Jasmine, you can't do this!" Eleanor shouts at her as she bolts past the haughty woman. Eleanor races around the barn, to the front of the building, where a large horse trailer rolls up the driveway.

"Stop!" Eleanor yells at the workers. "Don't do anything Jasmine tells you! She's trying to steal those horses!"

The horse-trailer driver parks his long rig, and Eleanor breathlessly paces back and forth. She has to think of something. This *cannot* be happening. She won't let Jasmine get away with this!

"Save your breath, darling, I am not selling them to the glue factory." Jasmine casually strolls up beside her, wearing a smirk of victory. "They are going to a family ranch on the other side of the state, who was willing to pay top dollar. At least through this sale I will end up getting something worthwhile out of this marriage."

"They're not your horses!" Eleanor growls at her.

She hears the front door of the horse-trailer's cab open, and Eleanor runs toward the driver. "Sir, sir, you have to listen to me! This woman can't sell you these horses, see it's not even legal!" She shows him the papers.

"Hmm…are you Jasmine Napp?" the wrinkly old man wearing a green John-Deer cap asks her.

"No, I am." Jasmine steps in, "Soon to be Jasmine Banjeree though, my rightful maiden name."

"Hmm…everything looks well and fine to me." The driver nods, satisfied with the papers. He hands them back to Eleanor.

"No," Eleanor whispers under her breath as the driver and Jasmine walk away to load the trailer. "No!" She cries out once more, then rushes back to the barn. She has to get help!

"Carl! Donavan!" She calls out the names of several longtime workers, "Carl, help! Donavan! Where are you guys?!"

Eleanor flies around the corner, nearly body slamming into Logan Sparks.

"Woah, woah, woah!" He grabs her elbows, attempting to keep her from falling over, "Is everything okay?"

"No, it's not!" Eleanor cries. Her mind is racing, and she doesn't even know how to begin to express the tragedy at hand. "Jasmine is selling Mom's horses! I don't know if this paper is fake or real, but Dad's gone and, and, I, I, I can't let this happen! I—"

"Do you mind if—" Logan is about to ask if he can see the documents, but Eleanor has already given them to him.

His eyes quickly scan the pages, and he frowns. He takes long strides ahead in his cowboy boots, and Eleanor follows.

Back in the front yard, half of the horses are already in the trailer.

"Excuse me, uh, can I speak with you for a moment?" Logan approaches the driver and holds out his hand, "Logan Sparks. I have a question, do you—"

"Hey, aren't you some kind of movie star?" the old man asks, cocking his head slightly. "Haven't I seen you in—"

"Not important right now," Logan gently interrupts him. "Where is this trailer unloading?"

Eleanor watches with bated breath. She is so anxious, she can't even breathe properly.

"Ridell Farms, eh, about six hours from here I'd say."

"Logan, this is none of your concern," Jasmine buts into the conversation. "These horses have already been sold. Mr. Ridell and I have a deal. He is depositing the money into my bank account this afternoon. It is already a done deal."

"Do you mind me asking how much you're selling these horses for?" Logan asks.

"Oh, Mr. Sparks," Jasmine giggles, "I do not feel at liberty to discuss my financial standings with you. Let us just say...I will be able to live quite comfortably after this."

"You know, I've actually been keeping my eye out for a good deal on a herd of horses. I'm willing to pay you double whatever Mr. Ridell is offering."

Eleanor's eyes widen.

Jasmine laughs, "Oh, dear, do not be ridiculous! Mr. Ridell is paying a pretty penny for this lot. If you knew what he has offered, you would change your mind!"

"Try me," Logan challenges her.

Eleanor's eyebrows pop up. Is he serious?!

Jasmine hesitates, then leans over and whispers an amount in Logan's ear.

Eleanor studies him, waiting for some kind of reaction. He's steady as a stone.

"I'll double that," he tells her without any hesitation. "I'll have the cash in your account by this afternoon."

Jasmine laughs, "Are you serious, boy?"

"Ma'am, I don't mess around about these kinds of things. My deal is on the table, either take it or leave it."

Jasmine pops out her hand, "It is a deal, Mr. Sparks!"

Logan nods and shakes firmly.

"So where am I taking these horses?" the driver asks.

"Nowhere," Logan tells him firmly. "Guys, go ahead and unload 'em! They're staying here. At their home. Where they belong."

Eleanor can't believe her ears. She wants to laugh and cry and twirl around and hug Logan all at the same time.

"And don't worry sir," Logan reassures the truck driver, "I'll reimburse you for your run out here. Thank you for your patience."

"Oh, it's no trouble at all!" The driver grins, "I finally remember where I saw you! My granddaughter is gonna go nutso when I tell her that I ran into you! Uh, do you mind if we uh, take a...whatcha' ma'call it?"

"A picture?" Logan asks with a smirk.

"No, a selfie!" the driver corrects him.

~*~

"I promise we will pay you back as soon as my dad gets home," Eleanor tells Logan for what feels like the hundredth time.

"You don't need to do that. I said I wanted to buy some horses, didn't I?" Logan smiles, "Well, now I've got twelve of them!"

"But you only wanted one!" Eleanor reminds him. "When you woke up this morning I know you didn't say, 'Oh, I would really like to buy a dozen horses today'. I seriously can't thank you enough for coming through for me like you

[152]

did, but I know that I speak on behalf of my dad, when I say we will *not* accept that kind of charity. We'll reimburse you."

"Eleanor, no." Logan shakes his head, "I've already made up my mind. I'm keeping these horses. And, I'll be paying for their feed and boarding, right here at *Napp.*"

Eleanor looks at Logan like he's crazy. "Why?" she asks, not taking time to filter out what she's thinking before it reaches her lips. "Why would you do that for me?"

"It's not just for you," Logan corrects her. "I told you I've been thinking about buying some land in Colorado, right? Well, when the time comes, I want to have horses out there. Real ones. It'll be a blast! And, if you decide my ranch is a suitable home for some of these fellas, then I'll be totally stoked to relocate them. That way you'll have some open stalls, and you can rescue more horses, just like your mom would've wanted."

Now Eleanor really wishes she could hug him. His words are causing her heart to melt like steam, and she can feel all the ten-foot walls of stone built around her soul crumbling to dust. She nervously adjusts the weight on her feet, wondering what she should say now. Logan is nothing like she thought he would be. Could the guy be any more wonderful? She finds herself aching with a strange kind of longing, brought on by his dreamlike words of establishing a ranch in Colorado. Is it insane that she can already imagine the metal welcome sign on the edge of his property?

"So, it sounds like *Cowboy Carson* is becoming a real cowboy?" Eleanor smiles.

"I guess so." Logan grins, "You know, it's kind of hard for me to explain what has happened to me since I've been here, but it's just been so great to slow down and return to the things that truly matter in life. Being here started to stir up a dream inside of me that I didn't even know existed. I was getting pretty drained from all the hustle and bustle of Hollywood, but I think God really sparked my inspiration again. And I have you to thank for it."

"Me?" Eleanor laughs, suddenly feeling shy beneath the light of his compliments, "What did I do?"

"You taught me how to ride! And that was huge. Being in the saddle helped me see things from a different perspective, and because of that, I have a few new ideas brewing."

"Ooh, will I get to hear these new ideas?" Eleanor asks playfully.

"Maybe in the future." Logan winks, "Right now I need to just focus on what's coming next."

"And what's that?" she asks, genuinely curious.

"Well, on Monday I'm reading for a new film downtown. If they decide to cast me, then I'll be headed to South Africa for a few weeks."

"Logan, do you mind if I ask you a personal question?" Eleanor asks boldly, heading into territory she isn't so sure about.

"As long as you don't sell the answer to the tabloids, go for it," he teases.

"You seem like a really smart, well-educated, compassionate, hardworking guy who just tends to care about the state of humanity in general," Eleanor starts slowly, "but what I can't seem to find the answer to is, *why* do you date a girl who disrespects the staff, struts around like she's an entitled

Barbie doll, and trash-talks everyone who doesn't make it on her 'cool' list? That just doesn't seem to add up to me."

"Huh? Wait, are you talking about Chelsea?" He almost laughs, then it's replaced with a serious look. "You didn't actually think that we're dating... did you?"

"Obviously." Eleanor grumbles, "I mean the whole 'babe' thing kind of tipped me off. Don't get me wrong, I'm sure she's a, uh..." Eleanor struggles to find a compliment, "talented girl and all, but I just thought someone of your decency of character might be able to do a little bit better than that."

"Chelsea's not my girlfriend." Logan chuckles, "Although I can see why you would think that. She has some uh, odd acting methods. Whichever guy she's co-starring with, she always explains ahead of time that she'll be calling him her boyfriend the entire time on set. She claims it helps her 'get into character', but if you want my opinion, I think it just helps stroke her ego."

Eleanor nods, relieved to realize Logan isn't interested in Chelsea. Finally, it all makes sense. Logan actually *is* the guy she thinks he is. Kind. Respectful. Generous. Selfless in decision making and encouraging to others–Eleanor stops herself. She needs to stop thinking about him like this. He's leaving tomorrow. She's not about to get emotionally wrapped up in someone she's never going to see again. She has to keep her head level and her heart steady.

"So, it's your last day on set, and your first official day as a certified horse owner!" Eleanor smiles, hoping to change the subject. "How does it feel?"

"Bittersweet, really." Logan reaches to stroke the head of one of his newest pets, "I'm totally stoked to be a Horse Dad, but

I feel kind of guilty for leaving them so soon. I wish I could hang out a bit longer and really get to know them, their temperaments, personalities, favorite treats—"

"Their names." Eleanor laughs.

"Yeah, that would be a good place to start." Logan releases a chuckle.

"Well, just make sure you check in on them every now and then, and visit as often as you can. Gifts in the mail are always a plus." She winks.

"Oh yeah? What do horses like to receive in the mail? New saddles? Bridles?"

"Actually, I was thinking something more along the lines of your *Cowboy Carson* soundtrack." She giggles, "That way they can listen to you sing when they're feeling extra lonely."

Logan laughs, "Are you sure this is the horses we're talking about?"

Eleanor gasps, "How dare you suggest such a thing? I would never stoop so low as to listen to a pop movie musical album like that! Even if it was recorded by the guy who just saved one fifth of our stables from being sold off."

"Come on, the soundtrack isn't gonna be that bad!" Logan insists. "At least promise you'll watch the movie? This is Prince's debut breakout role! You've gotta support him."

"Okay, okay," Eleanor sighs mellow-dramatically, attempting to hide her grin. "I'll watch it. But only for Prince!"

~*~

In Bella Adar…

"And so, we're recruiting as many men as are willing to join us in the fight," Captain Cepheus speaks, his authoritative voice booming across the boardroom table. "We will train here for several months to be sure that our men are ready for what lies ahead."

"With all due respect, Captain Cepheus," Jonathan tells the man, "I must return home as soon as I can. We're having a bit of a crisis on the home front, as my wife and I are in the middle of a possible divorce, and my sixteen-year-old daughter is by herself at the ranch, trying to keep everything afloat. I wish you and your men all the best, but I really need to be back there with her."

"Sir, I know you feel your place is back home in California, and understandably so." Captain Cepheus nods, glancing at Lena, Elizabeth, and Aurora who are all present. "But I want you to consider what is at stake here. Look into the eyes of these young women and tell me what you see."

Jonathan hesitates, knowing Captain Cepheus wants him to cave. He shifts uncomfortably in his chair. "I am very, very proud of the young women sitting here at this table." He smiles at Elizabeth, "They've chosen to do something unbelievably selfless, and it will require great courage." He looks at Lena, "You will be in my prayers. But as much as I'd love to stay and help, as far as I can see it, my duty here is done." He looks back at the Captain, "All of the girls are safe, and they are ready to rightfully claim what is theirs and take back the throne."

"Have you forgotten, Jonathan, that there are *four* Royal Princess daughters?" Captain Cepheus asks.

All of the girls turn to look at Cepheus. They had nearly forgotten about their fourth sister!

"I suppose I had," he replies slowly, hoping the Captain isn't about to give him a new assignment. "You've kept the identity of the fourth so well under wraps, I'll admit she hasn't even come to mind."

"We thought it would be wise to keep her identity concealed for as long as possible." The Captain continues, "But perhaps now it is time to unmask the truth. Jonathan, your daughter, Eleanor, is the fourth Gem."

"I beg your pardon?" Jonathan chokes. The words slip out of his mouth like an impulse reaction. Did he just hear what he *thought* he heard? Or are his ears deceiving him?

"It's true, Jon," Captain Cepheus nods. "Do you think it was just coincidence or a goofy happenchance that the URIA reached out to you several years ago? We weren't just flipping through the phonebook searching the coastline for random, American males between the age of forty and fifty! Eleanor is just as much an heiress to this nation as these Princesses are."

"Tha-that's impossible!" Jon stutters, feeling his heartrate increase and his blood pressure shoot through the roof. He launches out of his chair, "This is insane! There's no way! The adoption agency never said anything about, about–" he shakes his head, feeling overwhelmed as threatening tears come to his eyes, "My daughter looks *nothing* like these girls!"

"We're not identical sisters. I look nothing like Aurora, nor Elizabeth," Lena speaks up quietly, knowing full-well what kind of life-changing shock the man is going through. The wild range of roller-coaster-esque emotions were something each girl in this room had gone through when discovering the truth about her royal identity. "Perhaps your daughter looks like me?"

"No," Jonathan shakes his head, "she doesn't." He looks back at Captain Cepheus, "This has to be a mistake. A huge mistake! My daughter is NOT related to the girls in this room! Her birth certificate didn't say anything about being born in Bella Adar!"

"No, it did not." Captain Cepheus explains, "But the document you possess is faux. We created it for the purpose of keeping her safe. I know it's hard to believe Jonathan, but Eleanor is a rightful citizen of Bella Adar. Not only a citizen, she is the Daughter of Queen Isabella and King Tyrone. And these young women are her sisters. We have the authentic documents, her birth certificate, thumbprints, and social security number for you to look at, if you don't believe me."

"This…this just…" he looks at the girls once more, "This can't be true."

"The bottom line is that your involvement in the URIA isn't just about these girls and their safety." Captain Cepheus continues, "It's about much, *much* more. It's about this country, innocent civilians, fighting for what's right, justice prevailing, and now…it's about your daughter. What kind of a future do you want for her, Jonathan? What kind of nation do you want her to inherit?"

~*~

"Alright, I've got our airline tickets!" Miss Maggie announces triumphantly as she opens the door into the girl's small, shared, underground room. "I had to get the Captain's permission to use the computer in his office, as the Wi-Fi signals down here are dead as a doornail, but I finally got us booked! We leave first thing in the morning."

Miss Maggie sounds relieved. She reaches under her bunk bed and pulls out her suitcase. She plops it onto the mattress and unzips it. "I know it's going to be tight, but I'm pretty sure we can make it back in time for your show in Milwaukee. And boy, was *Bubblegum* relieved to hear that! With absolutely no word from us or any activity on your social media accounts, they thought perhaps you'd disappeared for good! Let's just say, it scared them a little. Anyway, I've notified your Show Runners that everything is back on schedule!"

"You're leaving?" Lena asks quietly.

Aurora opens her mouth, but no words come. She doesn't know what to say. As much as she wishes to stay, she knows she cannot. She's torn between two entirely different universes. Her desire to stay and help Lena is frightfully overpowering. She's dangerously tempted to tell Miss Maggie that she refuses to return to the States.

"Oh dear." Miss Maggie lifts a concerned hand up to her mouth. She twirls around, "Sweet Elizabeth, I didn't even think about asking if you wanted a ticket as well! I know you've only just arrived, but now that you're here and see that all is well with Lena, I'm sure you want to return home too. Have you talked to the Captain? Is he making arrangements for you or should I run down and see what flights are open?"

"No," Elizabeth tells her boldly, "that will not be necessary."

"Does this mean…" Lena is almost too excited to speak the words, "you're staying?!"

"I cannot return home," Elizabeth confesses. "At least, not right now."

"What do you mean?" Aurora asks, wondering what has brought a sudden shift to Elizabeth's mind. "Is it like, your conscience won't let you?"

"I was forced to make a choice." Elizabeth sighs, "A choice between my old family and my new family. Ma said that if I left..." Elizabeth's voice tightens up, as tears surface. "Ma and Da do not understand. And now, I am not strong enough to endure the pain of returning home only to be...shunned."

A small knife slices into Lena's heart. "Shunned?" she echoes, struggling to imagine such a thing. She can feel the heavy weight of her sister's agony. "Does that mean your parents threatened to never speak to you again?"

"That is exactly what it means," Elizabeth nods. "I was so terrified. But somehow, deep down inside, I knew it was what must be done. Now I am confident that God will not reject me, nor forsake me, even though I am far from home. I believe what the Bible says, and though I do not know much, I am ready to learn more. I believe Jesus is the only Way to the Father, and He will watch over me while I am here. I will return home. Someday. But not before my heart is ready to see the shame and disappointment in my parents' eyes."

"Oh, Elizabeth!" Lena breathes, compassionately enveloping her sister in a hug.

Aurora flinches as she watches from the sidelines. How has Elizabeth done such a thing? How has she found courage to give up her entire world in exchange for the frightful unknown?

Elizabeth's shoulders shake as she begins to cry. Heavy sobs are released from her chest, and Aurora's heart falls.

"It's okay to cry." Lena gently strokes her sister's back, feeling tears of her own welling up. "I know. I know. You have lost so much. Just let it out. I'm here for you. I promise, God is going to help you through this. You're going to make it through this, Elizabeth."

Aurora comes behind her sisters and adds another layer to the hug. She sighs, desperately wishing there was something she could do to snap her fingers and make everything better again. It's not fair. The cruel way that Lena lost her family, and now the heartbreaking way that Elizabeth has given up hers. Meanwhile, Aurora's selfish little self doesn't even want to talk to her parents? Aurora feels tears coming as well, all too aware of her pathetically-prideful state.

Elizabeth cries even louder, feeling as though she is drowning beneath a roaring river of sorrow. "I left Jonah!" she confesses through choked up tears, "I left the one person whom I ever truly loved!"

Elizabeth's heart stings as his precious face is plastered to the forefront of her mind. She has memorized every priceless detail of the treasured young man. She adores everything about him. She wanted to spend the rest of her life with him. And now—now, she has said goodbye. Forever.

She can still see the look in his painfully beautiful eyes as they stood quietly in the Dawns' kitchen. After calling Jonathan and asking him to come pick her up, she had explained the entire story to Jonah. He listened intently, with a distressed look etched into his face. She told him she would not be returning to Amish country. At least, not for a very long time.

"I will wait for you," he had told her, his frantic eyes searching for an ounce of hope. "I know you are the woman God has for me to marry! I will not lose you to the

Englishers' world! I do not understand why you are leaving, but I know that you must do what you must do. When you return, I will be here. I will wait as long as I have to."

"Oh, Jonah," she had cried, unable to stop the tears, "You should not. It is wickedly unkind what I am doing to you. I do not want you to wait. For I do not know if it will ever be in God's will for me to return."

"You cannot change my mind, Elizabeth Stoltz." Jonah was on the verge of tears himself, "I will wait. As long as I have to, I'll be here. I give you my word."

Elizabeth squeezes her eyes tighter, wanting to forget the unwelcome memories. She clings to her sisters, "Oh God, I need Your strength! I need Your strength!"

"Help my sister, dear Lord," Lena joins in the prayer. Her voice is much stronger than Elizabeth's. "She is shaking, but I know You are greater! Hold her Lord! Surround her with a great hug of comfort and set her heart at peace. Let her know that even though she appears to have lost everything, Your reward for her is greater. You are all she needs. She is clinging to You, Lord. Do not let her down. Be her support and her rock!"

Aurora glances at Miss Maggie, who has paused from packing and is now sitting on the bed quietly with her hands folded. She is praying too. Aurora takes a deep breath and reaches for the Bible on Lena's bed. She remembers a verse she learned when she was little. Perhaps it will help Elizabeth right now.

She flips to the book of Matthew and scans for the right words. It takes a few moments, but finally the letters leap out at her.

"Anyone who loves their father or mother more than Me is not worthy of Me. Anyone who loves their son or daughter more than Me is not worthy of Me. Whoever does not take up their cross and follow Me is not worthy of Me. Whoever finds their life will lose it, and whoever loses their life for My sake will find it." She looks up from the passage, "Elizabeth, I know God has to be pleased with you. You've truly given up everything for Him and His Kingdom, and you're doing what you believe is right."

She stands up, and Elizabeth looks at her through blurry tears. "I know it hurts right now, but this really wise chick once told me," she winks at Lena, "if God has called you to this, the rewards of your obedience in the future will far outweigh any pain you may have to endure for the moment."

"Thank you," Elizabeth sniffs, accepting the Kleenex that Miss Maggie offers. "I know I have to trust God. And I do. But thank you for letting me cry."

"Any time." Lena smiles, wiping a tear from her cheek, "Grandmary used to say that crying is a way of pouring out all our weakness at God's feet, until we are empty, and He can fill us up with His strength again. I know God is going to give you all the strength you need to get through this."

Just then, the door opens, and Peter enters. Everyone looks at him. His face turns a slight shade of pink, feeling as though he has just bombarded a very private moment.

"Uh, I can come back later." He starts to close the door, but Lena stops him.

"No, it's alright!" She smiles, "Elizabeth here could use your prayers."

Peter is relieved to know they still want him to enter. He shuts the door behind him and cautiously steps in. "Is everything alright?" he asks Elizabeth.

"No," she replies honestly, "but it will be. In time."

Peter nods, satisfied with the answer. "Lena, may I speak with you for a moment?"

She peers into the hearts of her sisters, wanting to be confident that all is well for the moment. Elizabeth gives her a knowing nod, and Aurora smiles as well.

"We're all good here." Aurora grabs Elizabeth's hand, promising to stand by her for moral support. "Looks like farmer boy needs you."

Peter frowns. As much as he cherishes and admires Lena, he doesn't think too highly of her empty-headed sister.

Lena tosses Peter a sympathetic glance, as if she's apologizing for Aurora's off-handed remark. She follows him out the door and shuts it behind him.

The two stand in the dingy, dimly-lit hallway. Lena shivers. It's colder out here. She gives herself a hug, attempting to warm her arms. "What is it you wish to speak to me about?"

Lena looks at Peter. Beneath her casual façade, she is quite nervous. She doesn't know what Peter is going to say. And after their last encounter, when he grabbed her hand and— Lena's heartrate involuntarily speeds up. She can feel a touch of color in her cheeks. Now isn't the time to think about such things.

"I'm joining the army, Lena," Peter reveals suddenly.

The abrupt words are unexpected.

"What?" Lena breathes. Her mind races with panic, "You can't!" The volume increases in her voice, "Peter, why?!"

"I know how important this country is to you, Lena." Peter explains calmly, "And there's no way Raymond will be removed from the throne without bulking up Bella Adar's military forces. The URIA's numbers are mournfully low and they're desperate for recruits. After seeing those attacks, Raymond bombing that school…" Peter's voice trails off. He shakes his head, "There's no way we can leave someone like that in charge."

"But what about your family?" Lena asks, her voice breaking. "What if something were to happen to you?! No, I can't take that chance. I won't stand here and be responsible for such a thing! Your family needs you, Peter! Think of your parents and your siblings! Why, they would be devastated if–" Lena can't bear to finish her sentence.

"I know it's risky." Peter takes a deep breath, "But there's no way to win a war without taking chances like these."

"No!" Lena bursts out, feeling tears come to her eyes. "I can't lose you!"

Peter quickly draws her into a hug. Before Lena can blink, his comforting arms are wrapped around her. But that doesn't do anything to stop up the desperate sadness stirring in her heart. If anything, his closeness only makes it worse.

"Lena, it's okay," Peter tells her quietly in a soothing tone, "you're not going to lose me. I promise."

"You don't know that!" She pulls back from the hug, angry with his decision. "And don't go around making promises you cannot keep! You are not God! Nobody but Him knows how all of this is going to turn out. Everybody 'promised' that Grandmary and Theodore would be safe, and they weren't! If you enlist, the same thing could happen to you! Peter, my heart can only take so much. I can't lose my best friend!"

"Lena, where is your faith?" Peter asks, his eyes gazing upon her with a deep sense of love. "You yourself said you believe we can defeat Raymond. Me enlisting is my way of showing you that I believe the same thing! I'm behind you Lena, one-hundred-million percent! You're not in this alone. We're going to win this war! And I'm not going to lose my life. You have to trust me. It's all going to work out like it's supposed to."

"But how do you know that?" Lena asks, feeling as though she wants to sink onto the ground in a pile of doubt and weakness. "There is no way of knowing what the future holds."

"Sometimes, you just know things," Peter speaks passionately. "Deep in your gut, somewhere far beyond the doubts in your mind or questions in your heart, you just know. It's like an anchor, and no matter what, it doesn't move. That's how I know we're going to be okay, Lena. No matter what happens, I love you. I always have, and I always will."

All at once, Lena stops shivering. The coolness in her bones is melted away by Peter's warm words. She is unable to think straight, as he gently clasps her hands. It's as if the gesture is serving to re-affirm his words.

Her wide eyes are beneath the gaze of Peter's dancing ones. Despite the severity of the moment, there is a deep joy twinkling from somewhere in his soul. Like the sparkling ocean, his eyes are attempting to remind her that all is well.

"I love you, Lena," he repeats himself, "with every inch of my heart. I've spent my whole life trying to impress you, attempting to prove my faithfulness and devotion toward you. Lena, I want to spend the rest of my life with you. Your friendship is the greatest treasure God has ever given me."

Peter slowly kneels down before her, resting on one knee. Lena releases a small gasp. Is he–?! Surely he's not?! He isn't going to–

He gazes upward affectionately. The small dimple in his chin lights up with joy.

"I wish there were ample words to express how I feel right now." Peter is glowing, "But this is how I've always felt. Lena, you're not going to lose me. You never have to lose me! I don't want to go through this life without you. I want to give you everything and be your everything. I pledge my heart to be yours forever. Lena Bodner," he pauses several seconds before finally asking, "will you marry me?"

Lena is utterly speechless. "Oh, Peter," she finally whispers after several quiet seconds, "I–"

"I know this isn't very formal!" He quickly explains, "I don't have a ring or a house or a plan or land of my own, but I promise it will come! After I get my first paycheck from the URIA and–"

"Peter," Lena stops him from rambling on. She tenderly reaches for a strand of his hair and removes it from falling in front of his precious eyes. "Oh dear, sweet Peter."

Peter's smile disappears. He knows that tone. He can hear the high dose of common sense and hesitancy in her voice. He slowly stands up, bracing himself for her response.

"You know I care for you. You are my dearest and truest friend," Lena starts. Peter's eyes frantically search hers for an answer. "But I wish you hadn't asked such a thing." She continues, "Have you forgotten where we are? What we are in the middle of?" She looks upward at the dingy lights, "We're underground in an army base! Preparing to march forth into war and attempt to rebuild a shattered nation! Surely now isn't the time for such things. For such…" she searches for the right word, "changes."

"I know," Peter breathes. "Perhaps the timing is terrible. But what does it matter? I love you, Lena! I had to get it off my chest and proclaim the truth! I've been silent for far too long, and I need you to know how I feel. And now that you do…" he clears his throat, "I understand if you need some time to think about it. I would never force you into a decision as large as this one."

"Thank you." Lena bites her lip, suddenly feeling awkward beneath the intensity of his gaze.

What has just happened?! In a matter of seconds, everything she knew about their solid friendship suddenly shifted, as Peter rambled on about his intense feelings for her.

Had he seriously just *proposed* to her?! Is that even legal!? Aren't they just kids?! Lena doesn't know how to think through all that has happened. "It's getting late," she tells him. "My sisters are waiting for me inside."

"Very well." Peter nods, now appearing slightly insecure about his outburst. "I should return to the barracks as well. Tomorrow morning, I'll be enlisting. I don't know yet what my schedule will look like, but I know that from here on out, nothing will quite be the same."

"Right." Lena nods, attempting to regain her composure and move on as well. "Goodnight, Peter."

He gives her one last squeeze of the hand then makes his way down the long hall.

Lena watches him, her heart exploding with an unwelcome mixture of joy, pain, adoration, sadness, and utter confusion.

"How true those words are, dear Peter." Lena sighs, whispering for no one to hear but herself. "Nothing is ever going to be the same again."

~*~

Episode 5

"So, I guess this is goodbye." Lena clenches her hands together. "Again."

Aurora stares at her sisters, not wanting to speak the dreaded words.

"Captain Cepheus, thank you for your hospitality, as always." Miss Maggie smiles, delighted to be leaving, "And thank you for keeping the girls safe."

The group lingers by the mouth of the elevator, preparing to board. Rachel hauls Aurora's heavy suitcase off the back end of the cart. She struggles to regain her footing and haul it forward. "Here you are, Your Majesty!" the breathless woman proclaims. "Have a safe journey."

"We'll miss you," Lena tells Aurora, attempting to keep her voice steady. "A lot."

"And remember Your Majesty, no word of this to anyone." Captain Cepheus reminds her of the importance of keeping everything top secret.

"Well, we'd better get a move on it if we don't want to miss our flight!" Miss Maggie grabs her suitcase handle and pulls it up, rolling it toward the elevator.

"Miss Maggie, wait!" Aurora suddenly bursts out. Her voice is marinated in anxiety.

She stops.

"I…I'm not going," Aurora tells her anxiously, shocked by the words coming out of her mouth. "I can't."

"Aurora, don't be ridiculous," Miss Maggie scolds her. "I know how much you love your sisters, but you can't stay here. You've got fans waiting at a sold-out arena in Milwaukee!"

"I know this might be hard for you to understand," Aurora inhales courage, then speaks boldly, "but I can't go back with you. My sisters need me." She smiles at Lena, "And I don't know, maybe somehow, in a weird kind of way, this country needs me too."

Lena's eyes beam with pride for her sister. Elizabeth shares in the joy, offering a smile of her own, delighted to hear that she's staying. She knows what a challenging decision this is for her.

"And what am I supposed to tell your parents?!" Miss Maggie bursts out. "They're trusting me to take care of you and make sure you're safe! They're going to be livid if I leave you here! Aurora, stop and think about this for a moment. This is crazy! I cannot stay here with you."

"I know," Aurora nods, "but isn't that what the URIA is for? Protecting me? I'll talk to my parents and explain everything. I'm sure they'll understand. I mean, we kind of have a national emergency on our hands."

"And what am I supposed to tell *Bubblegum*? And your Show Runners? And the fans?!" Miss Maggie's mind races, as she realizes that she may be losing one of her biggest clients.

"Tell them I died." Aurora's voice is firm with determination, "Because the old Aurora is gone."

"Aurora, don't be so dramatic!" Miss Maggie is flabbergasted, "Now, we need to leave right now before we miss our flight!"

"I'm not being dramatic!" Aurora raises her voice, hoping that this will be the last time she ever gets in such an argument with Miss Maggie. "I know I've been selfish and immature and a terrible jerk to put up with over these past few weeks, but Miss Maggie you have to listen to me! There's nothing you can say right now to change my mind. I've prayed about this and I know this is where God wants me to be. And if my career has to die in order for this country to be safe, then it's a price worth paying." She grabs Lena's hand, "My sisters had to make heartbreaking sacrifices to be here. Can't you see? God is giving me a second chance at making my life truly matter! I'm not going to stand on the sidelines and continue barreling down that selfish road, deceiving myself into thinking life is all about me. It's not anymore. The old me is dead. It's time to discover who I was truly meant to be."

Lena resists the urge to let out a wild cheer. She can't believe how inspirational Aurora sounds right now! She has made her choice! God has finally gotten through to her!

"Very well." Miss Maggie nods, quietly accepting the defeat. "I can see this is very important to you. I don't have a *clue* how I'm going to handle things back in the states without blowing your cover." She sighs, "But I'll try to think of something." She presses the elevator door button and waits for it to open. "Even though I don't agree with your decision and feel like pulling my hair out right now…" she hesitates, "I am proud of you, Aurora. Now, promise to stay in touch, okay? And if you ever need anything, I'll be back as soon as I can. Emma and I will be praying for you." She looks at the other girls, "For all of you."

They bid their final farewells, and the elevator door shuts. Just like that, Miss Maggie is gone, and Aurora is still standing hundreds of feet beneath the ground.

Lena quickly tackles her in a small hug. "You stayed! You stayed! Oh, praise the Lord, you stayed!"

"That was a wise decision, Your Highness." Captain Cepheus smiles, "I know the three of you will be far stronger together. A three-stranded chord is not easily broken."

"That was the scariest thing I've ever done in my life." Aurora giggles, and lifts up a trembling hand, "See, I'm still shaking!"

"But you did it!" Lena encourages her. "And that's all that matters!"

"Shall we load your things back on the cart, now that you are staying?" Captain Cepheus asks. "We'll give you a lift back to your room, so you can unpack."

"No, that's okay." Aurora smiles, "I think I'd like to stretch my legs a little. You don't mind if I walk, do you?"

"Not at all, Your Highness." Captain Cepheus nods, "But we will at least take your luggage, for convenience sake."

"Thank you." Aurora nods kindly.

After Captain Cepheus and Rachel disappear down the long tunnel, Aurora takes a deep breath. She's in the mood to explore. "This place is huge!" She turns to Lena, "Have you looked around much?"

"Not really," Lena replies honestly, "I've had far too much on my mind to think about sightseeing. Besides, there's not really anything awe-invoking about these earthen walls. I miss the fresh air."

Elizabeth nods in agreement. It's frightening being tucked down here deep beneath the grass.

The girls slowly begin walking down the hall. A small motor vehicle passes them on the left. Aurora catches a glimpse of the rider in the passenger seat. It's that handsome young prince from Tarsurella. She makes eye contact with the lad as they buzz by.

Lena wonders if he's headed to the Mess Hall to eat. Her stomach grumbles ever so slightly. It is about that time.

"Well, there is one perk to being stuck down here in the middle of nowhere," Aurora giggles mischievously. "This place is crawling with cute guys!"

"Aurora," Lena scolds her, "now is not the time to be thinking about such things!"

"I guess you're right," Aurora sighs, attempting to get ahold of her whimsical thoughts. "I'm sorry," she quickly apologizes. "That was the old Aurora. But she's a total goner, and you're not gonna hear from that flakey, boy-crazy chick any longer. In fact, if either of you hear from the old Aurora, feel free to slap her. Because she doesn't have permission to live here anymore. The *new* Aurora doesn't care about guys. No matter how stinkin' gorgeous they are."

Lena wrinkles her nose. It's so strange to hear her sister speak about the male species in such a flamboyant, animated way. Lena has never given much thought to romance. As a little girl, it was a rare occurrence for her to daydream about such things. She was usually far too occupied with building tree forts, racing through the creek, and nursing baby birds back to health. The only young man she ever had the experience of being around was Peter. Until, of course, she met Jack.

Now, even though she's older, Lena is absolutely certain she doesn't know a *thing* about young men and relationships. Peter's sudden proposal was so unexpected. So abrupt and sudden! It sent her heart and mind flying in several different directions at once. She didn't even know what to think!

Without anyone in her life to offer her wise council about such important matters, Lena feels entirely clueless.

Of course, she cares for Peter. His valiant devotion to her is so very obvious. Her heart softened with such a tender feeling at the revelation that he loved her. But what did that even mean? They are just teenagers! Are they even mature enough to know what true love is? And does she love him? Or does she just care for him like a brother?

Lena doesn't know if she can trust what she's feeling. What is she feeling, anyway? At any rate, despite Lena's confused emotions, his request is ridiculously out of timing. The idea sounds ludicrous! They're in the middle of a war, are they not? How can Peter even think about marriage at a time like this?!

Lena wishes she could speak with someone older and wiser, such as Grandmary. Grandmary would know exactly what to say. She would have wise words to counsel her questioning heart. But now, Lena is at an absolute loss. What should she tell Peter? Should she accept his proposal? Should she turn him down? And if she does, how can she do so without shattering his poor little heart?

"So, what do we do next?" Aurora asks, breaking into Lena's thoughts.

"Huh?" Lena asks, looking at her, trying to focus on the conversation.

"Now that we're all here, what are we going to be doing?" Aurora asks. "If the army has to train for several months before we invade the palace again, what are we going to do in the meantime? I mean, what's our job? Why does Captain Cepheus need us here? I mean, surely he's not thinking we're just gonna sit around and knit."

"That's a really good question." Lena ponders the new thought, "We need something to focus our energy on. I, for one, know that I must stay busy, otherwise the worries will overtake me. Let's go to his office and ask him about it."

"Perhaps we could prepare meals for the men?" Elizabeth suggests, wondering what they might do to assist on a practical level.

"The kitchen workers already have that taken care of," Lena tells her. "But I'm sure we could help out on occasion!"

"Kitchen work?" Aurora shakes her head, "Oh, no, no, no, that's not what I'm talking about. I'm talking about doing something real. Something that actually matters! Like training in Taekwondo or kick boxing! I'm ready to kick some bad guys' behinds!"

"You're right, Aurora," Lena agrees. "We should be partaking in some kind of training. If Captain Cepheus thinks we're just going to sit around and let the guys have all the fun, he is terribly wrong. And if we learn how to defend ourselves, we won't need people watching over us at all times. We need to learn how to fight!"

Elizabeth's eyes widen with fear, "I would much rather help out in the kitchen."

~*~

"Hmm…that is a very wise suggestion." The Captain nods thoughtfully.

"It was Aurora's idea!" Lena exclaims excitedly, wanting to give honor to the source of the brilliant thought.

"I'll have my men develop a training schedule," Captain Cepheus thinks out loud. "It will involve archery, target practice, and martial arts for self-defense, as well as your usual school studies, as you do not want to fall behind in those."

"We'll be ready to start tomorrow." Lena nods, excited to put her hand to the plow. "We are your students, Captain Cepheus. Anything that you think would be necessary to learn, anything that would be helpful for the fight ahead or for our royal role as Queens, we are willing to learn."

"Very well," Captain Cepheus nods. "Is there anything else or will that be all?"

Just then the door opens, and Jack appears. "Oh, forgive me, Your Majesties."

"You're fine, cadet, we we're just finishing up our meeting." Captain Cepheus welcomes him, "Please come in."

He nods at the girls respectfully then turns to the Captain.

"I come before you, Captain Cepheus, to humbly request several days off. An emergency has come up at home, and I am needed there as soon as possible." Jack sounds concerned.

"I'm sorry to hear that, Cadet. I hope everything is okay. I suppose I can grant a short leave if you check out with your Sergeant." Captain Cepheus nods, "Your request is granted. And," he turns back to the girls, "if you'll excuse me, I have an important video conference call coming up with France. Unless there's anything else of urgency you wish to speak of, I request you leave me to my call."

"Thank you, Captain," Jack nods. In the same moment, Lena says, "Of course! Thank you for your time!"

They glance at one another, surprised to have spoken at the same second.

With nothing else to say, they leave the room and are in the dingy hall once more. Elizabeth shivers. She knows it's only early morning, but it feels like midnight. Without any natural sunlight, the darkness is tiring.

"Is everything alright back home?" Lena asks. The sweet faces of the orphans and widows Jack calls his family flash across the movie screen of her mind.

"Though I wish the circumstances were better, it is nothing to concern yourself with, Your Majesty," Jack tells her. "But I must be leaving as swiftly as possible. Good day."

He turns to leave, but Lena stops him.

"Jack, wait!" she calls out.

Aurora tosses a suspicious glance toward her sister.

"I, um," Lena quiets her voice, "may I speak with you a moment?"

Aurora looks at Jack again, wondering if something might be going on between the two. *And why wouldn't there be?* she thinks with a smile. *He's quite perfect looking.*

"Of course, Your Majesty," Jack is eager to serve.

"Are you hungry, Elizabeth?" Aurora asks but doesn't wait for an answer. She grabs Elizabeth's arm, "I could totally eat a mongoose right now! Lena, we'll meet you down at the Mess Hall!"

Aurora leads a confused Elizabeth away, and Jack is suspicious of Aurora's odd behavior. He's always had an unsteady feeling about her. He can only hope she won't cause too much trouble in the weeks and months to come.

"How can I help, Your Majesty?" Jack asks again, very official sounding.

"Jack, I have something important to discuss with you," Lena tells him, slowly finding the courage to open up and express what's on her mind. "But I want to speak with you as a friend, not as your Queen."

Jack nods, discerning that perhaps this is a more sensitive topic. "I'm all ears."

"I hope you don't find it strange that I'm talking to you about this." Lena hesitates. Is it unwise to say these things? Will he think she's crazy? But she's already up to her knees in this river of discussion, and it's too late to back up now. "There's no one else I can speak to about this. As much as I love my sisters, I'm not sure they would understand. I need a second opinion about something, and I want you to give it. With brutal honesty."

"I can do that," Jack nods. "What is this about? The Kingdom? The war strategy? Your sisters?"

"Not quite." Lena takes a deep breath, bracing herself for his response. "It's about Peter."

Jack doesn't reply, but his eyes appear to understand. So, Lena keeps going.

"Last night, he pulled me aside for a private conversation and revealed some things that I had suspected but wasn't completely certain about." Lena struggles to find the best way to express her thoughts, "Peter cares for me. And while he was giving his heartfelt discourse of all the reasons why, he asked a most shocking question. Now, we all know Peter can be passionate, and a bit of a firecracker, allowing things to fly out of his mouth without even thinking about them, but I'll admit that even for Peter, this was a shock! The question he asked…he…I just don't know what to think. It's a question which I cannot even begin to make sense of." She looks at Jack, wondering if she'll be able to read any clues in his eyes, "He asked me to marry him."

Jack's eyeballs increase in size. Lena spots a small vein on his forehead increase. His Adam's apple tenses, then he lets out a small laugh. "You're right, that's pretty outlandish, even for Peter!" He shakes his head, looking as if he deeply regrets something. "Oh man, the poor kid doesn't have a clue. Does he not realize that we're in the middle of rebuilding a nation?!"

"That's what I told him!" Lena agrees, hoping Jack doesn't think she had encouraged it. "But the timing didn't seem to faze him. He said his proposal still stands, and now, he's waiting for an answer."

"The things that go on between you and Peter are none of my business," Jack begins. "But it *is* my business to protect the Crown and see to it that the destiny of this nation is fulfilled. If the circumstances were different, I would have no right to raise my voice and offer an opinion. But Your Majesty, you have to zoom out from the emotions of the moment and look at the bigger picture. Whoever marries you is going to be Bella Adar's next King. That is an offering of power so enticing that it could easily cause even the most level-headed of men to do unthinkable things."

"Peter isn't interested in becoming King." Lena laughs, "It's not like that. He would never—"

"Propose just to climb the ladder of power?" Jack asks.

"I've known Peter my entire life." Lena defends him, "He would never do such a thing! I know him better than anyone."

"If you know him so well, then why are you asking me for a second opinion?"

Lena isn't sure how to respond.

Why *is* she asking to hear his thoughts? Had she secretly hoped he would be angry with Peter? Did she foolishly think that perhaps if she shared what happened, Jack would then express his own interest in her?

Lena's face turns red, suddenly realizing the unknown reason she hadn't instantly said yes to Peter's offer. Something was stopping her, and she didn't know what. Until now.

It was Jack.

"Your Majesty, it sounds to me like you already know what you need to do," Jack tells her calmly. "You're very wise, and I know you'll make the right decision."

~*~

"Greenwood!"

Peter closes his locker door. He spins around, responding to the call of his last name. Whoever spoke it doesn't sound happy.

He is surprised to see Jack, just inches away from his face. He can smell his strong, minty aftershave.

"May I help you?" Peter asks sarcastically, not even bothering to hide his irritation.

"What the heck do you think you're doing?" Jack's nostrils flare as he confronts him.

"Moving my stuff to another room," Peter snaps, wondering why Jack is all up in his face.

"Drop the innocent act. Don't pretend like you don't know what I'm talking about!" Jack cuts straight to the chase, "What kind of idiot proposes to a sixteen-year-old girl the day before he enlists, smack in the middle of a blasted war?! For someone who claims to know her so well and thinks he's the only person on the planet who can give her everything she needs, your blunt display of misjudgment is embarrassingly pathetic."

"Woah, who died and made you dictator?!" The volume in Peter's voice increases, "Lena's personal life is none of your business!"

"Peter, wake up! Things are changing! This isn't some little girl you used to pick daises and play hopscotch with! Lena is the rightful Queen of Bella Adar, and she deserves the respect which that position holds! And you're right. In typical circumstances, overstepping into Lena's personal life wouldn't be my measure. But in case you haven't noticed, Lena's life is *not* typical! The fact that you're messing with the Crown, playing with our Queen's emotional well-being, and tinkering with the possible outcome of the future of this nation, *makes* it my business!"

"You have no idea what you're talking about." Peter shakes his head, unable to remove his sour stare from Jack's hard face, "You don't care about her! You're just like everybody else in the URIA, treating Lena as nothing more than her title or an expensive game-piece on the playing board, only wanting to use her to dethrone Raymond!"

"Oh, so the URIA doesn't care about her?" Jack laughs, shaking his head at the foolishness of the young man standing before him. Peter is only three years younger than he, but sometimes Jack feels like they are lightyears away in maturity. "And you do? If you care for her even half as much as you claim, I hope you would've at least possessed enough sound judgement to know how utterly cruel it is to present such a life-changing question in these uncertain times! If you truly love her, you would've waited for a kinder timing!"

Peter is appalled by his words. In a knee-jerk reaction, Peter lurches toward Jack, fists clenched, wanting to prove that his devotion to Lena is real. He's ready to fight for her.

Jack steps out of the way, causing Peter to continue flying forward, nearly hitting the wall on the other side.

"Save your energy, Peter." Jack reaches for his knapsack beneath his bunk-bed. It's already full of the supplies he'll need to travel back home. "I'm not worth swinging at. If you really want to fight for something, take it to war. That is, if you even make it to the frontlines." He chuckles, "You're gonna need all the energy you've got just to get through Basic Training."

And with that, Jack swings his bag over his shoulder and exits the barracks.

~*~

Miss Maggie anxiously looks at her flight schedule. She's attempting to get through airport security as quickly as possible. She impatiently taps her foot as a guard scans the man in front of her with his metal detector. She lets out a huff, knowing that there are still half-a-dozen people in front of her, and Bella Adar security seems to be taking its own sweet time.

She watches the line of people waiting to pass security checks in order to enter the country. She spots a young Filipino man with a thick black head of hair and defined eyebrows. She admires his warm eyes and wonders why they don't cast more culturally diverse men in Hollywood's leading blockbusters. Surely a young guy like that would be the heartthrob of many!

"Lady, put your items on the belt!" A sudden voice interrupts Miss Maggie's nonsensical thought of making the young man across the room into a massive star.

"Oh! Sorry!" She quickly moves forward through the line.

The young Filipino man continues to wait patiently. Finally, it's his turn to pass through customs. The woman in charge of the security checkpoint opens his passport. "Name?" she asks lifelessly. It's the question she asks hundreds of times each day.

"Kehahi Julyan."

The woman opens his passport and gives him one last glance, making sure the images match.

Yup. Same face. She stamps his passport and hands it to him.

"Next!"

Kehahi steps forward, relieved to make it through security. He glances around the swarming airport, both anxious and exhausted. He's far, far from home. A sudden lurch of homesickness jolts in his heart. He makes a beeline for an empty seat near the wall and flips open his phone.

"I just landed in Bella Adar!" His fingers dance across the screen, "It was a good flight. I'm almost to the base. Not sure if we will have any reception there, or if we will even be allowed to use our phones…but I will call you as soon as I can. Tell my sisters I said hello, and I miss their goofy little faces already! I love you, Mom. –Kehahi."

He signs his name at the end of the text which is sent in his native language, Tagalog. He closes his phone and releases a sigh. As tired as he is, Kehahi knows his journey is not over yet.

His next step? Finding the URIA base.

~*~

Kehahi pauses to rest his back upon the moss-covered tree. Though it is no pillow, it strangely resembles one.

He reaches for the nearly empty water bottle which he purchased before leaving the airport. He tips his head backward and allows the last few drops to settle on his tongue. He shakes the bottle unhappily, realizing the drink is emptied. Perhaps he should have gotten two bottles for this journey.

His back slides down the trunk of the tree, allowing himself to rest temporarily on the hard ground. He reaches for his handy-dandy cell phone and takes another glimpse at the map, wanting to be perfectly certain he's heading in the right direction. Even though he is without cell service, the map which the URIA sent him has been saved in a file accessible offline. As long as his battery remains strong, he should have no trouble finding the URIA base.

Kehahi knows he needs to keep moving. He's expected to arrive today and was ordered to make no unnecessary stops. It's of utmost importance he be keenly aware of his surroundings and make sure no one is following him.

Kehahi glances around, quite positive that nobody would ever be able to find him out here, even if they wanted to. Though

Kehahi isn't concerned about anyone from the city being on his trail, he would like to reach the base as quickly as possible. He releases a small groan and drags himself to his feet. Kehahi wants nothing more than to stop and take a nap, but he knows soldiers are not allowed such luxuries.

He carries onward, thoughtlessly pulling a green fern up from the ground before stepping onto a moss-covered rock. Though the terrain is mostly level, there are many buckling roots and–

"Uuugahhh!" Kehahi lets out an involuntary shout as someone smashes into his side, knocking him off the rock and tackling him to the ground.

Kehahi struggles to get his breath back, shocked both from having the wind knocked out of him, and from this unexpected visitor.

Though Kehahi attempts to fight back, the struggle is short lived. Before he can blink, there is a gun in his vision. The sound of a cocking trigger overwhelms his senses.

And then,

It all goes black.

~*~

Back in California...

"I want adventure in the great wide somewhere; I want it more than I can tell!" Julie's crystal voice floats through the auditorium, nearly bringing Emma to tears. The woman is so unbelievably talented! She is bringing Belle to life!

If Emma closes her eyes, she can almost hear the longing behind each lyric. The desperate ache for a thrilling adventure resounds deep within Emma's spirit. Belle's desire to break free and separate herself from the status quo, being a wild lion among a culture of bland and boring sheep—Emma hears her loud and clear! She can relate to the struggle of wanting something so desperately yet being too afraid to open her mouth and say so. Belle longs for change, but the only place she can find a vice for adventure is in her books.

"For once it might be grand, to have someone understand." Julie stares off mellow-dramatically into the distance and Emma resist the urge to cling onto the empty seat beside her. *UGH.* Emma mentally tells no one but herself, *It's just so beautiful! Julie is nailing this role! And she's not even in her costume yet! Once she wears the signature dress and belts out those notes, Julie will officially be Belle!*

Emma smiles. *Well, I may have forgotten one minor detail. Julie's baby bump. A pregnant Belle isn't exactly congruent with the original fairytale. But, the cast is determined to make it work. We'll do whatever we need to do to hide it. Desperate times call for desperate measures. And right now, this show desperately needs a Belle!*

"I want so much more than they've got planned!"

Yas, girl, yas! Emma mentally cheers her on. *You're totally owning this character, Julie!*

"Ptsss, Bates."

Emma feels a sudden prick on the back of her bare neck. She slaps her neck in fear, whipping around with an unfriendly face.

"Dude, jumpy much?!" Jeremiah is seated behind her, wearing that smug smirk of his.

Emma resists the urge to release an audible growl. "What?!" she snaps, wondering why in the world he would be poking her like they're in second grade or something.

"I need to talk to you," he insists. "It's about Aurora."

"Jeremiah, I am not your personal messaging system. If you have something you want to say to her, and she's not answering her phone, that is not my problem."

"She broke up with me."

Emma's face doesn't hide her surprise. "Really?" Emma's voice is hopeful.

"Geesh, don't sound so happy."

"Well, of course I'm happy!" Emma grins, "I couldn't be prouder of her! She finally came to her senses!"

"Um, ouch." Jeremiah shakes his head, "Can't you be at least a *little* bit sensitive here? I really liked her, Emma. This is kind of a huge blow for me."

"Oh, I wouldn't be too worried. I'm sure you'll find some other helpless victim, desperate for a boyfriend who will come along and be your arm candy soon enough." Emma rolls her eyes, offering no sympathy whatsoever.

"Okay, maybe I deserve it." Jeremiah sighs, running a hand through his hair, "I totally blew it. But I never intended to make out with Savannah. It's just, we were talking and the next thing I knew–" Jeremiah pauses, "I was kind of a jerk.

"Kind of?!" Emma isn't satisfied with his lame description, "More like a major-league, home-running, award-winning, blowing away every other jerkish person in your own stupid category, jerk!"

"Okay, okay!" Jeremiah throws his hands up in surrender, "I confess. I'll own the crime. I was the King of all jerks. It was a huge mistake, and I regret every second of it. It just kills me to think Aurora is going through that kind of pain right now."

"I didn't tell her. If she broke up with you, it wasn't because of anything I said. She still doesn't know what happened between you and Savannah."

"She doesn't?" Jeremiah appears confused.

"I wanted to tell her," Emma sighs, "but I couldn't."

"Wow." Jeremiah scratches the back of his neck, "I guess that makes a lot more sense now, looking back at our conversation. The whole time she kept saying it had nothing to do with me, and how she just needed time to focus on God or become who she really was or something like that…but I thought she was just trying to be nice. I didn't know that she doesn't know about uh…you know. The whole jerk thing."

"Yeah, Aurora is going through a lot right now. And the last thing she needs in her life is a boyfriend."

"Our connection was really spotty, and I had trouble catching everything she said." Jeremiah fishes for more information, "Is everything okay? I mean, where is she? She mentioned something about family issues, but is she alright? Is she in some kind of trouble? Rehab?"

"We really shouldn't be talking about this. If Aurora doesn't feel comfortable sharing any more information with you, then neither do I. For now, you're just going to have to respect her privacy and give her some space."

"Not the answer I wanted," Jeremiah sighs. "But I guess I'll have to live with it."

~*~

"How does this sound, Em?" Miss Maggie clears her throat and reads Emma the email. "Aurora Jasper is taking time off to attend to personal and family matters. She understands her fans' concern and disappointment as this was highly taken into consideration before making her decision. She sincerely apologizes to anyone who is affected by her choice, but asks that you respect her personal life and," Miss Maggie pauses to release her frustration, "Ugh, there's no way they're going to be satisfied with a statement like this! The more we try to cover up, the more questions are going to be raised, and the deeper inquiring minds are going to dig!"

"Jeremiah asked if she was going to rehab." Emma giggles, not knowing how else to respond to the oddity of the situation. "If only it were that simple. Hollywood can understand a substance abuse problem, but a top-secret undercover Princess? Yeah right. Who has a grid for that kind of information?"

Miss Maggie's head falls into her hands as she shakes it tiredly. "We are in way, *way* over our heads here."

"Just think how Aurora must feel." Emma sighs, wishing she could be in Bella Adar with her right now, secretly observing every crazy, exciting happening. Oh, to be a fly on the wall in those board rooms as they strategize about invading the castle and removing Raymond from power! Emma can't help but feel like Belle, longing to break out and join the fight somehow. Instead of living adventures, all she gets to do is hear about them through Aurora's scattered narrative.

"I'm actually really, really proud of her," Emma adds. "She finally broke up with Jeremiah, and it sounds to me like she's truly making an effort to focus on her relationship with God and continue to bond with her sisters."

"I don't have time to finish this," Miss Maggie announces in a defeated tone as she closes her laptop. "My statement will have to wait. *Acid Rain* has a concert on the beach tonight. I never thought I would say this, but it'll be such a relief to get back to one of my 'normal' clients!" Miss Maggie smiles as her thoughts shift, "Helping Arden is such a joy. And at least we know he isn't living some kind of freaky, double life."

"Actually, Mom, I wouldn't be too sure with that kid." Emma smiles, "He seems kind of Peter Parker-ish to me. Totally unsuspecting, yet completely capable of being Spider Man."

"Oh goodness, don't even mention such a thing!" Miss Maggie laughs and pretends to tug on the ends of her hair. She shakes her head, but the smile doesn't disappear, "I've gotta go get ready. Are you coming to the show tonight?"

"I guess so." Emma shrugs, attempting to act nonchalant about it. Truth is, she's been low-key looking forward to the concert ever since Arden first mentioned it. She doesn't know why she's thinking about the event so favorably. But she doesn't mind the fact that she is.

"Yay!" Miss Maggie lets out an excited sequel, "My daughter is actually leaving the house to do a normal teenage activity! You have no idea how happy this makes me!" She playfully grabs Emma's arm and the two head upstairs to prepare for the evening. "You know, if I didn't know any better, I'd say Arden is starting to rub off on you! It seems as though the two of you are becoming great friends, am I right?"

"Mom, it's not like a big deal." Emma wrinkles her nose.

"Oh, but it is!" Miss Maggie insists. "You know I love you sweetheart, but I've always been a tad bit concerned about Aurora being your only friend. But now with Arden on the scene, the two of you really seem to be bonding! I think it's wonderful that you're branching out a bit and expanding your palate of friendships! I've never said this before, but sometimes having just one 'best friend' for everything isn't very ideal. It might seem like the thing to do in grade school, but as you grow older, you'll see there is a great need for all kinds of friends in life. Like my grandma used to say, 'Friends are like vegetables! The more variety you have, the healthier you'll be!' Aurora is your carrots, and now Arden is your broccoli!"

Emma makes a strange face. "Broccoli?!" she laughs. "If we're going to categorize Arden into kind of food group, he most definitely is a curly fry."

~*~

Emma's Converse-clad toes make contact with a thick, black wire. She loses her footing yet manages to miraculously catch herself mid-air. She presses her hands on a tall speaker, relieved that she didn't face plant onto the stage.

"Woah, watch the mic cords!" a stage worker offers her a delayed warning.

Emma tries to give him a reassuring nod. It's accompanied with a cheesy thumbs-up. Emma hopes to convince him she's completely fine.

"Are you tripping over thin air, or just giving a mellow-dramatic demonstration of what the audience is gonna do when we play?" Arden asks. He hands her a bottle of water. "Fall over in amazement."

Emma gratefully receives the bottle. The California sunshine is merciless today. With several more hours of hanging around before the sun takes a nap and the show starts, Emma will take all the hydration she can get. "I would typically go with A, thin air." Emma untwists her bottle, "But today I have an excuse." She glances at the cord. "Bulky wires."

"I have to say, I'm pretty shocked to see you up here. I thought you were like, allergic to stages or something."

Emma's eyes dart to where a man is tuning a guitar, and another is setting up mic stands. Jay and Matthew, Arden's bandmates, are attempting to shoot some kind of artsy photograph of themselves jumping off an amplifier. Emma's mom is chatting with stage management about where to set up the merch tent, and several other conversations are happening amidst *Bubblegum* bosses and employees, all at the same time. Emma returns her focus to Arden.

"Hey, I don't have a problem with stages, so long as nobody is watching." She looks at the empty lot and tumbling ocean on the other side of the sand. "I could actually get used to a view like this."

"Yeah, it's pretty epic, isn't it?" Arden grins, clearly elated with his current lot in life. He stands next to her, admiring the glorious ocean in the nearby distance.

"Are you nervous?" she asks, wondering if she'll get an honest answer.

"Nope. We've already sung *Obsession* so many times, I could literally sing it anywhere. I could sing it in my sleep, I could sing it while sky diving, I could sing it while hanging upside down from the Eiffel Tower, I could sing it while being attacked by sharks, I could sing it—"

"Okay, okay, I get the idea!" Emma laughs, "You know the song really well. You're not nervous. That's good."

"Are you nervous?" Arden turns the question on her.

"Me? Why would I be nervous? I'm not the one who has to perform in front of a crowd!"

"Not for tonight, silly. For your show!" Arden pops his hands out to the left and right, wiggling them like he's narrating a story with his hands, "The unforgettable, life-changing, mind-blowing presentation of the Broadway spectacular: *Beauty and the Beast*!"

"Oh, yikes, I hope the audience isn't expecting all that!" Emma laughs, "If they are, they're going to be sorely disappointed. Although, Julie is doing an amazing job with Belle. I think the play will turn out alright. But again, why would I be nervous? I'm not even going to be onstage."

"But you have such a massive role!" Arden insists. "I mean, hello, prop lady! Without you, there are no wigs. No faux flowers in fancy pots. No dining utensils!"

"Do you drink coffee?" Emma asks with a quizzical brow. "Because if you do, I think you need to cut back a little. I've never heard anyone quite so passionate about silverware."

"It's called adrenaline, Em." Arden continues talking with high enthusiasm, "And its way more hyper-inducing than coffee! I don't know how that bad boy works, but it starts pumping through my blood before every show and WOOO! I'm stoked man. So totally stoked. Just watch. It'll hit you on opening night. You're gonna take *Beauty and the Beast* backstage management to a whole 'nother level."

"I highly doubt that." Emma dares to disagree, "If anything, I'll be bringing the boring, wet-blanket of chill. My night backstage will probably consist of shushing all the little kids, reminding them to be quiet, several hundred times."

"That's no fun. But, I guess someone has to do it." Arden shrugs, "Anyway, I'll be out there in the auditorium, telepathically cheering you on."

"What?" Emma laughs, never ceasing to be surprised by the things that come out of Arden's mouth. "Wait, you're not actually coming to the show, are you?"

"Of course, I'm coming!" Arden nudges her in the side, "You think I'd miss an opportunity to watch a bunch of school kids put on a low-quality reenactment of a super-cheesy Disney story?" Arden winks, "Besides, I've gotta get a load of this Jeremiah guy and see if he's really as much of a Gaston as you say he is."

"Oh." Emma is struggling to recalibrate. Really? Arden is planning to come to the show? She's not sure why, but the news causes an unexpected bout of nerves. "Don't you have something else going on that night? I mean, recording session, photoshoot, interview…anything?"

"Nope, my schedule is completely clear." Arden sounds quite proud, "I already bought my ticket."

"Okay, we need a level on the vocals!" An important looking man who sounds like he knows what he's doing, makes the announcement. "Arden and Jay, let's get you on mic two and three. I just need a quick vocal check, and we can take *Obsession* from the top."

Oops, that's Emma's cue. It's time for her to exit the stage. She descends down the metal steps, careful not to trip.

She leaves the boys to work out their audio issues and approaches her mother below. Maggie is still in the middle of a discussion about where to put the Merch Tent.

Emma's eyes drift back to the stage.

"I've been trying to get your attention," Jay begins, "been, been trying to get your attention, but you just keep looking the other way."

"I wanted to be your superman, but you're treating me like I'm Peter Pan, thinkin' I'm a lost boy, a lost boy, thinkin' I'm a lost boy ohhhhhhhh" Matthew croons. His volume increases.

"There's only so many ways you can break my heart, but it's like you've got a check list, and you're killing me right from the start." Arden sings his line, and Emma's stomach does an excited flip-flop. Arden's voice is unreal. It's almost not even fair.

She watches as they break into the chorus, and next thing she knows, a dopey smile has slipped across her face. They're just so good! Even Miss Maggie and the Merch Guy pause from their conversation to listen to the song.

The guys prance around the stage, passionately belting out each word, and Emma can't help but feel that Arden was truly made for performances like this.

She sighs, secretly wondering what it must feel like to have finally found your 'thing.' Finding what you're created to do seems amazingly simple for people like Aurora and Arden. It's as if God loaded them with incredible talents, and all they had to do was wake up one morning and begin pursuing what was already in their hearts.

Pastor Brian has been talking about 'Making an Eternal Impact' in Youth Group, and he believes that God places dreams and desires inside the heart of every young person. He says that those dreams are like roadmaps to finding your destiny. Emma purses her lips. It sounds easy enough. And it probably would be, if she had those kinds of aspirations. But she doesn't. Emma doesn't have the shadiest hint of a clue what she wants to do with her life. What is she created to do? What is she good at?

Lord, she finds herself praying right in the middle of *Acid Rain's* sound-check, *what do You want me to do with my life? I want to make an impact. I want my time on this earth to count for something. But I don't know where to begin! I'm not a long-lost Princess who's called to save a European country, or a flamboyant popstar who rocks out onstage. I'm just Emma. The bland, drab, usual, non-spectacular and outlandishly boring 'behind the scenes' girl. Sometimes I feel so 'normal', it's pathetic. Lord, if invisibility is my superpower, then I have no idea what it's any good for.*

As Emma quiets her heart, a strange thought floats into her mind. It's so soft and quiet, she nearly misses it due to the loud speakers pumping *Acid Rain* through the airwaves. *'There is no such thing as a small role.'* She remembers telling little Emma those same words when she was discouraged about her fork status. But the thought continues, *'Having even the smallest role in any production is a huge honor. Emma, you've been cast in My story. I am the Director and I have created you to be the Emma that you are! Speak your lines with passion. Don't doubt where I've placed you. You're not just a 'fork' on the sidelines. Trust Me, I know what I am doing.'*

Emma's shoulders relax as a deep peace settles over her. She must keep her thoughts centered in the right place. The Lord is right. He knows what He's doing, and Emma has to trust that. Even still, she wishes she could see a bit more clearly in her attempts to make sense of everything.

"Wow, who are those guys?" Three teenage girls come up behind Emma and Miss Maggie, "They're so cute!"

"*Acid Rain*! Miss Maggie tells them excitedly. She hands them each a little business card, "They're playing tonight at 7! Come back then and bring your friends!"

"Oh, my goodness, look at the guitar player!" One of the girls excitedly nudges her friends. "Talk about cuteboys.com!"

Emma attempts to keep her face from reacting negatively. *Yikes.* Emma keeps her disturbed thoughts to herself, *Have some respect, ladies!*

"I call dibs on the guy in the middle!" another girl announces.

Emma's heart stops. She's referring to Arden! An unwelcome anger stirs deep in the pit of her stomach. She bites her tongue, reigning back her desire to bark, 'Get a life, girls! You can't place 'dibs' on other human beings! That's so desperate and immature!'

The girls exchange exited giggles then make their way toward the stage.

Emma's breath is short. She has a sick feeling about these girls. They're like a heard of golden lioness pouncing in on their helpless prey. As they approach with flirtatious struts, short shorts and spaghetti-strap tanks, they're bound to get the boys attention. Ugh, Emma can't even watch.

The song ends, and the girls have pressed themselves up against the iron gate. They're standing as close as physically possible to the stage. Arden offers them a wave, and they all giggle hysterically.

Emma feels like she's watching a bad horror movie. Someone make it end! Quick!

Jay starts talking with the girls, and even though Emma can't hear what they're saying, it deeply concerns her. She notices another small crowd of six, long-limbed teenage girls curiously joining the group. Emma feels like smashing her head into the cement below. It's happening! The fangirls are multiplying! Emma feels a strange need to take several steps closer and monitor the situation.

Without warning, Arden hops off the stage and is in the crowd with the young ladies. Emma hurries her steps forward. *Arden Laverne, don't you dare make a fool out of yourself. Keep your dignity, boy!*

But it's too late. The girls are already giggling like a heard of mindless hyenas as Arden chats easily with them, easily wooing them with his endearing charm.

"You guys are so good looking," one girl comments. Emma can't believe her ears. Would someone actually say that out loud?!

"We're good looking?" Arden laughs, "No, no, no, you ladies are all beautiful." Arden smiles sweetly, "Wanna snap a group selfie?"

The girls are obviously in. Jay and Matthew leap off the stage, bringing more flirtatious comments and infectious giggles to the group.

Emma wants to gag.

"Okay, let's try to squeeze everyone in!" Arden instructs, attempting to hold his phone far enough away to catch the group.

"My pleasure," a girl giggles as she presses close to Arden, her hand flirtatiously touching his back.

"Oh! Em!" Arden suddenly tosses her his phone. Miraculously, she catches it. "Can you get this shot?"

Emma wishes to boycott it, but she doesn't want to be ridiculous. She frowns and holds up the camera, attempting to find everyone in the frame.

She bites her lip as Arden comes into view, front and center. He's glowing, flashing that devastatingly beautiful smile of his. He's surrounded by girls. She takes a deep breath, knowing that this is just the first of many, *many* moments like this to come. Like it or not, Arden is on his way to the top. And now, Emma has to find a way to regretfully share him with the rest of the world.

~*~

Eleanor's heart soars with joy. She steps back several feet, just short of tumbling over the thick bed of hay. She doesn't recall being this tired in years. After staying up the entire night, all of the stress, anxiety, and patience required to endure has finally come to an end. The newest family member of the Napp's ranch has arrived. A brand-new foal has entered the earth!

She lovingly admires the tender scene, as a proud mama nurses her tender baby.

"Sundance was a true champ!" The vet expresses what everyone in the stall is thinking, "I was a little concerned about the size of her foal, but she really pushed through. Looks like this little guy is healthy as can be. Good job, Eleanor."

"I didn't do much!" Eleanor smiles, leaning against the stall door, "I was just here for moral support. It was all Sundance."

"Any ideas for his name?" the vet asks, basking in the glow of the miraculous moment. As a vet, there is nothing more fulfilling than assisting new life coming forth into the world.

"Spark," she tells him. "Because his birth is just what we needed to bring a fresh little spark of hope around here."

The vet nods, and everyone in the stall seems to agree that it's a wonderful name.

Eleanor sighs, half longing for her pillow, and half far too tired to think about sleep. The past twenty-four hours were quite batty. Shortly after Logan and the movie crew left, Sundance started experiencing labor pains. Eleanor wasn't too concerned, knowing it would take a while for her to be dilated. But she kept the vet's number nearby, just in case anything abnormal occurred. She had witnessed many births, and even helped her mom midwife some deliveries, but this was the first time Eleanor would be completely responsible for whatever happened. With Dad gone, and several of the usual workers on break, Eleanor was nervous. If a crisis occurred, she wasn't sure she'd be able to handle it.

Truthfully, Eleanor was thankful for the distraction of Sundance's labor process. Even though she had to drop all other chores and monitor Sundance, it helped get her mind off things. Mainly, the absence of Logan, and how quiet things were now that the crew left.

Eleanor knew it would be strange with them gone, but she didn't anticipate feeling quite so…disappointed. Though she would never admit it to another living soul, she was actually going to miss Logan. They had become friends, and it was a blessing having someone else around her age to chat and hang out with. Though the world Logan grew up in was far,

far different than her own, they actually had more in common than she ever thought possible.

Several hours into Sundance's labor, Eleanor's dad called. And his news was quite unsettling.

"Ellie, sweetie, I know this is going to be hard…but I have to stay in Europe for several more months. There's a lot happening right now, and they really need me here."

Eleanor couldn't make sense of the situation, nor would he share any kind of details with her. Eleanor grew angry, feeling as though her dad was hiding something. "What are you doing over there? Why do you have to be gone for so long? Why does everything have to be so 'top secret', I'm your own daughter, why can't you tell me?!"

But Jonathan was tight-lipped, and his answers left Eleanor dissatisfied.

"I don't want you to be at the resort by yourself," he told her. "In fact, I would feel much more comfortable with the situation, if you were with family right now. So, I've talked to your Aunt Lydia and asked if she wouldn't mind you going to Colorado and staying with them until I get back."

"What?!" Eleanor was blindsided by the news, "And leave the ranch? Dad, I can't! We're just starting to get things back in working order, now that Jasmine is gone. You know I love Aunt Lydia, but I can't leave for months on end! Dad, this is our home."

"Ellie, I love that you want to help get things re-established and fill the gap Jasmine has left in our administration, but that is not your responsibility." Jonathan reminded her, "For goodness sakes, you're a sixteen-year-old girl! You're taking on far too much stress and carrying a load that is not yours to carry. I'll handle all of those details."

"But Dad, how can you? You're not even here!"

"Ellie, these are not your decisions to make. I am your father, and I know what's best for you. And right now, I don't want you staying at the ranch by yourself. Understood?"

Her father's determined words ring in her thoughts. There's no changing his mind.

Eleanor attempts to refocus on the delightful sight of mare and foal tenderly enjoying one another's company. Her heart aches as she thinks of her mother, and how much she would've enjoyed this moment.

Eleanor can feel a tight restriction forming in her throat. Why do things have to be like this? First, she loses her mom, and now she's nearly lost her father to those stupid top-secret business trips. She doesn't want to leave the Napp's ranch. Not for a month, a week, or even a day! She can't leave everything Mom has started. Someone has to stay here and see to it that things are run according to her original vision. And she wouldn't even *have* to leave, if her father didn't keep disappearing! What is he doing in Europe anyway?

Eleanor feels a twinge of distrust, suddenly wondering if this stupid URIA company is even a real thing. What if it's not? What if her dad has just made up an excuse to jet off and—

"Ellie!"

Eleanor slowly spins around, wondering who would be calling her name so excitedly.

A trim woman dressed in solid cowgirl boots, faded blue jeans, and a black leather jacket scurries through the stable alleyway with open arms. She leaves her small, black, rolling carry-on bag at the stall door and unhooks the latch. Before Eleanor can say anything, Aunt Lydia has her enveloped in a hug.

"Oh, Ellie darling, I can't believe how big you've gotten! Look at you! You're beautiful! Just like your mom!" Aunt Lydia pulls away from the hug and holds her niece happily by the shoulders, "I can't believe it's been five years since you've been out to visit us!"

Eleanor doesn't know what to say. A flood of conflicting emotions overwhelms her. She's not ready to see Aunt Lydia. She's not ready to leave. The last time she was in Colorado…was for her mom's funeral.

Still, her aunt's striking resemblance to her late mother is strangely comforting. Though Aunt Lydia's strawberry blond, hair dye assisted style is vastly different from her mom's brunette locks, they share the same loving hazel eyes, petite nose, and inviting smile. Eleanor resists the temptation to start crying all over again. Seeing Aunt Lydia is like beholding the vivid, real life ghost of her mother.

~*~

At Aunt Lydia's and Uncle Sky's Ranch in Colorado…

Eighteen-year-old Obadiah Mason hauls a hefty hay bale across the barn aisle and tosses it into an empty stall. He removes his pocket knife and quickly slices the thin strings holding the bale together. The bale unravels slightly. He uses a rake to separate the cuddled-up hay chunks and spreads them across the stall floor.

In his peripheral vision, two pink cowgirl hats whizz past the stall door. He smiles, knowing there are two very excited kids running beneath them.

"Come on, we're gonna be late for our trail ride!"

It's against the rules to run and make loud noises in the stables. But their family dude ranch is frequented by American families from all over the country who don't have a clue how to behave around horses. Thankfully, their livestock is used to all the commotion, and they don't have fidgety horses who react negatively to all the hustle and bustle.

The summer rush of tourist season is nearly over, and soon things will quiet down for a season as school resumes. Then again, the word 'quiet' is all relative. There's never a dull moment at Sky Dude Ranch, and Obadiah knows better than to think things will ever truly slow down. He exits the stall and reaches for another heavy bale. With dozens of horses, six rental cabins, riding lessons, rodeo competitions, and their own personal family happenings with seven siblings, the to-do list is ever enduring.

"I would've creamed you if it wasn't for that shortcut!" a male voice calls out, his words thundering through the hollow stables. All of the horses are turned out for the afternoon, and every noise bounces off the empty walls.

"Are you kidding?!" a young woman laughs. "I wasn't even riding at top speed. I was taking it easy on you guys, since you're both total newbies."

Obadiah recognizes the voice. It's his younger sister, Sarah. His ears perk up. He drops the bale and listens intently, trying to make out the male voices.

"Newbies?! What a burn!" Another young man pretends to sound affected by her words, "We've been here for a solid five days, and we still haven't reached expert status? It's a good thing you're so pretty or else I'd be blaming our riding instructor."

Obadiah's jaw tightens. He can hear Sarah's playful laughter in response to his offhanded comment. Obadiah is ready to, if need be, put those little twerps in their place. As much as he loves Sarah, she seems quite oblivious to the way their male guests fawn over her. Although innocent Sarah has never so much as gone on a date, Obadiah considers it his personal responsibility to see that she's treated with respect and honor. Throughout the summertime rush, there can be some real creeps frequenting this place.

"I think Dad needs to send out a public notice statement," sixteen-year-old Harmony floats onto the scene, hauling a saddle past the stall where Obadiah is working. She pauses to rest the saddle on the stall door. "The purpose of this ranch is to learn how to ride and fall in love with Colorado. Not with his bubbly, blonde, curly-haired daughter."

"I wouldn't worry about it, Mony," Obadiah tells his next youngest sister in the Mason lineup. He pops his head out of the stall and peers down the alleyway. "I'm keeping my eye out for her. I'm not afraid to use my shotgun."

"It's kind of disgusting," Harmony huffs, pressing her hands anxiously against the saddle. "I mean, doesn't she know that laughing like an airhead is just encouraging them? She acts like she doesn't know what she's doing, but I think she does."

Obadiah tosses her a questionable glance, "Jealous much?"

Harmony gasps. "Yeah right! Gosh, I can't believe you'd suggest such a thing. Why in the world would I be jealous of getting attention from creepy guys who just get in the way of riding?"

Obadiah laughs, "You're the only sixteen-year-old girl I know who still thinks guys her age have cooties. Don't ever change, okay? Your realistic view of the male species is spot on. Just one of the many reasons I adore you, sis."

"Duh!" Harmony grins playfully, tossing her high-centered brunette ponytail over her shoulder. "I plan on staying single forever, being one of those crazy cat ladies, remember? I'll sport the ugly, bulky knit sweaters to bingo night, and everything."

Obadiah laughs, knowing his sister is only half joking. "I didn't know you were so into cats. I thought you were gonna have dozens of horses."

"That too." She winks, "But I'm not planning on sleeping in the barn, so the cats will keep me company."

"I'm slightly disturbed you have this all planned out." Obadiah laughs, opening the stall door and reaching for his next bale of hay. "You might change your mind. Maybe you should leave things a little more open-ended for destiny to take over and do its thing?"

"Okay, okay!" Harmony throws her hands up in mock surrender, "If God so happens to have it in His plan for my life, to bring along a guy who adores horses, is down with my dream of letting me be a vet tech, and thrives off of ranch life, then I *might* be open to negotiation. Maybe then I can do without all the cats."

"Enough about the future." Obadiah grins, "The present is calling. Give me a hand with those bales? I've still got seven stalls to go before we turn the horses in."

[208]

"I'd love to help, but actually I need to go clean my room." Harmony's face forms a quick, concerned frown. "Like, desperately. Mom asked me to do it before she left for Cali, and now it's even worse. Mom's gonna be back in just a few hours. If Eleanor steps foot in there right now, she'd probably suffer a minor heart attack."

"Are you cool with sharing your room?" Obadiah asks. "I mean, I know Eleanor is family, but we haven't seen her in like what, five years?"

"I was eleven last time they were out here," Harmony replies thoughtfully, "And unless Ellie's turned into a total diva or something, I don't mind at all! We actually had quite a lot of fun as kids. We were both horse crazy. I remember Mom and Auntie took us all out to camp by the cabins one night, and we slept under the stars. We roasted marshmallow and looked for constellations. Whenever Ellie would visit, we had a total blast together."

"A lot can change in five years, Mony," Obadiah cautiously warns her. "I just don't want you to be disappointed if Eleanor's a totally different person now."

"I don't think I have anything to worry about." Harmony giggles, "For girls like me and Ellie, it takes a lot more than five years to remove the 'horse crazy' fever from our blood. Think about who are moms are! It's part of our DNA. There's no way we can escape it."

~*~

Episode 6

"Miss Emma, Miss Emma, my hat is missing!" Eight-year-old Timothy forcefully tugs on the back of Emma's grey T-shirt.

Emma turns to face him, "What do you mean your hat is missing? It should be in the Townspeople costume box, right where you left it."

"I'm not lying, it's truly not there!" He continues to pull on her shirt, wanting her to come instantly and discover that he's right.

"Miss Emma, I did something bad," ten-year-old Skylar joins the conversation. "Something really, really bad."

"Did you steal Timothy's hat?" Emma asks.

"No." Skylar looks down sadly toward the ground, "But I forgot my costume."

"What?!" Emma screeches, "Miss Julie reminded you guys like sixty times not to leave the house without your costumes!"

Emma lifts a frustrated hand to her head. It's only 10:30 AM but she's already put out dozens of mini-wildfires. It seems as though this morning, on the day of their first (and last) dress rehearsal, everything that could possibly go wrong, is going wrong.

"I'm sorry!" Skylar apologizes. "But my mom is at work now and she's gonna be *so* mad if I ask her to come and bring it! What am I gonna wear? Miss Julie said street clothes are not allowed! This means I'll have nothing but my underwear?!"

"No, Sky, we're not going to make you go onstage without a costume." Emma does her best to hide a smirk. Despite the stress and last-minute insanity of attempting to pull together a production like this one, these kids never cease to make her chuckle.

"Ow, I've got makeup in my eye!" Little Emma lets out a small scream, "Ouch, ouch, it hurts, it hurts!"

Emma rushes to the makeup table, swooping up the girl and rushing her to a nearby water-drinking fountain. Emma gently sprays water in her eye, hoping it will soothe the pain and remove whatever particles of mascara are not supposed to be in there.

"I didn't mean to!" One of the older girls, who is in charge of doing the Little Fork's makeup, reveals her regrets. "She was just so wiggly!"

After being confident that Emma Junior is okay, Emma claps her hands to get everyone's attention. "Okay, new plan! We are now going to play the silent game!"

Several of the teens release audible groans.

"I hate that game!" Little Emma protests, placing unhappy hands on her hips.

"But this isn't just any old silent game," she tells them, thinking on the fly, hoping to create a solution that will help decrease the headache-inducing volume happening backstage. "This is the super-duper dramatic silent game! Meaning, as your lips are zipped and you're keeping your hands and feet to yourself, you must think of your favorite character and dramatically act like them in your head!"

"But nobody can hear us?" Emma Junior isn't thrilled about the rules.

"That's right!" Emma hopes the excitement will catch on, "And that way you can be as dramatic as you want, cracking up nobody but your own silent little self. Ready? Set? Go!"

All at once, a miraculous hush sweeps across the group. Emma is in awe. She can't believe they're all actually being quiet! She moves quickly, knowing this state of bliss isn't going to last very long.

Little Timothy wiggles his hand into the air, and Emma reassures him, "Don't worry, I'll find your hat. And Skylar, I'm going to see if there are any extra costumes in the Green Room."

She quickly pushes through the black door and into a small room where Julie, several volunteers, and the older teen girls are getting ready. Emma's eyes widen. Helping hands are attempting to fit Julie into Belle's ball scene costume.

"What in the world?" Julie marvels, "This fit last week?!"

"Julie, your baby bump is getting bigger!" One of the teens giggle, "We're gonna have a hard time covering that up."

"Oh, no." Julie's face is bright red. She's completely flustered, "There must be a way to fix this! Maybe I can take out the hem on the sides and add more material. Oh dear, little Savannah was skinny as a rail…there's got to be a way to make this work." She looks at Emma, "Anyone here know how to sew?"

Emma's face doesn't hide her concern. This dress isn't working for Julie. As glorious as the lavishly-gold gown is, there's no way it's going to fit around Julie's widening tummy. A deep sinking feeling attacks Emma's chest. This play is going to be a disaster. She just knows it. With kids who don't know their lines, missing costumes, and a pregnant leading lady, Arden is going to be laughing his head off. She hates the fact that he's going to be here to witness such a disgrace. This production will be just another item on Arden's long list of things he can tease her about.

"Don't worry, you guys!" Julie is staying deliriously positive, "There is always an answer! I'm trusting God with this thing, and I know He's going to make a way!" She suddenly reaches for her stomach. "Oh! I think I just got an amen from our little one! Our babe is kicking in agreement!"

"But what are we going to do about your dress?" Macy, a concerned Townsperson asks. "It's obviously not working. We can't have the dance scene without Belle's epic dress!"

"I'll call my friend Taylor!" a sudden thought pops into Julie's head. "She's dabbled around with sewing, maybe she can think of a way to add more fabric!"

~*~

"Tale as old as time, true as it can be, barely even friends, then somebody bends unexpectedly." Mrs. Potts begins the classic ballad.

Emma watches from the side stage with a nervous hand up to her mouth. Even though Celia, the fifteen-year-old who plays Mrs. Potts, is a bit pitchy, she's doing alright. Her tea-kettle costume makes the whole thing feel much more real.

"Just a little change, small to say the least, both a little scared, neither one prepared—"

"Ooomp! Ow!" Belle suddenly stops dancing and releases a small wince of pain. The furry beast quickly removes his fuzzy costume head. "Miss Julie, are you okay?!"

Emma's eyes widen in fear, as Julie is leaned over, attempting to catch her breath.

"Yeah." She takes a deep breath, finally able to speak, "Oh goodness, I'm sorry." She stands up and rubs the small of her back, "Sorry guys, I don't know what that was. Phantom pains, I guess. Okay, my bad, let's take it from the top." She places her arms out, prepared to resume the dance number.

Emma bites her lip. The Beast places his head back on, and Mrs. Potts takes a deep breath.

The music begins, and everyone tries to get back into character.

"Tale as old as time, true as it can be, barely even friends, then somebody bends—"

"Agghh!" Julie releases a sound of distress and nearly falls to the ground. The quick-thinking Beast catches her before she crashes to the floor.

"Julie!" Emma cries, racing onto the stage. She rushes to her side, grabbing her arms for support. "Oh, my word, are you okay?!"

Julie is struggling to breathe. Her face is pained, and she's clenching her abdomen. "Ow! Agghh! Emma, call—" She struggles to find her next breath, "Call Brian!"

"Cell phone, cell phone!" She shouts to the kids in the auditorium, "Quick, who has a cell phone?!"

Jeremiah races onto the stage, but Mrs. Potts has already handed her phone to Emma. Emma's trembling fingers quickly dial Julie's husband. Though Brian isn't in Celia's contacts, Emma has a strange knack for memorizing numbers. Her eyes are wide with fear, as she watches Julie struggle with pain.

"I need—I need to sit!" The Beast helps Julie onto the hard stage floor, all the while she is groaning and releasing pain-filled noises.

"Jeremiah!" Emma orders as she waits for Brian to answer, "Call 911!"

~*~

"Okay, Celia's got the kids in the other room playing Freeze Tag," Emma announces as she enters the Green Room. A small group of teens are waiting there for her.

As soon as the ambulance came for Julie, Jeremiah suggested Emma get the younger kids occupied in a game then call an emergency meeting with the older cast members. Emma was experiencing so much shock and horror, she was hardly able to think straight. And so, she followed Jeremiah's suggestion.

Now, with the small crowd of frightened faces awaiting her direction, Emma doesn't have a clue what to say.

"Is it over?" one of the girls asks. "Are we gonna have to cancel the show?"

"Brian promised to call as soon as they know what's going on," Emma tells them.

"Do you think she's gonna have her baby?" Jeremiah asks.

"Julie is way too early in her pregnancy to be experiencing labor pains." Emma's voice is heavy with concern, "We can only pray that if it is some kind of early labor everything will be okay. But I desperately hope that's not it. Right now, her baby needs to be in her womb. Not outside of it."

"So, what are we going to do?" Celia asks. "It's impossible for this show to happen without Julie!"

"We don't know for sure what's going on, and we can't cancel until we do." Emma tries to look on the bright side, "Maybe it's just something simple, and Julie will be back in a few hours. All I know is that she wouldn't want us to stop rehearsal. We can't give up so easily."

"But we don't have a Belle!" Macy argues.

"We don't need Belle right now to keep practicing." Emma stands firm in her decision, "Julie obviously knows her lines, and she's nailing the musical numbers. But everyone else still needs to rehearse! We've got Silverware who are missing their ques, and Townspeople who are still forgetting their lines. We need to run those scenes over and over until we get them right. Now I don't know about you guys, but I am not ready to give up. Let's do this. For Julie."

"Alright!" Jeremiah cheers, attempting to get everyone in the room pumped up, "Emma's right! This is what show business is all about! Insane stuff happens, but you gotta keep pressing on. There's a ton of little kids out there who have been dreaming about this musical for weeks. We can't disappoint them. Besides, they're gonna be looking to us to set the tone, so let's keep the energy high, smiles wide, and high-fives slapping! We've gotta stay excited for them." He stands up, "We're gonna smash this production out of the park! You guys with me?!"

Emma smiles. Naturally, all the girls jump on the band wagon and are excited to do anything Jeremiah suggests. They all let out cheers of their own, and soon the entire room is pumped up again, ready to conquer the realm of the impossible.

~*~

"Beauty and the Beast Cast!" Jeremiah arrests everyone's attention from onstage, "I need all eyes and ears looking this way! Emma here has a very important announcement to make, so keep those lips zippity-zipped!"

The bustling auditorium quiets down, and Emma takes a deep breath. Dozens of little faces are looking at her.

"Miss Julie's husband, Brian, just called me, and he had some news to share." Emma doesn't allow her voice to quiver, despite the deep concern she feels with these words. "Julie is in labor right now. But as you guys may have noticed, her baby is still very small, and she's several months away from her due date. Both Julie's and her baby's life are in danger. I know we all want her to be okay, so I'm proposing that we each close our eyes and take a few moments to pray for Julie." Emma takes another deep breath, "I know that many of you might not believe in prayer or believe that there's a God in heaven who cares about what we have to say. But I do. Because of Jesus Christ, I have a personal relationship with God, and I know He hears my prayers. And I believe that if we all join together and pray for Julie and the baby, God is going to take care of them. Do you guys agree?"

There are several nods from the littlest cast members in the front row.

She glances at Jeremiah, and he removes his hat, bowing his head. Several others follow suit, and soon most of the kids have shut their eyes.

Emma clasps her hands together and focuses her heart and mind on God. She prays quietly for several moments, passionately petitioning heaven for the lives of both Julie and her baby. She knows this situation is entirely out of her control, and as much as she wishes she could be there to help

Julie in her hour of need, she knows that she has to surrender it to the Lord.

"Okay," she whispers before opening her eyes, "it's Yours, Lord. Amen."

~*~

"I thought I told you to come down to dinner!" the Beast shouts up the stairs.

Silence lingers as he imagines Belle's response, then continues. "I am the master of this castle, and I am telling you to come down to dinner!"

"Emma, why is he talking to himself?" Timothy asks from offstage.

"He's just pretending Belle is there," Emma tells him quietly. "It might look strange, but it helps develop his acting skills."

"Is that what he's going to do tomorrow night?" Timothy asks. "Cause my mom will think it's weird, coming to a show where people talk to themselves."

"No, there will be someone there tomorrow night, don't worry," Emma attempts to reassure him.

"Who? Will Miss Julie be back from the hospital on time? Doesn't it take a while to have a baby?"

"Emma, you should at least get out there and read Belle's lines." Jeremiah comes up from behind, "This is totally confusing the little kids. I was just talking to Chip, and he's clueless as to how he's gonna do his scene with Belle."

"Okay." Emma huffs, "If it will help dissolve the confusion."

"Here's a script." Jeremiah hands it to her.

"I don't need that." Emma waves her hand in the air. "I'm not hungry!" Emma shouts while still offstage.

The Beast pauses. He looks toward stage left, where Emma is standing. He smiles from within his costume. "I am the master of this castle, and I am telling you to come down to dinner!"

"Master, that may not be the best way to win a girl's affections," a candle stick tells the Beast.

"Don't you have any manners?!" Emma bursts onto stage, confronting the Beast for his uncivilized ways. "You're a cruel bully, shouting whatever vain thing pops into your mind! Do you have any idea how to treat your guests?!"

"Woah!" Timothy gasps from side stage, "Who knew Miss Emma could act?!"

"Deep breaths, Master, deep breaths," the candle-stick coaches the Beast.

He crosses the stage angrily, opens his mouth to shout at her, then lowers his paw. He attempts to be pleasant. "Would you...uhh...be so kind as to join me for dinner?"

"Please!" The clock coughs, "Say please!"

"Uhhh....please?"

"No." Emma crosses her arms angrily. "No, I will not."

Jeremiah laughs. "Finally! She's taking out all that feisty sass on some other loser!"

"Fine! Then starve!" the Beast shouts in her face, turns his back, and storms offstage. "If she doesn't eat with me, then she doesn't eat at all!"

~*~

"Ah, ha!" Emma announces triumphantly, "Here are the missing Townspeople hats!" Emma quickly picks up the box and moves it to where it's supposed to be. She takes a deep breath, relieved that all the young children have gone home. The Dress Rehearsal, all things considered, actually went well.

The kids are as ready as they'll ever be for their performance tomorrow night. Emma's heart falls as she remembers one major, devastatingly-discouraging detail: their Belle is in the hospital.

"Emma, you killed it out there," Jeremiah tells her as he collects several props and places them in the correct boxes.

Emma glances at the young man who stuck around with several other of the teens to help clean up. "You should've heard the little kids backstage!" Jeremiah continues, "You've definitely got a fan club growing. I mean, I knew you were dramatic, but where'd you learn to act like that?"

Emma laughs, "Oh, goodness! I was just goofing around. I am not an actress."

"What do you mean you're not an actress?" Jeremiah looks at her like she's insane, "You owned that stage! I mean, you were totally into character. And how did you know all of Belle's lines?!"

"I don't know." Emma shrugs, "I mean sure, I had fun today, but I could never do that in front of a real crowd. I guess I just read the script too many times. And Belle's always been my favorite Disney Princess," she adds with a smile.

"Emma, you have to be Belle tomorrow night," Jeremiah insists. "You're perfect for the role."

"There's no way." Emma shakes her head violently, "I'd be way too nervous! It makes me nauseous just thinking about it! On stage? With real people watching? No, no, NO way."

"But Emma, you're our only hope! Even if Julie were to have her baby, like right now, and it was perfectly healthy with no complications, you and I both know she's not gonna be ready to leave a premature birth and join the show tomorrow. Emma, you have to do this. We don't have any other options."

"Yes, we do!" she insists.

"Like what?" Jeremiah crosses his arms, waiting for a response.

"Like…um," she nervously shuffles her feet around, wishing there was a way to avoid this question, "maybe…"

"Reality check. It's too late. Either you're our Belle tomorrow night or there's no show."

~*~

"Mmm, I love a bowl of chili on a beautiful fall afternoon." Miss Maggie serves a heaping spoonful of steaming beans and beef to her dinner guests.

"Mrs. Bates, it's like 90 degrees outside," Arden reminds her. He watches with a grumbling stomach as Miss Maggie hands him a delicious-smelling bowl.

"True. But soon this wretchedly hot summer will be over, and it'll be time for sweater weather! All of your friends will be going back to school, and *you* will be traveling down the road to your destiny!"

Emma stares into her bowl. Her appetite is nowhere to be found. The day's events have zapped all her energy. Her mind is flooded with worries, and her heart is congested with fear. Miss Julie is still in the hospital, and she hasn't gotten any updates from Brian. On top of all that...Jeremiah is right. Unless Emma walks on that stage and brings Belle to life, there will be no show. The thought is both debilitating and terrifying.

"Any word from Brian?" Miss Maggie asks as she sits down, noticing her daughter's distressed state.

"No." She sets down her empty spoon. "Um, I'm really not hungry. Do you mind if I'm excused?"

"Oh, but sweetie, we were going to talk about Arden's schedule and possible–" Miss Maggie stops herself, sensitive to Emma's distraught state. "Okay, dear. But consider joining us for dessert? I've got chocolate brownies and mint ice cream!"

Emma slowly pushes her chair back and apologizes to Mrs. Laverne who is sitting beside her. "Sorry. I just need to go, um, pray for a while."

She opens the screen door and steps outside.

~*~

Twenty minutes later, a familiar figure plops into the sand beside Emma.

"Well, you look elated about tomorrow night." Arden's voice is heavy with sarcasm.

"This isn't a joke, Arden!" Emma snaps. "Julie's life is in danger! And so is her child's!" Her voice softens, and she instantly regrets attacking him so viciously. Her eyes soften as well. "Brian just sent a text and said they're gonna try a C-section. But the odds are..." Emma can't finish her sentence.

"Hey, Emma, it's okay, nobody's laughing." Arden speaks sincerely, "I know how tough this is. Does this mean Julie's gonna cancel the show?"

"I'm sure this show is the last thing she's thinking about right now. Even so, she loves those kids so much. She would never want to disappoint them. For some of those little guys, it's their first time *ever* onstage. Emma said her mom bought her a special dress, and they're going out for dinner after the show to celebrate…it's a big, big deal for some of these kids. They would be absolutely crushed if we canceled. But the only way we don't is…" Emma hesitates even speaking the outlandish words, "If…" She looks away from Arden, afraid he might start laughing. "If I play Belle."

She flinches slightly, bracing herself for the sarcastic jab which is bound to come her way.

Surprisingly, Arden is quiet. She looks at him.

"Why aren't you laughing?"

"Why would I be laughing?" Arden appears confused, "I think you playing Belle is an epic idea! I mean, you're pretty much her. The only difference between the two of you is that she walks around singing while she reads. And I've never heard you sing." He cocks his head slightly to the left, "Wait. Can you sing?"

"No!" Emma quickly spits out, "Of course I can't sing! I mean, sure I can sing, but not in front of people!" She shakes her head, feeling all the familiar anxieties flooding over her, "There's no way! Me being Belle would be impossible! I just… I can't. No. There's no way."

"You don't seem like the kind of person who would allow the word 'impossible' to be in their vocabulary. Emma, nobody's asking you to perform for Hollywood critics. This isn't the Oscars or the Teen Choice Awards or some high-budget production. This is a play! With elementary students and homemade costumes…nobody's says you even have to be any good! You just need to have fun."

"But Arden." Emma isn't giving in that easily, "There are going to be people there. Real, living, breathing, thinking, pointing, laughing people! If I mess up–"

"Then you'll make a joke and play it up!" Arden grins, "It's called improv! If you forget your lines, just think of something Belle would say and roll with it. A laughing audience is totally a good thing. Emma, you can do this. I know you've got what it takes."

"But what if I throw up!?"

"Then you blame Lumiere and the kitchen people for food poisoning!"

Emma giggles. Arden can be ridiculous sometimes. But, he does know how to make her feel better. "I can't believe I'm actually considering this. This is crazy!" She shakes her head, feeling excited and short of breath.

"Not any crazier than dancing on tables, and you've already done that, so what's a silly school play?"

A smile slowly creeps onto Emma's face. "Promise not to laugh if I completely ruin the entire show?"

"Are you kidding?!" Arden laughs, "I'll be the first one rolling on the floor!"

Emma's eyes widen in horror.

Arden is surprised to see her take the comment seriously, so he quickly recovers, "Emma, it was a joke. I'm going to support you. No matter what, I'll be there. If anyone laughs when they're not supposed to, I will personally make it my business to remove them from the theater and see to it that they don't laugh off cue ever, EVER again!"

A deep chuckle travels from Emma's tummy and out her mouth. "Oh my!" She places shocked hands up to her cheeks, "Please don't!"

"You get my point though, right?" Arden asks.

"I do." Emma nods, "I'm taking this whole thing way, waayyyy too seriously, and I just need to relax, have fun, and let whatever happens, happen."

"Couldn't have said it better myself." Arden grins.

Emma's pocket is vibrating. She quickly reaches for her phone. She glances fearfully at Arden, dreading what the message might say. She flips it over and bites her lip, knowing the message will be from Brian.

She's here! Our little Miracle weighs one pound and eight ounces. Julie is stabilized, but Miracle is still fighting for her life. Stand and agree with us in prayer that she is our living Miracle!

Emma clutches her chest as tears form in her eyes, "Oh, thank You, Jesus!" Unable to read the words out loud, she hands her phone to Arden and allows him to read the words for himself.

"Wow," Arden breathes. "If God can handle all that, He can most definitely handle this play."

"You're right." Emma nods confidently, making the official decision to embrace the challenge. "Impossible isn't going to be in my vocabulary. God is obviously in the business of working miracles. And tomorrow night, he's gonna have to work another one."

~*~

Emma's right hand is nervously clutched to her neck. Her eyes are glued on the velvet red curtain. It's only a thin bolt of fabric, separating her and the audience. She can hear their lively conversation as the auditorium is buzzing like unorganized bees. Emma's breathing is heavy, and she can hear her own heart pounding. She knows that both Arden and her mother are out there. She reaches for her stomach as it flops around wildly.

She's dressed in Belle's opening outfit, holding a book in her hand and a basket of baguettes. The ill feeling is overwhelming. Without warning, she quickly whisks off the stage, heading for the Green Room door. That's it. She's not doing it. There's no way she's going to stand out there in front of all those people and sing!

"Emma, the show's about to start!" the assistant director calls after her in an irritated whisper. "We need you behind the curtain!"

But Emma doesn't care.

She storms through the Green Room door, feeling as though she must find a restroom to empty her stomach of all this fear. She nearly smashes into Jeremiah, who is bulked up in his ridiculous, clunky-armed Gaston costume.

"Woah, woah, woah!" He grabs her by the shoulders. "You're going the wrong way."

"I can't!" She pants, "I'm not, I'm not..." She is struggling to find her breath, "I'm not going out there!"

"Emma, breathe." Jeremiah tries his best to sound calm, "Yes you can. You're going to do this, and you're going to be amazing. You've inflated this whole thing up way too big in your mind! It's just a play, Emma! The kids just want to have fun. Your fears? They're not even real. They're like my buff arms." He wiggles the flimsy fabric, "Completely fake."

Emma doesn't laugh. "Don't tell me my fears aren't real! I know what I'm feeling right now, and it's real alright!"

"There you go, get mad!" Jeremiah encourages her. "I know how much you hate my guts…use it to your advantage! Take it onstage, filter it as adrenaline, and give Gaston a look that is *so* wickedly fed up. A glare that only Emma could give. Oh. Yup. That's the look. Own it, Emma. You've got this!"

He slowly spins her around and gently maneuvers her forward by the shoulders. She's so frightened, she doesn't even have the clarity of mind to resist him.

"Good luck, Belle!" one of the little Townspeople tell her as she passes by.

"You don't say good luck in theater, that's bad luck!" another kid corrects him. "You have to say break a leg! Break a leg, Belle!"

Jeremiah plants her in place, right behind the curtain, "Stay here, he tells her. He opens her book and hands it to her, "Read."

And with that, he exits stage right. Emma wants to dash away, but she feels as though her feet are cemented in place.

In that very moment, far before she's ready, a most terrifying thing occurs. The velvet curtain slowly opens. An eerie hush settles over the audience and the tinkering of piano keys from the orchestra pit fills the air.

[227]

Emma can't think. A lone spotlight finds her, streaming down upon her face. In the absolute silence, she cannot speak. She cannot move. She cannot leave. She is trapped, completely frozen by an overpowering fear.

She knows her cue. She must begin singing. The whole show is waiting for her to start. She glances down at her book, wondering what Belle would do in a situation like this.

Most certainly, Belle would read.

Emma opens her book and lowers herself to the stage. She settles there and allows her eyes to scan the pages. Having never read the prop before, she realizes that the book is *Alice in Wonderland*. She flips to the first page, hoping to completely forget about the audience. She's just going to sit here and read.

The audience waits for a few moments before growing suspicious. The piano player grows nervous. He restarts the song, concerned, as she's missing her cue.

Everyone waits for Belle to do something.

But she's just sitting there. Reading. Acting as if she's completely clueless that the show has really begun.

Offstage, the cast explodes with anxiety.

"What is she doing?!" Celia whispers loudly, "Why isn't she singing yet?!"

"Emma, come on!" Jeremiah urges her on, hoping that perhaps he can telepathically tell her to get a move on it, "Go! Go!"

Emma appears to be completely contented, soaking in the words of her newest novel. She flips to the next page, finding herself settling into a world where everything is right. Reading calms her pounding heart and settles her mind. Finally, she is at peace. She's not thinking about the audience or the show or all the dreadful mistakes she could make. She's just becoming Belle.

"We have to do something!" Celia freaks out, "Should one of us go out there?!"

"Crap, we're gonna need to improv!" Jeremiah scratches his head, anxiously racking his brain, attempting to think of something. "Emma! What are you doing?" he murmurs, even though he knows she can't hear him.

"Hey lady!" A voice suddenly shouts from the crowd.

Emma looks up from her book, searching the crowd for whomever has spoken. She lifts a hand to shade her eyes, attempting to see past the blinding spotlight.

She cannot make out any faces, and the auditorium is nothing but a sea of darkness.

The critic stands up and continues with an animated voice. "Are you gonna start the show or what?!"

Emma's heartbeat quickens. She attempts to suppress a smile as she realizes who is speaking. It's Arden.

"Oh my!" Emma pretends to be surprised by the outrage. "I didn't even see you there!" She giggles, sounding just like the famous Disney darling. She closes her book and rises to her feet, "Have you ever been so immersed in a good book that you've completely lost track of all time? That happens to me on nearly every occasion." She laughs again, "But I suppose it is time to put my book away and tell you a story. Would you like to hear one?"

Jeremiah, Celia, and the rest of the cast breathe a massive sigh of relief, amazed to see that Emma has unfrozen.

"Yeah!" some little kids in the front row call out. A few audience members clap, and Arden lets out a little holler, "Woo! Let's hear this fairytale!"

Emma flips her hair over her shoulders and travels to center stage. "Wonderful!" She clasps her hands together, feeling that promised adrenaline that Arden spoke of, pumping through her veins. "Excuse me, Mr. Piano man? Let's begin!"

The piano player sighs mellow-dramatically, causing some of the little kids to giggle. Emma takes a deep breath, closing her eyes, attempting to remember who she is. Belle. And Belle loves to sing.

"Little town, it's a quiet village." She begins softly, hoping to find the right notes, "Everyday, like the one before."

Confident that she isn't completely messing up the song, she increases both her volume and her animation, "Little town, full of little people. Waking up to say…"

"Bonjour! Bonjour!"

The full stage lights flash on, the set behind her is uncovered, and the sleepy little town is awakened. The stage is loaded with lively characters, and the fun begins…

~*~

"Miss Emma, Miss Emma, you were amazing!" Emma Junior throws herself into Belle's poofy dress while attempting to give her a hug.

Emma laughs and crouches down, knowing it's hard to give hugs past all that golden material. "So were you! I've never seen a fork have so much fun!"

"That's because you were Belle!" Little Emma insists. "You made it such a blast for everyone! I never want to forget this night! So, I made a memory book, and I'm going to have the whole cast sign it!" Emma sweetly hands her a small autograph book, "Will you be the first to give me your autograph?"

"Aw, I would be honored." Emma's heart bursts with fireworks of love and bliss. The show has finally ended! All of the cast shone brightly, nailing their characters and pulling out impressive improv lines through any mistakes that were made. They sang, danced, laughed, shouted, and cried. It was a true theatric experience. But for Emma, it was so much more than just a silly little show. That night something changed.

Emma uses a thick black sharpie and signs Belle's name with big, cursive letters.

"No, I want your name!" Little Emma insists.

"My name?" Emma laughs, "Why?"

"You might be famous someday!"

Emma laughs again. "Uh, I wouldn't get your hopes up, sweetie."

"But I already have!" Emma continues chatting excitedly, "I think you're even better than Aurora Jasper!"

That *really* causes Emma to laugh. "Well, that's a first."

She hands little Emma her book and gives her one last hug. Little Emma happily skips off, eager to find her mother and go out for that pleasantly promised dinner outing.

A whole heard of small Townspeople approach her, carrying on about what a wonderful job they think she did. Emma can only blush and return the favor. She gives them all hugs, and despite the joy of the moment, there's a tad inkling of bitter mixed into the sweet. Their one night, only performance is over. She won't be seeing these kids again for a long time.

"Emma, you were ah-may-zing!" Celia and several of the other teens excitedly compliment her. "Like seriously. You were electric. And your singing voice is so pretty!"

"Aw, thank you." Emma sighs, happily resting her hands in the lap of her dress, "You were all just as spectacular. Like really, the whole cast went above and beyond."

"We did it!" Jeremiah gives her two excited high fives. "As always, you did a fabulous job at hating my guts."

"My pleasure!" Emma grins, "I mean, you make so easy, I'd hardly call that acting."

Jeremiah laughs, knowing her comment is all in good fun.

"Any word on how Julie and Miracle are doing?" Emma asks, hoping someone backstage might know.

"Not yet." Celia bites her bottom lip, "But sometimes no news is good news."

Emma nods, "That's true." She chooses to continue trusting the Lord, and allows her mind to switch gears, "I know everyone wants to get home before it gets too late, so I asked Mr. Garbonzo about us coming back to tear down and pack up tomorrow. He said that'll be fine. So, I guess I'll see all of you back here at noon? And if any parents want to come help, that would be greatly appreciated! We'll use all the extra hands we can get!"

After the group agrees to return tomorrow, Emma smiles and makes her way toward the Girls Dressing Room. She is *so* ready to get out of this heavy gown!

She enters the empty room, shocked to see someone standing there. It's Arden. With a bouquet of purple roses!

"I believe these are for Belle." His smile is like whipped cream with a cherry, topping a perfectly magical night.

Emma is floored. She doesn't even know what to say. And so, to keep herself from melting into a speechless little puddle of admiration, she opens her mouth and playfully asks, "Who let you back here?"

"I've got connections." He winks, handing her the bouquet.

"Thank you," Emma breathes, attempting to keep her voice steady. "Truly." She looks at him, "For everything. You saved me out there."

"Yeah, what was that about?" Arden asks with a laugh, "Were you planning on sitting there and reading the whole time?"

"Pretty much." Emma admits, "I was terrified. I didn't know what else to do."

"You know your mom is totally freaking out, right?"

"Huh? Why?" Emma asks, suddenly wondering if something is wrong with Aurora and the girls.

"Because her whole life revolves around trying to discover new talent. Meanwhile, her own daughter is sitting under her nose, acting completely nonchalant about everything, pretending like she's too cool for showbiz, while she's secretly hiding these killer talents! Emma. Your voice is amazing. And your acting? Crazy entertaining! I think your mom just found her new secret weapon."

"What?" Emma shakes her head, disliking the words coming out of his mouth. "No, that's ridiculous! My mom would never want me on her talent roster, and even if she did, I would refuse. Hollywood is such a mess!"

"So I've heard." Arden smiles.

"Be warned, I'm coming in!" a voice calls from outside the door.

Emma turns her head, just in time to see Jeremiah come through the door. His eyes are squeezed shut, and when he doesn't hear any screams, he opens his eyes. He's relieved to find Emma dressed, but surprised to see a random dude accompanying her.

"That was quite the entrance." Arden chuckles.

"It's the Girls Dressing Room," Jeremiah replies in a snooty tone, sounding as though his odd entrance should be easily understood. He turns to Emma, "There's someone here to see you."

"Who?" Emma asks, wondering why whoever it was doesn't just come backstage.

"I don't know, it's just some random chick and a super-tall dude who said they wanted to talk to us." Jeremiah doesn't offer much explanation.

"Well, that helps." Emma giggles.

"I don't know, they just sounded like it was important." Jeremiah shrugs, "Come out as soon as you're ready."

"Sure thing, boss." Emma rolls her eyes.

He leaves as quickly as he had appeared.

"Yup," Arden smiles, "I am definitely getting those Gaston vibes from him."

"The kid needs help." Emma shakes her head sadly.

"I'll wait for you out in the lobby," Arden tells her. "Your mom ran to put more money in the parking meter. We're a few blocks away, so I'll walk back with you. And then we're taking you to *Sour Apples* to celebrate. Oh! Don't forget your flowers."

Arden leaves, and Emma finds herself staring after him, wearing a dopy smile. She looks at the roses and sighs. "Best night ever," she whispers to no one but herself.

~*~

Emma escapes the Green Room, slightly disappointed to give up her ball gown. As relieved as she is to be wearing her comfortable old street clothes again, she can't deny the fact that dressing up was pretty magical. Like, when else will she ever be able to wear a golden ball gown again?

Finally, she spots Jeremiah on the empty stage, chatting with yes, just as he described, a super-tall dude and a random chick.

Well, we know Jeremiah is never going to be a writer. Emma smiles, getting a small dose of amusement from the thought.

"Wonderful performance tonight, Miss!" The tall man with a receding hairline and a large bald spot compliments her. "Your reenactment of Belle's tale swept me away!"

Emma thinks he appears too young to be going bald. He's perhaps only in his mid-40's or 50's?

"Thank you." Emma blushes, not sure what to do with all these dramatic compliments. Why is everyone making such a big deal about this? Sure, she had fun, but she wasn't *that* amazing.

"I'm Kendra Johnson, and this is my husband George." The curly-haired woman flashes a smile, locking her gaze on Emma. "We almost didn't make it tonight. But wow, what a huge mistake that would've been!"

"Aw, well I'm glad you guys came." Emma does her best to be kind and civil. Now that the show is over, her stomach is back to normal and is begging for food. She hasn't eaten anything all day! She's ready to leave and go stuff her face with appetizers at *Sour Apples*. "Do you have children in the show?"

"No." George shakes his head, "But we attend a lot of local musicals and actor showcases. We're talent scouts for Anderson's Academy of the Arts. Every year, the school grants us the honor of scouring LA and its surrounding suburbs for students we believe would flourish at Anderson. And every once in a while, we're lucky enough to stumble upon teens like you two. Fresh young talent who we believe would be deserving of the Betsy Dane Scholarship."

Emma glances at Jeremiah. Does he know what these people are talking about?

The excited expression on his face tells Emma that he does. Emma has never even heard of the Anderson's Academy of the Arts.

George digs into a folder tucked beneath his arm and pulls out two crisp certificates.

"And so, on behalf of Anderson Academy, we are so excited to present the two of you with full-ride scholarships to Anderson's Performing Arts High School!" Kendra hands

Emma a certificate, then gifts one to Jeremiah. Emma struggles to grasp what is actually going on here. She stares at the certificate, reading the words in fancy lettering. *So what, this is some kind of elite prep school for snooty kid actors?*

"Wow!" Jeremiah gasps, "This. This is unbelievable! I mean, this school costs a fortune! And the Betsy Dane Scholarship? Seriously!? I don't even know what to say right now, I'm literally freaking out inside!"

Kendra laughs. "This would be the perfect moment to toss confetti and give you balloons, but we didn't want to make a mess for the custodian to clean up!" She looks at Emma, "How are you feeling right now? Too happy for words?"

"Um," she looks up from the certificate. She hates to burst these people's bubbles, but what in the world is this? Some slick marketing scam to make people come to their high school? "This might sound like a stupid question, but who is Betsy Dane?"

"Who is Betsy Dane?!" Jeremiah's jaw drops. "Are you for real? Emma. Do you live under a rock or something?! Betsy Dane is the multimillionaire who helped build this school! The tuition fees are sky high, and before Betsy died she set a bunch of money aside for the school to use for scholarships and hand out to whoever they like."

"Not whoever we like," George corrects him. "You make it sound so casual! We typically only give away five or six scholarships a year. The waiting list for Anderson is a mile long, and there are thousands of kids around the city who wish this scholarship could be theirs. But we picked you guys!" The man appears particularly proud of himself. "We're looking forward to seeing you at our Open House on Saturday!"

"And then for orientation at the beginning of the school year!" Kendra flashes her luminescent smile once more and shakes Emma's hand. "We can't wait to work with you at Anderson!"

George shakes Jeremiah's hand and then Emma's. "Have a wonderful evening!"

Emma watches as the couple exits the scene. She glances once more at her certificate, folds it in half, and stuffs it in her denim bag. She is *so* ready to eat.

Jeremiah watches her in horror, acting as if she's just thrown her sacred Bible across the room. "What are you doing?!" he pounces on her with a condemning voice. "You're getting it all wrinkled!"

Emma looks up from where she's zipping her bag. She lifts an eyebrow. "Calm down! It's just a piece of paper."

Jeremiah acts as if she's just spoken blasphemy. "Just a piece of paper?!" he screeches. "That's your Golden Ticket to Anderson!"

"Yeah, a ticket to a place I'm never going." Emma heads down the stairs, "Come on, I think we're the last ones here. We need to lock up."

"Woah, Emma!" Jeremiah quickly follows her down the steps. His voice is frantic. "Do you not realize what just happened?! We just had a head on collision with destiny! Anderson Academy has produced some of the finest actors in Hollywood! Everybody who wants to be anybody is dying to get into that school! The tuition is insane. Opportunities like this don't just happen every day! I'm serious. Google Anderson. Find out how much that ticket is worth. It's going to blow your mind."

Emma flips off the main breaker and the entire auditorium goes dark. All they can see are red Exit lights several feet away. Emma quickly makes her way to the door, pushing through to the Lobby where she knows Arden is waiting.

"You ready?" Arden asks. His face is bright.

Emma smiles, "Yep. I'm starving."

"Emma, I know you don't take me seriously, but you have to realize the value of what's in your hand right now." Jeremiah then looks at Arden, "Make sure she doesn't throw away her lottery ticket."

Jeremiah swings his backpack over his shoulder and pushes through a door to the parking lot, "We'll finish this conversation tomorrow." He points a long finger in her direction, as if he's scolding her for something very important. Then he disappears through the door.

"What's that all about?" Arden asks.

"Oh, nothing important." Emma sighs, "He's just being dramatic about the fact that some uppity prep-school talent scouts are trying to get us to attend their Performing Arts School."

"Talent scouts?" Arden laughs, "Did you tell them your mom already claimed that job? I wouldn't be surprised if she booked for your first audition already."

Emma groans as she turns the pins on all six auditorium doors, making sure they're each locked. "You're kidding."

Arden opens the seventh door, knowing that will be the one they'll use to exit. "Not so much. You should've heard her after the show! You completely blew her away. Actually, I think it's safe to say, you blew everyone away."

"Well, I hope she's not going to make a big deal out of it," Emma tells Arden as they step outside. "Because *Beauty and the Beast* was my first acting gig and my last. The sooner my mom understands that, the better. Now I'm hungry, sweaty, burned out, sore, and mentally exhausted. All I ask is that she let me eat my onion rings in peace!"

~*~

"And to think you've been wasting your beautiful singing voice all these years for nothing but the shower!" Miss Maggie exclaims.

Emma's hand tiredly dips a corn chip into her small dish of queso. The glorious platter of appetizers set before them is slowly dwindling away. The onion rings, mini-tacos, and French fries have vanished. All that's left is a bowl of chips and several last dips of queso. Mom and Arden are finished eating. Emma's almost there.

Even though the food is nearly gone, Miss Maggie's energy-filled opinions are nowhere near being over. Emma knows when her mother is on a roll. She's just getting started.

"Oh, if only you would let me take you to one audition, sweetie!" Miss Maggie reveals the deepest desire of her heart, "I just know you would love it!"

"Mom." Emma sets her chip down, attempting to remain calm and kind. But after twenty minutes of hearing her talk like this, the woman doesn't know how to take no for an answer. "I already told you. I'm not going to any auditions. I'm not your next client, I'm not becoming an actress, and I'm not gonna be some stupid star! So, would you please, *please* stop talking about this?!"

"Sometimes I just don't understand you, Em." Miss Maggie shakes her head, "Hiding all these wonderful talents from us, acting as if you—"

"Hey, Miss Maggie, what did you think of that Jeremiah guy?" Arden suddenly jumps in, hoping to change the direction of the conversation. He can see how exasperated Emma is with her mother. She's on the verge of exploding, and he doesn't want her perfect day to be ruined by a massive blowout disagreement. From what Arden has observed of Emma's mom, she's somewhat like a puppy. Her attention can easily be diverted to become fixated on another topic entirely.

"Who?" Miss Maggie asks.

"Gaston." Arden reaches for a chip and dips it into the queso dish, "He was pretty impressive. I mean, his vocals left room for improvement, but his character was pretty convincing."

Miss Maggie still isn't getting it.

"You know, that guy Aurora was dating?" Arden reveals the final clue.

"OH!" Miss Maggie clasps her hands together, "Yes, him! He did have quite the stage presence, didn't he? Although, I have to disagree, I don't think theater quite suits him. But with a face like that, he would be an absolute treat for film though!" She gasps, "Ooooo, I wonder if he has an agent? Em, do you know, is he already a working actor?"

"No." Emma twists her lip, trying to remember if he's ever mentioned anything in the past. "He's really into competitive surfing, so I don't know if he has the time. He might be going to that Anderson Arts school though. He sounded pretty through the roof about it."

"Oh, honey, a school like that wouldn't get him anywhere!" Miss Maggie waves a dramatic hand through the air, "What he needs is an agent! Someone who can take him to auditions, help him make connections, and give him the experience he needs!"

"Someone like you?" Arden asks.

"Why, yes!" Miss Maggie is thrilled, "Someone exactly like me! Honey, do you have his number? I need to reach out to him before someone else does!"

"Mom, can't this wait 'til morning?" Emma groans. "This has been a crazy-long day. The last thing Jeremiah needs right now is a hyped phone call from you."

"I suppose you're right, the poor dear might be sleeping already." Miss Maggie sighs, "I'll wait until morning." She glances at the bill sitting on their table, "Well, if you two are finished, I'll go pay!" She pops up from the table and goes to the front of the restaurant.

"Thanks a lot," Emma speaks sarcastically, wiping her fingers off with a napkin.

"I was just trying to get your mom to stop bugging you about becoming her next project! Gaston seemed like a perfect distraction."

"And that might've been a good idea," Emma gives him half a complement, "until my mom actually signs him to her talent roster, and we have to sit here and watch his head inflate several sizes larger. If he becomes famous someday, I'm never going to forgive you."

"Hey, that'll make two of us." Arden laughs.

~*~

In Bella Adar...

Lena's shaking arm pulls the tight string of her bow as far back as her muscles will allow. Her arm tenses up, feeling resistance from the exercise. She firms her grip, careful not to let go before it's time.

As intense as the pulling-backward motion is, she knows it will only help launch the arrow forward with speed and precision. She gently bites the inside of her cheek, feeling as if it will somehow help her aim properly.

"And...now!" Captain Cepheus gives the go ahead, and Lena lets go. The arrow launches forth from her bow and penetrates the atmosphere. Within seconds it has landed in the target, just slightly off from the red center of the circular bullseye.

"Well done!" Captain Cepheus congratulates her, "I'm seeing great improvement! I find it hard to believe you've only been working on this skill for a few days and are already performing so impressively."

"Peter and—" Lena quickly catches herself mid-sentence.

She was about to say, *Peter and I used to practice archery in the woods.*

She quickly rephrases her thoughts. "I've had a bit of practice in previous years. The bow string was not as heavy, but I'm sure it helped with my aim."

She lowers her bow, unhappy with herself for speaking so freely of past times with Peter. Ever since Peter's sudden proposal, dozens of memories from their childhood and young adolescence have been floating through her mind. As much as she dislikes the distraction, she can't seem to come to a settled place within her heart concerning him. She has yet to give him an answer concerning his life changing question.

Lena is thankful for the focused time and energy required to master the skill of archery. It helps center her thoughts and rid her mind of anything other than meeting her target. Archery practice is not the time to be thinking about Peter. She shakes her head then hands her bow to Aurora. It's her turn.

Lena takes several steps back, knowing Aurora's skills are raw and untamed. The girl has a fierce determination about her. She just doesn't quite know how to aim yet.

"Fall back, everybody make room, back up!" Captain Cepheus announces.

Aurora twists her lip and places an unhappy hand on her hip. The young soldiers who practice archery at the range right beside them quickly collect their arrows and move out of the way.

"Oh, come on, I'm not that bad!" Aurora broadcasts to everyone within hearing distance. The large training room is dedicated to equipping the URIA for all sorts of important tasks. With an archery field, a small shooting range, and even a rock wall to help build stamina, their setup resembles a large, oversized gym.

"With all respect, Your Highness, you nearly nicked the ear of one of our men yesterday," Captain Cepheus reminds her.

Aurora squints her eyes. It's not like she forgot. "Maybe I was just trying to give him an earring." She shrugs.

Lena giggles. Oh, Aurora. She is truly one of a kind.

"You know, the URIA could use some serious wardrobe improvements. There's nothing wrong with a little bit of bling! This all black thing can be a little depressing." Aurora glances down at her outfit. She's officially conformed to the URIA dress code. With black combat boots, black pants, and a black tank, she's feeling ready to kick some serious bad guy behind. "I mean, yes, black is good for that whole sneaking around the woods in stealth mode thing, and I won't lie, I feel a bit like Katniss with my boots and my bow, now all I need is a braid and—"

"Your Highness, just aim." Captain Cepheus attempts to keep her on track. He already knows Aurora has the propensity to talk way too much. It also seems to be an excuse to buy time when she's nervous about performing a task.

Aurora steadies her feet in position and takes a deep breath. She gently lifts the bow, taking her own sweet time to make sure everything's centered. She doesn't want to make a total fool out of herself. Again.

She glances to the left and the right, making sure everyone has cleared out of the way. She would hate to injure an innocent bystander.

"Your Highness, keep your eyes on the target," Captain Cepheus reminds her. "Your arrow is going to fly wherever your eyes do. Stay locked in. No distractions."

Right, Aurora tells herself, *no distractions. That should be my new theme song.*

Adjusting to life in the URIA hasn't been easy. No, no, that line is far too gentle. For Aurora, living here isn't as simple as an outfit change. Everything in her entire universe has been flipped upside down and turned inside out. Nothing about her schedule, her company, her goals, ambitions, or the way she spends her time are anything like life back home.

Her new, intense training schedule has her doing pushups, running laps, and attending intense taekwondo sessions. She's never experienced such a dramatic life change. There's more than enough to keep her mind occupied throughout the day. But every night, as she flops into her tiny bunk bed, her body aching for a soak in the non-existent hot tub and her toes begging for a massage, she can't help but mourn over everything she's giving up. She thinks of Jeremiah, and Emma, and Miss Maggie, and her comfortable bed with a balcony overlooking the ocean. She thinks of her music, her career, her tour, and her fans. She even thinks of the annoying paparazzi and media monsters who never leave her alone. And now, they're gone.

The old Aurora has truly died. Her social media accounts lay barren as her fans message, sending thousands of questions about what's going on. It's in those moments, lying in bed, wide awake until midnight, when the tears come. The distractions, the doubts, the fears and the questions.

It's in those moments she's struck with panic, concerned that she's making a terrible, terrible mistake. But then she prays, and the Lord helps settle her heart. She remembers what's important and why she's here. She thinks of her sleeping sisters; sweet Lena and beautiful, innocent Elizabeth. Of everything they've given up to be here. And in the wake of those heartbreaking thoughts, Aurora remembers that her sacrifice is nothing compared to theirs. All at once, her pain doesn't seem quite so intense, and there's a small voice, whispering somewhere deep from within her heart, reminding her it's all going to be worth it.

No distractions. She tells herself again, attempting to zero in on the bullseyes. *The only way you're going to win this war is if you stay completely focused.*

Just then, a motor cart whooshes onto the scene. Though it isn't odd to see carts frequently whiz by, whoever it is hasn't been warned of her archery session. Aurora wears a determined look, wishing to prove to whoever's passing by at the moment, that she can do this. She's not going to be distracted. She can be just as good as Lena.

"Your Highness, wait!" Captain Cepheus warns, realizing she's ready to release the arrow.

But it's too late. Aurora has already let go and the arrow is flying forward. Except, it's not headed for the bullseye. It's going toward the cart!

"Look out!" Captain Cepheus warns.

Aurora lifts a horrified hand to her face, desperately hoping it won't hit the driver. The driver slams on the breaks, jolting both him and the passenger into a sudden jerk forward. Aurora's eyes grow even wider as she realizes who the driver is. It's Prince Asher of Tarsurella!

The arrow lowers itself, piercing into the front, right tire of the cart. Aurora gasps, relieved she hasn't injured anyone.

Asher leans over the steering wheel, examining the damage that's been done. His face is completely astonished, wondering how the Princess could manage to have such terrible aim. They weren't driving anywhere *near* the target!

He glances at his passenger, Liam Henderson, who wears a small smirk. Asher can tell he's trying to keep himself from full out laughing.

"Looks like I'm in time for target practice," Asher finally jokes, unsure of what else to say.

Aurora still has a horrified hand up to her face. She wishes she could sink even deeper into the ground. Her face is hot.

"My apologies, Your Highness!" Captain Cepheus bursts out. "As you can see, we are still very much in the beginning stages of learning this skill."

Aurora frowns, displeased to hear the Captain speak so negatively of her. "Here, let me go again, I demand a do-over."

"Perhaps," Captain Cepheus slips the weapon out of Aurora's hand, "we'll let your sister have a turn. Elizabeth, you're next."

Aurora huffs, unable to shake the embarrassment. She glances at Prince Asher as he makes his way toward them. He's accompanied by another man whom Aurora has seen around the base with him. She places an unhappy hand on her hip, wishing she had a second chance to prove she isn't such a dimwit. There's nothing she hates more than when guys don't think she can do something. Especially cute guys.

Elizabeth nervously receives the bow from Captain Cepheus. She doesn't want to do this. Her skills are far worse than Aurora's. Elizabeth feels shamefully inadequate compared to her sisters. They both seem to be growing better and stronger with each passing day, but Elizabeth doesn't sense any kind of improvement at all. It's quite clear she was never intended to do these kinds of things. Elizabeth knows it's not a woman's place to fight. The rigorous training schedule doesn't bid well with her. She's shed more than just a few tears. Everything about her new life in the URIA is painfully hard. The only true joy she finds in her days is the moments she spends reading the Bible.

God's Word, the book that was closed off to her for so many years, is finally coming alive. Even after their exhausting days, she stays up for several hours in the candlelight, reading as much as she possibly can. Every story and every line is like nothing she's ever experienced before. She had no idea that God's ways were so mighty and powerful!

She's been wonderstruck by the miracles of Moses and how God parted the Red Sea for his people. She has been baffled by Shadrach, Meshach, and Abednego not burning up in the fiery furnace, and comforted by Daniel being protected in the midst of the wicked lion's den. She's been strengthened by Esther's resolve to save her people, and heartbroken by Jesus' perfect sacrifice on the cross. With each new discovery, Elizabeth feels her heart coming alive. With each sentence, it's as if her old self is being stripped away, and someone new is forming and coming out of a barren cocoon.

Elizabeth had no idea she was in so much bondage. She didn't know her people were following legalistic rules God never intended for her to follow. After speaking with Lena and asking many questions, she finally found the courage to remove her Prayer Cap and white apron. Even though Elizabeth is slowly changing on the inside with each passing day, she's not ready to change the outside yet. She remains in her black dress and wouldn't dare exchange it for the close fitting black pants her sisters wear. Even though she is free in Christ, Elizabeth knows that some things about her modesty and personal beliefs will never change.

The one thing she *does* wish would change faster is her weak and tired muscles. She's been sore for days, and all these silly activities only make her feel that much worse. Lena says the only way to get stronger is to first break the muscles by making them weaker, but Elizabeth isn't sure if she agrees. She'll have to search the Bible and see if there's anything like that mentioned.

Elizabeth tries with all her might to pull back the heavy string, but it slips too soon, and the arrow falls to the ground. Her shoulders sag and she can feel tears lingering dangerously close to the surface.

"May I offer a tip, Your Highness?" Prince Asher kindly speaks up.

Elizabeth helplessly looks at him, quite frankly wishing for no such thing.

"Yes, we will take all the assistance we can get!" Captain Cepheus speaks up on her behalf.

Asher takes several steps closer, and Elizabeth cannot erase the hard, unfriendly look from her face. She hates archery.

"I've learned from personal experience that your form is super-important," Asher begins. "The posture you begin with directly effects where your arrow is gonna go. Try again, but this time focus on making your elbow as straight as possible."

Elizabeth unwillingly lifts the bow, her weak arm already shaking from having to pull it back so hard.

"See, your elbow isn't aligned with your forearm." Asher corrects her, "You want to form a perfect T. Think about making your arm as flat as a board, perfectly in line with your sights."

She glances at the young man, surprised to see him standing so close to her. His kind eyes and dark wispy hair nearly startle her. All at once, she realizes who he reminds her of.

Jonah. She feels an unwelcome lump in her throat as the memories return.

He gently reaches for her arm and softly lifts it higher, helping her come into the proper alignment.

"There you go." He smiles, "Now relax your fingers and take a deep breath before releasing. Focus on the target and think of nothing else other than something that makes you feel total peace."

Elizabeth does her best to follow his instructions, but his nearness makes her even more nervous. She tries to set her mind on something happy. Something that will settle her. She thinks of Jonah and their last picnic together. She imagines that he's here, standing beside her, offering her a word of encouragement. Elizabeth inhales deeply and releases the arrow with her breath.

Suddenly, the arrow is gone, and it hits the bottom of the bullseye.

Her mouth falls open. She didn't hit the floor this time!

"Well done, Your Highness!" Captain Cepheus lets out a small clap of applause.

"Way to go, Elizabeth!" Lena cheers.

Elizabeth can't help but smile. She actually did it! Perhaps she's not a total failure when it comes to these sorts of activities after all!

"Thank you." She looks at Asher, remembering to thank him for his tips. "That was the first time I hit the target!"

"And it definitely won't be your last." Asher smiles, "Don't thank me, I'm willing to help in whatever capacity you need."

He glances at his friend, "That's what Liam and I are here for."

"Break time," Captain Cepheus announces. "We'll resume in ten minutes." He turns to Asher, "Perhaps we should assess the damage done to that tire?"

The three men walk away, and Aurora makes a face. "It's just a tire," she murmurs to Lena. "I'm sure there's more where those came from."

"Oh, of course!" Lena smiles, hoping to offer her some encouragement, "A tire is easily replaced. But a functioning body part? Not so much."

"Ha, ha." Aurora rolls her eyes, knowing that her terrible archery skills have become an easy target for teasing. She heard some soldiers in the Mess Hall joking about it just yesterday. But she quickly set them straight.

"Don't worry, Aurora, you're getting much better!" Lena offers her a kind pat on the arm, "These things take time. Be patient with yourself."

"Says the girl who was like, born a champion!" Aurora nudges her, "You're so good at everything! Archery, taekwondo, kick-boxing…heck, even rock climbing!"

"I don't know," Lena quickly shakes her head. "You beat me pretty badly in that sparring match yesterday. Your roundhouse kick is quite power packed!"

~*~

"That's it, begin with your fighting stance. Feet planted, elbows tucked in, fists locked, ready to jab," the instructor tells Lena. "Your starting position is the most important. No matter what happens, if someone sneaks up from behind or confronts you in the front, you must get to your feet and find your fight stance. Any other posture is going to set you up for failure."

Lena nods, keeping her fists tight, prepared for whatever the instructor might say next.

Suddenly, without warning, he gently slips his foot beneath hers, causing her to tumble backwards onto the ground. Thankfully, a fluffy, blue mat breaks her fall.

Elizabeth winces from where she watches on the sidelines. These training sessions make her so nervous! They never know what their instructor will do next!

Lena scrambles to her feet, returning to the fight stance as quickly as possible.

"Faster," he tells her, "I could have killed you already."

His foot knocks hers out once more, and she gets up, quicker this time.

"Even faster, you have to be back on your feet before I can blink." He topples her over one last time.

Lena leaps up, and the instructor is truly impressed. "Nice. Elizabeth, you're next."

Elizabeth's eyes grow wide with fear. She hates fighting in the ring. Even more than archery.

As soon as she arrives, the instructor is already critiquing her, "You look terrified. You have to believe and be bold. Fight stance, go!"

Elizabeth tries to remember what she's supposed to do. She clenches her fists and lifts them near her face.

Before she can think about what comes next, she is on the floor.

"Umph!" Elizabeth lets out a small cry of discomfort.

"Up to your feet, up to your feet, go, go go!"

"Come on, Elizabeth, you can do this!" Lena cheers from the sidelines.

"You got this, girl!" Aurora joins in to encourage her. She knows how hard this is for Elizabeth.

She tries to stand up, but it's not fast enough. As soon as she's standing, her instructor knocks her over again.

She feels like crying. She hates being on the floor! She stands up, but it's not fast enough.

The instructor sighs, "Okay, change of plan. Let's practice your roundhouse kicks. Begin!"

Elizabeth racks her brain to remember what she must do. While attempting to rehearse the steps in her mind, the instructor barks, "Fight, chamber, pivot, extend, react, recover!"

Elizabeth is still on the second step, attempting to chamber by lifting her leg then turning for a pivot. But as she turns, she loses her balance and falls over, face first.

Aurora sighs, truly feeling bad for her sister.

"I cannot do this!" Elizabeth cries as she stands up. "And I am not going to try, either!" Elizabeth quickly exits the ring, fighting back tears.

The instructor sighs, knowing Elizabeth is his weakest and most sensitive student.

"Aurora!" he barks. "Get up here!"

Aurora offers her sister's hand a squeeze before entering the ring. She walks confidently toward him, ready to show off what she knows. Strangely enough, Aurora actually enjoys their self-defense lessons. It's surprisingly fun learning how to fight.

"Roundhouse kick, go!"

Aurora whips into action, performing the kicks perfectly.

"Front kick!" he calls, wanting her to perform each action on demand. "Drop kick! Back kick! Side kick!"

"Very good." He nods, pleased with her display, "Show me your first kata! Go!"

Aurora walks through the series of familiar steps she's been working hard to memorize. She tries her best to stay focused, but a distraction is brewing in the distance. A group of new recruits are moving in. Aurora knows she shouldn't allow herself to be caught off guard, but it's hard to stay focused when there are men in uniform in the room.

Sergeant Crawdad is barking off commands of his own, telling the men to pick up the pace and run like their lives depend on it. "Move, move, move it!" His loud voice echoes through the training facility, "Is that as fast as you men can go? I shouldn't even call you men! You're not deserving of the title! My grandmother can run faster than you!"

Lena glances over her shoulder, wondering if Peter might be in the group. She sighs, wondering how he is faring with all the intense training. It's not like anything he's used to. Peter is such a free spirit, she can't imagine Peter willingly subjecting himself to obey the commands of a harsh Sergeant.

As the men pass by, her breath catches. Sure enough, Peter is there, running in the third line to the left. His face is flush red, and he appears as though he could fall over at any second. She quickly looks away, not wanting to make eye contact with him. She hates that she's been avoiding him. But she just doesn't know what to say, or how to act around him. Why did Peter have to go and make everything so awkward?!

All at once, Sergeant Crawdad calls for the men to stop moving. "HALT!" he shouts at the top of his lungs, his voice slightly cracking in pitch.

The men stop running.

Okay, Aurora is really distracted now. What's going on?

"How dare you men think you can just jog on through here without stopping to honor our most noble Princesses?!" Sergeant Crawdad scolds them.

Lena can't help but giggle. This Sergeant seems a little wacky. Wasn't he just telling them to run faster? Which command does he want them to obey? Poor Peter must be so flustered.

"What do you think, the URIA is nothing but a pack of barbaric wolves?! We're not just training soldiers, we're training gentlemen! So, stop and honor the Princesses, who are deserving of your adoration!" Sergeant Crawdad yells. He then turns to Princess Lena and softens his voice. "Forgive us, Your Majesty, for passing through in the middle of your training session. We did not know you would be here."

"Oh, it's no problem!" Lena grins, "Us three girls are not any more important than the rest of you. We all must train, as we are in this together."

"You heard the Princess, back to training!" Sergeant Crawdad announces at the top of his lungs. "What are you doing just standing around here, gawking over these beautiful ladies for?! Put your eyes back in your head where they belong and get a move on it!"

Several of the men begin to move, thinking they're now supposed to run, but Sergeant Crawdad chews them out for it.

"What do you think you're doing?! Did I tell you to move out of formation?! Drop and give me thirty!"

The clueless men stare at one another, unsure as to what they're supposed to do. "NOW!" the Sergeant reinforces his command.

The men drop to the ground to begin their pushups.

"And for the rest of you!" Sergeant Crawdad chews out the other men who are still standing in formation, "When I say run, I mean run! Why, I've never seen such pathetic runners in my life! I'm tempted to write home to your mothers and say, 'Ma'am, you did not send us men, you sent us worms! And they all run like GIRLS'."

"Hey!" Aurora snaps suddenly, her voice echoing throughout the large room. She stops in the middle of her taekwondo lesson and addresses the sergeant. "*What* did you just say?"

Lena can't help but smile. It appears as though Aurora is about to give the Sergeant a taste of his own sour medicine.

"I said they run like girls, Your Highness!"

"Oh really?" Aurora places sassy hands on her hips, "I would think that would be a compliment. I hope they fight like girls too."

"Don't mind fighting like girls, as long as we don't fight like *those* girls," a quiet voice remarks from the line of solders. It's enough to cause smirks on the faces of several young men.

Aurora's eyes search the crowd, wondering who would speak such a thing.

"Watch your mouth, cadet!" Sergeant Crawdad appears to know exactly who spoke it. "Everyone with the exception of Cadet Julyan, move out! NOW!"

The men quickly fall out of formation and run out of the room.

Lena watches her sweet Peter pass and wonders how he's managing all of this new stress.

Aurora leaves the ring to address the young man who spoke so rudely.

After the crowd of soldiers have dispersed, Sergeant Crawdad is standing alone with Kehahi Julyan.

"Apologize to the Princess, Cadet!" Sargent Crawdad tells him.

"I find no need to do so, Sergeant," Kehahi speaks with determined eyebrows. "From what I've seen, Her Highness is in no place to hope we would fight like them. If we did, Raymond would defeat us in nothing less than a heartbeat."

"He's right, Sergeant," Aurora snaps. "He doesn't need to apologize. He just needs to be proved wrong. From what I've seen of your platoon, the men are struggling just as much, if not more than we are."

The Sergeant opens his mouth, but it is clear he has completely lost control of this conversation.

Kehahi laughs, "Oh really?

"Really." Aurora takes a determined step closer, "All *you* guys are doing is running around, doing pushups, bouncing through relay courses, and climbing that silly little rock wall thing. Meanwhile, we're learning how to actually fight."

"You want me to fight you, Princess?" Kehahi reacts with an unexpected fire in his eyes, feeling as if she's taunting him. "Because our men know how to bring it in the ring."

"It would be my pleasure to beat you, Cadet." Aurora is way too hyped up to back down. She's been waiting for her first real fight, and now it's about to happen!

"Your Highness–" Sergeant Crawdad struggles to regain control of the situation, "With all due respect, you, uh, the Cadet will, uh…."

"What? Are you scared he's gonna hurt me?" Aurora snaps, clearly not thinking logically. The guy is a whole head taller than she.

"Actually, I am." Kehahi laughs, "I wouldn't want you to break a nail or something."

"The only thing that's gonna be broken is your egotistic male pride," Aurora warns him before turning on her heel and heading for the ring.

Kehahi grins, pleased with the challenge. He had no idea the Princess was such a fiery little twerp.

"Cadet, I command you not to do this!" Sergeant Crawdad warns him.

"Sorry." Kehahi's smile doesn't disappear, "It appears to be my royal duty at the moment." He winks and joins Aurora in the ring.

"Aurora, don't be so foolish!" Lena warns her. "He's going to beat you!" She quickly looks away, "Oh dear, I can't even watch."

She and Elizabeth exchange concerned glances then hide their faces in one another's arms.

Aurora quickly finds her fight stance.

"Oh, taekwondo. Is that what we're doing?" he asks playfully.

"What else is there?" Aurora looks at him like he doesn't have a clue.

"Judo, Jujutsu, boxing…take your pick. Unless of course, you'd rather play Bingo or something you'd actually have a chance at winning."

Aurora has had enough talk. She lifts her leg, ready to smash him with a roundhouse kick. But Kehahi grabs her leg and knocks her to the floor.

It takes her a second to realize what has happened. She quickly gets up, dusting off her legs and her pride. She *is* going to beat him. She's determined. Aurora attempts to surprise him with a front kick, but it's almost as if he knows what she's going to do before he does it.

He grabs her leg, and she attempts to wiggle out of his grip. She quickly flips down to her hands, doing half a somersault, using her free leg to smash him in the stomach.

Surprising enough, the blow causes Kehahi to lose his grip on Aurora's leg, and she's back on her feet.

"Oh! Elizabeth, look!" Lena encourages her to open her eyes, "She's still standing!"

Aurora attempts several other kick combos, but soon Kehahi is throwing punches. Aurora ducks, somewhat terrified as his large fist comes her way. Okay, maybe this was a bad idea. They haven't gotten into punching in their training yet! She quickly thinks of ways to avoid him and attempts to toss a punch of her own. When her palm nears his face, he grabs her wrist and quickly twists it backwards.

It doesn't hurt, as Kehahi is careful not to injure her. But it's still wildly frustrating.

As she fumbles to escape, the next thing she knows, he has her in a headlock.

Aurora turns her head toward his chest and quickly jabs him in the stomach.

"Wow," Kehahi nods as she scurries back to her standby fight stance, "you're determined. I'll give you that much."

"I'm still on my feet, aren't I?" She grins, "And at the end of the day, that's all that counts."

Aurora gets ahead of herself, suddenly excited with her mini-victory. She lets out an intimidating shout, hoping it will add to the fear factor, and pounces on his back. She locks his head beneath her elbow, scheming an on-the-fly plan to get him to the ground from here.

But Kehahi isn't fazed.

Next thing Aurora knows, he's flipped her onto the floor and has firmly pinned her to the ground. "One, two, three," he counts, his eyes clearly pleased with his accomplishment. "Winner."

He lets go of Aurora, stands up and offers a hand to help her to her feet.

She frowns but takes it anyway. "This isn't over," she tells him.

"Actually, I think it is." He chuckles, turning to exit the ring.

"I'll fight you again!" she calls after him.

"When?" He shakes his head, wondering why the feisty little thing just won't quit.

"Tomorrow. At noon."

His puzzled explanation is asking for more info.

Aurora continues, "You clearly know what you're doing, and I need to learn from the best. You'll be a great teacher because I know you won't take it easy on me or let me win. Sergeant Crawdad will see to it that your schedule is clear to assist in my training from now on."

Kehahi's eyebrows challenge her, but he almost appears pleased with the command. "Is that all, Your Highness?"

"Yes." She nods spunkily, "It is. You're dismissed, Cadet."

~*~

Episode 7

"Emma! I hope your bags are packed!" Miss Maggie bursts into Emma's bedroom.

She looks up from where she's sitting on the edge of her bed, tying her skinny, white Converse laces. "Why, where are we going?" Emma feels a spark of excitement. Perhaps Aurora needs them in Bella Adar. Now *that* would be an adventure.

"Obsession just landed in the Billboard Top 200!" Miss Maggie resembles a shook-up bottle of Pepsi poised to explode, "They're number 164! *Bubblegum* is giving the green light for *Acid Rain's* music video!"

"Oh yeah, Arden just texted me. He's through the roof excited!" Emma stands up and grabs her denim, long-sleeved, button-down shirt. She slips it over her grey tank top and catches her reflection in the full-length mirror. For some reason, she always manages to get her buttons crooked if she's not paying close enough attention. "Aren't they gonna film it in LA?" she asks, focusing on clasping each tiny button.

"Nope, the *Bubblegum* creatives had a far better idea! They want to shoot select scenes in London and Paris!" Miss Maggie squeals, "Which means we're going to Europe!"

"When do we leave?" Emma asks. She's just headed out the door to tear down the *Beauty and the Beast* set.

"Tomorrow!" Miss Maggie's sing-song tone tells Emma she's thrilled with the development, "The boys have several meetings today, then we're off for their next big adventure! Eeeep, honey, it's happening! *Acid Rain* is climbing the charts! I knew all this investment in Arden was going to pay off!"

"I know he's one of your clients, but that phrase just sounded creepy. Like he's responsible for paying our bills."

"I know it must be strange for you," Miss Maggie sympathizes, "mixing business with friendship, but in Hollywood this *is* business. And to be completely honest, with Aurora currently AWOL, it's important for me to have a client doing well financially."

"I understand." Emma sighs, "But try not to put so much pressure on him, okay? He should be doing music for the love of it. Not for the money."

"Of course, sweetie." Miss Maggie smiles, "So, are you ready to go?"

"Yup." Emma follows her mother out the bedroom door and down the stairs.

"I just got an email this morning with some fresh leads." Miss Maggie reaches for her car keys on the counter, "Pilot season is coming up, so as soon as we get back from Europe, I'll get some of my clients hitting the pavement with auditions and hopefully booking some jobs. Emma dear, it's the perfect time of year for you to play around and get your toes wet! In fact, I was just reading about a new show where they're looking for a Caucasian, female lead, exactly your age–"

"Mom," Emma stops her. "We already talked about this. I am not auditioning. End of story. Haven't I already made myself perfectly clear? I don't want anything to do with Hollywood."

"You have," Miss Maggie admits, "but what I just can't seem to understand is why? Are you afraid of performing? Are you worried about failing or not booking a job? Emma, you're a very talented young woman! And with a little bit of vocal training and several acting classes, I believe you could go far in this business! You've been hiding away all these talents for years, and now that they're out, I don't want to see you bury them all again! Just think how much fun this would be for us!"

"Fun for us?" Emma echoes, unable to hide the harshness in her voice. "Since when have you cared about doing anything with *us* in mind? Everything you do is for Hollywood! It's all about finding your next big client, then micromanaging every aspect of their lives, completely forgetting about what it means to be a family!"

"Emma." Miss Maggie places a hand on her hip, "That's not fair. Just because I take my work very seriously and pour my heart into it, doesn't mean that I don't have time for you."

"Yes, it does, Mom!" Emma insists, feeling her emotions growing shaky. She wasn't planning on having this conversation. Especially not now, on their way out the door. "When's the last time you and I spent some real, quality, mother-daughter time together? When's the last time you turned off your cell phone, forgot about everybody else, and sat down undisturbed for a one-on-one conversation?"

"Emma, you know things have been crazy lately." Miss Maggie attempts to defend herself, "With everything going on with Aurora and Arden and all the budget cuts at *Bubblegum*, you know I've had a lot on my plate! And don't place all the guilt on me! You've been just as busy with your musical!"

"When's the last time, Mom?" Emma stands firm with her question, "Do you even remember?"

Miss Maggie hesitates then finally admits with a sigh, "No. No, I suppose I don't."

"It was the first day Arden came. He and his mom showed up on our doorstep and completely barged into our time together. You promised we were going to do tacos and PJ's, and that work wouldn't get in the way. But it did. It always does."

"Well, what do you want me to do Emma, quit my job and go crawling back to your father, begging for money?!" Miss Maggie sounds as if Emma has struck a deep nerve, "As much as I'd love to stay home and dance around in our PJ's, someone has to pay the bills! Just think what might've happened if I told Arden and his mother to go home that afternoon?! Do you think *Acid Rain* would be in the place they are today if I would've done that?!"

Emma bites her lip. Her poor, frazzled mother, is showing obvious signs of stress and concern over their current lot in life. Emma knows it isn't fair to accuse her mother of being a workaholic. But isn't it true? Shouldn't her mother wake up and face the facts?

Emma quickly looks away, wondering if she should continue to speak what's on her mind. Should she just suppress her feelings and forget about it? Like she always does? Stuffing everything inside and never finding a good way to talk about things until she suddenly explodes like an overbaked potato in the microwave?

"Maybe not," Emma speaks just above a whisper, "but at least I'd know you care enough to spend an entire day with me."

~*~

"Last night was lit!" Jeremiah continues to chat excitedly as he rolls up the long, fleece backdrop with the image of Beast's castle imprinted onto it. "I was up 'til 3 AM Googling

[266]

Anderson Academy. You should see their campus, Emma! It's like a miniature college! The dorm rooms are huge, their theater is twice the size of this one, and their outdoor cafeteria has a built in Chick-fil-A!"

"So, I'm assuming this means you're planning on going?" Emma asks as she rolls the background up from the other end. Jeremiah won't stop talking about the school. Clearly, he's excited.

"Of course!" Jeremiah suddenly changes his tune, "Well, maybe."

"What's wrong, not sure you want to eat Chick-Fil-A every day for lunch?" Emma teases.

"I haven't told my parents yet."

"Why not?" Emma is curious.

"Well, my dad isn't really down with the idea of me becoming an actor," Jeremiah explains. He and Emma meet in the center of the stage, after their opposite ends roll up and join together. Jeremiah picks up the bulky roll, which resembles a tightly wrapped burrito. He maneuvers it onto his shoulder and cautiously descends the stage steps.

"Surely you don't have to be pursuing acting professionally to go to that school," Emma shares her thoughts. "It's a full-ride scholarship, right? Can't you just go because you enjoy acting as a hobby, but don't want to make a career out of it?"

"Exactly!" Jeremiah lifts up a frustrated hand as he drops the backdrop, wishing his parents were listening to Emma's words right now. "But my dad thinks acting is a total waste of time. He says I should be out on the waves, training for the surf circuit. Not prancing around onstage like Peter Pan."

"It's kind of funny how parents think they know what their kids should pursue." Emma reaches for a metal bar, beginning to detach the sturdy frame where the background once hung.

"Tell me about it!" Celia jumps into the conversation, "My mom has this obsession with organic soaps. She pours all these natural, essential oils and herbs into her mysterious mixtures and gets so giddy over it, like she's won the lottery! She wants me to learn how to make them and help with the business. But what *doesn't* she get about the fact that I don't care about soap the way she does?"

"I think parents mean well," Emma speaks thoughtfully, thinking of her own overly passionate and overbearing mother, "but they have to realize that their dreams are not always our dreams. And the more they push, the more we're just going to go the opposite direction."

"Yeah!" Celia agrees. "It's like *High School Musical*!" She turns to Jeremiah, "And you're like Troy, the basketball boy who doesn't want to follow his dad's plan for his life." She giggles, "Except he wants you to be a surf star, not a basketball jock."

"But I love surfing," Jeremiah sighs, "and that's part of the problem. I thought I'd be totally down with continuing to do the surf circuit, not even thinking about acting again. Until Anderson came along. Now I'm not even sure what I want anymore." He looks at Emma, "What about you?"

"What about me?" she asks slowly.

"Are you going?"

"Of course, I'm not going!" Emma speaks what she believes to be the obvious. "I already told my mom that *Beauty and the*

Beast is my first and *last* onstage appearance. I have no desire whatsoever to become a professional actress."

"But didn't you just say that you don't have to go pro to be at Anderson? What if you just went for fun? It's totally free, isn't it?"

"I would go, I would go!" Celia bursts out. "Ugh, you two are so stinkin' lucky! Emma, if you're not going to take the scholarship, can you at least give it to me?"

"I'm sorry, but the last thing I want to do with my life is attend a crazy expensive school with a bunch of stuck-up rich kids who wear brand name clothing and claw each other's eyes out for the next big breakout role." Emma shudders, "Sounds like a nightmare."

"Wow, you really don't know much about this school, do you?" Jeremiah shakes his head, "Anderson isn't Hollywood. The kids who attend that school aren't trying to be Disney Channel stars. They're studying to develop their craft, dig deeper into the roots of creative arts, theater and music theory. Anderson is all about the love and history of the arts, not some big, flakey star machine obsessed with cranking out generic teen actors."

Emma is surprised. If Jeremiah is speaking the truth, which Emma still can't be sure of, then this Anderson Academy sounds far different than what she previously thought. She recalls her mother's words from last night when they talked about Jeremiah's potential acting career. 'Oh honey, a school like that wouldn't get him anywhere. What he needs is an agent!'

It's a far different perspective for Emma. Living with her commercial driven mother has nearly brainwashed her to forget that there are people out there who enjoy acting, theater, and the arts, all for the simple joy of artistic expression.

"Well, I hope you're right," Emma tells him as she unhooks another set of metal bars. "Because the last thing we need in this world is a school full of starry-eyed high schoolers inflated with false hope and impossible dreams. I've never seen any kind of true integrity in the arts, but I like the idea of it. Sadly, the long line of people waiting to become Hollywood's next disastrous train wreck is *way* too over populated."

~*~

"Good morning, Sleeping Beauty."

Emma's head bobs forward as the plane comes to a halt. She forces herself to open her eyes and remove her head from where it's smooshed against the window pane. She has a terrible, sleepy taste in her mouth, and all her muscles hurt.

"Have a good cat nap?" Arden persists, attempting to jog Emma from her state of zombie-like sleepiness.

She releases a groan and attempts to crack her neck to the left. But the tight kink doesn't come out.

"I hate sleeping on planes," she grumbles.

"I dunno, you looked pretty comfortable to me."

Emma casts her tired eyes toward him, suddenly feeling awkward about the fact that she fell asleep beside him.

"Just FYI, you talk in your sleep."

"I do not!" Emma argues.

"Yes, you do."

Emma's glare intensifies. If Arden doesn't stop his yammering on about nonsense, Emma is liable to smack him alongside the head. Emma is particularly gifted in the area of being grumpy after she wakes up. Especially if it's mixed with jet-lag, European airports, and hyper guys who are un-humanly excited about plane rides.

"You were calling out my name over and over again!" he teases in a mellow-dramatic tone, "Arden, Arden, ARDEN!"

Emma's eyes widen as he practically shouts on the plane. She grits her teeth together, hoping he'll quiet down. Why does he have to be so embarrassing?!

She punches him in the arm, "Shhh!" She scolds him, "Goodness gracious, we can't take you anywhere!"

"I heard her too, man!" Jay pops up from behind them. He removes his seatbelt and stands, even though the airline stewardess hasn't given permission for him to do so yet. "She was singing lines from Obsession." He winks.

Emma's heartbeat quickens as her nerves flop around like freshly caught fish. Surely these guys are just kidding, right? Even though she secretly enjoys the song, there's no way she's singing it in her sleep. Is she?

"Just the first among millions in the UK!" Arden broadcasts excitedly. "Look out London, the next hit boyband has arrived!"

"The weather is clearly excited that you're here," Emma mumbles, turning back toward the window. A dreary, heavy grey sheet of rain slams upon the plane.

"It's *Acid Rain*." Arden shrugs.

Emma smiles, even though she's staring at a crazy rainstorm. As exhausted as she is, she's secretly excited about whatever wonderful thing might be coming next.

~*~

"There it is!" Miss Maggie squeals, "The glorious Tower Bridge! The place where we will, very sadly, not be filming your music video."

Emma leans toward the window on the bottom level of their double-decker bus. The city is suffering the blow of a torrential downpour. As beautiful as the bridge is, she's happy they're not filming. Standing out in the rain wouldn't be any fun.

"Dude, look, it's the Thames River!" Jay bursts out. "James Bond filmed some of his most epic scenes there! Miss Maggie, I just got a killer idea for the video! We should rent jet-ski's and ride them down the river!"

"What does that have to do with *Obsession*?" Miss Maggie cocks her head, wondering how it fits with the video storyline.

"Nothing." He shrugs, "But we would look so epic on wave runners!"

"Where is the logic behind this?" Emma observes, "We came all the way to London just so you guys could go to a studio and film inside with a green screen? How does that make any sense?"

"Well, that wasn't the original plan," Miss Maggie answers. "We were hoping the boys were going to film outdoors. But it's supposed to rain for the next four days." She frowns, unhappy with the forecast on her iPhone.

"So, when do we get to try the local grub?" Arden asks. "I've been dying to try Pie and Mash, ever since I saw it on *Doctor What!*"

"I'm hungry too," Emma agrees. "But I think I'll just stick to fish and chips."

"Oh, come on Emma, live on the wild side!" Arden encourages her yet once again to break through her usual boxes of mundane living, "Expand your horizons and wet your palette with jellied eel!"

Emma shudders. She can't imagine eating such an awful thing.

A few blocks later, the bus pulls over and *Acid Rain's* entourage filters out. They dash into a darling little café and find an empty table.

Emma scans the menu, even though she already knows what she's getting. She finds it rather fascinating to read about all the unique foods. She can hear the boys' rambunctious conversation swirling all around her.

"You might want to give a second thought to the eel, Arden," Sensible Matthew suggests.

Emma looks up, having already observed that his personality is far different from the other two. Arden and Jay are like two extremely hyper, shamefully immature hyenas who excitedly feed off one another. But Matthew, the platinum blondie, is more like a wise lion, doing his best to keep them grounded and orderly. Emma hopes he won't try too hard. She knows from experience that attempting to keep Arden's energy corralled is a very taxing job. Arden is not for the faint of heart.

"Yeah, if you end up kissing our music video girl, you don't want your breath to smell like sea food!" Jay adds.

Emma freezes. Wait. Music video girl. What? This is the first she's heard of such a thing.

"Huh?" Emma can't help but ask the question. She needs answers. And pronto.

"The video girl. You know, the love interest?" Miss Maggie answers. "I'm told that *Bubblegum* has cast a darling young woman for the role. I still haven't seen her yet, which I'm not too thrilled about, but I'm sure she's going to be just perfect." She grins through clenched teeth, "At least, we can only hope she will be."

"I don't get it." Emma feels herself growing oddly uncomfortable with the idea, "Why do they need some random chick in their video? What's she supposed to do, just dance around and serve as eye candy? That's completely disrespectful to women all over the world!"

"Oh, no, honey, she's not a dancer." Miss Maggie shares what she knows, "She's the girl *Obsession* is about! The storyline is that all three of the boys are in love with the same girl. They're following her around the city, attempting to get her attention, but she won't give them the time of day."

"Well, that's original," Emma grumbles sarcastically. *Seriously? Are they going to ruin Acid Rain's amazing song with some fake Barbie girl, and a stupid plot that's been done ten-million times? But I guess that's Hollywood for you.* She sighs. *They squeeze out every ounce of creativity and uniqueness in exchange for cookie cutter, pop-culture mania. Even so, the demographic eats it up, so they continue feeding them 'what works'. Isn't it time someone breaks out and changes the mold?*

Emma was hoping that perhaps *Acid Rain* might be just the guys to do that. But apparently, it's not in the grand plan.

"It's too late. I'm already committed," Arden tells his band members. "I'm going for the eel. I've passed the point of no return."

Emma makes a disgusted face, then leans over to drink her lemon water. Ugh, it makes her queasy just thinking about a dead eel. Let alone it being on someone's plate! Emma adjusts her straw and—

"Oh, my goodness!" she suddenly bursts out.

"Em, relax, it's just a wiggly little critter, one of God's yummy creatures just like everything else we eat." Arden tries to console her, "I'm sure it'll taste like chicken."

Emma doesn't respond. Arden follows her gaze, wondering who, or what, she's looking at. He waves a hand in front of her face, "Uhhhhh, hello, earth to Emma?"

"I can't believe this!" Emma lifts a shocked hand to her face, "I think I'm actually fangirling!"

"Well," Jay puffs out his chest mellow-dramatically, "you know, *Acid Rain* tends to uh," he whisks his hair backward and Miss Maggie laughs, "have that effect on people!"

"I don't even know what to say right now!" Emma isn't paying any attention to them, "I mean, I knew she hung out here sometimes, because of entries posted on her blog, but I didn't think I'd actually get lucky enough to see her!"

"Emma, who in the world are you talking about?" Miss Maggie asks, feeling slightly concerned for her daughter.

"Jane Akerly!" she excitedly reveals, trying to keep her voice hushed. She doesn't want to act like a total freak.

"Who is Jane Akerly?" Miss Maggie asks.

Emma's jaw drops. "Who is Jane Akerly?! Only one of my all-time favorite authors ever!" She looks at everyone at the table, but no one seems to be trekking with her. "She wrote *Unaccounted Involvement*! The breakout *New York Times* best-seller for teens?!" Her hands fall to the table, "You've got to be kidding me. Nobody here has read her book?!"

"I don't read unless it's no longer physically impossible to avoid it," Jay tells her.

Emma's eyes widen.

"Nope, never heard of her," Matthew adds.

"Me neither." Arden shrugs.

"And you guys are supposed to be Hollywood's next big thing?!" Emma gasps, "Un. Believable." She shakes her head, "I can't even fathom how shamefully uncultured this table is. I shouldn't even be sitting here right now."

"Well, why don't you go sit at her table?" Arden chuckles. "Maybe the two of you will be able to hold a 'cultured' conversation with finesse."

Jay tosses him a look of surprise.

"Oh yeah, I can use fancy words when I want to!" Arden grins.

"Yes, honey, if you're such a big fan, you should go get her autograph!" Miss Maggie suggests. "I can take a picture!"

"Her autograph?!" Emma echoes. "I can't just walk up to her! She's Jane Akerly!"

"Emma, where's your chill?" Arden laughs, "You share the same air with celebrities all the time. I'm sure this Jane person is just as normal and friendly as Aurora. Just go talk to her."

"How can you compare someone like Aurora to *Jane Akerly*?!" Emma has a far different perspective from everyone else at the table.

"Yo, Jane!" Arden calls across the restaurant.

Emma gasps and fights the urge to dive under the table.

The tall, slender, teen girl turns her head toward them. Emma's face is bright red.

"Got a second?" Arden calls. "Mega fan over here!"

Jane smiles and makes her way toward them. Emma's heart rate quickens, and her palms grow sweaty. She can't believe this is happening!

Jane kindly approaches the table with a cautious smile and Arden points to Emma. "This chick, right here. Talking to her will totally make her day." He looks at the other guys, "And uh, no offense, but nobody else at this table reads."

"Hi there!" Jane offers a polite hand to shake, "I'm Jane!"

Emma stands up, bewildered by the fact that such a legend is standing before her. "Hi!" Emma's excitement is evident, "Wow, I can't believe I'm actually talking to you! I mean, I read your blog all the time, and I knew you're living in London now, but I never dreamed I'd actually bump into you! Not to freak you out or anything, but I am seriously such a huge fan. I've read *Unaccounted Involvement* three times already, and I don't know how it's possible, but it just keeps getting better with each re-read. Wow, okay, now I'm rambling, but seriously, I never thought I'd get the chance to actually meet you!"

"Aw, thank you," Jane replies with a humble smile. "Your words mean a lot to me! It still feels like a completely surreal experience every time I meet someone who says they've read my book. So, thank you. So, so much."

"No, thank you!" Emma's eyes continue to shine, "Um, do you mind me asking...are you working on a sequel?"

"Well, I probably shouldn't tell you this," Jane lifts a shy hand up to her mouth, "but I'm going to anyway." She giggles, "Yes. I am definitely working on my next novel. We haven't officially announced it yet, but it is coming, I promise you that."

"Yay!" Emma claps her hands together excitedly, feeling like a giddy little kindergartener who just found out that recess would be extended an extra fifteen minutes.

"Well, I'd better let you get back to your food, but it was a joy meeting you, Emma!" Jane sweetly excuses herself and returns to the opposite side of the café where she was about to order.

"Wow," Arden chuckles, "I didn't know you were capable of fangirling that hard. Well done, Emma. Well done."

"Ahh!" Emma plops into her chair, attempting to lower her voice in hopes that Jane won't overhear, "I feel like I just drank an entire case of *Red Bull*! That was incredible! I just met Jane Akerly." She can scarcely believe the words. She repeats them, just to make sure they're real, "I just met Jane Akerly. And she's coming out with a new novel! And, oh my goodness, she was so incredibly sweet, can you believe how sweet she was?!"

"Oh my, darling, if I had any idea you were so over the moon about your favorite authors, I would've taken you to a meet and greet a long time ago." Miss Maggie chuckles, "I'm with Arden! It's quite the treat seeing you this giddy and animated! Just imagine what would happen if we could transfer all this spunk and excitement into the acting industry!"

Emma frowns. "Mom. Meet and Greets are so overrated. I mean, who wants to stand in line for hours and hours, just to have a five-second, completely forced encounter with a tired author, walking away with nothing less than an autograph? I just met Jane in real life, at one of her favorite British hangouts! That to me is way more amazing than attending some fabricated event for publicity purposes. Wow." She sighs again, feeling as though her time in London has already been spectacular, "So I wonder what Jane's next book is going to be about?"

~*~

"Come on, man, if anybody can make those guards laugh, it's gonna be you." Jay attempts to give his buddy a pep talk. He places encouraging hands on Arden's shoulders and takes a deep breath, "You got this."

Emma playfully crosses her arms, attempting to readjust her umbrella. Even though the immense downpour from earlier in the week has settled down a bit, there's still a steady drizzle. The weather just can't seem to make up its mind. One moment the sky is shouting with angry thunder, and the next moment the sunshine appears, and a sweet little rainbow releases its colors. After spending three days on the *Acid Rain* video shoot at an indoor studio, the youngsters are finally free to explore London. Tomorrow, they'll catch a train for Paris and see if they can shoot some outdoor scenes in France.

Emma shakes her head. These boys are crazy. "You're not going to be able to do it. It's practically impossible."

"I thought you said impossible wasn't going to be in your vocabulary anymore?" Arden reminds her.

"Yeah, don't be such a Negative Nancy!" Jay chimes in. "Arden was born for this moment."

"Alright, the Instagram Livestream is starting now, go!" Matthew announces. "Tell the fans what we're doing, Arden!"

Emma quickly jumps out of the way, careful to make sure she's not in the shot. Despite the stupidity of the moment, Emma's eyes still hold a smile. *Acid Rain's* off-the-wall, impromptu live-stream sessions are quickly becoming a favorite pastime for the group. But Emma can't scold them for it. They *are* kind of hilarious.

"Good afternoon, chaps!" Arden turns on a cheeky British accent and speaks to Matthew's iPhone, "Today we're here in the rainy city of London, mentally preparing ourselves to take on the challenge of a lifetime!"

"Arden, is that the best you can do?" Jay insults him in a British accent of his own, "Everyone this side of the pond knows that's not the way to greet a live-streaming audience! The proper way to address them is..." Jay lifts his voice and raises a triumphant hand into the air, "Cheerio!"

Emma shakes her head, desperately hoping nobody is watching them. But she knows better. Whenever she goes somewhere with *Acid Rain*, people are definitely watching. She can feel their disapproving stares of petty judgement. Emma is confident their group has been labeled as "the moron American tourists." Their ridiculous attempts at such classy accents are completely labeling them as out-of-towners.

"As you can see, we've got this dashingly dressed palace guard standing beside us here at Buckingham palace," Arden explains, "and today we're going to see if we can cause him to crack a smile!"

"All part of a special segment we like to call, Laughing in London!" Jay jumps in front of Arden like a hyper little jack-in-the-box.

Emma glances over her shoulder, trying to hide her grin.

"Alright." Arden's face turns serious, "Quiet on set, as I need complete and total concentration right now." He dramatically sucks for air, "I can do this." He turns to the guard, "So, there once was a watermelon and a cantaloupe. The watermelon said, 'Let's get married!' the cantaloupe said, 'I'm sorry…but I can't elope.' Ah, hah!"

Jay mimics the sound of a smashing drum set and Arden frowns.

Matthew gets a close-up of the frowning guards face.

"Well, clearly that didn't work." Arden tries again, "Why do seagulls fly over the sea?"

"Gee, I dunno, Arden!" Jay attempts to help him out.

"Well, if they flew over the bay, they'd be called bagels!"

The palace guard continues to frown. Emma's eyes sparkle with amusement. If these boys want to make a guard laugh before sunset, they'd better get funny, real fast.

~*~

"I'm glad you decided to leave your Hobbit Hole and come join us today," Arden tells Emma as the group strolls through the downtown area.

"My Hobbit Hole?" Emma laughs. "Hey, just because I didn't join you guys at your silly video set doesn't mean I've become a social recluse! Ten hours a day locked in my hotel room with nothing to do but read, think, and pray has been an absolute dream. Especially, after all the craziness with *Beauty and the Beast*, it's been nice just to have some 'me' time. Introverts need ample recovery time to recharge, you know."

"Oh yeah?" Arden stuffs his hands in his jean pockets, "I thought maybe it was because you didn't like the idea of another girl being on set."

Emma nearly drops her umbrella. Arden's words catch her completely off guard. Her mind races, as she fears that perhaps he really *can* read her mind. How could he possibly know she's weirded out by the idea? Surely it's not that obvious, is it? Her mother always tells her that she tends to wear her emotions on her sleeves, but Emma dares to think otherwise. As much as she doesn't want to admit it, Arden's words hold a ring of truth to them. It makes her heart cringe to think about Arden getting along so flawlessly with another young woman. Especially a flirty, attention-seeking, self-absorbed, ridiculously pretty, video girl.

"I know you'd never admit it to a soul," Arden continues, "but you can't stand the idea of *Acid Rain* having groupies, can you? And I know, I get it, you were here first, and you knew us before we were famous, and blah, blah, blah, but it's a reality you're just going to have to come to grips with." He winks, "You can't always be the sole proprietor and reigning Queen of our fan club, Emma. You're gonna have to learn to share the royal court with a few others."

Emma laughs. She isn't sure if it's because Arden actually thinks she'd desire such a ridiculous position, or if she's low-key nervous and doesn't want him to see the fact that he might be onto something. "Let's get a few things straight here." She clears her throat, "First of all, you guys are *not* famous."

"Yet!" Arden grins, "Yet, yet, yet."

"Okay, yet." She sighs, at least giving him that much. "Secondly, I already told you, there's no way I'm going to be the president of your fan club, or whatever you call it. And I can totally handle the groupies! My main concern is that your video is going to give your fans the wrong idea about who you truly are. Running around like maniacs, chasing some girl with your tongues hanging out of your mouths is totally disrespectful and inappropriate! I know that kissing complete strangers in Hollywood is a supposedly 'acceptable' thing, but–"

"Emma, you haven't even seen our video yet!" Arden interrupts her. "How can you already be making this much of an intense pre-judgement about it?"

"Because I know Hollywood!" Emma argues. "I know *Bubblegum Pop*, and I know the direction they're going to try to take you guys. And unless you stand up for what's right and decent and moral, you're going to be just as trashy and disappointing as every other mainstream boyband out there."

"Oh yeah, you're one to talk!" Arden laughs bitterly, "Because that's all you ever do is talk! You seem to know exactly what everyone else should do with their lives, how they should make their videos, what kind of music they should write, and how a person can navigate their way through Hollywood without selling their soul to the devil.

You ramble on and on about what a garbage bin Hollywood is, and how everything is cutthroat and evil and how it's all going to hell in a handbasket. But have you ever actually stopped to consider what you could be doing to make a difference? Instead of throwing your empty opinions around from the safety of your book-bedroom, why not actually have the guts to do something with your life?!"

Emma stops walking. "Well, that was harsh," Emma snaps, not even sure how to process everything he's just said.

"Yeah, I guess it was." Arden stops walking as well and turns to look at her. A moment of silence passes between them.

Arden finally speaks again. "But sometimes friends need to give each other a loving slap in the face." His voice softens, "Emma, please don't take this the wrong way. You have a good heart. But sometimes I feel like all you ever do is talk about the problems of Hollywood, and well, as long as you're not making any actual effort to be part of the answer, then I don't know how qualified you are to be running your mouth." He runs a handful of fingers through his hair, "And the most frustrating part, is that your mom is right! You're crazy talented! You have the potential to make an impact on this world! I just don't get why you're so freaked out to take a risk and give something a shot."

Emma's mouth pops open. As much as she wants to defend herself, she can't. She wants to argue with Arden, but she doesn't have the heart. Because, as painful as his slicing words are, the most excruciating thing about them is that they might actually be…true.

~*~

In Paris…

"Are you sure you don't want to come with us to the video shoot, honey?" Miss Maggie asks her daughter one last time. "It's such a gorgeous day! We're going to be getting some fun scenes of the boys riding mopeds in the streets, and even running around the Eiffel Tower! Ah, this video is going to be such a cinematic treat for the eyes!"

"Hmm…would I rather explore The Louvre, and soak in some of the most brilliant masterpieces of all time, or sit in a golf cart and watch three teenage boys run around filming their silly video?" Emma pretends to be weighing her options, acting as if the two could actually face one another in the gladiator ring. "You know, Mom, I think I'm gonna go with the historical monuments and trillion-dollar paintings."

"Okay, suit yourself!" Miss Maggie doesn't appear overly disappointed by her choice, "Just remember, we're all meeting up at Café Le Jardin Du Petit for lunch! Remember to keep your cell phone on, and don't talk to strangers!"

"That shouldn't be a problem," Emma giggles, "I can't speak French anyway."

"Alright darling, enjoy your day!"

Miss Maggie scoots out of the hotel room, and Emma sighs.

Finally, peace and quiet again.

She props up a pillow on the bed and attempts to make herself comfortable. A familiar weariness plagues her body as she fights the urge to take a nap. Her eyelids are heavy. Last night she was up late video chatting with Aurora. Now that they're temporarily in the same time zone, Aurora's been giving her the inside scoop on everything happening at the URIA.

As much as Emma enjoys hearing about it, she can't help but feel an unwelcome dose of jealousy. With each passing day, Emma feels a deeper and deeper cry of discontentment. It's bubbling up from somewhere deep inside her soul. Even with her jet-set lifestyle, sight-seeing expeditions in Europe, and highly entertaining people to keep her company, Emma can't help but feel like the core of her is still dry. She's still aching. She's still longing for more.

Arden's words from yesterday afternoon float into her mind. Her initial response to his hurtful sting was to bite her tongue and walk away. She felt a shield of offense mushroom in her heart, bubbling up like cream rising to the top of an Amish milk pail. But then, after a few sour moments of selfish grumbling to the Lord, a new thought entered her mind. Perhaps Arden had a point. What *is* Emma doing to make a difference and impact the world around her?

Arden was right when he said she's loaded with opinions. But the pathetic part is that she's never, as Arden said, done anything to attempt making Hollywood a better place. Meanwhile, while Aurora's off trying to save the world, Emma can't even find space in her heart to be kind and intentional about the daily interactions she's having with the people around her.

"Oh, Lord, I need Your help," Emma prays. Her eyes are wide open, as she imagines Jesus to be right there in her hotel room, listening to her every word. "I want to make a difference with my life. I don't want to, like Arden said, just throw everything away. Maybe the reason I'm always hating on Hollywood is because I actually have a heart to see things change. I can't stand all the nonsense, and it's so depressing to think of all the people who are hurt and deceived by that crazy machine. But what could I possibly do to help? I mean, I'm only one girl. A girl who hates being onstage, speaking in front of an audience, or drawing any kind of attention to herself. How can I make a difference when I'm practically invisible?"

Emma allows the questions to linger in the air. She listens for an answer, but there is none.

Frustrated, she plops onto her back and wonders if God is going to answer her this time.

~*~

"There she is!" Miss Maggie calls out from across the café, relieved to spot Emma within the bustling crowd. "Yooo-hoo! Over here, sweetie!"

Emma spots her mother who rambunctiously waves and jumps up and down. It appears she's signaling in a jumbo jet. Emma smiles. Talk about over-dramatic.

"So, how was the Louvre?" Miss Maggie asks eagerly.

"I'm sure it's amazing. But I didn't actually get a chance to see it." Her smile disappears as she sheepishly tugs on the edge of her sweater, "I fell back asleep."

"Well, you sure missed an exciting morning!" Miss Maggie is still wound up from her cappuccino, "The boys are doing an incredible job! And oh my, you should see some of the scenery shots! If their director doesn't win an award for this video, I will be utterly shocked! I wasn't sure how soon you'd be here, so I already ordered us some macaroons!"

Emma sits down at the small table across from her mother and glances over her shoulder. Arden and the guys sit on the opposite side of the café. A large group of crew members accompany the group. A firework of laughter travels across the café, and for a split second she almost wishes to go join them. Then she sees her. The video girl. Emma quickly looks away.

"I'm telling you, Emma, this video is going to be off-the-charts amazing!" Miss Maggie squeals, "I must confess, I'm quite impressed with how Arden is handling himself on set. Very professional, just as I had hoped. Once again, this trip confirms my previous beliefs that we really struck gold with that kid. Oh no, there's no cream for my latte!" Miss Maggie shoots up from the table and hops in the long line at the main counter.

Emma reaches for a purple macaroon and glances over her shoulder again. The video girl doesn't look anything like what Emma was expecting. For starters, she's not blonde. The short, petite, black-haired young woman appears to be of oriental decent.

Arden catches her gaze, and Emma quickly looks away. She sets her focus on her plate, feeling like a goon for being caught staring in their direction. Seconds later, Arden appears.

"Hey! How was the Louvre?"

"I didn't quite make it there," Emma admits. "I guess I needed to catch up on some extra sleep."

"Oh nice, you're actually talking to me!" Arden smiles. "For a minute there, I wasn't sure. After what I said yesterday, I thought you might pull out your icy silent treatment. But even if you did, it's not to say I don't deserve it. Emma, I was totally out of line for–"

"No, you weren't," Emma interrupts him. "You don't have to apologize. In fact, I'm glad you said what you did. I'll admit, at first it stung a little bit. But your point was completely legitimate. And it's caused me to think about some really important things. I guess you could say I've been asking myself some of those more intense, deeper, introspective questions this morning."

"Really?" Arden is pleasantly surprised, "And have you gotten any answers yet?"

"Not exactly." Emma twists her lip, "But, as strange as this sounds, I have been thinking a bit about that Anderson Performing Arts School."

"Seriously?" Arden slips into the seat across from her, clearly interested in what she has to say. "Does this mean you're actually considering pursuing acting as a professional career?"

"No way!" Emma quickly shakes her head, "I've already made it perfectly clear, I don't want to be an actress. But I was looking at the school's website, and they have a pretty impressive Film and Production program. As much as I can't stand all the drama of Hollywood, I've always been kind of drawn to the 'behind-the-scenes' aspects of movie making. If I had the opportunity to work on a smaller, low-budget, independent film someday, I wouldn't hate it." She smiles. "Some kids grow up knowing exactly what they want to do with their life and are driven by some kind of invisible passion to pursue their dreams. I've never been like that. I don't know what God has planned for my life or why I'm even on this planet, but I can't help but think about the uncanny way this scholarship just fell into my lap. As random and completely out of the blue as it seems, I don't know, maybe it's God's way of showing me what kind of direction my life might be headed?"

"Wow." Arden nods his head, "So have you talked to your mom about this?"

"Not yet," Emma confesses, "I mean, I haven't decided yet if this is something I want to do. It's all pretty new. I'm not sure how Mom would react." Emma glances at where her mother is chatting with the cashier, "I've never done anything like this before. I've been homeschooled my entire life, and it's always been just her and I, traveling all over the place and working with clients. This would be a major adjustment for the both of us."

"Well, I'd better get back to the guys." Arden stands up, "But keep on trekking down this deep, introspective, life-changing road, because I like where it's headed!" He grins, "Sure you don't want to come over and join us?"

"No, that's okay." Emma crunches into her macaroon. She thinks about the video girl and a deep pain clenches her stomach. She can't stand the thought of watching some girl mindlessly flirt with Arden. "It looks a little crowded over there anyway."

"Rose doesn't take up very much room." He glances over his shoulder, looking directly at the young Chinese girl.

Emma nearly chokes on her macaroon. How does he know she was just thinking about her?! Emma reaches for a napkin and releases a cough.

"She's not your typical video girl." Arden continues to explain, "She's a local Londoner, with manners that rival the Queen. But that's because this isn't your typical boy band video either. Contrary to your snap judgement yesterday, *Bubblegum* went totally classy with Rose's character. She's a wealthy, sophisticated, shy girl who plays violin, cello, and is obsessed with reading. We spend the day chasing her around, and at the end she dumps freezing cold smoothies on our head and scolds us for acting like such freaks. If I didn't know any better, I'd think you were one of the writers!" He chuckles, "I'm pretty sure you'd give the Emma stamp of approval."

Emma's eyes widen. A sudden wave of relief washes over her. This must mean…there's no kiss! She slowly smiles, "Wow. It sounds like I might actually be able to watch your video without gagging after all!"

Arden laughs and heads back to the other side of the room.

Emma's smile lingers. She takes another bite of her delicious macaroon, and her mother reappears.

"Alright, coffee round two!" she proclaims. "Let's try this again, Café Le Jardin!" She takes a sip and releases a heavenly sigh, "Oh, I love Paris! So many bittersweet memories." She sighs, "This is where your father and I came on our honeymoon."

"Oh, yeah." Emma remembers hearing that from the past. She isn't sure what else to say. It isn't often her mother talks about Dad.

"I was completely over the moon!" Miss Maggie reminisces, "We were broke college students, so our wedding consisted of a simple dress, my maid of honor, his best man, and a quick trip to the Courthouse! Your grandma was so distraught over the fact that we didn't have a real wedding in her church. When Dave pulled out our passports and tickets to Paris, I was in shock! He had been saving for several years and wanted to surprise me. He was very sweet about those kinds of things." Miss Maggie smiles, "It was my first time in Europe! Oh, I'll never forget seeing the Eiffel Tower all lit up, sparkling and dancing with glitter and lights! We rode bikes around the city, explored Chateau De Versailles, and strolled through the Le Marais District! I'll always cherish that trip."

"Do you…" Emma starts slowly, apprehensive of the words about to fall from her lips. "Do you ever…miss him?"

Miss Maggie sets her coffee cup down. Silence lingers several long seconds. Finally, Miss Maggie speaks wistfully. "The man I miss is the man your father no longer is. The old Dave? The Dave I met and fell in love with in college? He was an absolute dream to be married to. But then," Miss Maggie's airy voice is drained, and her throat tightens. Her voice drops to a heaver tone, snapping herself out of the happier days and returning to reality, "then the financial struggles came. Along with the stress, arguments, and verbal shouting matches. Next thing I knew he was drinking, gambling, and destroying our entire life savings for his next high. That Dave? I don't miss him at all."

Emma nods, knowing her mom made a wise choice in leaving. She did what she thought was best for both her and Emma, and even though Emma can't help but wonder what life might've been like with her dad in the picture, she knows there's nothing either of them can do to change that now.

"But enough about him." Miss Maggie reaches across the table and pats Emma's hand, "Let's talk about you! It's not very often we get to sit down and chat, just the two of us. Anything on your mind?"

Emma is surprised her mother has stopped talking about *Acid Rain*. She cocks her head, almost wondering if it's a trick question. No, maybe it isn't. Maybe her mother actually, finally, wishes to just spend one-on-one, quality time with her.

"There is, actually," Emma speaks bravely, despite her underlying nerves. "You remember me telling you that Aurora's old boyfriend, Jeremiah, got a scholarship to that Anderson Performing Arts School?"

"Oh, yes!" Miss Maggie nods, "Which reminds me, I need to contact that boy as soon as I get back to the states! He might be my next big client!"

"Well," Emma takes a deep breath, mentally preparing herself for her mom's reaction, "something happened after our *Beauty and the Beast* performance that I haven't exactly told you about yet."

"What do you mean?" Concern seeps through Miss Maggie's words.

"Jeremiah wasn't the only one to receive a scholarship." She looks nervously at her empty plate. "I did too."

Emma doesn't dare look up, fearful as to how her mother might react. There are several seconds of uncomfortable silence.

"Oh, my goodness!" Miss Maggie bursts out. "Honey, that's incredible! Are you serious?! Anderson High awarded you with a scholarship?!"

Emma looks up. She nods.

"Oh, Emma dear!" Miss Maggie's voice is thrilled, "Why didn't you tell me sooner?!"

"I don't know." Emma's pointer finger traces the empty plate, "You were making such a huge deal about me going into acting and I felt like you were putting way too much pressure on the subject. And then, after your negative response about the school, it didn't sound like you thought too highly of it."

"Oh no, that isn't the case at all!" Miss Maggie explains, "I merely said Anderson Academy isn't going to help aspiring actor's book working jobs or anything they'll get paid for right away. But for someone as new to the industry as you, someone who desires to practice their skills, grow their craft and slowly flourish like a sweet little flower, oh honey this would be so perfect for you!"

"But I don't want to be an actress, Mom."

"But Em! You're so talented!" Miss Maggie insists. "And a full ride scholarship to Anderson is worth a small fortune! How could you just throw something like this away, taking no mind of the fact that—"

"Wait, just hear me out okay?" Emma calmly attempts to make herself heard. "I didn't say I don't want to go. All I said was that I don't want to be an actress. Anderson actually has a really cool Film and Production program. Mom, that's something I might be interested in."

Miss Maggie pauses, considering her daughter's words. "Film and Production? Hmm…wow, yes, that's an interesting field to get into. There sure is a lot of money to be made there! Come to think of it, you would make a wonderful producer, always paying attention to small details everyone else misses. Hmm…I think I could envision you wearing a producer's cap! Oh, Em, this is just thrilling! Tell me more about the school, tell me everything you know! How do we get you enrolled? When does orientation begin?"

"Woah, Mom, slow down! I didn't say I'm ready to sign up. I simply wanted to mention that I've been thinking about this. But I am certainly not ready to make any hard and fast decisions. Going to a school like that would dramatically change my life. I mean, am I actually ready to attend a boarding school where I share a bedroom with complete strangers, wake up when it's still dark, eat all my meals in a cafeteria and be forced to socialize with people on a daily basis?" She shakes her head, "I don't know if I'm ready for all that."

"You're right, it would be a big change." Miss Maggie slows down, attempting to consider all the pros and cons of such a choice. "Come to think of it, I don't know how *I* would feel about that either. You've always been my little travel buddy, tagging along and ever present as we take on the world together! It would feel so empty without you on the road with me! Aw, honey." Miss Maggie frowns, "I would miss you too much!"

Emma's heart is warmed by her mother's words. "Really?" she asks in wonderment, surprised to hear what her heart has longed to be affirmed of. "You would?"

"Of course, I would! Now, I know I run around like a chicken with my head cut off most of the time, blasting through my appointment books and always placing this business as my top priority. It's just one of my many, many character flaws." She sighs, "I'm a perfectionist, Em, and I want to do everything with utmost excellence. But I'm ashamed to say that oftentimes it has come at the price of placing motherhood on the back burner. I'm so sorry, sweetie. I'm sorry for all the times I've made you feel pushed aside or less important than the things on my desk. The truth is, I love having you around and I never want you to feel like a burden or just some random person blended into the background. Emma, words cannot even express how much I love you! You're the most important person in the world to me. And I don't want you to forget that. Ever."

Emma can feel sweet tears coming to her eyes. "Thank you," she whispers. "That means a lot."

"When I was a teenager, I didn't want anything to do with my mother." Miss Maggie continues, "The more she tried to control and be part of my life, the more I rebelled! Sadly, I don't have the best relationship with Grandma today. But I don't ever want things to be like that between us, Em. So, if it feels like I'm backing off and giving you too much space, it's because I want you to grow and become more independent! As a mom, it's so easy to spread out our Mama-Hen wings and not want our children to grow up. As much as I dislike the idea of not having you around for my future travels, the truth is that you're getting older, and like it or not, things are going to change. I know that you going to Anderson would be an amazing developmental stepping stone for your future, no matter what you decide to do with it afterward. Now this is completely your decision, and you can do whatever you think is best...but I think you should do it, Emma. I think Anderson High needs a Miss Emma Bates on their attendance roll!"

"I can't believe I'm actually talking about this." Emma feels a shiver of fear trickle down her spine, "It feels so out of character for me to even be considering such a wild thing. I mean, me? Emma. The Webster's Dictionary definition of a shy, quiet, moody introvert, attending a high school full of animated, mellow-dramatic, high-strung, totally-hyper, professional actor and actress wannabes?! There's no way I would fit in." She shakes her head, "I'm nothing like those other kids."

"Which is why you should do it," Miss Maggie smiles. "Because you're different. The last thing that school wants is another average, cookie-cutter, run-of-the-mill, Disney-Channel-Star lookalike! Yes, you're different. But that's a good thing! Standing apart from the crowd is exactly why they gave you this scholarship in the first place, honey. Being just like everyone else is overrated! Besides, you can't make an impact on the world if you're just like it."

~*~

At Aunt Lydia's and Uncle Sky's Ranch in Colorado...

Eleanor scrubs the bottom of the raised, marble bathroom sink, careful to erase the line of mildew crusted around the drain. She turns on the faucet and gives the sink one last rinse, satisfied with her cleaning job. She wipes her hands on a nearby towel which boasts a bold moose imprint. Eleanor almost smiles. The rustic theming in Aunt Lydia and Uncle Sky's rental cabins is pretty adorable.

She reaches for her spray bottle of Windex resting on the toilet seat and spritzes the mirror with it. She's careful not to bump into the fragile, faux deer antlers which are affixed to the mirror frame.

"Alright, living room and bedrooms are done!" Eleanor's cousin Harmony pops her head into the bathroom. "Two down, one to go!"

Eleanor is impressed with how quick Harmony moves. It's clear that the girl knows her stuff.

"Two seconds," Eleanor tells her, quickly finishing the mirror. She knows they're on a time crunch. Their new guests will be checking in within the hour, and its Harmony's and Eleanor's job to make sure that three of the six cabins are spotless. Aunt Lydia and twelve-year-old Heaven are cleaning the other three.

As much as Eleanor doesn't want to be here, she's impressed with the way the entire family pitches in to make things happen. Running a dude ranch is no small feat, especially when new visitors are constantly filtering in and out. Unlike *Napp Resort*, Uncle Sky and Aunt Lydia's ranch doesn't have a large staff. All their children work extremely hard to make sure their bases are covered. Eleanor misses that. She remembers the days at their ranch, when it was just up to her, Mom, Dad and two stable hands to make sure everything got done, before they went all mainstream and commercial. If only things could get back to the way they used to be.

Maybe they will, Eleanor thinks, *once Dad gets home, now that Jasmine is out of the picture.*

She wipes the mirror with a paper towel, careful not to leave any streaks.

"Done!" she announces. She quickly collects her cleaning supplies and follows Harmony out of the bathroom. They cross through the living room. Although Eleanor doesn't have time to stop and study the details, she appreciates all the design elements in this cozy cabin. It reminds her of how her own mother would have decorated. With chestnut hardwood floors, forest green couches, a stone-adorned fireplace, thick cedar wall beams, and plush brown Aztec pillows, Eleanor enjoys the atmosphere. In her mind, this is what rooms at a ranch should look like. Comfortable and homey. Not expensive and hotel-feeling.

They push through the screen door and onto the small porch. Eleanor takes a deep whiff of the fresh, Colorado air. One thing she enjoys about staying here is that they're truly in the heart of horse country. The scenery is absolutely breathtaking and there are no shopping malls, parking garages or sports complexes for miles around.

"Thanks for your help!" Harmony tells her as they hop onto the dirt path and head toward the last cabin. "I really appreciate it."

"Oh, no problem!" Eleanor's response is genuine.

"Things are always a little hectic around here!"

"Oh, but I love it!" Eleanor smiles, "I grew up on a ranch too, remember? So, I know there's always something that needs to be done. Even though ranch life is crazy busy, it's so much better than sitting around doing nothing."

"Agreed!" Harmony laughs. "Free time? What's that? Who needs it?"

Eleanor laughs. As much as she would prefer to be at home, Aunt Lydia and Uncle Sky are truly treating her like a member of the family. They've assigned her chores, given her a bedroom to share with Harmony, and expect her to behave just as the other kids. Eleanor finds their demeanor refreshing. No special treatment, and she really appreciates that.

After conquering the final cabin, they dash back outside and rush to the barns, to give a group of Green Horns a trail ride. (Green Horns are what they call visitors at the Dude Ranch who are clueless when it comes to horses.) Eleanor thinks of Logan and what a terrible rider he was when he first arrived at *Napp*. She smiles. Perhaps there's hope for the Green Horns after all.

Harmony snatches a clipboard off the barn wall and glances at her list. "Oh great, we've got Tyler and Tyson on the list." She frowns, "They've been here all week. Let's just say, they're far more interested in flirting with Sarah than they are with learning how to ride."

"That's a shame." Eleanor sympathizes with her cousin. "Some people just don't know how to keep their priorities straight."

"I know, right?!" Harmony laughs. "Who needs boyfriends when you've got horses?!"

"Finally, someone who understands me!" Eleanor laughs, "Seriously though. I need a bumper sticker with that phrase."

The girls giggle once more, and Eleanor's eyes continue to smile. Another sweet blessing about being at the ranch is reconnecting with Harmony. Her and Eleanor's personalities are clicking flawlessly, as they seem to agree on just about everything. They both have an unhealthy obsession with horses, couldn't care less about boyfriends or shoe sales, and know how to get things done. She and Harmony definitely have the most in common out of all of her cousins. They're also the same age.

They step back outside to meet Sarah, as it was her job to tack up horses for their trail ride and deliver them to a nearby pen. Dry dirt kicks up from beneath their cowgirl boots as they scurry down the path.

Obadiah, the eldest cousin, carries a canoe over his shoulder with the help of another staff member. Eleanor watches as an excited family with two little kids skips behind him, clearly elated about their upcoming canoe ride. For the wide-eyed visitors, there's always something fun happening at the ranch.

"Oh, my gosh, look, it's a real cowboy!" A girl from a nearby walking path squeals, "Can we take a picture with you?"

Eleanor resists the urge to giggle as Obadiah lets out a frustrated huff. They lower the canoe to the ground and Obadiah tips his hat toward the young woman, attempting to be polite. Eleanor has already seen three people run up to him with their phones, snapping photos, acting as if they're capturing a famous tourist attraction.

"Oh yeah, let's all get in the picture!" the girl's father exclaims, motioning to his other family members to hop in.

Eleanor shakes her head. Apparently, the city slickers think it's great fun to see a 'real' cowboy.

When they reach the pen, Harmony isn't happy to see Tyler and Tyson laughing with Sarah.

"Oh no, if you fall off this horse, I am not going to be there to help you back up!" Sarah laughs.

"But what if I need CPR?" one of the guys asks.

"You fell off a horse, you're not drowning," Sarah snaps, clearly disgusted by his offhanded comment. She flips her hair over her shoulder and struts away, climbing over the fence and landing on her feet, right beside Eleanor and Harmony.

"They're all yours." Sarah rolls her eyes then saunters off, clearly happy to wash her hands clean of them.

Harmony frowns. "Only two more days and these guys are history," Harmony mumbles to Eleanor. "They'll go back to their sunny little home in Florida, and we'll see who the next round of Green Horns are."

Harmony unlatches the gate to the riding ring and Eleanor follows her inside.

"Hey, where'd your hot sister go?" one of the guys asks.

Harmony is clearly displeased with his comment. "Please. There are little children present. So, get your crazy teenage hormones under control and start acting like gentlemen."

Eleanor raises an eyebrow. Yikes. Harmony sounds just like her. She couldn't have said it better herself!

Harmony clasps her hands together and attempts to smile, "Okay Ranchers, let's find our horses and get ready to ride! Please remember to stick to the basic ground rules we've been covering all week. No loud shouts or screams, avoid abrupt or jerkish movements and approach your horse from the front or side, not from the behind."

"Miss Harmony, I need help. I can't reach my pony's saddle!"

Harmony smiles at a little girl struggling to lift her leg into the tall stirrup. She quickly helps her, and Eleanor observes the group. It appears everyone knows what they're doing. They're all mounting, so Eleanor turns to Heaven, the twelve-year-old version of curly, blonde-haired Sarah.

"Here, you can ride Comanche!" Heaven motions to a nearby buckskin.

"Thanks." Eleanor smiles and approaches the beautiful gelding with a pat on the side. "Hi there, cutie pie. My, aren't you a handsome fella!"

"Comanche is one of Harmony's horses," Heaven explains. "He's also an amazing barrel racer."

After several moments, Harmony leads the group they slowly head on out. A thick dust bath is left behind them as their horses' hooves kick up the dry ground. Eleanor is happy to be back in the saddle again. She shifts herself and comfortably settles in, slightly excited about the ride to come. Even if it is just a slow walk with a bunch of Green Horns.

"So, what's it like in California?" Heaven asks eagerly. "It's my dream to go to Cali! Do you go to the ocean often? Oh, I would love to live near the ocean! Have you ever tried surfing? Or snorkeling? What about parasailing?!"

Eleanor isn't surprised Heaven is being such a chatterbox. It's one of her trademark personality traits. During breakfast, dinner and lunch, even though there's lots of conversation happening around the table, Heaven is always talking the fastest and the loudest.

"The ocean is really beautiful. But my favorite beach activity is riding."

"So, you've never been parasailing?!" Heaven's blonde eyebrows knit together, "Wow, if I were you and was blessed enough to live that close to the ocean, I would be hanging out there every single day! The *last* thing I would do is go horseback riding. Ugh, what I wouldn't give to go on a real vacation! One without horses and hay and manure. If I went to the ocean I would definitely try parasailing. And surfing! We've never actually been on a real vacation. The only time I've even left Colorado was for Harmony's barrel racing competition and that was just in Nebraska! Ranching means we never get to leave, so I've never seen much of the outside world. Hashtag, sheltered homeschool girl probs."

Eleanor laughs. "You know, being stuck at home isn't such a bad thing. I mean, look at this place. Your property is gorgeous! For all your paying guests, this is their vacation. I'd say you're pretty blessed. Home is the most special place in the world."

"But I've never been anywhere!" Harmony continues. "So many places are calling my name! California, Florida, the

Bahamas, Hawaii, Bora Bora! I'm struck with a deep sense of wanderlust and nobody in my family gets me."

Eleanor wonders why people can't be more content and just appreciate where their roots are. Eleanor loves being home. It's her favorite place on the planet. Just like her mother was, she's a total homebody. She wonders if maybe that's why her dad is running all over the place. Has he been struck with an unquenchable dose of wanderlust as well?

Eleanor looks up toward the sky, wanting to appreciate where she's at in the moment. Even though it isn't her home, it sure is gorgeous. The big blue sky is stretched out like a royal tapestry. Today there are only a few wispy white clouds floating around. In the distance, rising hills which slowly arch into the foothills of magnificent purple mountains, linger ahead.

The group of riders reach a wide-open meadow, and Eleanor can't see any distinguished trail heads. Unlike the Napp's ranch, it appears everything is wide open beneath the sun, without trees or man-made signs mapping out the way of travel. Eleanor can't help but wonder if they'll see any wildlife critters today.

"Dad says this land is our inheritance and that someday we'll be glad we made the sacrifices required to keep our property." Heaven continues, "But would it be *that* hard to squeeze in just one, measly little vacation? I'm not asking for a trip to Disney World, I just want to get out and do something, somewhere, anywhere besides here! Everyone in our family is head-over-heels in love with horses, but just because I didn't get bit with the horse crazy bug, does that mean I have to stay here and suffer while my future is calling!?"

Eleanor glances at her cousin, secretly wondering if she has an off button. Can't she just be quiet and enjoy the view?

"We all know Obadiah is gonna inherit the ranch anyway." Heaven adds, "So for me, being the fourth in line, it really doesn't matter all that much. Harmony says she wants the land and would take way better care of it than Diah, but whenever they start bickering about it, Dad reminds them of the fact that if they don't figure out a way to share it, he could easily sell it to a land developer with the snap of a finger! That shuts them up real quick!" Heaven laughs, "The list of men pestering Dad to sell has been a mile long for years! A lot of nearby ranchers and neighbors are giving in to the pressure as the amounts of money being offered are through the roof! But then there are the older, more traditional ranchers like Dad who joined together and formed a union, trying to do whatever they can to stop developers from purchasing nearby land. The fight around these parts is getting pretty intense! Oh, but get this! There's a rumor going around that Logan Sparks is trying to purchase land and build a massive studio out here!"

Eleanor's eyes slant toward Heaven. She doesn't know how to respond. Has Heaven just said what she *thinks* she just said?

"Logan Sparks." Heaven repeats herself, wondering if perhaps Eleanor has never heard the name. "You know, that big movie star guy?"

"Yeah, yeah, right." Eleanor nods, realizing she must have a pretty-stupid look on her face right now. She wipes the bewilderment from her eyes. "I know who you're talking about."

"Okay, so can you imagine that guy building a TV studio out here?! Some of the locals think it's a great idea and are trying to convince my dad's board that it'll be good for business. But then Dad and the rest of the traditionalists are completely livid, sticking their boots in the mud, determined not to let it happen. As for me, I'm not really sure which side I'm on yet. As cool as it might be to have a big-name star build something nearby, it seems kind of silly he would choose Colorado of all places to do so! I mean, why doesn't he pick California or New York, or someplace exciting?! At least go where the action is! Not where the ranches are."

Eleanor listens as Harmony continues to chatter on. Eleanor readjusts her fingers on the reins and considers this newfound information. Could this be true? Is Logan actually going to be building something nearby? Is this the new and exciting idea he mentioned to her before leaving *Napp*?

But a TV studio? Something about the information just doesn't compute.

Eleanor decides to shake her head and let it go. Besides. Heaven said it's just a rumor, right?

~*~

Episode 8

"Your Highnesses, may I have your attention for a moment?"

Aurora flings her head back and allows the fresh gulp of water to travel down her throat. She removes her water bottle and reaches for a towel to wipe sweat from her forehead. She and her sisters just finished running laps around the training area. She flings her high ponytail and settles her attention on Captain Cepheus.

"On behalf of the URIA, I would like to let each of you know how proud we are of your hard work and determination to press through these training courses. I know it hasn't been easy." He looks at Elizabeth, "You miss your families, your comfortable beds, and all the luxuries of living life in the manner that you so choose. But, I am confident that your sweat and hard work will pay off in the long run. Not only will it benefit you but learning to discipline both your bodies and minds will greatly benefit our nation. And so, we'd like to give Your Highnesses a night off and host a special party in your honor!"

"A party?" Aurora echoes. Her fingers thread through her high ponytail. She unfastens the tight clip and allows her long hair to tumble down her shoulders. Yuck. She's in desperate need of a shower. "What kind of party?"

"A celebration." Captain Cepheus smiles, "Honoring the regal hearts and amiable character of our beloved Princesses. After the conflict ends and Raymond is removed from the palace, we'll host a magnificent ball! But for now, we can think of this as a 'practice party' of sorts. We'll provide refreshments and invite the army for an evening of fellowship and dancing. The everyday, routine life in the army can become very dull and monotonous. It is best if we keep the soldiers' spirits up and have a bit of fun!"

Lena has worry lines on her forehead. She doesn't think it sounds like a very wise idea. "But why should we celebrate when the Kingdom is still in turmoil? Surely we should wait until after the victory for such a party."

"Sometimes, when the war is long and the fight lingers, it is easy to grow weary and discouraged," Captain Cepheus explains. "Everyone at the URIA must remain positive. And taking time to stop and celebrate the little things in life always helps strengthen us for the days ahead!"

Elizabeth's eyes are wide. She doesn't like the idea either. The last time she attended a party, Aurora's big birthday bash in California, things were pretty awful.

"Captain Cepheus is right!" Aurora grins, "Everyone needs to learn how to stop, drop, and party! I think a night off is just what we need."

~*~

"What to wear, what to wear, what to wear." Aurora digs through her suitcase, searching for just the right thing. She pauses. "Seriously girls, what are we going to wear? If only the URIA had a built-in mall!"

"I think any old thing will do," Lena shares her thoughts on the matter. "We shouldn't invest that much time and mental energy into it anyway. We need to remain focused on what truly matters. Winning the war."

"Lena, why do you have to be so intense about everything?" Aurora stands up, "Didn't you hear what the old Captain said? He wants us to have a good time tonight! Stopping and enjoying ourselves is actually part of our training!"

"No, it isn't," Lena gently argues.

"Actually, it is." Aurora insists, "I've been reading the Bible a ton these past few days and I am truly amazed by all the times it tells us to rejoice! If the joy of the Lord is our strength, then surely, it's important to stop and enjoy ourselves every once in a while. I was reading about these dudes who wanted to take an enemy camp, but they had these massive walls built up and everyone was freaked out. So, what did God tell them to do? He told them to march around the walls seven times and then blow their little trumpets, and the walls would fall down! That must've sounded ridiculous to them! I can only imagine their leaders wanted to strategize and get all serious, and meanwhile God was just like, 'Yo, people. Relax. Listen to me. Let's have some fun.' And boom! The walls fell down! We've been working so hard and unless we pause to take a break, we're not going to have enough strength for when the *real* battle actually gets here!"

"Aurora might be right," Elizabeth speaks softly. "As much as I do not like the idea of going to a party, we have been working very, very hard. Even the Amish take time to stop and enjoy the blessings God has given them. Without resting, we might wear ourselves out."

Lena looks at Elizabeth. As much as she doesn't want to give in to the idea, if Elizabeth is on board then maybe she should think twice about it. "Okay," she finally huffs, "maybe you two have a point. I suppose a little bit of fun will not set us behind *too* terribly on our progress."

"Yay!" Aurora squeals. "This is the perfect opportunity to give the two of you a makeover!" She rushes back to her cosmetics bag, "Even if our clothes are totally drab, we can at least make up our faces and do our hair!"

"Who says your clothes have to be drab?" Rachel enters the room just in time to hear the tail end of their conversation.

"You mean we can take a trip to the mall?!" Aurora pops up.

"No," Rachel chuckles. "Not quite. But I do have some dresses that you girls might like to try on."

"What?" Aurora is completely surprised, "Dresses? Where are you keeping them? How'd you smuggle them down here?"

"I didn't smuggle them." Rachel chuckles as she opens her tiny, compact closet door. "But I have been saving them for a special occasion. I knew the Royal Highnesses would need gowns eventually, and although that's the last thing the URIA would think of when executing their top-secret plan to save the world, it's always good to have a woman onboard. Men plan wars, but women plan the party to be had after the war!"

Aurora's jaw drops as Rachel pulls out several dress bags. All the girls excitedly gather around her. "Rachel!" Aurora squeals, "You're like our fairy godmother!"

Rachel begins to unzip the bag, then stops herself.

Lena senses something wrong. "Miss Rachel, are you okay?"

She sets down the bag and turns to face the girls. "I was there the night your parents were murdered."

"You knew our parents?" Lena exclaims.

An eerie silence settles over the room as they all wait for her to continue.

"I did," Rachel nods, her eyes becoming watery. "I worked in Her Majesty's court. Queen Isabella was the kindest, most gracious, loving woman I ever had the privilege of meeting. She never spoke to the staff as if we were beneath her or treated us like we were any less important than she. Oh, she was so excited to become a mother! I sewed several of her maternity gowns."

"You're a tailor?" Aurora asks.

"Yes." Rachel nods with a smile, "She talked about you girls all the time. She couldn't wait to meet each of you! At the time of her pregnancy, she talked about the kind of young women she hoped you would one day become and asked that I sew special gowns for…" she stops, choked up by the memory, "your sixteenth birthday. She continually said it would be a most monumental day in your lives."

"And it was," Aurora speaks, completely breathless to think that her mother knew that would be the day everything changed for them. "The day Elizabeth and I met."

"Her Majesty had a very close walk with God and sometimes spoke of things that nobody else knew of, before they happened. But once they came to pass, we remembered what the Queen had said, and it was clear she had a prophetic gifting from the Lord. She asked that I create each gown by her exact specifications. She acted as if she knew exactly which daughter would someday wear which gown; although I have no way of knowing who each dress was intended for, now." Rachel looks back at the dress bag, "With that being said, I'll leave it up to each of you to decide which you'd like to wear."

Rachel slowly unzips the bag and Lena gasps. A glorious, floor-length, emerald green gown is revealed. The bodice is adorned with sequins and tiny crystals. The A-line skirt tumbles to the ground in a waterfall of chiffon.

"That one's for you," Aurora nudges Lena. "It's green like the meadows where you grew up. It's every bit of elegant and classy as you are."

Lena reaches out to touch the material in wonderment. She's never laid eyes on anything quite so stunning. "I feel as though I am dreaming," she whispers.

Rachel hands her the dress, and the next stunning gown is exposed. A long, slender, floor length, black dress. It doesn't have all the sparkles and fancy beading as it's sister dress, but it is beautiful, nonetheless. Elizabeth can scarcely believe how plain, yet lovely it is.

"Wow," Aurora breathes, "Elizabeth, that's your dress."

Elizabeth slowly reaches for the gown, wondering if it will be okay to have her bare arms exposed. How will God feel about that?

The next dress brings tears to Aurora's eyes. The flaming red gown is a full-blown, ballroom-style, work of art. Off the shoulder, full-length, red lace sleeves mesh perfectly with the fitted bodice.

"That's yours," Lena smiles. "Fiery and determined, just like you are."

"How could she have known that we'd all be so different?" Aurora marvels. "Each of these dresses are…are completely perfect for us."

Aurora removes her dress from the bag, and they see the fourth and final gown. It's a stunning, sapphire blue, mermaid-style ensemble. The girls exchange glances, knowing they're all thinking the same thing. Who does that dress belong to? Where is their other sister, and what is she like? Will they ever meet her?

"On the night of the attack, I knew I had to grab these gowns," Rachel reveals. "I was going to wait until the official coronation to give them, but I feel Queen Isabella would want you to have them right now. She was all about celebrating the small moments in life. Moments like this one." She wipes away a stray, sentimental tear and clears her throat with a smile. "Well, what are you girls waiting for? Let's try on these dresses!"

~*~

Elizabeth flinches as the scissors slice through her hair. She doesn't dare open her eyes.

"Oh, my goodness, Elizabeth, you look ah-may-zing!" Aurora proclaims in a sing-song tone. "You're going to love this!"

"She's right, Elizabeth." Lena gives her reaffirming vote of confidence, "Aurora is doing a lovely job. You will be very pleased with it."

Elizabeth's heart is pounding. Even though it doesn't physically hurt to feel her long locks falling to the floor, she can feel the pain of the scissors in her heart. This is yet another step carrying her further and further from Amish country. In her mind's eye, she can see Ma and Da's horrified looks. If only they knew what she's doing right now! Wearing an Englishers dress, cutting her hair, and breaking so many of the Ordnug rules!

Elizabeth takes a deep breath and desperately prays. *Lord, I need Your help! I know I am not sinning or breaking Your Word, yet I still feel so very guilty! I am trying my best to renew my mind in Your Word and think about life the way You think about it, but I still feel the effects of my childhood and all the teachings Ma and Da gave me seeping into my mind. It is not so easy to get rid of! Help me trust You, Lord! Help me not to worry about what anyone else may think of me, but only live to honor You. And please, Lord, give Ma and Da mercy in their hearts to forgive me. I pray that there would be peace between us so that I may see them again on this earth, and that our family may be reconciled yet once again. And if not...I still trust You.* A familiar verse flutters into her mind, *Though my mother and father forsake me, the Lord will receive me. Lord, thank You that You love me...even if they don't.*

"Okay, you can open your eyes, Elizabeth!" Aurora announces.

"I do not think I can!" Elizabeth admits, "I am far too scared!"

"Elizabeth, it's okay!" Lena tires to comfort her, "If anyone is in Christ, He is a new creation. The old things have passed away, and the new has come. This is all just part of the new. You're like a butterfly, remember? Breaking out of that old caterpillar cocoon. Now on the count of three, open your eyes and we'll be right here to help you through it. One..."

Elizabeth clutches Lena's hand.

"Two."

Elizabeth clutches Aurora's hand.

"Three!"

Elizabeth's eyes pop open and she studies the face of the young woman staring back at her. Elizabeth takes a deep breath. A small, short frame of shoulder length hair surrounds her face. She blinks, taking a closer look at her eyes which are popping out dramatically, due to the light amount of mascara Aurora has applied.

"You're an absolute showstopper!" Aurora croons. "Those soldiers are going to be getting in fistfights over you."

Elizabeth's eyes widen in horror as she turns away from the mirror to face Aurora.

"She doesn't mean that!" Lena quickly tries to recover. She tosses a warning glance toward Aurora, "What she means to say is, you're beautiful."

"Thank you for trimming my hair, Aurora, but there is no need to make a fuss over it," she tells her sister confidently. "It is a vanity to stare at yourself for too long." She stands up and reaches for the door handle. "Are we ready? May we go and get this party over with?"

"Not yet!" Aurora thinks of one last thing, "We need jewelry!" She quickly digs into her bag. "Let's see, what did I bring with me…"

"Elizabeth!" A sudden thought strikes Lena, "Did you happen to bring the crown necklace Aurora gave to you?"

Elizabeth's anxious gaze softens. "Yes."

"So did I!" Lena squeals and rushes over to her bunk.

"Oh, my goodness, no way, me too!" Aurora laughs, "We truly must be sisters!"

"Indeed, we are." Lena giggles.

~*~

Prince Asher of Tarsurella looks up from the snack table. His attention is captured by the dramatic entrance of the three Princesses. A reverent hush falls over the room as every young solider turns their heads.

Lena can feel herself blushing. Why are they all looking at them!? She wonders if perhaps they're supposed to say something. She anxiously searches the crowd for Peter, secretly hoping he won't be in the room. With each passing day that she avoids him, the more intense their awkward and uncomfortable tension grows.

Lena still hasn't spoken to him since Peter posed his life-changing question. Lena knows she needs to speak with him and face the matter in a sensible and practical, adult-like manner. But she is very much dreading the moment. So, for now, she chooses yet again to sweep the issue under the rug and find something else to do with her time.

Lena lifts her heavy skirt an inch from the floor. As breathtakingly beautiful as the dress is, it sure doesn't fair well for the practical things in life. She had nearly tripped on her way down the long hall.

Lena nervously leans toward Aurora. The glowing girl looks like a magnificent Queen in her glorious red dress, holding her head high with confidence. She doesn't appear nervous at all.

Elizabeth, who is on the opposite side of Aurora, is just as scared as Lena. She hates the way everyone is staring at them. She wishes to run out of the room and lock herself in a closet.

"Now that our Royal Highnesses have arrived, let the celebration begin!" Captain Cepheus announces.

And with that, a peppy, 1950's-sounding dance song begins blasting through the PA system. Aurora smiles with delight. *Nice music choice Captain C!* she thinks to herself.

Several female soldiers partner with their male dancing buddies and begin to boogie on the dance floor. There are only a few, brave enough to perform such moves in the presence of Royalty. The rest of the men timidly step to the sidelines and continue drinking their pink party punch, carrying on with casual conversations.

Lena spots Peter chatting with a fellow solider. "Perhaps I'll go see if they need any help in the kitchen!" Lena pipes up, the sudden thought striking her. She quickly turns on her heel and buzzes out of the room.

"I will help as well!" Elizabeth announces, taking advantage of her quick escape.

"Not so fast." Aurora grabs her sister's wrist. She gazes into Elizabeth's terrified eyes, "You're not the fearful, frightful girl you used to be, remember? You have a backbone now! You have courage and confidence! So, use it girl! Practice being in a room with strangers and exercise those social skills. I promise, I'll be right here with you. You're going to be fine."

"Excuse me, Your Highness," a voice cuts in.

Aurora releases her sister's wrist and turns to face the young man standing before her. It's Kehahi Julyan.

"Would it be breaking royal protocol if I asked you to dance?"

Aurora observes the dark-eyed fellow. She's been quite enjoying getting to know the snarky guy. He's prideful, opinionated, and carries a male ego larger than the state of Texas, but not without reason. His Martial Arts skills are even more advanced than Aurora's URIA Instructor's. After attempting to beat him in the ring and miserably failing, Aurora's been benefiting from his daily coaching. He acts as though he's completely irritated with her, endlessly teasing and pointing out her weaknesses, but Aurora is only growing stronger through his merciless jabs. He's an outstanding teacher, and Aurora is determined to someday conquer the master.

"Dance?" Aurora echoes. "Don't I have to spend enough time with you as it is already, in the ring?"

"Dancing and fighting are not that different from one another," Kehahi tells her. "They both require complicated foot work, an internal rhythm, and complete concentration on your opponent."

"Are you challenging me to a dance off?" Aurora asks. "Because if you are, you just asked the wrong girl. You might be able to kick my behind in the ring, but this is where the tables turn. I'm going to cream you on that dance floor."

"I'd like to see you try." Kehahi's voice is firm.

Elizabeth watches with bewildered eyes as Aurora follows the young man to the center of the dance floor. Elizabeth frowns. So much for her sister staying with her the entire time! She remembers all the travesties of Aurora's birthday party, and Elizabeth observes that this atmosphere is much gentler. There are no strobe lights, fog machines, or tone-deaf punk bands pounding on their drum sets. Even though worldly music floats through the sound system, at least it's at a quieter, more tolerable volume.

Elizabeth glances around nervously, unsure of what to do next. She remembers that Emma led her directly to the snack table, so Elizabeth heads in that direction. Even though her stomach is anxious, a fancy cupcake platter grabs her attention. Elizabeth *does* love cupcakes.

"Good evening, Your Majesty." Prince Asher greets her in a friendly tone.

"Oh." Elizabeth is surprised by his greeting. She tries to think of the proper response, "Uh…good evening."

The Prince turns back toward his friend who stands nearby, devouring several crackers and chunks of cheese.

"So, I was trying to convince Captain Cepheus that there could be a deeper plot at work," Asher continues, sounding as though he was in the middle of a very important conversation. "But of course, he didn't believe me. Nobody ever does."

"You can't blame the Captain for not wanting to run down that rabbit trail of another conspiracy theory," Liam replies. "With no hard and fast evidence, a practical military officer like himself isn't ready to spend the time, money, and man power required to explore a theory based off nothing more than a gut feeling."

Elizabeth removes her cupcake wrapper and continues to listen.

"But this isn't just a theory!" Asher argues, clearly passionate about whatever he's speaking of. "Charlie has evidence! What if the AA16 code is being used to control the minds of King Raymond's closest allies? Why else would his men bomb schools, kill innocent children, and oppress the citizens of Bella Adar with such evils?!"

"Ash, I know this is hard on you," Liam sympathizes. "You've been carrying this burden around for two years now, wanting to take action, yet not sure how. But can't you see that our hands are tied? Our role in Bella Adar is to serve their leadership however it's needed, not project our own ideas and suspicions onto them."

"I get that!" Asher huffs. "But if you saw a deadly, poisonous snake crawling around, wouldn't you speak up and say something about it?! I don't care if they don't believe me. And I'm going to keep running my mouth until somebody does."

"Oh, hey it's time for me to video chat with your sister." Liam pulls his cell phone out of his pocket and glances at the time. "But we can talk more about this later, if you like."

"Whatever. Go." Asher waves his hand through the air, and Liam quickly leaves, his face lit up like a four-year-old boy, clearly excited to escape this conversation and converse with Bridget instead.

Asher sighs and stuffs frustrated hands into his pocket. He glances at Elizabeth and wonders if there's something different about her appearance. He can't quite put his finger on it. Did she cut her hair?

"Excuse me," Elizabeth sets down her cupcake, "what is this snake you speak of?"

"Oh, it's not a literal snake," Asher tries to explain, wondering if perhaps the Princess is confused.

"But you think the people of Bella Adar are in danger?" Elizabeth asks.

"Yeah." Asher is pleasantly surprised by her asking. He takes a step closer, "Actually, I do."

"How so?" Elizabeth's question is simple.

Asher runs a quick hand through his hair. "Yikes." He shakes his head, "Your question is an easy one, but the answer? Not so much. Where should I start? Okay, this is going to sound pretty outlandish, but just hear me out for a minute. I have reason to believe that Raymond is using radio frequencies, implanted in various forms of technology, to influence and control the minds of his workers, and possibly even the minds of the Bella Adar citizens at large. Now people usually shut down when I use the words 'mind control', but it's been scientifically proven by my friend Charlie that this kind of technology is not only possible, it's actually happening! We believe it's being powered by something called the AA16 code and…" Asher pauses, "Have I completely lost you?"

"No," Elizabeth shakes her head, "not at all. I believe that mind control is real," she confesses.

"You do?!" Asher's eyebrows elevate.

"Yes. I used to be subject to the same kind of control and manipulation."

Confusion knits Asher's brows.

"I was Amish. And although we did not have any cellular phones or forms of technology to where those kinds of evil frequencies might be sent out, we were still being controlled. By fear. My life was dictated by rules and regulations that are not in the Bible. But we were all deceived."

"Wow," Asher breathes, "that must've been crazy. What made you decide to leave?"

"I believed what God was speaking to my heart was true. I believed the words of John 3:16 and discovered that my salvation is in Christ alone, not in a set of rules. When I thought Lena was in danger, I finally decided to leave it all behind and come support my true family."

"That must have been really hard."

"It was," Elizabeth admits. "But what is harder, with each passing day as I remain here, is attempting to win this battle in my mind. It's as if there is a war between the person I used to be and the person God is calling me to become. Some days I do not know which girl to be. But, as hard as it is, I make it my goal, as the Apostle Paul said, to forget the things which are behind and press onto the things which are ahead. I know that renewing my mind in God's Holy Word and ridding my thoughts of all those terrible lies from the past are the only way to rid myself of the terrible mind control which once plagued me."

"Wow, I've never thought about things from that perspective before." Asher ponders her words, "The fact that mind control doesn't have to come through a digital frequency. It can simply be from the way we were raised, or by things we've always thought about ourselves that weren't true. Interesting."

In a sudden, terrifying flash, Elizabeth feels as though she's speaking with Jonah. She quickly looks away. How strange it is that they look so much alike! She takes a deep breath. "Well, it was nice chatting with you. I'd best go find my sister."

And with that, Elizabeth takes off to locate Lena in the kitchen.

~*~

"Peter!" Lena gasps as she turns out of the kitchen and nearly collides with him in the hallway.

"There you are!" Peter's voice is genuine with concern, "I've been looking all over for you!" His eyes dance with delight, "You look absolutely beautiful tonight. As you always do."

[322]

Peter's arms are still gently holding her elbows, allowing her to regain balance. Thanks to her poofy dress and wobbly shoes, she had nearly toppled over completely. His gaze arrests hers and Lena can feel herself squirming. She knows he loves her dearly. So why doesn't she feel as confident as he does with such affections?

She carefully slips out of his grip and takes a simple step backward. This conversation will be far easier if they're not standing so close.

"Peter," she admits, "I've been avoiding you."

The light in Peter's eyes diminishes as a frown slips onto his face. "You have?" He sounds as if he doesn't believe the words.

"I'm so sorry," she admits, just nearly above a whisper. "It's just....I haven't wanted to have this conversation."

Several soldiers pass, laughing as they joke with one another, going to enter the party.

"Perhaps this isn't the best place to talk," Lena observes. "Shall we go in another room?"

"Yeah." Peter tries to think of a place. "Our bunkhouse should be quiet. Everyone has gone to the party."

"Okay." Lena sighs sadly, truly hating what is to come next. "That will work."

~*~

"I stand corrected," Kehahi tells Aurora. "Your dance moves are far more impressive than I expected. After seeing your cringy *Glitter Girl* music video, I was expecting nothing short of a horror show."

[323]

"Rude much?!" Aurora gasps. They're standing by the sidelines, finally finished with their dance-off for the evening. After three old-fashioned, high-energy, swing-dance style songs, the melody switched and turned into a slow, romantic waltz. That quickly ended their competition. No way were they going to slow dance with one another. "I filmed that video five years ago! And I thought it was pretty good for my tiny little mini-me, thank you very much."

"Hey, I'm just reiterating a common fact that everyone around the globe knows!" Kehahi lifts up his hands in defense, "American popstars are the worst when it comes to dancing."

"Oh, please!" Aurora sticks her chin up, "Compared to who? Your robotic, synchronized Filipino pop bands?"

"Princess, are you blind?" Kehahi snaps, clearly enjoying the lively argument. "Our pop bands could dance circles around you, any day! Not only do we dominate martial arts, we also kill it at karaoke. We're pretty much the best in the world." He grins.

"So," Aurora crosses her arms, "I'm curious. How did a Filipino boy like yourself end up serving in the URIA? I mean, how did you even find out about this? Were they accepting applications through Facebook?"

Kehahi laughs. "Actually, I was recruited." He speaks proudly, puffing out his chest, ever so slightly, "Captain Cepheus contacted me shortly after the disaster ensued, and asked that I come and serve. Our dads used to be close friends, and I guess as they continued to stay in touch over the years, the Captain figured I'd be a good addition to the team."

"So, you left a family behind? Girlfriend?" Aurora is fishing for more information about this mysterious character.

"My mom and three sisters," Kehahi tells her. "No special lady in my life, except the obnoxious next-door neighbor my mom keeps trying to set me up with. But she's obsessed with American pop music, so clearly that would never work."

Aurora tosses him a perturbed face.

"Your Highness," a short, pale solider comes up to Aurora and wipes sweaty hands on his pants. "May I have the honor of this dance?"

Aurora hesitates. She knows that after dancing with Kehahi, it would be completely rude to turn this pasty-white guy down. But she wishes to stay and continue chatting with Kehahi. He's intriguing.

"Of course," Aurora grins, trying to be polite.

She follows the young solider to the dance floor. She resists the temptation to peek over her shoulder and see if Kehahi is watching her.

Aurora is slightly irked by the fact that she can't seem to figure the guy out. Does he like her? Is he teasing her because he thinks she's attractive, or because he's truly irritated with her immature and girlish ways?

Aurora frowns. *No distractions, Aurora, remember?!* She scolds herself. *You're not about to fall head over heels for a guy you know nothing about. This is not the time to allow your heart to become romantically entangled. You need to stay focused. No distractions.*

~*~

Elizabeth stands by the snack table yet once more. Lena has disappeared, and Aurora is occupied on the dance floor.

Elizabeth reaches for another cupcake, not sure of what else to do with herself.

Prince Asher appears at the table again as well. "Hey! Back for round two?!" He smiles.

"I suppose so." Elizabeth gives her mouth the liberty of cracking a small smile, "These cupcakes are very, very good."

"Will it completely damper the mood of this party if I keep talking to you about what I think is going on with Raymond's plot?" Asher asks. "I'm sorry if this is too much, it's just, I can't stop myself from thinking about all of this! My mind is running down this crazy track and I know I'm not going to sleep tonight unless I talk to someone about this."

"Talking is good," Elizabeth tells him simply. "And I do not like parties anyway."

"Well, I guess that makes two of us." He reaches for a cupcake of his own but is far too immersed in what he's about to say to think about eating it. "So, my friends, Charlie and Jane, have been researching this topic for the past two years, and the information they've dug up clearly proves that the AA16 code is being used for destructive purposes. Our only problem is, we don't know *who* has their hands on it, or if it's spread among multiple world leaders. Raymond appears to be the perfect suspect to investigate. I mean, he's acting like a total Nazi and only someone as insane as him would actually try to test out this kind of technology on innocent, human guinea pigs. Part of the reason I came to Bella Adar is to propose the idea to you and your sisters that we send in spies to discover what Raymond is really up to. If he isn't using the AA16, then fine, that's great, I'll move onto the next suspect. But if he is, then we've got a serious problem on our hands, and this entire nation is at risk. Maybe even the world."

"What do you mean?" Elizabeth asks, struggling to understand the fullness of what they may be up against.

"If Raymond is using frequency technology on his confidants and citizens, then he'll be able to sway the minds of the population in whatever direction he pleases. Meaning, even after you dethrone Raymond and remove him by military force, the people will still be on his side, responding to his every move like an army of robots."

Elizabeth's eyes widen. "Oh no! The people must be free to think for themselves! There is nothing worse than being controlled by another human being or organization! How can we stop it?"

"We need to convince the Captain to send in undercover agents to Raymond's network." Asher's voice is all seriousness, "Unless we can get in there and clearly see what's going on, they're going to maintain the element of a sneak attack, which could be deadly for us. So long as their works are shrouded in darkness, they're safe and we're in danger. But once we shine the light on their plot, we'll know *exactly* what needs to happen to combat it."

~*~

"Peter, there is no easy way to say this." Lena hesitates.

They're standing in the empty bunk room and Lena already feels like crying. Why are her emotions such a mess? Why can't she just say how she truly feels?

Peter is silent, his eyes heavy with concern.

"I love you, Peter," Lena stutters. "But I love you, like a brother."

"Well, I'm glad you finally got that out of your system." Peter winces. "Took you long enough." Because of his bleeding heart, Peter grows visibly angry. "*Now* you tell me this? After making a complete fool out of myself and declaring my undying devotion to you!?"

"Peter wait, let me explain!" Lena attempts to calm him down, "We're still so very young! Why, I am just merely sixteen years old! How am I to know what true love is? Try to think about things from my perspective for a moment! Here I am, struggling to gain my footing in this newfound calling of leadership, learning to fight and think, and become who this nation needs me to be! I've just lost Grandmary and Theodore, the only family I've ever had, and there's no one for me to turn to, to discuss such things! I don't have time to sort out all these newfound feelings and emotions! I do care for you, Peter! I really, truly do. But I am not ready to be married. Goodness, I am not even ready to begin a courtship or explore a possible relationship because I don't even know how I feel right now! It's all so very confusing. Please, Peter, you have to understand why I am saying these things. It's just, your timing of such a question couldn't have possibly been worse."

"Or perhaps it was just the wrong person asking the question," Peter snaps, his eyes burning with flames of frustration.

"What?" Lena is stumped by his comment.

"Oh, you know what I mean!" Peter raises his voice, "If big, buff Jack would've asked, you would've said yes right away!"

"Peter, that's not true!" Lena scolds him, "How can you say such a thing?"

"Oh, don't try to pretend you don't like him!" Peter crosses his arms and suppresses a bitter laugh, "I've seen the way you look at him."

"Is that what you think this is about?" Lena shakes her head, "Cadet Conway has nothing to do with this! Peter, can't you hear what I'm saying? My decision has nothing to do with you, or Jack, or anyone else! This is about me, and what I must do for myself at this time. The last thing I need is a heart jumbled up and intertwined with such intense emotions! My heart and mind must be clear for serving my country!"

Peter takes a deep breath, attempting to calm himself down. "So, I guess that's it then." His voice is flat and frighteningly lifeless, "Our discussion is over?"

"Peter, I don't want things to grow sour between us," Lena speaks gently. "You're my best friend."

"Maybe Jack's right," Peter speaks slowly, his eyes washed over with a fresh wave of brokenness and devastation. "Perhaps you're not the same girl I used to know. Maybe it's time for me to bow out and let you handle this royalty thing on your own. After all. I am just a lowly foot solider."

"Peter, please—" Lena attempts to ease the wound, but it's too late. Peter is already damaged.

"Good evening." Peter walks away, then remembers to turn with a quick and bitter bow, "Your Majesty."

~*~

"Oh, my goodness, that was so much fun!" Aurora laughs from the back of the cart where Captain Cepheus is driving them back to their room. "We should have parties *far* more often."

"You certainly were the Belle of the Ball, Your Highness!" Captain Cepheus comments. "Thank you for dancing with our men, I am sure it will be the highlight of their time in the underground! I know it helped raised their spirits."

"My pleasure." Aurora laughs. "Can I do archery? Not so much. But dancing until midnight is definitely something I can handle!"

She glances at her sisters who are sitting on either side of her. They both appear completely depressed.

"Well, don't you two look cheery!" Aurora comments sarcastically. "Goodness, you're like deflated party balloons! Didn't you have any fun?"

"I am just tired," Elizabeth speaks quietly. Truthfully, her mind still lingers on the discussion she had with Prince Asher. They spoke together most of the evening, discussing the possible strategies as to how they might stop Raymond from accomplishing his vile plot.

Elizabeth has never felt quite so a part of the world and its frantic goings-on's until tonight. Finally, it makes sense to her. She's beginning to understand why this country needs her and her sisters to stand up and set them free from the heartless oppression they're currently suffering under. Before speaking with Asher, Elizabeth simply thought God had called her here to focus on her own self, renewing her mind in God's Word and letting go of the past. But now she sees a far, far greater picture. Perhaps God has called her here to help set others free from the very chains that used to cling to her so tightly.

"So am I," Lena adds. She doesn't want to speak about her heartbreaking conversation with Peter. It hurt her heart to see him aching so deeply. She knows her words stung him to the core.

After the girls are back at their room, Aurora plops backward onto her bed. "Oooo, we are going to sleep good tonight!"

"Thank you for these beautiful dresses, Rachel," Lena tells Rachel in the doorway. "Your works of art truly are masterpieces. I look forward to the day we can wear them again."

"Aw, you are completely welcome, Your Majesty!" Rachel glows from the compliment, "It made my soul soar with happiness to see each of you in them tonight!"

"And perhaps," Elizabeth adds with a careful glance toward the lone, zipped-up dress bag hanging on the other side of the room, "on the next occasion, our fourth sister will be with us."

Aurora lifts her bed sheet, eager to change into her cozy jammies and crawl in. She is surprised as a piece of paper tumbles out of the sheet. She quickly grabs it, wondering how it got there. She hurriedly opens it, realizing that it's a note.

Princess,

Thank you for dancing with me. This time, let's do it without the crazy crowd. Meet me in the kitchen. —Kehahi

Aurora feels color rush to her cheeks. She quickly stuffs the note away and continues making her bed, hoping her sisters didn't see it.

~*~

Aurora flops to her side. She can hear Elizabeth's gentle breathing in the bunk above her. Their bedroom is completely dark with the exception of a small nightlight coming from the kitchenette.

Aurora squeezes her eyes shut and tries to focus on sleep. But it's quite pointless. Her mind is fixated on Kehahi's mysterious note. Her eyes pop back open. Should she go? Should she sneak down the corridor and meet him in the kitchen?

She turns to the opposite side, battling with her blanket in the same way her mind is battling with itself. Perhaps it's too late. How long has she been laying here?

She can hear Rachel's quiet snoring, and Elizabeth hasn't even stirred. Surely everyone is asleep.

Aurora, don't, she tells herself. *This guy is nothing less than a big, compelling, handsome distraction. You promised you weren't going to be distracted by guys! The whole reason you broke up with Jeremiah in the first place was so you can be completely focused on God, devoted to your faith, and committed to helping your sisters take back their country. Hanging out with Kehahi is going to be a total waste of time.*

But we're not just hanging out! she argues with her conscience. *He's helping me learn how to fight! Being around him is helping me become a better warrior. At least, when we're in the ring. I don't know how dancing in the kitchen is going to help in that arena…*

Aurora smiles. *That's kind of ridiculously sweet for him to ask though! Dancing without any music. Totally adorable.*

Unless, of course, it's a trap! What if he just wants me to come all the way down there, only to find he's going to tease me and accuse me of falling for a stupid little trick! And even worse, what if he's not down there at all? What if he's just playing with my mind? What if he sent

[332]

this note as a screening process to find out if I like him or not…and then if I do show up that means I like him? But I don't like him. Do I? I mean, he's not hard to look at, but—Aurora stop!

Aurora argues with herself for several more moments. Finally, she comes to the conclusion she's not going to get any sleep unless she ventures out and investigates for herself.

She cautiously tiptoes out of bed, careful not to wake any of the sleeping bodies. She slips a navy-blue sweater on over her tank top, and a pair of jeans over her pajama shorts. She doesn't want to look completely ridiculous.

She reaches for the door latch, and Rachel jerks up to a seated position. "Your Majesty?" she asks in a groggy tone, as if she's attempting to get a grip on her surroundings.

Aurora's heart pounds. She quickly thinks of an excuse. "Yeah, it's me," she confesses in a loud whisper. "Can't sleep. I'm going to steal a cupcake from the kitchen."

And with that, she quickly slips out the door.

She stands in the hall for a few seconds, nervously waiting to see if Rachel is going to run out after her. Thankfully, she doesn't. Aurora breathes a sigh of relief, then continues down the long corridor.

As she nears the entryway, she can see Kehahi waiting in the kitchen. She smiles. It wasn't a complete setup after all! He actually wanted to meet with her.

But Kehahi doesn't appear nearly as pleased to see her as she is to see him. He's wearing a painful, frightened look. His head shakes, as if warning her not to take another step closer.

His destressed look is puzzling. Aurora decides to laugh and playfully enter the kitchen, "Having second thoughts about the—"

"Aurora, run!" he shouts in a frantic tone.

Before Aurora can respond, she feels the weight of a full-grown man pouncing on her back and shoving her to the kitchen floor. She is pinned to the ground by this heavyweight. Struck by the shock of the unexpected attack, Aurora's mind frantically attempts to recall her Taekwondo moves.

She jerks her arms backward and attempts to hit him in the stomach, but her efforts are fruitless. The man yanks her to a standing position and drags her out of the kitchen by her hair. Aurora releases a pain-filled yelp. Kehahi is nowhere to be seen.

"Help!" Aurora screams at the top of her lungs, desperately hoping there's someone nearby to hear her. "Help!"

"Now! Now! Now!" The man who has Aurora in his clutches shouts at two men fumbling with wires on the Cafeteria floor. Their nervous fingers tinker with tools.

"We've got it, run!" a shady man with a long, jagged scar beneath his left eye shouts. He bolts toward Aurora and her captor, "Go! Three minutes before this thing blows!"

Aurora's eyes widen in horror as she realizes what's happening. Someone has planted explosives!

Aurora is drug out of the Cafeteria and into the Main Corridor. "Faster!" her captor shouts. "Unless you want to blow to smithereens with everyone else in this godforsaken base!"

"It's a bomb!" Aurora screams, hoping someone from the URIA can hear her desperate echo traveling through the empty halls. "There's a bomb! Everybody run, there's a bomb!"

The enemy is clearly irritated with Aurora's warning calls, so he picks her up and hikes her over his shoulder. She wiggles and kicks and attempts to break free of his grip, but it is to no avail. His bulky hand muffles her screams.

The scrawny man with a sagging tool belt quickly unscrews a round, bronze plate in the ceiling and attempts to lower the emergency escape ladder.

"Hurry, hurry!" the heavyweight man who holds squirming Aurora barks at him. "We're running out of time!"

At that very moment, Prince Asher and Liam are seen walking past the cross hall ahead.

Aurora chomps down on the finger of the man, and he releases a yelp.

"Help!" Aurora screams, taking advantage of the seconds her mouth is free. She knows it might be her only chance to save herself, and everyone else in the base. "There's a bomb!" she screams. "Get everyone out of here!"

Liam and Asher quickly bolt toward her, and the scrawny man attempting to free the escape ladder accidently drops his screw driver.

"Hurry, you dimwit!" the massive man barks.

The scarred man scurries to fetch the fallen screw driver.

"Asher, go warn everyone!" Liam calls over his shoulder. "Call for emergency evacuation! Get everyone out of here! Go!"

Asher doesn't have to be told twice. His boots stop, then pound in the opposite direction. Liam continues charging forward and slams into the sumo-sized man holding Aurora. The force of impact causes Aurora to slip from his arms. Aurora lands on her feet and gasps for air.

"Go! Get out of here!" Liam shouts.

Liam is fully engaged in a violent fist-fight with the bad guy. Aurora ducks as the men punch and dive and avoid one another's swings. She prepares to run to the opening ahead, but the man with the haunting scar grabs her leg.

Aurora screams again and tries to continue running. But he has a firm grip on her ankle, so she doesn't go very far. She tries to kick him with her opposite leg, but he secures his capture. Aurora is pulled tightly into his chest before he yanks her up the ladder, quickly climbing into a dark, fearful tunnel which points upward.

Aurora's pounding heart thunders with fear. What's happening?! Where are they going?!

Aurora looks downward as the man continues to drag her ever higher. The glance makes her dizzy as she realizes they're already several stories high. Pretty soon they'll reach the top and be standing on level ground again.

An unexpected drop of water falls onto her cheek. She cranes her head upward. She can see an opening in the distance. Another drop hits her forehead. The drops of rain intensify as they near the surface.

With only three ladder rungs left to go, Aurora hears a terrifying boom. Aurora releases a scream as the ladder shakes.

The man scurries out of the hole and pushes Aurora forward. She tumbles onto the soggy grass. Its pitch black. She scurries to her feet, but the man has her in his grip again. He continues running, dragging Aurora through an opening in the forest. She's paralyzed by fear. The sound of another explosive is heard behind them.

Her mind is so polluted with shock and fear, she can't even think properly. Where is he taking her?! Did the others make it out in time?!

Suddenly, the man trips on a buckling tree root and almost releases Aurora. She fights and kicks with all her might, knowing she must break free from his deadly claws.

Liam reappears in the dark, downpour-drenched scene and tosses a punch into the man's stomach. But Liam isn't alone. Within seconds, the other two grimy villains appear and knock Liam to the ground.

All at once Aurora releases the loudest, most intense war cry that has ever been released from her lips. She shouts at the top of her lungs and kicks the man with all her might. He loses his grip and Aurora bolts.

She struggles to see through the darkness as she runs forward. Her breathing is frantic.

Suddenly, two bright lights appear ahead. A small truck whips into the clearing. The two, intense headlights temporarily blind her. Out of the corner of her eye, she can see the men toss Liam into the back of the truck and lock the door. Aurora's stomach is lead. If she doesn't get out of here now, she knows she'll be trapped in the truck as well.

She screams once more and tries to escape. But she is no match for the three conniving men. Next thing she knows, she's smushed into the front seat of their truck, sandwiched between her captors.

"Go, go, go!" one man shouts at the other.

"I'm going, I'm going!" He slams on the gas and the car flies forward. Windshield wipers ferociously slap away the pounding rain.

"Mission accomplished!" one of the men declares triumphantly. "Report to King Raymond." He offers Aurora a wicked grin, "We've got her."

~*~

Lena grabs Captain Cepheus' hand as he pulls her up the final rung of the escape ladder.

"Where is everyone?!" Lena cries. A wild wind and freezing-cold sheet of rain whips through her hair and into her face. "Where are they?" she shouts. "Did they escape?! How will we know?!"

"Your Majesty, we need to keep moving!" Captain Cepheus commands. "I know you're concerned but right now your safety is our utmost priority! We need to get to higher land and find a cave or some shelter where we can hide. It's no doubt Raymond poured water into our ant hill, hoping we would scatter out like frantic bugs, with no manner of protection. We will not give him the satisfaction of finding you! Come, we must move quickly!"

Lena obeys his command as they dash into the woods, but her heart screams at her. Where is Elizabeth?! How could they have possibly gotten split up!?

When Prince Asher pounded on their bedroom door in the middle of the night, frantically shouting about a bomb, nobody knew what to do other than grab their shoes and bolt into the hallway. Everyone was manic, desperate to rush to the nearest escape routes. One minute Elizabeth was beside her, and the next she was gone! When she turned to look for her, Captain Cepheus insisted she hurry up the ladder. And what about Peter?! Had he made it to one of the twelve emergency exits?!

"Shh!" Captain Cepheus suddenly hushes her, even though she's completely quiet. He gently grabs her and sinks to hide behind a thick tree. "Someone's out there."

Lena drops to her knees, hardly even able to think. There's no way this can be happening. It's like a dream. A terrible, heart wrenching, dream. It must be. She's even still wearing her long, white nightgown.

"Sound off!" a man calls in the distance. "Roll Call!"

Captain Cepheus suddenly shoots to his feet. "It's Sargent Crawdad!" he announces. "I would recognize that voice anywhere!"

A tidal wave of relief crashes over Lena as she remembers that Sargent Crawdad is the leader of Peter's platoon. He must be safe!

"Sargent, is that you?!" Captain Cepheus calls out.

"All stand at attention for Captain Cepheus!" the Sargent commands his men.

Lena and the Captain step deeper into the woods and soon find the small pocket of men. Lena's eyes frantically search the crowd. Though it is nearly pitch black and the moon is covered by thick clouds, Lena still hopes to see Peter.

"Praise be to God, your platoon made it out alive!" Captain Cepheus tells the sergeant. "Are you all numbered and accounted for?"

"All except three, Captain," Sargent Crawdad reports. "They broke rank and I'm not sure where they went. My guess is they tried to help whoever else they could find and assist in their escape."

"Who were the men?" Captain Cepheus asks calmly.

"Stephan Brown, Conner Cox, and Peter Greenwood."

~*~

Elizabeth presses on through the driving rain, completely unsure of which direction to go.

"Lena? Aurora?" she cries out at the top of her lungs. "Rachel? Captain Cepheus? Anyone?!"

Her tiny little frame shivers as her bottom lip turns purple. Her crossed, bony arms which cling to her chest are not keeping her warm enough. Every part of her is numb. She knows she needs to find shelter soon. But even more desperately than she desires a warm place to rest, she desires to find a familiar face.

She continues walking, praying, and asking the Lord for mercy.

"Oh Lord, lead me to someone! If they are alive p-p-please let me find them!" As cold, exhausted and afraid as she is, she tries to keep her mind fixed on the Lord and on His Holy promises.

"Wh-wh-when," she shivers, "when I am a-a-fraid, lead me to the rock that is higher than I."

A sudden thought comes to mind as she recites the Psalm she just read yesterday. She needs to find rocks. She doesn't know why, but she feels as though it is vital to find a rocky area. Perhaps it is the Lord speaking to her, telling her which direction she should go?

She presses onward, straining her eyes through the darkness, trying not to trip over branches, mossy logs, and clumps of thick ferns.

Finally, she spots something that appears like a raised, large rock in the distance. Elizabeth's heartbeat quickens with hope. Could it perhaps be a cave of sorts? A place where she can rest for the night and get out of this merciless rain?

She continues trudging forward and finally comes to the thick stone which forms a wall taller than she. She rests her back on the raised rock and gasps for air. There. She has found it. Now she just needs to see if there's an entrance of sorts. She allows her hand to guide her along the edge of the stone, searching for whatever it is God wants her to see next.

Her eyes do a double take. It appears there are two figures in the distance!

"Hello?! Elizabeth calls out, hoping it's not her imagination playing tricks on her. "Hello, is anyone out there?!"

Meanwhile, several feet away, Prince Asher and Jonathan struggle to see through the dark as well.

Jonathan had been on his way up the escape ladder, just moments before the explosion, when he saw the young Prince running back toward the Cafeteria area where the bomb was set. 'No!' Jonathan had shouted, 'Don't try to be a hero, there's not enough time!' Thankfully Asher listened, and Jonathan escaped just in the nick of time.

"Do you hear that?" Asher now strains his ears through the roaring down pour.

"Yeah." Jonathan nods. "It sounds like someone's calling out. Hello?!" Jonathan shouts back.

"Help!" the quiet voice cries again. "It is me, Elizabeth! Who is out there?!"

"It's the Princess!" Asher is shocked to hear her voice in the distance.

"Elizabeth!" Jonathan speaks her name like a reflex, as he thinks of his own daughter. "Elizabeth! Keep walking, it's Jonathan! You're getting closer!"

"Jonathan?" Elizabeth gasps, relived to recognize the voice. "Oh, thank You, Lord!" She whispers the heartfelt praise as she is on the verge of tears.

Next thing she knows, Elizabeth is standing before Jonathan and Prince Asher. Jonathan quickly envelops her in a hug.

"Oh Jonathan!" she cries. "You have no idea how relived I am to see you!" Elizabeth can feel tears pressing, "I, I was so s-s-s-scared that I might walk forever a–a–and–"

"Shhh, you're okay." Jonathan hugs her just as he would his own daughter. Relief blankets his soul. He was completely rocked by the thought that perhaps Eleanor's blood sisters, the ones she knows absolutely nothing about, might be dead. "Don't cry," he coaches her, hoping to offer comfort. "Everything is going to be just fine."

"I k-k-k-know you are r-r-r-ight" Elizabeth shivers.

Jonathan grabs her hands, "Oh, no. She's stone cold." He turns to Asher, "We need to find shelter and build a fire before she goes into shock."

"R-r-rocks," she stutters, "we must find r-r-rocks."

"Here, take my jacket." Jonathan quickly slips off his black leather jacket and drapes it around her shoulders. "You two stay here. I'll go see if I can find an entrance to that cave."

"Wait." Asher grabs Jonathan's arm, not ready for him to wander off. "You can't go in unarmed. What if Raymond's men are lodging there?"

"Good point," Jonathan reaches for a large, broken tree branch on the ground below. He nods, satisfied with the thickness of the walking stick in his hand. "Hopefully I won't have to use this." He looks at Asher, "If I'm not back in ten minutes," the words catch in his throat, "don't come in. Your priority is to get Elizabeth to safety. No matter what." Jonathan attempts to walk away, then he stops himself. He turns back to the two, "And if something happens…please tell my daughter I love her."

~*~

Aurora tumbles out of the truck, feeling as if she's trapped in the middle of an inconceivable horror film. She trips in the mud and nearly tumbles over. One of the wicked men catch her and Aurora hits him in the arm.

"Let me go!" she shouts.

"She sure is a feisty one." He shares his lofty commentary with those who are listening, "We should've killed her when we had the chance."

A man opens the back end and yanks Liam out. Aurora stares helplessly at the man who tried to save her. A fiery look of determination is still ablaze in his eyes. Aurora interprets that look to mean he still believes there is hope of escape.

"The King said he wanted her alive." The guy who sounds like he's in charge, speaks. He shoves Aurora forward, causing her head to turn and face the castle for the first time.

Aurora's heart falls. There's *no* way this can be the central icon of the country they've been fighting for. The castle is nothing she imagined it to be. Instead of a dazzling whitewashed exterior with towering bulwarks and sparkly windows, the medieval castle looks like a cold and miserable dungeon. The ancient stone appears as though it could topple over and crumble apart at any second.

Demonic bolts of lightning and evil thunderclaps cause the entire experience to feel even more traumatic for Aurora. She strongly resists the temptation to cry in fear. She doesn't move any closer to the craggy castle. But the men continue to push her forward, and it is clear she has no choice.

They pass a rusty, black iron gate and once they enter, it slams behind them. The loud CLANK sends tremors of horror through her soul. Aurora is completely trapped. They pass through a terrible-smelling courtyard and finally step into one of the thick, black bulwarks.

The leader lights a torch. Although they're out of the rain, Aurora is far from comforted. Thick stone walls are illuminated by the light, revealing nothing but more stone, and three cruel, iron gates. Aurora gasps, finally realizing what lies beyond those iron bars.

Prison cells.

They open the first gate and toss Liam inside.

"What about him, why are we keeping him alive too?" one of the men asks. "He's got this look in his eye that thinks he's gonna escape."

"Eh, chain him to the wall," the man says. "And if he tries to pull some Houdini escape trick on us, we'll shoot him."

Aurora watches in horror as Liam's hands and feet are bound with ancient chains. He won't even be able to sit down or rest his legs in the cell! An immense feeling of guilt and desperation crashes into her core, as she realizes this is all her doing. If only she hadn't gone down to the kitchen and–

They move Aurora to the next cell over and open the door. Her heart frantically pounds.

"Your lodging, Princess." The man speaks of her royal title like a sarcastic byword. He tosses her into the cell and slams the gate behind her.

~*~

"There, this fire should help you get warm," Jonathan tells Elizabeth.

Elizabeth sits in the stillness of the dry, dark cave, shivering by the glow of blazing flames. Elizabeth's trembling hands near the flames as they thaw in the heat. "Th-th-thank you, Jonathan," she tells him, truly grateful for all he has done to take care of her. "You are too kind."

"Don't thank me." Jonathan crouches down beside her, desiring to warm himself as well. "Thank Prince Asher, here. He's the one who got this fire started."

"Someone should keep watch." Asher's eyes flicker toward the cave entry, "We still don't know if Raymond's men are lingering nearby."

"I've got it covered." Jonathan stands up, "You kids need to get some sleep. We're going to have a long day ahead of us tomorrow."

[345]

Jonathan leaves and Asher takes his position. Elizabeth looks at the young man and wonders what time it is. Dark circles beneath his eyes proclaim it hasn't been an easy night. She guesses it to be about two or three AM.

"Do you t-t-think they all made it out alive?" Elizabeth asks the dreaded question.

"I don't know," Asher admits honestly, "I sure hope so."

"I know that the Bible tells us not to be afraid, but I am greatly failing. I have never experienced anything like this before."

"I have." Asher sighs, recalling challenging times just as traumatic in his own family. He looks at Elizabeth, "And it wasn't easy. But somehow, God brought us through it. And he'll get you and your sisters through this, as well."

"Oh dear, I just pray that they're still alive!" Elizabeth clasps her hands anxiously. "And that they are all safe, with shelter and company. I cannot bear to think of either of them wandering around all alone."

"Well, worrying certainly isn't going to help anything. Jonathan is right. You need to get some sleep."

"What about you?" Elizabeth asks, wondering why he refuses to rest.

"Someone needs to keep an eye on things."

"Is that not what Jonathan is doing?"

"He's guarding the entrance of the cave," Asher speaks calmly. "But nobody knows how deep or far this tunnel goes, or what might be on the other end. I don't want any more surprise attacks."

"Oh." Elizabeth senses his wisdom. Still, she wishes that he would at least give himself some time to rest. "Very well." She rolls up Jonathan's jacket and lays her head upon it, "So long as you do not allow your mind to worry, either."

Asher doesn't reply. He continues staring into the crackling fire, and Elizabeth closes her eyes.

~*~

Episode 9

Emma bites her bottom lip as she nervously kills time in the waiting room. She hates hospitals. She's not sure if it's the pasty white walls, the generic clean chemical smell, or the squeak of orthopedic shoes rubbing on the floor as nurses scoot by. Whatever the reason, it has never been Emma's favorite hangout place. But then again, whose is it? Nobody likes to be at the hospital.

Emma closes her book, her left leg jittering nervously.

"Are you okay, Em?" Miss Maggie asks, "Are you nervous about meeting Miracle?"

"She still only weighs several pounds." Emma reveals her fear, "Even though they have her most vital organs stabilized, she's still not out of the woods yet. I just don't want to break down and start crying. Julie and Brian have been so strong through all of this."

"They've been troopers, that's for sure." Miss Maggie sets her magazine back on the nearby side table, "I can't imagine going through something so traumatic with your child." Miss Maggie's eyes lovingly gaze toward her daughter. A loud ring bounces through the waiting room and Miss Maggie dives into her purse, frantically searching for her phone. She can feel the irritated looks of those sitting nearby. "Oh dear, I thought I had it on vibrate!"

"Miss Bates?" A doctor wearing a pale blue scrub with matching pants appears. "Julie and Brian said you can come on back."

"Go ahead, honey! I'm sorry, I have to take this. I'll be there in a few!" Miss Maggie quickly answers the phone and covers her ear. She scoots into another room, careful not to further bother those who are already irritated with the Aurora Jasper ringtone.

Emma stands up and follows the doctor down a long hall. She wants to cringe. More squeaky shoes.

They turn a corner, and Emma reverently steps into a small room where Julie and Brian are gathered around something that looks like an incubator.

"You made it!" Julie embraces her, "Aw, we're so happy to see you! How was your time in Europe?!"

"Oh, it was good." Emma is distracted by the incubator. Is Miracle in there? Her throat tightens. "How are you guys doing?"

Brian gives her a hug. "Well, it certainly hasn't been easy." His eyes are bloodshot and the dark bags beneath them speak of his exhaustion, "But with coffee, prayer, and a whole, *whole* lot of grace, we're making it. Miracle is improving on a daily basis, which is the most important thing."

"Do you want to meet her?" Julie asks excitedly.

Emma doesn't know what to say. Of course, she does. But her emotions are already raw.

Julie grabs her hand and slowly directs her toward the incubator. Emma nearly gasps. There, nestled among a little purple blanket, is a miniature human being with pink skin and tiny tubes sticking out of her from every direction. Miracle is just a smidge larger than Emma's hand. Emma can't believe it. The premature baby should still be developing in her mother's womb. She shouldn't be out and kicking in the world yet! Emma can feel tears threatening dangerously close.

"God is faithful," Julie testifies, despite the heartbreaking hardship. "All of our friends and church family have been incredibly supportive, and God has already been teaching us so much through this process." Julie's eyes clog up with tears, "But I wish…" A lump comes to Julie's throat, "I wish I could hold her. She just…"

Brian quickly hugs his wife, offering her emotional support. "I know honey, I know." Brian sighs, appearing to be on the verge of tears himself, "We can't hold her, so we have to trust that God is."

"She's beautiful," Emma speaks in wonderment, unable to take her eyes off the little darling.

"And to think they abort children the same size as her." Julie shakes her head, unable to fathom such a tragedy, "So many mothers discard their unborn babies, while we're here fighting for our daughter's life!"

Emma's heart is heavy. Julie is absolute right. Since when has human life become so common and disposable? The little girl breathing, taking in doses of oxygen and depending on God to keep her alive, is a true miracle.

We're all miracles, Emma thinks. *We're just as weak and dependent on God as Miracle is. We need Him to supply us with air and food and health, and every need we could possibly have. And He does it. So faithfully. Day after day after day.*

"You guys are amazing." Emma looks up at Brian, "Your faith through this whole process is so inspiring to me."

"Oh, it's not us." Brian shakes his head and points heavenward, "It's all Him. Grace upon grace, upon grace."

"If we're talking about amazing, the person we should be talking about is you!" Julie grins, "The girl who saved our entire play! Miss Belle! I'm *still* getting texts from the kids raving about how much they loved you and your performance! Emma, the Lord truly used you to not only meet a need but impact the lives of others around you! Brian and I are so proud of you!"

"Yeah, we wish we would've been there to see it," Brian adds. "We hear you rocked the house."

"Well, I don't know about that," Emma giggles. "But it was amazingly fun. And I think the Lord used it to help me conquer some fears, as well as open up some new possibilities."

"Oh yeah?" Julie smiles, "What kind of possibilities?"

"Actually," Emma slowly breaks into a grin, "I got a full ride scholarship to Anderson's Academy of the Arts."

"What?!" Julie bursts out, "Emma, that's incredible!" She rests excited hands on Emma's shoulders, "Congratulations!"

"Wow!" Brian's tone reveals how impressed he is, "That's no small accomplishment! They don't hand those scholarships out to just anyone!"

"I know." Emma sighs, "Which is why I'm so torn. I don't know if I'm going to accept it or not."

"Why not?" Julie asks.

"Well, I've been talking things over with my mom, weighing the pros and cons, and it seems like the 'Reasons Not to Go' side is pretty heavy." Emma explains, "First of all, I've never done anything like this. I've been homeschooled since birth, so the idea of attending a real school is slightly terrifying. I also wouldn't be able to travel around with my mom and her clients. Not to mention the fact that I know absolutely nothing about performing arts."

"Reasons *to* go?" Brian asks.

"It might be an opportunity God has opened up for me," Emma speaks slowly. "But then again, maybe it's not. I don't know!" She releases a frustrated huff, "How are you supposed to know what God's will is for your life?"

"Oh dear, the famous question!" Julie laughs, "The question that I ask myself pretty much every week! We could delve into such a deep, multifaceted conversation about that topic. But I think the most important question to ask right now is, what if this *isn't* God's will for your life? What then? What would happen if you took a leap of faith, went to this school, and found out it wasn't what God wanted you to do?"

"Then, I would be a complete and miserable failure and ship myself home ASAP?"

"Maybe," Brian laughs. "Or maybe you'd learn something through the process. Maybe you'd learn that God isn't going to freak out and condemn us if we accidently go to the 'wrong' school or audition for a play, instead of working at Chick-Fil-A. Sure, God has a good and perfect plan for all of our lives, but sometimes I think we're so concerned with finding that 'perfect path' that we're afraid to make any kind of decision at all, and we end up never getting anywhere because of fear. I really like the attitude the Apostle Paul had. Even though he wanted to be led by the Spirit of God and move within the realm of His plan, it appeared there were times when Paul really didn't know what to do next. So, he took a step of faith. And, sometimes God showed up and told him to stop or redirected his footsteps. Proverbs says the footsteps of a righteous man will be ordered by God. But I think we have to stand up and start moving in a direction, even if it's the wrong one at first, so God can redirect our paths while we're at it."

"Brian is right. So, what if you go to the school, try it out, and find out it isn't your thing? That's completely okay! You're still *so* young, Emma. Nobody's demanding that you get your future all figured out right now. You'll be trying something new, and if performing arts isn't your thing, that *doesn't* make you a failure. It makes you a girl who had enough guts to step out! And wouldn't that be better than looking back on your life, years from now, wondering what things could've been like?"

Emma considers their advice. She can definitely see their point. She doesn't want fear to stop her from living life.

"And who knows?" Brian asks. "Maybe God will have an assignment for you there. Maybe there are other kids who need to meet you and be impacted by Jesus shining through you. Maybe this school will help train and equip you for whatever's coming up in your future. There could be so many epic possibilities! But there's only one way to find out."

~*~

"Mom, I think I should do it." Emma takes a deep breath, feeling as if she's about to jump headfirst off a thousand-foot cliff. "I think I should go to Anderson."

"Really?!" Miss Maggie glances at her daughter from where she is maneuvering through LA traffic, "Are you sure?"

Emma bites her lip. She hates making decisions. Especially ones as life altering as this. But she's already committed. She's not going to back out now.

"Yes," she nods confidently. "And if for some reason this school isn't the right thing for me, well God can certainly make that obvious and send me home. But honestly, Mom…I think this might be the next step."

"Yay!" Miss Maggie lets out a victory hoot, "Oh honey, I am so, so proud of you! This school is going to open up a whole new world of opportunities and experiences for you! But is it too late?" Her smile suddenly disappears, "You were gone for orientation, will they make an exception for you anyway? When is the deadline for enrollment? When is your first day? When do we have to have you moved in by? Oh, we'll have to go shopping for some cute little dorm items! Just think, we can buy you a new lamp and a matching laundry basket, and all those cute Target items they sell to college kids! Oh Em, this will be such a blast!"

"Slow down, Mom!" Emma laughs, "I still need to contact the school and find out all the details."

"This calls for an ice cream celebration!" Miss Maggie cheers, "If I can just get into this other lane and–" Miss Maggie's eyes are focused on the wild, six lanes of whooshing traffic.

Her purse is vibrating.

"Oh, Em, can you get that?" Miss Maggie attempts to change lanes, "It's probably *Bubblegum*! They're going to let me know the status on *Acid Rain's* possible tour options. They want to get those boys out, but with Aurora gone, we need another tour to hook them up on."

"It's a text," Emma explains as she removes the phone from her mother's purse. "And it's from *Bubblegum*. It says, after three highly animated confetti emoji's, Obsession just climbed to number ten on the Top Billboard 200!" Emma's voice increases with excitement, "Jamie Drift wants them as a tour opener, starting next week!" Emma looks up from the phone. "Mom, that's crazy! Jamie Drift's sold out stadium shows are even bigger than Aurora's!"

"Oh, My Kale Chips!" Miss Maggie cries out. "Emma! That's massive!"

"Wow." Emma breathes, attempting to soak in the news. "So, I guess that means you and Arden will be leaving soon, huh?" Emma suddenly feels a strong dose of homesickness, deep in the pit of her stomach, "And I'll be at Anderson?"

"I guess so, sweetie." The excitement deflates from Miss Maggie's voice. "But I'm sure you'll be having so much fun at that school, you won't even miss us for a second! But me on the other hand? I'm going to miss you like—"

The phone rings and Emma glances at the caller ID. "Aurora's parents?" Emma questions the ID.

"Here, I can talk to them really quick." Miss Maggie gestures for her daughter to hand her the phone.

Emma isn't sure if it's safe for her mom to talk in this much traffic, but it's not often Aurora's parents call. She quickly hands the phone over.

"Hello?" Maggie's voice is full of ginger and sweet spices. Suddenly, all the flavor from her voice evaporates and a shaky, gravely tone of dread overtakes her. "Oh, my Lord. Dear God, have mercy." She quickly pulls off to the side of the road.

Emma's heart is pounding. Her eyes frantically search her mother's as she strains her ears to catch their conversation. *What's going on?* Her mind screams, *Why does Mom sound like that?*

"Oh my. Oh my." Miss Maggie's eyes are glossed over with tears, "Okay. Okay. Oh dear, Lord. Yes. Yes, okay, call as soon as you hear anything. Okay. Okay. Bye."

Miss Maggie hangs up the phone, and Emma stares at her.

She's far too afraid to ask.

Miss Maggie's voice is shaky. "Emma." She turns to her daughter and chokes out the words, "There's been an explosion."

~*~

Eleanor's cowgirl boot-clad toes rest on the bottom rung of a whitewashed fence. Her stomach is pressed against the higher rung as she watches a swarm of dust kicked up from within the riding arena.

Harmony appears to be weightless in Comanche's saddle. The thundering horse performs hairpin turns around a course of barrels, whipping through the tight corners at breakneck speeds.

Eleanor is impressed. Her cousin is crazy talented.

"Mony, you came in too tight on that last turn!" Obadiah offers what he believes to be helpful pointers, "There goes five seconds! You've gotta give Comanche more room there!"

Harmony releases a frustrated huff. "Obviously," she grumbles. She knows what she's doing wrong. She doesn't need Obadiah to point out her flaws.

"Obadiah and Harmony have a really odd relationship." Heaven pulls herself up onto the fence beside Eleanor. "One minute they're arguing like a crabby old married couple, and the next they're best friends, coaching one another and attempting to smash record barrel-racing times. Mom says they've been like this practically since birth."

Eleanor doesn't respond. Heaven is more than eager to offer her commentary on everything, giving her a play-by-play of every second. As much as she loves her cousin, Heaven's endless chatting can be a little bit draining.

"You guys have a lot of malls in California, right?" Heaven asks.

"Um, yeah." Eleanor keeps her eyes fixed on Comanche's gait. She's never tried barrel racing. At least, not at the intense level her cousin competes at. Her mom taught her to guide some of their rescued horses around obstacle courses, just for fun as well as assisting the horses in overcoming fear. But Eleanor finds herself captivated by Comanche's movements. Barrel racing looks like a total blast.

"Ugh, I'm so jealous!" Heaven bursts out. "The nearest mall for us is forty minutes away! And we never go, because there's always work to be done here. Even when I *try* to convince Mom and Dad that I am in desperate need of new clothes, that happens to be the time when they so conveniently open up a new box of hand-me-downs. If I lived in Cali, I would be at the mall *all* weekend."

"Big city life really isn't all it's cracked up to be." Eleanor's voice is flat, "And a lot of those stores are far too overpriced anyway. You'll either get bored or run out of money, whichever happens first."

"Which is why I want to be a professional surfer," Heaven continues excitedly. "Or a swimmer. Something where I can be at the beach all the time! Or maybe I'll be a professional YouTuber! Then brands would be begging me to come to their stores and give me free clothes, just to feature their outfits in my videos!" Heaven sighs, "Isn't it crazy exciting and cool to think that people actually do that for their full-time job!? Ugh, now *that* would be the life."

"You're taking the corners too cautiously." Obadiah flails his arms, "You're tightening up and Comanche can sense that! You've gotta keep your speed up! Ride it again, but this time go solely for speed. Don't think about your corners, let Comanche lead, he already knows how to take those, I think you're just tightening up."

"How are they looking?" a voice calls from behind.

Eleanor glances over her shoulder. Uncle Sky and Aunt Lydia approach. Eleanor quickly looks away and sets her attention back on Comanche. It's so strange seeing a woman who looks, talks and dresses just like her mother did.

"A little rough," Heaven reports honestly, "but I think Harmony is determined to keep her Rodeo Queen title."

"Obadiah, Mony, let's reign in for a few minutes, okay?" Aunt Lydia's voice is heavy. "We have some news."

Harmony pulls Comanche to a stop and Obadiah gives his parents his full attention. "What's wrong?" His eyes are drenched with concern.

Aunt Lydia regretfully clasps her hands together, not ready to share the news. Uncle Sky clears his throat as if he's nervously buying extra time, and Eleanor realizes they're looking directly at her. She slowly lowers herself from the fence.

"There's no easy way to say this." Aunt Lydia hesitates before continuing, "Eleanor, we just got a call from the company your dad works for. The base he was working at has suffered a serious accident. Apparently..." Aunt Lydia draws a sharp breath, "an explosion went off within the basement."

"Is he okay?" Eleanor asks quickly. Surely he is. Surely the only reason Aunt Lydia looks so solemn is because of the financial loss of the company, right? Surely nothing has happened to her dad.

"We don't know yet." Aunt Lydia speaks matter-of-factly, keeping her voice even, "Many of the workers ran out, trying to find safety and escape the fire as quickly as possible. Most of the men are accounted for, but there are several missing."

"He's okay. Isn't he." Eleanor speaks determinedly. "He *has* to be okay."

"Honey, I'm so sorry," Aunt Lydia reaches out for a hug. "We just don't know yet. But the URIA promises to call the second they discover where he is."

Eleanor rejects Aunt Lydia's outstretched arms. She doesn't want this woman's sympathy. Eleanor takes off, bolting like a frightened horse, completely unsure of where to run.

Aunt Lydia and Uncle Sky stare helplessly at one another. Should they go after her? Should they allow her some time to be alone?

"Oh, Ellie," Harmony breathes. Her heart is shattered for her cousin. She slips off Comanche's back and hands Obadiah the reigns. "This is terrible! Mom, Dad, how could something like this happen?!"

"We can't jump to conclusions yet." Aunt Lydia's voice is compassionate, yet firm. "It's highly likely Uncle Jon got out in time and is hiding out in the woods somewhere. The URIA doesn't want us to worry. But—"

"But what?" Heaven asks, her eyes just as wide and concerned as her sisters are.

"They want us to tell her."

"Right now?" Obadiah's jaw drops, "You're kidding! Mom, that news is going to completely rock her world! There's no way Ellie is going to be ready to hear something that life altering. Not right after she found out that her Dad might be—" Obadiah stops himself. "This just seems like really bad timing."

"I agree," Uncle Sky nods. "Which is why we're going to wait."

"But honey, the URIA said—" Aunt Lydia beings to argue.

"I know what they said." Uncle Sky is firm in his decision, "But Diah is right. Ellie isn't ready for this. We at least need to wait until we can reassure her that Jon is okay."

"Wait, I'm totally confused." Heaven scratches her head, "Tell her what? Is there some kind of secret going on that I don't know about?"

~*~

In Bella Adar...

Lena's eyelids flutter open. She releases a peaceful sigh and rolls over on her side. A steady drip-drip-drip pattering song creates a relaxing and tranquil lullaby. For a moment, she feels as if she's back home again, sleeping beneath the heavy quilt Grandmary made for her, listening to raindrops dance on their rooftop.

But suddenly, Lena remembers.

She's not at Grandmary's house.

Her head shoots upward. She rises to an abrupt sitting position and kicks the light sheet off her toes. She takes stock of her surroundings. Her makeshift bed is on the hard floor of the Bella Adarian forest. She's tucked beneath a small tent which Captain Cepheus set up for her last night. It was one of the few emergency items Sergeant Crawdad managed to grab before escaping to the woods. Lena is still in her nightgown, but she has nothing else to change into.

She unzips the tent opening and her bare toes step outside, squishing through the damp mud. She's only been awake for a few seconds, but her mind is already racing. She must find out what has occurred during her short slumber. Where is Peter and Aurora and Elizabeth, and the rest of the missing URIA men?!

Light sprinkles fall onto Lena's arms and head. Lena's heart sinks as she thinks of all the young soldiers who had to sleep out in the rain. The poor dears must be freezing and miserable! Her eyes scan the scene for Captain Cepheus. She sees him chatting beneath a small, makeshift tent. It's nothing more than a grey tarp, set up between three dangling tree branches. He is speaking with Sergeant Crawdad. Lena quickly makes her way through the rain.

"Good morning, Your Majesty," Captain Cepheus kindly greets her. "Did you rest well?"

Lena is somewhat irritated with his foolish question. Why should that matter right now? Everyone else has been forced to suffer all night beneath this miserable weather, while she has been treated like a duchess, resting oh-so warm and dry? Sometimes Lena grows frustrated with the way the URIA dotes upon her. She is not any more special than the rest of these men.

"Has anyone else been found?" Lena asks anxiously. "Aurora? Elizabeth? Peter?"

"No, Your Majesty." Captain Cepheus shakes his head sadly. "But there is good news. Sergeant Crawdad got his emergency radio working. We were able to reach the palace of Tarsurella. They dispatched a rescue squad and should be arriving at any moment to carry you to safety."

"But what about my sisters?" Lena's voice is desperate, "And the missing men?! We can't leave them!"

"Tarsurella is dispatching troops to continue the search. They'll return to what remains of our base, as well as diligently scour the nearby areas. We will find your sisters, Your Majesty. You needn't worry."

"I'm not leaving without them!" Lena cries.

"I know you wish they were here with you, but it is of vital importance that we remove you from the premises as quickly as possible. Raymond's men might still be lingering nearby. I insist you return to Tarsurella. Your sisters, as soon as we find them, will join you there as well."

A low rumbling is heard in the distance. Lena looks up. It isn't thunder. Two helicopters soar above.

"Thank heavens, they're here." Relief floods Captain Cepheus' voice, "Sergeant, tell the men to get ready. We'll need them to unload the tents, medical supplies, and food provisions."

"Yes, Captain!" Sergeant Crawdad offers him a respectful salute then marches through the frigid drizzle to go address his men.

"Your Majesty, get ready and collect your things. I'll escort you to your ride as soon as they land."

"I don't have any things," Lena speaks, perhaps too bitterly for the sensitivity of the moment. Has Captain Cepheus already forgotten that she's standing before him in her nightdress? "The *one* thing I have left in this world are my sisters. Captain Cepheus, I cannot leave them!"

"Your Majesty, I know you want to help them. But right now, the best way you can assist them, is by returning to safety."

"I've heard this all before." Lena crosses her arms, "I was fed these very same, lofty promises concerning Grandmary and Theodore that everything would be okay if I simply allowed myself to be whisked out of the picture. But it wasn't."

"I cannot promise that your sisters are okay," Captain Cepheus speaks honestly. "Anything could've happened to the Princesses. They could be lost in the woods, safely tucked away in a cave with Cadet Greenwood and the other men, kidnapped by Raymond's men and held hostage in his palace…or worse. Your Majesty, none of us knows what is truly going on here, except for God. And while I am not asking you to trust me, a mere human being, I am asking you to trust God Almighty. He is the only One who truly has the wisdom to handle all of this. Right now, to the best of my human judgement and flawed abilities, I believe it is safest for you to be in Tarsurella. Not here."

Lena watches with tired eyes as the helicopters land in a clearing in the far distance.

"Very well." Lena nods reluctantly, "I do not want to leave. But I suppose you are right. If Raymond attacks again, it will be best if I am nowhere near to stir up his wrath."

She regretfully gazes toward the helicopters then back to Captain Cepheus. "Thank you, Captain. For all you've done to help. I know your job isn't easy."

~*~

Jack Conway holds the frail hand of a dying young woman. Her boney fingers are weak and cold. Jack examines the face of his lifelong friend. Anna's eyes do not hold the same lively shine they used to. Dark bags add a frightful contrast to her pale skin, and Jack knows there isn't much time left.

Though Anna has been sick for years, the dark hand of death is reaching ever closer. Jack's heart is stinging, as he knows he will soon need to say goodbye.

"I-I want you to pro-promise me something." Anna struggles past stuttering lips.

"Quiet child, save your strength." Marie, a wrinkly widow speaks to the young girl. Marie dabs a cool washcloth on her forehead, hoping to sooth the intense fever.

Jack's heavy eyes meet Marie, who has been serving selflessly for days, attempting to keep Anna both comfortable and cared for. Although the widows in their community were doing their very best, the doctor declared that there was no hope for Anna. Their only tasks were to make the young teen as comfortable as possible before her passing.

When Jack first heard the news, he asked Captain Cepheus for permission to depart immediately. Because the Captain knew full well of orphaned Anna's history and Jack's special connection with her, the Captain didn't ask any questions. Jack wasn't sure how long he would be gone, but now it is starting to become clear. If Anna's health continues to fail at such a rapid rate, Jack may very well be returning to the URIA base as soon as tomorrow.

"No, I have to say this." Anna's voice is crackly. Jack winces deep inside. He hates seeing her like this. Anna has always been like a little sister to him. He's been fiercely protective of the girl, even though it's been quite clear she cares for him in a deeper way than just friendship. "Jack." She firmly states his name, even though she has his full attention. "Promise me you'll take care of Jamie."

Jack continues to stare at her. Jack is a man of his word. If he tells her yes, it's as good as gold. But her request isn't an easy one. Jack is in no position financially, geographically, or even mentally, to take care of Anna's young child. His commitment to the URIA makes the promise nearly impossible. "Anna, I—"

"Jack, he has no one!" Anna's eyes are on the verge of tears, "If I leave him, he's left without a fighting chance in the world! I want a better life for him, Jack. Jamie needs more than..." she glances around at the dark, dingy tent where she's currently dwelling, "this. He needs someone to care for him and show him what's right in the world. He needs a father."

"Anna, I'm not his father. But I promise that I'll..." he struggles to find the right words, while being completely honest, "I'll do my best to give him what he needs." Jack speaks, wishing for nothing less than the dying girl to know everything is going to be okay.

"Thank you." Anna's eyes pool with tears, "I don't deserve this. But Jamie does."

Jack swiftly wipes away her tears and offers her a reassuring hug, "Shhh, you need to rest."

A deep look of peace floods over Anna's face as she leans back into her pillow. "I can go now," she says calmly. "Now that Jamie is going to be okay."

"Oh, pickle root!" Marie calls out from the other side of the tiny tent, "I need more of my healing herbs."

Anna closes her eyes and Jack can tell she's exhausted. It's clear she needs to nap. Talking has completely worn her out.

Jack stands up and whispers to Marie. "Write down what you need. I'll run to town and grab your herbs."

"Are you sure you don't want to stay?" Marie whispers back, anxiously glancing back at Anna.

"I need to get out for a while," Jack tells her. Bedside duty can be draining. "The fresh air will be good for me."

~*~

Jack gazes up at the clear blue sky. The rainclouds have parted and the nasty storm that whipped through last night has completely dissipated. Jack stuffs his hands in his pockets and inhales deeply. It feels good to finally be out of that stuffy little tent.

His long legs stretch forward as he makes his way through the colorful morning market. Tasty spices float through the air. He passes a vendor selling ripe, juicy peaches. He pauses and chooses the best looking one. He tosses the man a coin, then continues on his way.

Jack searches for Amelia, the crazy old kook who affectionately earned the name, "The Wild Herb Lady." She's famous for whipping up odd concoctions from unknown roots and herbs which often perform miraculous healing results. Although both Marie and Jack know Anna is far past hopes of recovery, the herbs help settle and calm her through the process of her body slowly, and painfully, shutting down.

"Well, shiver me timbers!" Amelia gasps, "Are my eyes playing tricks on me? Or is it this Jack Conway?! Little Jack Conway who grew up like a sapling after a rainstorm?! Oh, My Tulips, come here, let me get a good look at you, boy!"

"Good morning Amelia." Jack smiles. He doesn't know what it is about all these elderly ladies who enjoy making such a grand fuss over him. "Here's Marie's list. I haven't even heard of all the items on here, so I'll let you look it over."

"Ohhh, yes." Amelia adjusts her eyeglasses and studies the list, "Mmm, hmm. Hmm, hmm. Yep, yep, couldn't have made a better list myself!" Amelia sets down the paper and begins tossing random herbs into small, brown paper sacks.

"My, my, we couldn't have asked for a more beautiful morning! Quite the happenings stirring in town! Goodness gravy, you should hear some of the rumors buzzing around here!" Amelia's chatter doesn't slow her hands, "Word on the street is that King Raymond has found and captured the daughter of King Tyrone and Queen Isabella!"

"What?" Jack questions, arrested by her words. Has he just heard her right? "What did you say?"

"I know!" Amelia nods her head, "That's what I said when I first heard the news! Jumping Jupiter, how could something like that be true?! But it is! The Royal jailers spilled the beans to the bakers, who spoke with the blacksmith, who spread the word to me! It's true, Jack! Our late King and Queen had a daughter, and she's the *rightful heir* to our throne! Talk about the drama!"

"But wait, what did you say before that?" Jack tries to dig into the most important information, "About her being captured?"

"Yep, yep, yep!" Amelia carries on gingerly, "Rumor has it that he threw her into the Royal Jail last night! Heavens only knows what he's planning to do to her!"

Jack instantly takes off in a run.

"Jack!" Amelia calls after him, "Wait, where are you going!? What about your herbs?!"

But Jack doesn't hear her. He only has one mission in mind. Freeing the Princess from Raymond's wicked grip.

How did this happen?! Jack's mind runs just as fast as his feet. *Who broke into the URIA base? How did they capture her? Where's the rest of the army? Why haven't they come for her yet? And how did they only get one Princess and not all three?*

But Jack doesn't have time to sit and ponder these questions. He needs to reach the palace gates as swiftly as possible.

~*~

The infamous castle looms ahead. The ancient structure could be a thing of beauty, if it wasn't for the heartless tyrant who dwells there. Jack finds no pleasure in its form or fancy stonework. It only stands as a reminder of everything stolen from him over the years. Jack's feet slow to a walk as he quickly devises a plan.

He knows it's not safe to attempt sneaking into the castle on his own. But he doesn't have any other choice. There's not enough time to trek through the forest and see how everyone at the URIA is faring. An urgency arrests his heart as Jack examines his surroundings. He's nearing the palace gate, where thick iron bars will attempt to keep him from entering. Jack knows he cannot blatantly approach and expect to be welcomed inside. He needs a subtle way of entrance.

He watches as a bakery truck rolls up and checks in with the security guard on duty. Suddenly an idea sparks. Jack turns around and heads back toward town.

~*~

Jack watches a friendly baker chat with a street vendor. Jack subtly nears the bakery truck, careful to see that nobody is watching. The baker releases a hearty laugh and Jack takes advantage of the moment. He lunges forward and ducks into the truck.

He quickly searches among the boxes of bread and cupcakes, anxious to duck down behind something. He makes his way to the back of the truck and slips behind a large box of bagels. His toes stick out and he tries to pull his legs tighter to his chest.

Jack hears another laugh, followed by the door slamming shut. Jack is surrounded by darkness.

He strains to listen. A soft rumble is heard as the engine starts. The truck moves, and Jack's head nears the ceiling as they hit a large bump. Jack struggles to keep his footing, not wanting to knock over any of the boxes and give away his hiding place. He tries to put the box back in its place, but it repeatedly tumbles over.

Several moments later, the truck stops. But it's not time to get out yet. He can hear the baker talking to the security guard. Jack gulps. What if the guard opens the back and searches inside? He quickly squeezes his eyes shut and prays no such thing happens.

Miraculously, the truck continues rolling forward. Jack breathes a sigh of relief. He's almost there.

The truck comes to one final stop, and Jack's large hands move quickly. He stops a massive box from plopping down onto his head. The door squeaks and Jack holds the box steady. He tries to hide both himself and his fingers, hoping the baker will start in the front and slowly work his way back.

The baker collects his first load, and Jack waits a few seconds. His timing needs to be perfect if he doesn't want to get caught. He quickly rises to his feet and heads for the doorway.

He peeks his head out, relieved to see the worker is strolling his goods on a cart toward a rear entrance to the Palace. Jack leaps out and heads for the stables.

He quickly ducks inside the darkened building and slips behind a tall pile of stacked hay bales. He needs to draw a deep breath, assess the situation, and make his way toward the ancient prison area.

The gentle clip-clop of horse's hooves meandering by echo in his ears. He waits until the coast is clear. He scurries toward the nearby Prison Tower entrance and sneaks up behind a fierce-looking guard.

In one quick movement, Jack releases a karate chop on a pressure point in his neck and the man falls to the ground. Jack quickly rips the man's keys from his pocket and leaps over him. He won't have much time before the guard awakes and calls for backup.

Jack runs down the cement corridor, searching for Her Majesty.

"Jack!" a voice calls out. Jack stops running and turns to see Princess Aurora behind bars. Jack wastes no time fiddling with the keys. He immediately unlocks her cell.

"Jack!" she cries again. Aurora flings herself into his arms and greets him with a relieved embrace. She fights back tears, "Thank God, thank God, thank God! Oh, my goodness, you have no idea how relieved I am to see you!"

"Shhh!" Jack hushes her. "We don't have much time! Hurry, I'm expecting company at the entryway."

"Wait!" she calls out. "Liam!"

Aurora yanks the keys out of Jack's hand and heads for his cell. But just as she anxiously tries to slip the key in the lock, three guards appear on the scene.

Jack flings into action, attempting to defeat two of the guards at once. The third guard charges toward Aurora, but she offers a quick sidekick. She smacks the man in the face, and Aurora releases an astonished gasp.

"Nice!" she tells herself. *You hit him! You actually hit him!* Adrenaline pumps through her entire being. She adds another kick in the stomach, just for revenge.

He groans and reaches for his abdomen, giving Aurora more time to get the key in place. Her hands tremble with fear and adrenaline. Finally, the desired 'CLICK' is heard and the gate screeches open.

She dashes into the darkened cell and zeros in on the chains cupping his hands.

"Aurora, behind you!" Liam calls out.

Aurora buzzes around just in time to dodge a grab coming from the guard. She leaps to the other side of the cell, but another man is there to snatch her wrist.

"Not this time!" Aurora calls out as she twists her arm and pops him in the nose with her elbow. Aurora fumes with anger and determination. The man stumbles back from the painful nose blow and Jack plows the second man into the wall.

Aurora digs the key in the ancient-looking, rusty lock and Liam's right arm is free.

"Everybody freeze!" a threatening voice calls out.

They all look up. A fourth guard stands firmly in the doorway with a pistol in hand. "I am not afraid to shoot!"

Aurora subtly slips the key into Liam's free hand. She bores holes of hatred with her bitter gaze into the guard's face. Aurora is determined. This man is *not* going to stop them from escaping. She quickly throws her hands into the air. But Jack knows she is far from surrendering.

Jack glances at Aurora, confident she has a plan brewing. Jack decides to take a leap of faith, knowing this might very well be their last chance.

"Arrgghhh!" He lets out a cry as he smashes the skulls of two guards into one another. The violent blow knocks them instantly unconscious.

The guard with the gun aims at Jack, but Aurora performs a quick sidekick. The gun falls free, and Aurora dives on top of it.

Liam has already freed himself. A guard storms toward him, but he overpowers the man and pins him to the wall. Liam

cinches the chains around the man's wrists. "Comfortable?"
He grins.

Aurora holds the gun high in the air, aiming at the shocked,
lone guard standing defenseless in the doorway. "Kindly let
us pass, or I'll be forced to use this."

The man appears unthreatened, so Aurora cocks the trigger.
He quickly steps out of the way.

Aurora sprints forward, Jack following close behind. But just
as Liam passes through the cell doorway, the standing guard
slams the iron door shut. Liam releases a bloodcurdling cry of
pain. The terrifying sound and look of sheer panic and
torture on Liam's face, causes Aurora to scream as well. His
leg is trapped!

Unsure of what else to do, she takes a vengeful shot at the
guard. Surprisingly, the bullet flies into his arm, and he
releases a sound of anguish as he clings to his arm and falls to
his knees. Aurora's face is white as a sheet.

Jack's eyes are just as horrified. He quickly lifts the iron door
with a groan, wishing to free Liam from such traumatic,
unimaginable pain. Jack can't even bring himself to look at
the bloodied and shattered leg. Liam groans in suffering as
Jack lifts him from the ground and dashes toward the Prison
Tower entrance.

"Aurora, run!" Jack tells her.

Aurora tosses one more horrified glance at the guard she has
just shot then dashes out behind the men.

~*~

Aurora anxiously sits in the medical waiting room. She
knocks her nervous fingers together and can't stop her leg

from acting like it's in a bounce house. She continues to glance over her shoulder, half-expecting one of Raymond's men to come in here and aim for her skull. She shudders.

She can scarcely believe they actually escaped. But now, after all the traumatic events have ended, Aurora's nerves are through the roof. She feels as though this uncontrollable anxiety is going to drive her insane. The glass hospital door which connects the waiting room to a long hallway automatically opens and Aurora nearly jumps out of her seat. Her heart thunders. It takes her several seconds to gain control of her breathing and realize that it's just Jack.

"Your Highness, you're okay," Jack tries to reassure her.

Aurora's thumping heartbeat is threatening to leap out of her chest. She needs to calm herself. "How…how's Liam?" she asks, tightly clenching her hands together.

"The doctor says his leg may be infected," Jack reports as he sits down beside her in a plastic blue chair. "The door smashed right into his calf. And because it was rusty iron, they're giving him tetanus shots and drugs to help with the pain. They're going to keep him overnight for observation then decide if any reconstructive surgery is necessary."

"This is all my fault." Aurora shakes her head. Her voice is trembling, "None of this would've happened if it wasn't for me."

"Why?" Jack's careful eyes search hers, "What happened? I tried to contact the base, but I can't reach anyone."

"It was awful," Aurora whispers, afraid to speak of the ghastly memories.

"Aurora, I need to know what happened," Jack demands.

"There was a spy in the underground." Aurora looks up, her heart searing with grief, anger and regret, as she thinks about Kehahi. "A double agent. I knew there was something off about him. I don't know how, I just had this gut feeling that he was bad news. But leave it to me to toss all common sense to the wind and get wrapped up in a handsome distraction." She feels foolish admitting these things to Jack, "He was helping me train for taekwondo. Then, last night, Captain Cepheus wanted to throw a party for everyone. He wanted to help the soldiers loosen up and enjoy themselves, so we had music, and cupcakes and dancing and this delicious cheese platter. Everyone had a blast. But then, Kehahi left me a note and said he wanted to meet me in the kitchen. I knew I shouldn't have gone. But I went anyway."

"Did he kidnap you?"

"No. He disappeared as soon as I entered the kitchen. But then, Raymond's men were waiting, and several of them set off a bomb."

"A bomb?!"

Aurora nods sadly. "I…I don't know if…if…" Aurora cannot finish her sentence. Her jaw quivers. Her voice falls to a whisper, "If anyone made it out alive."

Jack's breathing grows heavier. He is clearly distraught by the news. "Come on." He stands up, "We'll go back to my place. I'll try phoning the Captain again and see if I can get through."

~*~

Aurora steps into the forest green tent that Jack calls his 'home.' Aurora's nose curls upward at the scent. It's like a putrid mixture of old wet dog and rotten cabbage.

"Jack!" a little old woman calls out in desperation as soon as he ducks inside. "Oh, Jack." She shakes her head sadly. She reaches for his hand, "She's gone."

It takes a moment for the news to register. Jack's little friend, the sweet, bright-eyed, yet at times terribly frustrating and foolish young girl he had supported and loved for years, is now dead. A flash of sadness overtakes his eyes and Aurora watches with confusion.

He quickly pinches the bridge of his nose and looks away. He doesn't want Aurora, or anyone else for that matter, to see him cry.

"She asked for you," Marie reports sadly. "But she still looked peaceful as she passed. We can rejoice now, knowing she is forever free from her pain."

Jack's jaw tightens. He can feel a sob rising up from deep within. He quickly rushes into the yard and Aurora feels completely helpless. *What's going on? Who are these people? Has someone just...died?*

"Hello, dear," Marie offers Aurora a sad glance. "Thank you for coming to support Jack in this hard time. He may need a few moments alone though. He loved Anna more than anyone."

Anna? Aurora thinks to herself, *Who's Anna?*

~*~

Jonathan Napp nearly cringes as his boot steps on a loud twig. The snap echoes through the forest, and a nearby squirrel dashes away. Jonathan sighs and lowers his slingshot. So much for fresh meat for breakfast.

He regretfully stands up and makes his way back toward the cave. He hopes Elizabeth and Asher aren't too disappointed by his findings. The truth is Jonathan has never been stranded out in the middle of nowhere. And although he's attempting to convince the kids that he knows what he's doing, the sad truth is that Jonathan doesn't have a clue. All he's been able to round up for grub is a few stray acorns and a small handful of berries.

He wishes Siri could tell him whether or not the berries are safe to eat. But Siri isn't working. There is absolutely zero reception out here.

Jonathan sighs as he nears the cave. They need to return to civilization as quickly as possible. He thinks of Eleanor, and the fact that she hasn't heard from him. Thankfully, she doesn't know how much potential danger he's in. If Eleanor knew about his dire straits, her worry thermometer would be near the exploding point. That's one thing Jonathan can count as a blessing amidst these challenging times; Eleanor isn't here. She's safe in Colorado with Uncle Sky and Aunt Lydia, most likely having the time of her life on their ranch. She's enjoying the simple luxuries of being a teenager. Ellie is blissfully unaware of her royal pedigree, long-lost sisters, and all the drama ensuing because of it. Jonathan can't even imagine what things would be like if Ellie were present. Thankfully, he doesn't have to.

"Forward, and halt!" a voice cracks through the woods.

Jonathan stops walking.

"Aim, fire!"

A loud collection of gun shots is heard and Jonathan drops to the ground, carefully ducking in case of flying bullets. But the shots are far away. Jonathan can tell he's not in any direct threat or way of danger. He inches forward, searching the horizon for any signs of company.

Finally, he sees a group of people in the clearing ahead. A massive collection of troops is performing drills. They're responding to the commands of an officer. Jonathan strains his eyes. Surely that's not the URIA? They wouldn't be practicing drills out in the open like this. Especially not after everything that happened last night.

Jonathan's heart-rate increases. If it's not the URIA, it must be Raymond's men.

The innocent faces of Elizabeth and Asher flash before his mind's eye. They need to get out of here immediately! If Raymond's men discover where Elizabeth is, they'll be asking for far more trouble than Jonathan can handle on his own.

He runs into the cave, careful not to be spotted by anyone out in the field. They're a far enough distance away for anyone to notice him, but Jonathan doesn't take any chances.

Inside the dark cave both Asher and Elizabeth are awake. The fire is still flickering, but it is nearly dead. Asher stirs the embers with a long stick, attempting to keep the ashes hot.

"Did you get more firewood?" Asher asks.

"What about food?" Elizabeth asks.

"Change of plans," Jonathan speaks quickly. "Raymond's troops are rehearsing drills outside. We need to relocate. If they find us here…" Jonathan doesn't need to finish his sentence.

"We can't let them find Elizabeth," Asher speaks, knowing what the men are after. Asher grabs a larger stick and allows it to catch fire, serving like a torch. "Maybe there's an exit on the other end of the cave."

Jonathan nods and quickly stomps out the remaining embers. Elizabeth stands up and clutches her hands together. She doesn't know what today is going to bring. But after praying quietly for several hours, she's ready as she'll ever be.

Elizabeth finds that she's greatly missing her Bible. She dearly wishes she would've grabbed it on the way out of the base, but there just wasn't time. And so, she's rehearsing scriptures in her mind. She finds that they're very calming and strengthening, despite all the fearful unknowns.

Asher leads the way down the long, dark cave. Elizabeth crosses her arms and continues walking forward. The entire atmosphere is so damp and dreary. Quiet drips tip-tap down the cave walls. Elizabeth keeps her eyes fixed on the flame ahead. It's so cold down here without the fire. She releases a sneeze and the sound echoes ahead.

They walk for several long, quiet moments and Elizabeth wonders how long until they reach the other side. It will be such a blessing to come into the daylight again. She can scarcely wait.

Asher's determined face searches onward. His feet slow as he comes to a devastating realization. There's nothing but stone ahead.

"Where is the exit?" Elizabeth asks quietly.

"It's a dead end," Jonathan mutters. His mind quickly jumps from one thought to the next. How are they going to get out of here? How is he going to get Elizabeth to safety? If Raymond's men come in here while they're still present, their chances of escaping without disaster ensuing are slim to none.

Elizabeth sighs and leans up against the wall. As she does, a large stone shifts. The sudden movement causes her to lose her balance. "Woah!" she cries.

Jonathan catches her. "Careful!" he tells her, even though it's too late for a warning. "Are you okay?"

Asher holds the light in her direction.

Elizabeth nods, then touches the wall. "Who knew that cave walls could be so wobbly?"

Asher continues to study the wall. He takes a step closer and leans his hand against the stone. "You guys, look!" Asher bursts out. "It's an inscription."

Elizabeth and Jonathan lean over his shoulder.

"Wow, you're right," Jonathan responds, his eyes feeding on the strange letters and symbols. "What language is that?"

"What does it mean?" Elizabeth asks.

Asher continues to run his fingers along the words. His hand reaches a small, lose stone. He gently wobbles it, surprised with the stone-age contraption. It almost looks like some kind of lever or button, constructed by an ancient civilization long ago. He thinks of the secret underground passageways beneath their own palace in Tarsurella. His fingers continue to play with the lose stone. He turns it and presses it in, quickly figuring out the puzzle.

Elizabeth gasps as a large stone, far taller than her, begins to shake.

"Look out!" Jonathan calls, quickly grabbing her and pulling her away, not wanting anything to fall on her.

The large stone moves, rolling to the left, but Asher stays put. He's completely mesmerized by the movement, bewildered by the fact that something so high-tech could be hidden in a dingy old cave. Asher's eyes increase in size. After the rock rolls away, an old, stone door is revealed!

"Holy Indiana Jones!" Jonathan speaks in awe. He can scarcely believe his eyes. It's like he's watching a power-packed adventure movie unfolding. Except he's not sitting on the couch eating popcorn with his daughter. He's smack dab in the middle of it! "Okay, so I think this is the part where we're supposed to turn around and run, before we set off the booby trap, am I right?"

"But what if it's not a trap?" Asher insists. "What if it's our only way out of this cave? Here." He turns around and gives Jonathan the torch.

"This is a bad idea, kid," Jonathan warns him. He grabs Elizabeth's hand, ready to run if they need to.

Asher takes a deep breath and places his hand on the stone handle. He slowly cracks the door several inches. He waits for a few seconds, careful to make sure nothing's going to jump out at him.

Elizabeth holds her breath.

Asher pushes the door the rest of the way open. A dull glow illuminates the path ahead. Asher squints, struggling to make sense of what he's seeing. It appears as though there are dim ceiling lights hanging in a larger room. The enigma instantly captures him.

"What is this place?" he whispers, stepping inside.

Although the floor is made of the same, similar cave-stone pattern, the room itself appears to be something built by the hands of man. The ceilings are much larger, and for a moment Asher can't tell if they're still underground. There are no windows or doors, except the door from where he entered. It's clear that whoever built this place wanted it to remain a secret.

As his eyes continue to adjust to the lighting, he notices a raised platform, sporting racks of outdated computer equipment. The empty room boasts nothing else but large file cabinets.

"Looks like the coast is clear," he calls over his shoulder, giving Jonathan and Elizabeth the go-ahead to step inside. "Whatever this place used to be, it's completely abandoned." Asher runs his fingers along the dusty file cabinets and desires to look inside. Who built this? Was someone trying to store top-secret information?

"It looks like someone used to work here." Asher is thinking out-loud. Elizabeth and Jonathan examine the place with wide eyes. "Whoever it was had some seriously outdated software." Asher steps onto the raised platform and touches the dusty keys. "This stuff is like from the seventies!"

Asher's thumb accidently weighs down on the space key. He quickly pulls his hands back from the keyboard, instantly regretting his decision to touch the board. Suddenly, a loud hum is heard and a light flashes on the keyboard. It sounds as if a tired old system is attempting to rev up.

"Intruder! Intruder!" the system shouts at them.

"Time to bail!" Asher instructs, turning to leap off the platform. But it's too late.

They're already surrounded by men with machine guns on every side.

Asher's breathe catches. Where in the heck did these men come from? How did they appear so quickly?! There are six of them! Asher throws his hands up in surrender. Jon and Elizabeth follow suit.

"Don't move!" a muscular guard commands. He's wearing a tight pair of black pants, a tight black, breathable long-sleeved shirt, and a thick, silver breastplate of armor. Asher is distracted by his strange outfit. It's not like anything someone in Tarsurella would wear.

"Message to the Commander." The man continues speaking into his headset, "We've got a security breach in Sector B, two kids and a middle-aged man. Yes sir." He turns to Jonathan, "Well, you're in luck," he grins slyly. "The boss wants to meet you."

Someone nudges the tip of their gun into Asher's back. "Move!" The command pounds into Asher's eardrums.

They push the captives forward, and Elizabeth's heart is struggling to beat properly. "Where are they taking us?!" she asks.

But there is no answer for her.

The leading guard presses a stone, similarly to what Asher had done earlier. Asher watches, careful to memorize his movements. Another large, ten-foot rock shakes then rolls out of the way. A steel doorway is revealed, and the guard presses another button, this time a small red one, which appears to be connected to a modern electrical system.

Elizabeth takes careful steps ahead.

When I am afraid, I will trust in You! She prays as they march forward. *When my heart is overwhelmed, lead me to the rock that is higher than I! The Lord is my strength and my salvation, a strong refuge in times of trouble. I called upon the Lord and He answered me, He rescued me because He delighted in me! Lord, help us!*

Elizabeth strains to see ahead. But all her vision allows is the path down a dark tunnel and a dull light shining above them. She doesn't know where they're going. But God does. She looks downward as suddenly the light grows brighter. There's a light coming from beneath their feet!

She gasps as she realizes they're walking on a thin, iron walkway. Their boots clank on the iron bridge and there are railings on either side of them to keep them from falling. She carefully glances over the railing, wondering how it can be that they're getting higher. Are they not still underground? The pits below appear to be wide-open space, where people are walking around! Elizabeth shakes her head. This is all so confusing. What is going on?

She continues to look downward and realizes there are dozens and dozens of rows of soldiers, wearing the same silver outfits as these guards, training below. They move their arms in robotic-like motions, responding to the calls being barked off by their officers. *This is just like the URIA.* Elizabeth quickly puts the puzzle pieces together. *So, does this mean King Raymond has an underground army as well?*

They continue walking forward and move into a brighter, more illuminated area of the base. It's so bright, Elizabeth almost feels like she's walking around outside. Steel doors open yet once more and the long line pauses.

"Permission to speak with the Commander?" The lead guard speaks into a silver box hanging on the wall.

Elizabeth bites her lip as she waits for the response.

"Do you have the visitors?" An eerie sounding voice questions.

"Yes, Your Majesty."

"Bring them in."

Asher, who is at the front of the line, waits anxiously as yet another pair of doors parts before them like the Red Sea. Asher feels the familiar gun nudging in his back. He walks forward, surprised to find that this room is completely white. White ceiling, white floor, white walls, and a white desk. *Whoever works in this room must really have a thing for white,* he thinks jokingly, trying to keep his nerves at bay.

Asher instantly recognizes the man seated behind the desk. It's King Raymond; the profile of the wicked man responsible for destroying so much of Bella Adar, taking innocent lives and stealing the throne from the rightful Royals.

Raymond doesn't pay any attention to them at first. He's fingering through a pile of paperwork that someone has presented to him. Asher studies the back of a man standing before Raymond's desk in a long, vanilla, lab coat.

"Very well," Raymond nods, "this all looks up to par. Doctor Akerly, you are dismissed."

Asher's ears are ringing. His heart leaps, and his mind begins racing. He knows that name. Akerly.

It's the name Asher has been struggling to uncover the mystery behind for years. It's the name of the man who designed the Wall of Fire and the AA16 Code, and then mysteriously vanished sometime after. Asher's heartrate increases. He feels as though everything is happening in slow motion.

As the doctor turns around, Asher cannot believe his eyes. It's Walter Akerly! Jane's missing father! Walter Akerly!

Doctor Akerly abruptly exits the room. The steel door is slammed shut and Asher's head and emotions are reeling. *What's going on? There's no way this is happening?! There's no way that could be Jane's dad!*

"Well, what a pleasant surprise." Raymond casually collects his papers and stands up, "I went out in pursuit of capturing a Princess and ended up with a bonus catch! The young Prince of Tarsurella!" He chuckles.

"And who is this?" Raymond leaves the space from behind his comfortable desk. He nears Jonathan and examines the man. "A surviving URIA solider? You know, it really is a shame you survived the bombing. It would've been a much nicer, more humane way for you to go. If you were already dead, it would save everyone in this room a whole lot of trouble. It might've spared these two innocent and impressionable children from witnessing the bloody sight of your murder."

"No!" Elizabeth calls out in fear.

"And this must be the Princess." Raymond grins wickedly, "I've been waiting a great many years to meet you. It really is a shame that I'm going to have to murder you as well."

"She's no good to you dead," Asher quickly speaks up, attempting to spare her life.

"And she's no good me alive, either, young Prince. But you." Raymond's disgusting grin is still there, "You on the other hand could be very, very helpful. I understand that you have quite an impressive past when it comes to destroying peace and wreaking havoc on innocent civilians. You would be an impressive asset to our team."

Asher doesn't speak. As much as he wants to clobber the man with a good tongue lashing, Asher knows he has to be careful. One wrong word and they could all be killed in an instant.

Raymond returns to his desk, opens his drawer and pulls out a small, black gun.

Elizabeth's breath quickens.

"Now, I like to think of myself as a very merciful man," he speaks to Jonathan. "So instead of condemning you to a torture chamber, we'll get this finished very swiftly." He dramatically cocks the trigger.

"Stop!" Elizabeth cries, "You cannot kill him! He is a father, and he has a family back home! He must return home safely!"

Raymond poses a frown and rests the gun on his desk. "Aw, well isn't that touching. You're right, young lady. This completely makes me rethink my entire philosophy about life! How dare I attempt to kill a good, hardworking family man? What, am I mad?!" He lifts the gun again, "Indeed, I am."

"He is the father of one of the Princesses!" Elizabeth calls, desperate to say something that will stop the atrocity from happening.

"Oh really?" Raymond cocks his head, slightly lowering the gun, "So you're telling me, this man knows where the fourth and final wretch is that I need to exterminate?"

Elizabeth's heart is pounding. She instantly regrets her words.

Jon is silent.

"Perhaps you're right. He may be of some help to me after all." Raymond rethinks his plan, "Guards, take him to a cell."

And with that, Jonathan is whisked off. The door slams shut behind them once more.

"And now, removing a worm from this planet who is not fit to be here." Raymond aims the gun at Elizabeth, "I've been waiting a long, long time for this moment."

"Wait!" Asher shouts, suddenly throwing himself in front of Elizabeth.

Raymond raises an amused eyebrow.

"If you shoot her, you're going to have to hit me as well!" He boldly stands in front of her, fearlessly facing Raymond. "With us both dead, you're not going to be able to carry out your twisted, underground plan. We can help you."

"And how do you know that I have a 'twisted, underground plan'?" Raymond questions.

"Isn't it obvious?" Asher attempts to sound confident, "Bombing the base, splitting up the Princesses, setting up bait in this cave that you knew we were gonna take. You've got thousands of men training beneath your command and a highly sophisticated underground base you're pouring millions of dollars into. This isn't just about Bella Adar and keeping your power on the throne. Obviously, this is about something more. You don't seem to me like you're the kind of guy who would settle for the control of just one country. You want a monopoly."

"You are very observant, I'll give you that much." Raymond looks at Elizabeth and considers the cost of keeping her. "I'm still doubtful that she is going to be of any help."

"Can't you see, she's the perfect pawn? The URIA will do anything to get her back," Asher insists, hoping his words sound convincing. "Keeping her alive will cause the URIA to play right into your hand. But without her, you're going to lose the upper-hand advantage."

"You're a very good liar, Prince Asher," Raymond complements him, "and that is what I like about you. Guards, take her away! I need to have a chat with this young man."

~*~

Episode 10

Aurora peers out her window. Her jaw drops as a gentle spirit of wonderment sweeps over her. The helicopter gives a magnificent birds-eye view. She's seen the Palace of Tarsurella on magazine covers and in short tidbits through TV interviews. But she's never seen it in person before now.

Pointy peaks and ancient lookout towers stretch toward them, as the multi-dimensional castle stands a true masterpiece. Aurora can't believe how large it is. The frightening, unfriendly, crude castle in Bella Adar is measly compared to this one. Raymond's castle sent shivers of dread down Aurora's spine. But here, King Addison's welcoming estate causes her to take a deep breath and believe that everything is going to be okay.

She attempts to relax her hand, realizing it had been nervously clenched to her armrest the entire ride. *Take a deep breath,* Aurora tells herself, *everything is going to be okay now. You're not in Bella Adar. Raymond can't hurt you here.*

Even though Aurora knows her fears are irrational, she can't help but feel concerned as they hover toward the ground. They sweep over acres of beautiful, lush gardens. Aurora can see the grass swirling below, thanks to wild winds coming from their helicopter.

After landing, Aurora is escorted off the copter and toward the Palace by several security guards. As she crosses the walkway through the front gardens, Aurora is surprised to spot a handful of news and media anchors. They're all eager to see her.

"Aurora, Aurora Jasper!" they call out as Aurora's path goes right by them.

"Aurora, what are you doing here in Tarsurella?"

"Aurora, why did you choose Tarsurella as your secret getaway?"

Aurora presses her lips together tightly and continues walking forward. How did the press find her here?! She is in no way mentally prepared to face the world and discuss these things.

"Back up, give her some space!" one of the guards warns the media hounds who are moving in too close.

"Why did you leave your tour? What do you have to say to all of your thousands of disappointed fans who wanted to see you perform?" Microphones are shoved toward her.

"Are you quitting music?"

"Are you coming back? Is this the end of your career?"

"Aurora!"

"Aurora!"

Aurora quickens her speed and reaches the Palace doors. Thankfully, the media isn't allowed to follow in after her.

Aurora takes a deep breath and attempts to shake off the sudden shock of such an encounter. She doesn't know what's wrong with her nerves, but after spending a full night in a medieval prison, they're going absolutely manic.

Aurora doesn't have much time to admire the impressive Palace scenery. She's ushered to a large room, which looks like something one would encounter on a European tourist walk through a stately chateau. She's greeted by a woman who seems to know exactly where to take her. Up a flight of wide, marble stairs and into a room titled "The Tea Parlor."

The woman announces Aurora's arrival. Before Aurora can blink, Lena is tackling her in a massive, most wonderful kind of hug.

"Aurora!" she cries, clinging to her sister, allowing the grateful tears to fall freely.

"Oh, Lena!" Aurora squeezes her even harder, not wanting to let go. "Thank God, you're okay! Oh, I was so worried!"

The hug ends but the two continue to hold hands. Neither of them wants to release their grip. "Where's Elizabeth? And Peter? And everyone else?" Aurora asks, desperate to know if everyone has made it out alive.

"We don't know." Lena's gaze is struck with worry, "I haven't heard anything."

"Your Highnesses," the kind woman who escorted Aurora upstairs speaks up, "we have prepared some refreshments for you, so please feel free to partake of those whenever you desire. Captain Cepheus has requested we keep you posted on all the latest news, and he promises not to leave you girls in the dark. On behalf of the King and Queen, I invite you to please make yourselves at home. King Addison has invited you to stay here as long as needed. The staff is preparing your guest rooms. The King and his family will meet with you at their soonest convenience. If you need anything, anything at all, don't hesitate to call. My name is Deborah, and it is my pleasure to serve you." She offers a polite curtsy at the end.

"Thank you, Deborah," Lena tells her sweetly, you are truly kind. We appreciate the hospitality of King Addison and we wish there was something we could do to repay his kindness."

Deborah quickly exits to return to her tasks and Aurora hugs Lena once more. "I'm so glad you're safe!" Aurora expresses her relief all over again. "Where were you last night?"

"In the forest, with Captain Cepheus and a handful of our men," Lena reveals. "But, where were you?"

"Oh, didn't you hear?" Aurora chooses to make a joke out of the terrifying memory, "I was the lucky sweepstakes winner of an all-expenses paid stay at the palace of Bella Adar! And the best part?" Her voice falls flat, "My dungeon view."

Lena gasps, "Oh no! Please say you're joking! Raymond didn't really capture you, did he?"

"Thanks to his wicked little minion, Kehahi." Aurora crosses her arms, "I swear, if I ever have—"

"Aurora!"

Aurora looks toward the doorway. Her eyes widen. It's her parents!

"Mom!" she cries. She dashes toward them, and they run to meet her as well. "Dad!"

"Oh, Aurora! Our baby girl!" Aurora's parents envelope her in a long-awaited group hug. Tears are flowing, and Lena lifts an emotional hand to her mouth. She now wants to cry as well. What a touching scene! To be safe in her parents arms yet once more.

In the midst of the emotional reunion, two more figures enter. It is King Addison and his sister, Princess Bridget. Aurora doesn't notice their quiet entrance.

"Excuse me for interrupting," Addison speaks gently as he approaches Lena, "but I just had a break in meetings and wanted to come as quickly as I could."

Everyone's eyes drift toward the crying parents and child, so Aurora attempts to pull herself together. There's so much she wants to say to her parents. So much she wishes to apologize to them for. But now isn't the time. A King has just entered the room!

Aurora sniffs and turns her attention toward him. She runs a quick finger beneath her eyes, attempting to dry her face. She's sure she must look like an absolute mess. Raccoon eyes from tears, no sleep, and running mascara.

"I wish we were meeting on more pleasant circumstances, but it is an honor to finally meet you, Aurora." Addison offers a friendly handshake.

Aurora shakes his hand, pleased to find that the famous King is even more handsome than he is on TV. All at once, Aurora feels a little bit nervous. The King and Queen of Tarsurella are a *huge* deal back in the United States. All the fangirls have been watching their fairytale unfold over the past few years. Even Aurora watched the Live Broadcast of their wedding. It isn't often Aurora is star struck, but she feels like she's in the presence of a legend!

"Th-thank you." Aurora struggles to find the right words, "I mean, obviously I'm a huge fan. I've always been! Oh, and these are my parents."

Addison quickly exchanges introductions, then draws his sister Bridget into the spotlight. Aurora nearly gasps. She's been a massive Bridget fan for years! The gorgeous, mega-rich Princess has her own clothing line, accessories, makeup products, and cute little plush dolls. Again, she can't believe she's actually standing in her presence.

"Wow, it is such an honor. Like, seriously." Aurora shakes her head, "You two are amazing. I feel like I'm dreaming."

"It's lovely to meet you as well," Bridget grins. "Your music is quite popular over here! Jillian and Millie will be thrilled to have you stay with us for a while."

Aurora smiles. Jillian and Millie are just two of the eight Royal siblings. Aurora is looking forward to meeting them all.

"Liam said you had quite the traumatic evening last night," Bridget continues, "so I hope you'll rest well here."

Aurora's smile disappears. Suddenly, she remembers. Liam, the young man whose leg got smashed in the prison cell. "I'm so sorry," Aurora gushes, feeling guilty for placing him in such danger. "The poor guy should've never suffered such a thing. I can't even imagine how worried you must've been!"

"He'll be home tomorrow." Bridget smiles, "And even though I'm immensely relieved, this family is no stranger to hardship. I'm just thankful he's alive and well. Without Cadet Conway's brave act of heroism, I fear that things could have been far worse for you and Liam. How did Cadet Conway even find you guys there?"

"You mean Jack is alive?!" Lena suddenly perks up.

"Yes," Aurora nods, "he's the one who broke Liam and I out of Raymond's trap. It's kind of a long story but—"

"Your Majesty," a tall man dressed in black enters the room. He's sporting a head of grey hair and an intimidating stare. He looks at King Addison, then at Lena. "I have an update from Captain Cepheus. They've searched the grounds, and the URIA base is officially deemed as unusable. The underground tunnels have all collapsed and nothing is salvageable. Thankfully, they found another platoon of men this morning, which means everyone is accounted for, except for Cadet Julyan, Jonathan, Prince Asher, and Princess Elizabeth."

"Everyone?" Lena speaks up. "Even Cadet Greenwood?"

"Yes, Your Majesty."

"But where are the others?" Aurora asks quickly.

"That is still unknown. But we will continue our search and bring word as soon as we hear something." He quickly bows and leaves the room.

Aurora bites her lip. Everything is happening so fast, she can scarcely keep up!

"That boy has a real knack for disappearing." King Addison shakes his head, attempting to lighten up the moment.

"He sure does." Bridget giggles, despite her deep fears.

"Wherever he is, I hope Elizabeth is with him," Aurora sighs. "I can't even imagine how terrified she'd be, trying to survive on her own in the woods."

"There's nothing we can do right now, other than wait, and pray." Addison sighs. Deep worry lines are pressed into his forehead and beneath his eyes. "Bridget and I have to excuse ourselves, but we want you to join our family for dinner tonight. Until then, please feel free to make yourselves at home and spend the day however you like. I don't know if the pool, spa, or golf course hold any kind of lure for you guys right now, but it might be better to find something to help pass the time."

"Thank you." Lena forces a small smile onto her face, "We truly appreciate everything you're doing to help us. Honestly, I don't know where we would be without Tarsurella."

"I just wish we could do more." Addison sighs then bids the girls farewell.

~*~

Lena stands on her temporary bedroom balcony and overlooks the scenery below. It's truly glorious. Vibrant hues of green border patches of pink and purple flowers. The gentle hum of a lawn mower buzzes in the distance. As tranquil as the scene is, Lena is in no mood to enjoy it.

Her nervous fingers cling to the marble balcony rim. She doesn't want to be anxious. But she is. Lena knows that God doesn't want her to worry. She tries to remind herself that He is still in control. Birds are still singing, creeks are still gurgling, and life is still moving at the usual rhythm in other parts of the world. But Lena's heart feels like it is the dead of winter. Everything is cold and barren. She has lost so very much. Grandmary, Theodore, the URIA base, and now, perhaps she has even lost Elizabeth.

You cannot afford to think like that, Lena scolds herself. *Surely, she is okay. God protected Peter. Surely, He's protecting Elizabeth too.*

Mrs. Deborah had insisted the girls take a few moments to get settled into their rooms and freshen up before dinner this evening with the Royal Family. Aurora was eager to shower, catch up with her parents, and of course call Emma back in California and let her know all that had happened. But Lena didn't have anyone to call. There were no friends or family eagerly waiting to hear from her.

"Your Majesty, excuse me, but you have a visitor," Deborah interrupts Lena's gloomy thoughts.

Lena twirls around, jubilant and overjoyed to see Peter standing before her.

"Peter!" Lena cries. His name feels as if it belongs in her mouth. It sounds so very sweet, she wishes to repeat it. "Oh, Peter!" She rushes toward him and throws her arms around his chest.

Peter is steady. He keeps his footing, despite the great speed at which Lena threw herself at him. "Oh, my dear, sweet Peter." She continues to embrace him, but notices something is different. Even though his arms are kindly returning the favor, there is no emotion in them. The embrace is empty and halfhearted.

She slowly steps back. Something is wrong. Peter is not acting like his usual self. His eyes are cold, and Lena notices that the ever-prevailing glow is missing.

"Are you okay?" she asks. "Peter, I was so worried! I don't know what I would've done if something happened to you!"

"We're fine." Peter's voice sounds reassuring, but his eyes tell her another story. "Myself and several of the other cadets made camp in the western woods, shortly after the explosion. I am glad to know that you are safe as well."

Deborah quickly whisks herself out of the scene, allowing the two to speak privately.

"Nobody will harm you here in Tarsurella," Peter continues. "And for that, I am grateful. Enjoy the rest of your evening, Your Majesty." And with that, Peter turns to leave.

"Peter." Lena grabs his arm, not wanting him to exit so abruptly. "What is this?" She confronts him on the sudden change of attitude, "Why are you acting so casual and cold?"

Peter's eyes grow more intense, but then, for a split second, Lena is sure she sees a line of deep hurt race across them. "You have made it perfectly clear to me where you stand.

You're to become Queen, and I'm not going to get in the way of you ruling this country as you see fit."

"Peter, I never said that I don't want you to be part of my life or that I wish to reject your help in winning back Bella Adar! I simply said that I don't care for you in the—"

"Save it." Peter holds up a hand to reject her flood of conversation. "I've heard it all once before. You don't need to remind me."

"But Peter, just let me finish what I'm saying!" Lena's voice is desperate.

"Things have changed, Lena!" Peter's eyes are wild with emotion, "The life we used to know has vanished, and with it, our friendship. I know my place. So, don't go trying to change things again." Peter's throat tightens up, "It will be easier this way."

Lena viciously shakes her head, "But Peter, I—"

"Good evening, Your Majesty." Peter quickly bows and exits the balcony.

~*~

"I know! I wish you were here with us." Aurora maneuvers her cell phone to another ear as something on the TV screen catches her attention.

Her parents have been quietly watching TNN, waiting for her to finish up her conversation with Emma. Until this point, the TV hasn't served as any kind of distraction. But in a moment, that all changes. Aurora's eyes widen as she sees her face on TV.

"Uhh, Em? I've gotta go." Aurora places a nervous hand on her stomach, "I know, I know, I love you so stinking much! Okay, we'll talk soon. Yes! Love you. Bye."

Aurora hangs up and dives onto the bed. She stretches her arm forward for the remote and quickly turns up the volume.

Her father looks up from where he's been munching on chocolate-covered strawberries, and her mother sets down her cell phone.

"Inside sources confirm that American popstar, singer-songwriter, Aurora Jasper, hasn't just been on a casual sabbatical. When the Hollywood sweetheart suddenly canceled her tour and dropped off the radar, Miss Jasper's management was silent." The perky news anchor reports, "With nothing more than a short press statement claiming the starlet needed time off to 'attend to personal and family matters', fans were outraged. Disappointed by the fact that Aurora's highly anticipated tour was a no-go, stories in the rumor mill quickly spread. But it wasn't until today that we finally learned the truth. This in, just moments ago, and I warn you, hold on to your hearts Aurora Jasper fandom, because I guarantee *none* of you saw this coming! Aurora Jasper is a Princess. That's right folks, a real, legitimate heir to the Bella Adarnian throne. If you've been following our stories covering the conflict in Bella Adar, you know that this tiny nation just below our southern border is struggling to gain its political footing. Nobody has known where Miss Jasper was, until today, when she was seen arriving at the Palace."

The scene flashes to a tired Aurora, trudging her way up the sidewalk, trying to avoid all the press attention.

Aurora frowns. That shot of her is *terrible*. And if she knows anything about the news, she knows they're going to be looping that same shot for the next twenty-four hours, or at least until the next big thing happens.

"How did they find out?!" Aurora quickly sits up and crosses her arms, "Who told them I was going to be here? And how do they know who my parents are?!"

"Maybe someone here at the Palace leaked the news," Mr. Jasper suggests sadly. "There's been so much hustle and bustle with all the staff, maybe someone decided to cash your secret in for a little bit of extra change. I'm so sorry, Aurora." He shakes his head, struggling to fathom what his daughter must be going through right now. "You shouldn't have to work through all this under the microscope of the public eye. What's happened to you thus far is bad enough already, let alone having the whole world watching as a critical audience."

Aurora quickly turns off the TV. "This is such a mess," she grumbles and shakes her head. "How are we ever going to figure this out? The base is destroyed, Elizabeth and Prince Asher are missing, the entire world knows my secret, and Raymond *still* has all the power! We're going to need a miracle."

"I know it's a lot, honey." Mrs. Jasper rises then sits down on the bed beside her. She places a comforting arm around her adopted daughter. Aurora allows her head to helplessly flop against her mom's chest, just like she did as a little girl. "But we'll get through this. Together. No matter what happens, your dad and I are going to be here with you every step of the way."

"Thank you." Aurora tries to smile, but her heart just isn't in it. She squeezes her mom's hand, "I know you mean that, but

I'm not sure I want your help every step of the way." She giggles, "I mean, I have been pretty independent for the last five years."

Mrs. Jasper laughs. "Of course! You wouldn't want your old dad and I to cramp your style!"

"Does this mean we can't come with you to dinner tonight?" Mr. Jasper sounds disappointed, "I mean, dining with the King and Queen would definitely be a huge item scratched off my bucket list."

"Nah, I guess you can come." Aurora winks playfully. "Just as long as dad promises to dress up a little bit and ditches the khaki shorts. Somehow I don't think the Royal Family of Tarsurella is going to be crazy about you wearing socks with sandals."

"But they're so comfortable!" Mr. Jasper argues.

Mrs. Jasper raises a questioning eyebrow.

"But then again, dress pants and polished black shoes can be comfortable too." He winks.

~*~

Aurora slips into her assigned chair near the head of the table.

Life is very, very odd. Exactly twenty-four hours ago Aurora was cutting it up on the dance floor with Kehahi. If someone had told her that she would later spend the night in Raymond's dungeon, be rescued by Jack, be flown to Tarsurella, and then get dolled up to eat dinner with the Royal Family of Tarsurella, Aurora would've thought they were insane.

"Thanks for joining us." Addison smiles and shakes Aurora's, Lena's, and her parents' hands once more. "I have to apologize on behalf of my wife. She really wished she could be here, but she's just not feeling well. She wanted to be sure and have me tell you that she's praying for you all."

Addison sits down, and they all follow his lead.

"We'll actually have a pretty small crowd tonight." Addison explains the empty chairs at the massively-long banquet table, "Just Bridget, Hope, Jillian and Millie."

Aurora eyes the gold-rimmed, porcelain dishes set before her. The table is decorated just beautifully. She takes a deep breath, realizing that there are multiple forks, knives and cups at each place setting. She hopes she'll be able to figure out which one to use in proper order. The last thing she wants to do is make a complete fool out of herself in front of the Royals. She glances at her father who is very much a finger food guy. Hopefully he'll have enough class to actually use his silverware.

Princess Bridget enters the Dining Room and Aurora smiles. She's surprised to see Bridget wearing a casual pair of blue jeans and a red 'All You Need is Love' T-shirt. Aurora gulps. She suddenly feels *very* overdressed.

"Sorry, I'm late!" Princess Bridget offers her apology. "But I just got bad news about Liam." She slips in beside her brother and everyone gives her their full attention.

"His leg is infected." Bridget reveals the melancholy news, "That's exactly what they *didn't* want to happen. He's running a fever and is in a lot of pain. They're trying to keep him highly-sedated, so he feels as little as possible, but they're concerned." Bridget takes a deep breath, "We need to pray."

Aurora flinches as she mentally relives the moment when the door slammed upon Liam's leg.

"Absolutely." Addison doesn't hesitate for even a second. He invites everyone at the table to join hands, and next thing Aurora knows, Addison is fervently petitioning Heaven for the health and healing of Liam. He also asks God to protect Asher and Elizabeth, to bring them home as safely and quickly as possible. He prays for the end of the conflict in Bella Adar, for the Princesses to have courage, and for Raymond's wicked rule to come to an end. They all agree with a wholehearted, "amen."

Aurora looks up, smiling at the King of Tarsurella. *Wow*, she thinks to herself, *I did not see that coming. This family really knows how to pray!*

"Thank you." Bridget smiles at Aurora, then at her parents. "I didn't want to be a Debbie-Downer and start our dinner off in such a foul mood, but in our family we pretty much share everything with each other. Especially things like this. So, thanks for praying with us."

"Of course, honey!" Mrs. Jasper reassures her. "We can't even begin to imagine what you're going through right now."

Aurora finds it amusing that her mom just called the Princess of Tarsurella 'honey'.

Several waiters enter the scene and reveal the first appetizer. "Spinach and Goat Cheese Tartlets," the French-sounding waiter tells the King.

"Thank you, Michael."

Aurora is impressed that King Addison appears to know each of his staff by name.

"Spinach and Goat Cheese?!" a little girl echoes from the other end of the table.

[404]

Everyone's eyes travel toward the youngest girl at the table, Princess Millie. "I mean…uh…" she twirls her fork in the air and smiles sheepishly, "Yum?"

"Don't feel bad, kiddo! I'm not a big spinach fan myself either!" Mr. Jasper expresses his thoughts on the dinner.

Aurora's eyes widen. Did her dad really just say that?!

"But I'll eat mine if you eat yours!" Mr. Jasper takes the small appetizer in his fingers and pops it into his mouth.

Millie giggles.

Mr. Jasper then leans over and whispers in her ear, "Or, we could just feed it to the dog."

"That could be arranged." Millie grins mischievously then stands up to call for their beloved Golden Retriever. "Oh, Mr. Darcy!"

"Don't even think about it," Jillian warns her in a stern voice. "You're going to make Darcy sick with all those extra table scraps. It's not good for him. He needs to eat his dog food, and *you* need to eat what's on your plate."

"I don't care how old I get," Millie broadcasts to everyone at the table, "I am *never* going to like vegetables. Even when I'm one-hundred-sixteen, I'm still not going to enjoy them."

"And you won't live to be one-hundred-sixteen if you don't eat your vegetables," Jillian grumbles.

Lena giggles. "So, tell me, what is it like growing up as a princess?" Lena asks the young girls sitting across from her. "It must be very lovely. To be surrounded by such beautiful rooms, with kind maids and butlers, to wear such fancy and fine clothes; does it all feel like some sort of a fairytale?"

"Oh, I wouldn't call it that," Princess Hope speaks up. "Don't you watch the news?"

"Hope." Addison criticizes his sister for the harsh comment.

"I'm not trying to be rude," Hope quickly defends herself. "But I feel like everyone should know by now that our lives are not like those old re-runs of *Leave it to Beaver*. The stirring rebellion has made it nearly impossible for us to leave the Palace, without fear of being harmed."

"I'm sorry, I was not aware," Lena sounds confused.

"Rebellion?" Aurora asks. "What kind of a rebellion?"

"It's complicated," Addison sighs. "But there's a group of young people who continue to grow more and more upset with the way we're running this nation. They're demanding that the monarchy end and a democracy be established. So, as you can see, the future of our nation is just as wobbly as yours is right now."

"How come I've never heard about this?" Aurora asks. "I mean, I'm not a huge news junkie, but surely they'd mention something about this in the States?" Aurora looks at Bridget, "The way they paint your lives to be so picture-perfect on the media, you're the envy of little girls all over the country!"

"We're trying to keep as much as we can on the DL," Bridget explains. "Of course the news catches wind of things here and there, but with everything so unstable right now, we're trying to keep the nitty-gritty details of our lives under wraps."

"And all while we remain silent, the rebellion continues to grow." Hope huffs.

Aurora looks at the Princess, picking up on the subtle fact that she sounds bitter about something. It appears as though Addison and Bridget are not happy with her negative comments.

"I understand," Aurora quickly sympathizes, finding yet another area in life where she completely relates with this family. "Living in a fishbowl isn't easy. The judgement and pressure can be harsh when your every move is scrutinized by the media." She glances at Lena, "Something Lena hasn't had to deal with yet. But she will."

"Actually, Deborah wants to talk to you two about the possibility of holding a small press conference tomorrow," Addison reveals. "You wouldn't need to go into significant details right now, but as long as Captain Cepheus gives the okay, we think it would be wise for you ladies to go ahead and address the public. They're pounding on our back door with questions."

"Well, you can't exactly blame them, can you?" Jillian speaks up. "I mean, Aurora Jasper secretly being a Princess is a massively-exciting story!" She smiles at Aurora and shrugs innocently, "Sorry, I'm kind of a huge fan. Your music is amazing."

"Aw, thanks!" Aurora giggles, finding it ironic that someone in the Royal family is a fan. Shouldn't it be the other way around?!

"Wasn't there a *Veggie Tales* story about this?" Millie asks, racking her brain in the attempt to remember. "Something about a princess and a popstar?"

Her comment brings laughter to everyone at the table.

"I still don't know how a kid who loved *Veggie Tales* can have such a strong distain for eating vegetables," Addison chuckles.

"What's with the empty chair?" Millie asks, referring to the wide-open seat beside her. "Didn't everyone who was supposed to be here already come?"

"I've invited Cadet Conway, one of the young men from the URIA, to join us," Addison reveals. "When I heard that he didn't fly here with you, Aurora, I called and requested he come separately. I want to thank him personally for performing such a daring rescue. Without his act of bravery, both you and Liam would still be in that prison. Deborah said he'll be here shortly."

Aurora glances at Lena, who appears pleased with the news. Aurora bites her lip. It's pretty obvious that Lena holds Jack on a pedestal of admiration. She's willing to bet Lena is harboring a secret crush. But then again, who wouldn't? Jack is ruggedly handsome, kind, and knows how to kick some serious bad guys' behinds. Aurora thinks of the young woman Jack was crying over and wonders who it was. She feels the sudden urge to tell Lena. But now isn't the right time.

The slim waiter reveals the next round of their dinner, Squash Soup. Aurora resists the urge to wrinkle her nose. She hates squash. She glances at Millie and wonders if she's going to make a fuss about it. Or even worse, her dad.

Just then, Jack enters.

"Jack!" Lena calls out his name excitedly.

But Jack knows proper etiquette. He addresses King Addison with a bow, and Addison rises from the table to shake his hand. He ardently thanks Jack, then introduces him to Bridget, Hope, Jillian, and Millie.

"I am truly honored to be here." Jack sits down at the end of the table beside Millie.

"How was your flight?" Aurora asks.

"Just fine, thank you, Your Highness," Jack tells her.

Aurora twists her lip. Jack acts so proper, it drives her nuts. She finds herself wondering if Jack has another side to his personality. Does he know how to kick back, relax, and have some fun?

"I can't believe you single-handedly broke Liam and Aurora out of a medieval prison!" Millie tells him excitedly. "How did you do it? Weren't there like, a ton of guards? And just one of you?"

"Oh, you heard about that?" Jack asks the young Princess playfully. "Word must travel fast around here." He winks.

"Of course, I heard about it!" Millie croons. "It sounds like such an adventure! How did you do it?! How did you manage to rescue them without getting caught?"

"Well, I snuck into the palace grounds on a bakery truck." Jack leans forward, his eyes flickering playfully as he shares his story with eager ears. Jack isn't the kind of guy to boast about his accomplishments, but he knows how much children enjoy hearing his tales. "Once I was safely inside the courtyard, I headed directly for the prison."

Millie's eyes were wide, as well as Lena's. Everyone at the table was thoroughly immersed in his story.

"In all honesty, they didn't have a very impressive security system. Which I assumed would be the case, seeing how

Raymond doesn't have much of a budget to work with. There was just one guard blocking the prison entrance, so I took care of him, snatched his keys, and dashed in to find Her Highness. At that point, I didn't have a clue which Princess it was, as I had only just heard about Her Highness's kidnapping from our local herb lady. Imagine my surprise when I see Aurora Jasper, America's favorite popstar, locked up behind bars." His eyes meet hers.

Aurora can't help but smile. Jack makes the entire ordeal sound so adventurous and exciting. Despite the trauma of it all, Aurora can't help but feel as if she's been part of something special. Something that belongs in a storybook. The kind of epic tale that Jack will tell his grandchildren someday. It makes her excited to think that her name might live long into the future, being echoed throughout the chambers of history, mentioned in stories and fables for years to come.

"As soon as I released Aurora, I might as well have walked away, dropped by the café and stopped for a donut break!" Jack is playfully expressive as he tells his story. "Releasing Aurora from the cell was like loosing a fire-breathing dragon!"

Millie giggles.

"No joke. She was one determined Princess. Whipping intimidating karate moves out of her back pocket, knocking out guards left and right, and with one swift move, unlocking Liam and clenching the chains onto one of the other guards! You should've seen the look on his unsuspecting face. Total surprise attack."

"Wow," Millie breathes. She turns excitedly toward Aurora, "Who knew you were so heroic! I might actually start listening to your music now!"

The entire table bursts out in laughter.

Jack continues to tell his story, and Millie adds in her lively commentary wherever she can. The table happily works their way through a six-course meal, laughing, chatting and immensely enjoying themselves.

Despite the intense reality awaiting them just outside these palace gates, for a few moments the dinner table serves as a fun and relaxing haven. It was as if they were able to slip away from reality and enjoy the simplest yet refreshing kinds of joy life has to offer: food, family, friends, and laughter.

Aurora smiles as she watches everyone flawlessly interact with one another around the table. By the time dessert is served, Aurora feels as though she, Lena, Jack, her parents, and the Royal Family have truly bonded.

None of them knows what tomorrow holds. Most likely it will be challenging. Exhausting. Faith-testing. And persistence-building. But for this temporary, fleeting moment, none of that matters. They all choose to focus on what is right in front of them and cherish the gift of the moment for what it is.

~*~

Back in Bella Adar...

Prince Asher is escorted into another glaringly-white room. Asher's intense eyebrows express displeasure with what surrounds him. His dark eyes hold steady as he frantically attempts to record and remember every detail of what's occurring. The bright, white walls are disturbing. It's as if they serve in some twisted way as a false attempt to bring light to the darkness of Raymond's soul. Prince Asher wonders if Raymond even *has* a conscience. Highly unlikely.

"And now, I introduce you to the greatest accomplishment of my lifetime." Raymond places his hand on a button, and it appears another pair of doors are about to open.

Asher squints, wondering why Raymond desires to reveal these things to him. Doesn't he know how foolish it is? Trying to convince Asher to partner with him?

"Let me rephrase that." Raymond pauses before pushing the button, "It is not *my* solo accomplishment. Rather, it is a corporate endeavor to which I have the distinct pleasure of heading up."

He creases his thumb into the button and doors part. Asher does his best to keep his gaze indifferent and unimpressed. He knows Raymond wants him to be impressed with the contraption. Despite the grand sight, Asher isn't going to give this man even an inch of satisfaction.

A long, torpedo-shaped machine, not any larger than a canoe, sits before Asher's eyes. The wide, donut-shaped opening on the end appears as if it's large enough for someone to crawl inside. Asher's heart jogs with anxiety. Is it some kind of weapon? Rocket? Torture chamber? The possibilities are chilling.

Three men dressed in long lab coats scurry around the machine, turning buttons and dials on a nearby control panel, closely monitoring and checking things with their digital clipboards.

Asher's heartbeat intensifies as he recognizes one of the scientists. It's Mr. Akerly.

"Doctor, would you please tell our guest what you have built?"

Mr. Akerly's head jerks upward. His look of surprise and confusion tells Asher that the man isn't used to company.

"This information is classified," Mr. Akerly speaks matter-of-factly. "If even the smallest detail falls into the wrong hands–

"Of course, it's classified!" Raymond snaps. "Just tell him what it does! And please, use small and bite-size terms that his brain will be able to understand. Not your dreadfully-long, droning, impossible-to-interpret, scientist-speak. English, Mr. Akerly. English."

"Of course." Mr. Akerly nods and shoves his glasses back up the bridge of his noise. Pride soars through his voice as he reveals his latest project, "What you see before you is a one-of-a-kind, experimental prototype for the JAA16. We have concluded, through several years of intense and excessive research, that the JAA16 possess the power to project frequencies to influence the mind in a particular direction. We have high hopes for this product, believing we can use it to better mankind, raise the IQ of those who are struggling, improve test scores, and perhaps even irradiate false doctrines and thinking patterns which are harmful for the human race."

Asher can scarcely endure the amount of pressure pounding in his head. His stomach is flipping with fear, and his mind racing in disbelief. Surely Mr. Akerly doesn't mean what he's saying. Does he even hear himself?! Asher's mind is frantic, *Better mankind? More like manipulate and control mankind! How could Jane's Dad build something like this?*

"Why don't we give the young Prince an example of how it works?" Raymond grins.

"Yes sir." Mr. Akerly nods and turns back to his dashboard. Two other scientists join him, and Asher's eyes are struck with icy fear.

Raymond places an unwanted arm around Asher's shoulder. "I'm not sure if you caught the drift of everything the doctor unveiled. But the machine you are beholding today is truly revolutionary. Doctor Akerly has harbored the power of the AA16 code, into something that will benefit everyone on earth. Leading scientists from around the world have partnered with us to condense the code into a chemical which we'll be able to sell commercially. Farmers are intrigued by this idea, being able to spray a light film onto their crops, which will mentally captivate their buyers into coming back for more. Investors are willing to pay out of their eyeballs for this kind of power! Frequency advertising is the wave of the future, and we're the first ones riding it. Car manufacturers are elated by the idea of being able to sell 'invisible ad frequencies' for massive amounts of money, which once implanted in each new model, will influence the mind of the buyer.

Just imagine, a man driving along in his brand-new car, has the sudden urge to stop and get a hamburger at Ronald's. Try as he may to fight the urge, it will overpower him. Millions of new drivers will be eating at Ronald's, vacationing in the Caribbean, or buying a new bottle of perfume; virtually whatever the frequency inside their car tells them to do. Quite genius, isn't it?"

"If by genius you mean sick and demented, then sure," Asher growls. "This isn't about monopolizing the business world." He shakes his head angrily, "Nobody cares that much about selling hamburgers and French fries." Asher can see right through the man, "What you want is control. And not just of their eating habits. You want control of their morals, beliefs, and daily life choices. Just like a demonized dictator would."

"And now, for the highlight of my day!" Raymond continues, "I get to induct you into the JAA16, and you'll forget everything I just told you." He chuckles, "It really is great fun. After your time soaking in the radioactive tube, the entire molecular structure of your brain will be rewired. Rewired to serve me."

Asher's heart is screaming as beads of sweat form on his face. The man isn't joking. Despite his wicked laugher, it's all real. It's all very, *very* real.

No! Asher thinks desperately, *This can't happen! They can't place me in there! I can't lose control of my mind! I need to get back and warn everyone, I need to tell Addison and Jane and Charlie! God, give me a way out of here!*

All at once, the grip of two doctors pressing their grubby fingers into Asher's arms, jolt him to action. He struggles to fight back, but they quickly strap him to a cushioned board which has descended out of the machine.

Asher puffs and pants, and kicks with his legs, but soon his ankles are strapped as well. He continues to struggle against the pressure, attempting to break free from his confinement.

"Your Majesty," Doctor Akerly speaks up, "We have a low level in the solar charge."

Asher looks up and attempts to calm his breathing, wondering if perhaps this is the miracle he has just prayed for.

"Meaning what?" Raymond barks.

"We need to give it ample time to recharge. This will postpone our start time. Depending on the current positioning of the sun, it could take anywhere from forty minutes, to six hours."

"Great," Raymond grumbles then glares at Asher. "Guards!" Raymond shouts at once, "Take His Highness back to his cell!"

Two buff guards appear and quickly do his bidding. Asher wishes there was time to speak with Mr. Akerly, but the guards are already pushing him out the door. He has so many questions. Why is Mr. Akerly doing this? Did they threaten him? Or is his heart just as dark as BellaAdar's twisted leader? Asher's chest is pounding.

His heart still hasn't settled by the time he reaches the cell.

"Praise God, you're still alive!" Elizabeth calls out as she rises to her feet. She had been sitting in the corner, praying.

The guards quickly disappear, and Asher pants several more times, attempting to control his breathing.

"Are you okay?" Elizabeth asks gently.

"Elizabeth, I need you to listen to me." Asher grabs her by the shoulders and expresses the intensity of their current disaster. "The AA16, the frequencies, the mind control! It's all real. It's real!" His voice shifts several octaves higher as it cracks with panicky nerves. He takes several strides and paces back and forth across their small, dark, cramped cell. "It's happening. It's happening, oh, God, what do we do!? What do we do!? Raymond has partnered with leading scientists in the world, and it's not a fluke! If he puts me in there..."

He stops pacing and his eyes dig into Elizabeth's once more, "He wants to put me through the system in just a few hours!

We need to find a way out of here! We need to escape and warn everyone before it's too late! If they take my mind, I'm not going to be able to stop this! I need to tell Jane, I need to tell Jane!"

"Asher, please, calm down! I know this is frightening, but we must think rationally. It is clear that Raymond wants us to be afraid. But we cannot give into his wickedness! We must pray!"

"But they're going to brainwash me!" Asher is frantic, "If I go in that machine, I'm not going to come out the same person! I won't remember anything he's told me, and I won't be able to stop any of this!"

"God is greater!" Elizabeth argues. "God is greater than any frequency or mind control! Surely, we can pray and believe God will protect you! His Word is a shield, and if you have hidden His Word in your heart, surely, He will protect you from the dangerous frequencies. He will help you keep a sound mind, Asher. I just know He will."

Asher only wishes he could be that confident. He slams an angry hand into the cell wall and Elizabeth jumps.

"We need to tell someone…we need to tell someone…" Asher continues pacing, "If we don't make it out of here, we need to tell someone!"

Elizabeth takes a deep breath and slips down to the floor. It is clear that Asher is far too worked up to listen to any sound reasoning.

Elizabeth closes her eyes and begins to pray.

Lord, You know the impossible trial we are in right now. It appears as though we are trapped, and there is no way of escape. But I know You are a God of miracles. All throughout the Bible You performed amazing signs and wonders, delivering Your children from the mouths of the lions, and from the enemy's sword. Lord, we need Your help! We are in a most desperate hour! Lord, please calm Asher. Help Him to relax and settle His heart on you. He is afraid, but He needs to trust You. Help him to think with a sound mind, and to see a way out. Surely there has to be an answer. Lord, reveal what that answer is. We need someone to deliver this message to those who can help us. As Asher has said, we must warn those who are in danger because of what Raymond is doing. Send us a messenger. Send us help! Send us a way out. In Jesus name, Amen.

Elizabeth opens her eyes. She glances at Asher who is still facing the wall opposite her. She looks back past the thick prison bars to where two guards are chatting in the distance. She thinks about Paul and Silas and the angels who came to deliver them from their chains. Elizabeth wonders if God still sends angels to help those who are in need today.

She sighs and continues to watch the guards. A third figure joins them, and Elizabeth's eyes widen. *Is that– No, it can't be! But it is! Kehahi! A URIA solider! The same young man who Aurora danced with!*

Elizabeth quickly flies to her feet. *What is he doing here?* For a split second, Elizabeth has the desire to cry out and ask him to save them. But something stops her from doing so.

Suddenly, a thought strikes her. *What if Kehahi isn't a good guy after all? What if he works for Raymond? It appears as though he does!*

Anger clenches her heart as she finally finds a face to blame for this catastrophe. *What if he is the soul responsible for the bombing?! How dare he pretend to be someone he isn't then turn his back and betray us all!*

"Asher," she whispers as she nears him, "look."

Asher turns around and instantly spots the familiar URIA solider.

"Can you believe it?! He was a deceptive double-agent!" Elizabeth whispers quietly. "He must've been the one who made way for Raymond's men to enter the base!"

"Maybe not," Asher says slowly, wondering if maybe he's come to break them out of here. Asher continues to watch Kehahi and his conversation with the men. Casual laughter floats through the hall.

After a few moments, the men leave but Kehahi remains.

"What did you say his name was?" Asher asks.

"Kehahi."

"Kehahi!" Asher suddenly calls out.

Kehahi glances over his shoulder, surprised to hear his name. He narrows his eyes and cautiously makes his way toward their cell.

"What are you doing here?" Asher instantly confronts him.

"I could ask you the same question." Kehahi's voice is cold and defensive.

"Listen, this isn't time for head games." Asher's tone is just as sharp, "Who are you working for. Raymond or the URIA?"

"You betrayed us!" Elizabeth instantly accuses him, "You're the one who opened up a portal for Raymond's men to enter, didn't you!? Didn't you!"

"Elizabeth, shhhh," Asher hushes her. "Let the guy talk."

"I'm not proud of what I did," Kehahi admits, "but I wanna get you two out of here. If I know anything about Raymond, it's that he doesn't keep his prisoners alive for very long. I'll come back at midnight. Then, the corridor should be clear, and I'll be able to snag a key from the office. I'll smuggle you two into the kitchen and–"

"No," Asher interrupts him, "no, it's going to be too late. Someone has to get this message to Tarsurella. Someone has to stop Raymond before he successfully establishes a new world order! If he gets the AA16 into our food, into the hands of our farmers, our car dealerships, and into the global economy…it's going to be too late. Kehahi, I need you to take this message to Tarsurella. It's simple, but absolutely vital it gets there safely! Tell my brother, 'The AA16 is in full throttle and I'm their next target. Mr. Akerly is here. Tell Jane. Tell the world'."

"Asher, we can't!" Elizabeth speaks up. "We can't trust him! How do you know he isn't going to turn on us?!"

"I don't," Asher admits, "but trusting him is a risk we're just going to have to take. Otherwise, it could be game over. For everyone."

"I'll do it," Kehahi promises. His voice sounds genuine, but Elizabeth is still concerned. "I'll get help. I'll deliver your message and return with reinforcements."

"Kehahi, this isn't just about us," Asher warns him. "It's about an entire planet falling into the grip of a man who wants to destroy it. You have to make it safely to Tarusrella. If neither of us make it out of here alive," Asher looks at Elizabeth, "or sane…nobody is going to know that someone is controlling their every move."

Kehahi nods, then quickly disappears.

Now it's Elizabeth's turn to freak out.

"Asher, what were you thinking?!" she scolds him.

"I know it seems crazy." Asher sighs, running anxious fingers through his hair, truly feeling as though he is at his wits end. "But we don't have any other choice here! The world needs to know what Raymond is doing!"

"Even if that means he kills us in the process?" Elizabeth fights back fear-filled tears.

"Elizabeth, I'm sorry." Asher lowers his voice, "I know how badly you want to get out of here. But sometimes, there's a greater price to be considered. Our attempt to find safety and freedom might've come at the cost of something far worse: the truth being silenced and an entire world subjected to the slavery of Raymond's cruel mind control."

"I suppose you're right," Elizabeth slowly agrees with him. "Perhaps there is a greater purpose. As frightful as it is to walk through the valley of the shadow of death, perhaps being here, right in the eye of the storm, centered in the middle of Raymond's evil project, is going to shed light on the very thing that has been hidden for years."

"He can't take my mind," Asher speaks determinedly. "He just can't."

"He won't." Elizabeth tries to encourage him, "God wouldn't bring you this far just to have it all end in this moment."

"But what if the machine actually works?" Asher is terrified by the words that tumble out of his lips, "What if I forget everything, and I become one of his brainwashed robots?"

"God will protect you, Asher!" Elizabeth is firm, "Surely His angels can guard you from those wicked frequencies."

"Oh, no." A sudden thought comes to Asher's mind, and almost causes his face to turn entirely pale.

"What?" Elizabeth asks.

"What if he tries to brainwash you?" Asher's eyes are wide with horror, "Oh no, I hadn't even thought of that! Of course, Raymond would want to control you. Gah, what was I thinking?!" He spins around and slams his head on the bar. "I should have had you leave with Kehahi!" He turns around and faces her again, "Elizabeth, I am so, so sorry. I didn't even think about the fact that—"

"Don't," Elizabeth tells him, placing a firm hand on his shoulder. "You made the right decision. There are far more important things at stake than our own lives. If God wants us to survive then we will. And if we perish, then we perish. But no matter what, we cannot fear Raymond's threats. Getting us worked up and anxious is exactly what he wants. So that means, we must refuse to do it. I am not afraid of mind control."

"You're not?" Asher asks.

"No." Elizabeth shakes her head. "I have already been through it. My mind was dominated by people attempting to control me for sixteen years of my life. If God delivered me from that, He can certainly deliver me from this too. Now that I know the truth, it has and *will* continue to set me free. Nothing can change that. Not even a stupid machine."

~*~

Kehahi's boots cross the grated flooring. Try as he may to be quiet, it isn't working too well. He sneaks past a series of closed doors, holding his breath, desperately hoping none of them open. As he scurries toward the exit, he knows he is

[422]

placing everything on the line. Leaving the base when he's supposed to be on duty is going against the grain of everything he's been trained to do.

He must escape into the woods before anyone notices his absence. If he doesn't get a far enough lead, he will be hunted down and shot. Kehahi knows how valuable he is to Raymond. Anyone who knows this much about both camps—Raymond's undercover operation, as well as the URIA—won't be trusted to return to civilization.

Beads of fearful sweat clog Kehahi's pores. He attempts to keep his anxiety under control. *You have to do this,* Kehahi tells himself. *Stay steady.*

The speed of Kehahi's heartrate increases as he nears the final exit. He knows that armed men will greet him with gunshots on the other side. Kehahi is all too familiar with Raymond's rules. Raymond controls his men with lifelong contracts of service. Trying to break the terms of that contract results in instant death.

Kehahi sucks air into his lungs, realizing these might be his last few moments on earth. Though he's faced the ugly threat of death many times, he's never felt quite this close to it.

His determined foot kicks down the door in front of him. Kehahi pulls the trigger of his own machine gun, quickly taking shots before he loses the element of surprise.

The first guard tumbles to the floor, and Kehahi continues running, bolting through the dark cave, unable to see where he's going. He can hear the angry shouts and rapid fire coming from behind. Kehahi's chest pounds, but his feet don't stop.

Within seconds, he can see an opening ahead. Although it is still dark outside, it's brighter than in the midnight-black cave.

Kehahi continues to tear into the woods, thankful for the darkness. Although it makes his vision a challenge, it will aid him in his desire to disappear.

His mind races as he senses they are gaining on him. He can hear the troops calling for backup, reporting his escape. With one impressive jump, Kehahi lurches himself up into a tree and climbs up several branches.

Two guards run past the tree, continuing their bounty-hunt. Kehahi watches carefully, as three more men stream out of the cave.

The men run to the tree and then slow. Kehahi ducks down, careful to make sure every part of him is hidden by the large tree trunk. If anyone sees him, it's all over.

"Who escaped?" one of the guys asks.

Kehahi holds his breath. He recognizes the voice. It belongs to one of his buddies, Konzopo.

"Kehahi."

"Kehahi?!" Konzopo echoes, surprised to hear the news. "What in the world? Why would he do a fool-headed thing like that?"

"Maybe he went soft on us," one of the older men huffs. "Maybe he decided to join the URIA."

"Kehahi would never do that." Konzopo shakes his head, "He's not a traitor."

"Oh yeah?" The man laughs, "Why else would he take off in the middle of the night like this? My guess is that his mission to spy on the URIA base made him soft. Probably fell in love with one of the Princesses, and now he's risking his life for her fair ladyhood." The man laughs at his own unoriginal joke.

"Let's split up," another guard suggests. "Von and I will search up toward the river. Konzopo, you guard the mouth of the cave, just in case he's got more men from the URIA out here, planning an ambush or something."

"Yes, sir," Konzopo nods.

The two guards run off, leaving Konzopo standing just several feet below Kehahi.

Kehahi bites hard on his bottom lip. He needs to leave. Every second he stays up here in this tree is another second Prince Asher's and Princess Elizabeth's lives are at risk. Kehahi needs to get a better view. Where are the rest of the guards? He attempts to climb higher, careful not to make any noise.

Kehahi's muscular arms pull him higher. He attempts to gain a firm footing for his left foot. He scoots higher toward a branch and–SNAP!

Konzopo gasps and twirls around, lifting his gun upward.

Kehahi clings to the tree limb, attempting not to fall. He quickly finds a firm place for the foot that was previously dangling in the air.

Konzopo's dark eyes meet his. Kehahi continues to stare downward at his friend. Surely he's not going to shoot.

"What are you doing, man?" Konzopo asks in a condemning tone.

"Something I should have done a long time ago," Kehahi explains. "The right thing."

"And what's that, running off and getting yourself killed?" Konzopo shakes his head. "You're not a saint, Kehahi. After everything you've done, the URIA isn't going to take you back either! Why did you have to go and mess everything up?" He shakes his head sadly, concerned for his friend's fate. "If our men don't kill you, the URIA will."

"But you won't," Kehahi speaks calmly, aware of the fact that Konzopo's gun is still aimed at him.

"You have ten seconds." Konzopo's voice is shaking, "Ten seconds to run before I pull the trigger."

Kehahi slips out of the tree.

"He's over here!" Konzopo suddenly bursts out.

Kehahi's eyes grow wide. He reaches for his own pistol and shoots before Konzopo has the chance. Kehahi winces as the blast of his gun sends a bullet into Konzopo's chest. Konzopo tumbles backward.

Kehahi instantly regrets what he has done. His heart is reeling with grief, shock and guilt. He wishes to stay and mourn, but there's no time. He has to keep moving. His feet pound forward, dodging through the woods, desperately remorseful about the choice to end the life of his old friend.

~*~

Kehahi spots a distant cave just as the sun begins to rise. After running all through the night, Kehahi can think of nothing but sleep. He knows Prince Asher needs him to deliver his message to someone in the URIA, or even the King of Tarsurella himself. But Kehahi doesn't have a clue where the URIA's new base is or how to get in contact with them.

The idea of reaching out to the URIA is causing Kehahi to doubt his intrepid spirit. If they figure out the fact that Kehahi was responsible for the explosion of their base, they might not believe him.

But then again, why should they believe him? Why would anyone believe him? Everything about Kehahi is an absolute fraud. His underhanded hypocrisy has everyone bamboozled. Including Kehahi. He doesn't even know why he's doing what he's doing. The choices he makes only bring deeper and deeper feelings of guilt and regret.

Kehahi tumbles into the cave, confident his attackers have given up the pursuit. He knows Raymond's men far too well. They're much lazier than they want Raymond to believe. Kehahi has heard their endless complaints and seen them cut corners on all their workouts. The laggards were most likely very eager to return to the base and get a full night's rest. The chances of anyone actually chasing him all night long are severely slim.

Suddenly, in an explosion of events, Kehahi's tired body is confronted by three men. The assault comes so quickly, Kehahi isn't prepared.

Before he knows it, he's on the floor, wrestling with two guys attempting to pin him to the cold stone below. Someone has swiped his gun, and Kehahi is defenseless.

He attempts to knock the two unknown men off him with his arms when a loud voice shouts, "Freeze! Don't move! State your name!"

Kehahi looks up. In the dark cave, it's a challenge to see the figure standing over him. His eyes travel upward, past black boots, black jeans, forest green shirt, and a frowning face topped with a matching green beanie.

Kehahi squints, highly aware that they have his gun aimed toward him.

"Kehahi Julyan," Kehahi speaks slowly, his deep, broad voice echoing through the cave.

"Who sent you here?" the guy continues to question. "Are you a spy?"

"Listen, I don't know who you think you people are," it's clear to Kehahi these men don't work for Raymond, "but I'm just passing through. I'm looking for a place to sleep."

"Where's your desired destination?"

Kehahi narrows his eyes. Whoever this guy is, he's way too nosey. "Tarsurella."

"Tarsurella?" The young man laughs, lowering the gun. "And you're going there on foot? Let up on the grip, guys."

Kehahi shakes the collar of his black jacket, relieved the men have finally let him go. He quickly stands up and offers the men who previously held him, a disapproving glare. He notices how young this group of men are. *Maybe men is a generous description,* he thinks bitterly. *More like little boys with handguns.*

"Sorry for the cold welcome committee." The guy apologizes as he takes a step closer. "But we can never be too safe out here." He offers a hand toward Kehahi, "The name's Luke."

Kehahi timidly reaches for his hand, still unsure if he can trust him. "Now if I can have my gun back, I'll be on my way." Kehahi reaches for his weapon. Surprisingly, Luke allows him to grab it without any resistance.

"You want some grub?" Luke offers. "You can rest here for a while if you like. We can keep an eye out, make sure whoever it is you're running from doesn't show up."

Kehahi studies the young man. How does he know he's running from someone? And why is he offering to feed him? "No, I need to be on my way," Kehahi turns down the offer.

"You sure?" Luke asks again. "We've got some fresh venison patties we were just gonna brown up for breakfast."

"And how do I know you didn't poison the food?" Kehahi's voice is hard.

"Woah, paranoid much?!" Luke laughs, "Man, I'd love to hear your backstory, 'cause I'm sure it's crazy interesting."

Another small group of young men walk past them, casually chatting with one another, heading for the mouth of the cave.

"How many men are down here?" Kehahi asks. His curiosity is lit. *Who are all these people and what are they doing, living out here in the Bella Adarian wilderness?*

"Come on, I'll tell you over breakfast." Luke nods toward the inside of the cave.

Kehahi weighs his options. Either he can go back outside and travel for several more miles before finding food, shelter, and a place to rest. Or, he can hang out in here and get all the above for free.

"You know, venison doesn't actually sound half that bad right now." Kehahi slowly changes his tune.

~*~

"There's about a dozen of us out here," Luke explains before biting into a burger. "Just camping, hunting, sitting around and telling ridiculous guy stories that nobody believes, but we all have fun telling anyway." He laughs.

"You have tents set up nearby?" Kehahi asks, wondering how far they actually are from Raymond's base. Kehahi would guess he's at least thirty or forty miles out.

"Naw." Luke shakes his head, "We're just sleeping in the cave. It's more fun that way."

Kehahi nods then bites into his burger. He is pleasantly surprised by the rich flavors. He hadn't realized how hungry he was until now.

"What about you?" Luke asks, "Got some kind of dark past you're running from? Or did you just wake up one morning with the sudden urge to walk across the country with no food, water, or supplies?"

"Luke, Luke!" A voice echoes through the cave.

Luke lifts his head, attempting to see who is frantically running toward the campfire. It's Fredrick, one of his friends. "We've got company! Elisha spotted eight armed men, just on the other side of the field while he was out this morning!" Fredrick is huffing and puffing, "He's pretty sure they didn't see him, but he said it's only a matter of time before they find the cave!"

"Snap!" Luke jumps to his feet and grabs a canteen of water. He dumps it out on the fire and calls to the men who are lounging nearby, "We need to clean this place up, pronto! Make it look like we weren't here!"

Kehahi anxiously stands up. "Is there an exit on the other end of the cave?"

"No." Luke shakes his head. "Wait. Do you know who these guys are?"

"I can't make any promises, but I think they might be here for me."

"Yeah, now might be a good time to fill me in on the whole big backstory thing," Luke frowns.

"Right, because you're one to talk," Kehahi challenges him as he crosses his arms.

Luke narrows his eyes, "What's that supposed to mean?"

"A camping trip?" Kehahi prods. "You expect me to believe that? The way you jumped up and are trying to cover your tracks? I'm not trying to throw stones of condemnation or anything, but I know what it looks like for a guy to be running from the law. And you've got all the classic signs."

"They're from Raymond's army!" Another young man runs inside with the newest report. "Cannon just spoke with them!" His eyes are wide, "Said they're looking for a traitor."

Everyone's eyes flash toward Kehahi.

Kehahi dives for his gun.

"Wait!" Luke calls out. "We do not support Raymond!" There is desperation in his voice, "We're from Tarsurella! We'll help you escape."

"Tarsurella?" Kehahi breathes. All at once, he knows what he must do. "This isn't just about me," he quickly explains. "In fact, this has nothing to do with me. This is about Prince Asher, and Princess Elizabeth. The URIA base was bombed, and Raymond has them as prisoners. Prince Asher sent me to get this message to the King." Kehahi's mind races as he attempts to remember each detail, "The AA16 is in full throttle and I'm their next target. Mr. Akerly is here." Kehahi pauses, attempting to remember the last part. "Tell Jane. Tell the world."

"Wait, you know Prince Asher?!" Luke's mind races. He turns to his friends who are still in the cave. He has his own share of history with the Royal Tarsurellian family. "Did everyone hear the message?! We need to get that to King Addison!" Luke gives commands to several of the guys, "Fredrick, Cannon, get Elisha and keep the guards occupied! Do whatever you have to do to keep them out of our hair! The rest of you make yourselves scarce and only jump into battle if absolutely necessary."

Luke pauses then looks at Kehahi, "Kehahi and I have a message to deliver."

~*~

Dear Reader,

YIKES. What a cliffhanger!

Want to be the first to know when *Regal Hearts: Season 3* is released, both in digital format and in paperback?

Visit www.livylynnblog.com and be sure to subscribe to my free email updates!

Other ways to get connected…

Instagram: @livylynnglittergirl
Twitter: @livylynnmusic
Email: livylynnauthor@yahoo.com
Blog: www.livylynnblog.com

Drop me a line! Let me know what you thought of *Season 2*, and what you're most excited about for *Season 3*!

Lots of love,

~Livy Lynn

Did you enjoy *Regal Hearts: Season Two*? :)

Leave a review on my Amazon page and let me know what you thought! I love hearing your feedback! Reviews also help spread the word about *Regal Hearts* and encourage others to check out the series! The more reviews, the more people we can reach! Thank you so much!

You Might Also Enjoy Reading…

Beauty Boys and Ball Gowns

When Life Feels Like a Taylor Swift Song

The Coronation (The Tales of Tarsurella #1)

The Rebellion (The Tales of Tarsurella #2)

The Wedding (The Tales of Tarsurella #3 – Coming Soon!)

Find these titles at livylynnblog.com or at amazon.com!

Made in the USA
Monee, IL
21 November 2023

47074240R00254